F. Chamier

The Saucy Arethusa

A Naval Story

SALZWASSER
VERLAG

F. Chamier

The Saucy Arethusa

A Naval Story

1st Edition | ISBN: 978-3-75253-423-8

Place of Publication: Frankfurt am Main, Germany

Year of Publication: 2021

Salzwasser Verlag GmbH, Germany.

Reprint of the original, first published in 1867.

THE

SAUCY ARETHUSA.

A Naval Story.

BY

CAPTAIN CHAMIER, R.N.

AUTHOR OF "LIFE OF A SAILOR," ETC.

"She is a vessel tight and brave
As ever stemmed the dashing wave,
Her men are staunch to their fav'rite launch—
Huzza! for the Arethusa."

LONDON:
FREDERICK WARNE AND CO.,
BEDFORD STREET, COVENT GARDEN.
NEW YORK: SCRIBNER AND CO.
1867.

CONTENTS.

THE SAUCY ARETHUSA.

CHAPTER I.

A SPOILED CHILD.

"COME hither, Walter," said Sir Hector Murray, "and listen to the advice of your father. Few years are left me before, according to the course of nature, I shall be swept from the living; and now that the infirmities of age begin to press upon me, I feel that I ought not to reckon upon a much longer continuance here. Listen to me then, and be attentive! it is the duty of youth to regard the monitions of age, and those who scoff at gray hairs may find an early and a disgraceful end. Alas! that the seeds of depravity should have already developed themselves in a boy—a mere child—an inexperienced youth of fourteen! I question whether it would be possible to produce a worse instance than is seen in you of a misspent youth. Many parents," continued Sir Hector, "would rebuke you angrily; I shall endeavour by kindness to command your affection. I would have you led by your love, not driven by your fear of me: he who is dreaded is seldom esteemed, and no father would like to hear the forced grief of his son as he lay on his death-bed."

Sir Hector paused to observe the effect that his remarks had produced on his son. Walter maintained a sullen silence, and did not even look at his father: his attention seemed rather to be engrossed by the various articles of the dessert than in listening to his father's serious advice.

Sir Hector eyed his son, not in bitterness, not in wrath, but in pity: it was evident that his earnest remonstrance had failed to produce any effect on the moody boy. The baronet had ever maintained towards his son an affectionate demeanour: from him had never fallen one word of disgust; his mildness, his evenness of temper—his love of his only son, the inheritor of his large fortunes—had been the astonishment of his friends. The father eyed his boy, and a deep, deep sigh escaped him. Walter looked up suddenly; he met his father's glance, and hung down his guilty head.

"Walter," began the father, "you are now past fourteen years of age, and although you have long since been able to distinguish between right and wrong, you have not the power, the strength of mind, to choose the one and to reject the other. I have heard from your master, who has just expelled you from his public establishment, that, in spite of all his care and all his attention, you disregarded his advice, you spurned his authority, you excited his pupils to rebellion; that in your playhours even those amusements which of themselves are sufficiently exciting to the schoolboy, were flat and insipid to you without the stimulus of gambling; that from your greedy disposition for money, and your wish to overreach your associates, you had not only risked your own money, but had endeavoured to win theirs in a manner not strictly honourable. Walter, this was not the worst of the complaints urged against you; there were others which, considering your youth, I can scarcely credit. You were expelled, not for ignorance, not for idleness, not for swindling, not for breaking through all restraint,—but—Heaven! that my old eyes should ever have read the word from the pen of that excellent man—for *theft!* As long as you live,—ay, you may well start, Walter,—as long as you live, that stain, that blot will never be erased from the book of your life. Into whatever society you go, some babbling boy will remember the deed and the punishment, and you must learn to bear with meekness the whispered reproach that Walter Murray was expelled from H—— for theft."

"He will not live," replied Walter, with a slow, steady voice, "to repeat it, father."

"I fear," replied his father, "that darker deeds will follow in due time; but I must not look too gloomily upon the future. I acknowledge that no little part of this blame most justly falls upon myself. Your mother, just before she was snatched from me, in the pride and beauty of life, warned me of your disposition. My love for you disposed me to view as boyish tricks what have since ripened into crimes; and the first false step on the inclined plane of vice has been followed with such impetus, that you have nearly slid into irretrievable ruin before you were aware of the gulf into which the smooth, deceitful descent has urged you.—Walter!"

"Well," replied the boy, starting; "did you speak, sir?"

"Did I speak!" repeated the old man, his eyes lighting up into a half-passion; then instantly relapsing into their wonted calmness, he continued,—"I spoke of your faults and your follies. You were listless when your poor old father was by kindness endeavouring to palliate them, or half to bear the reproach himself. The folly of the law has made you my heir,—the estates settled on your mother's marriage devolve upon her child, and I have no power to alienate them, or I should be half inclined to try what might be effected by placing the fortune into hands that would only relinquish it when you altered your behaviour."

"Thank you, father," said the boy, "for the kind disposition you show to make me wise by making me a beggar. Have you any more to say? for I have promised to meet one or two of my friends to-night."

"Yes, Walter, I have much to say, and to-night you certainly do not meet those friends. To-night we must resolve what profession you are to follow—how your education is to be conducted; for I will have no idler in my house, whose whole existence is to be a burden to himself and all those around him. The fortune I have earned was not acquired without much toil, much thought, much trouble: to that very toil and trouble I owe the happiness I now experience in all but the conduct of my son. The day was too short for my occupation; the flying hours never lagged upon my hands; constant employment was but a pleasing prelude to my evening's domestic comfort; and in my office and in my room I learned that true happiness is not to be found, but to be made."

"I find just the contrary," said the saucy boy; "for in this room I have no happiness, and out of it I sometimes do find pleasure. To be sure, I have had some delight here to-night, for I fancy you cannot send me back to school again."

"If your mother had not been as virtuous as she was fair," said his father, "I should much doubt your being my son; for there does not seem to run one kindred drop of blood in our veins."

"What's bred in the *bone*, father, you know ——" and the youngster sat back and laughed.

"Silence, sir!" said the old man; "your remark is a sufficient rebuke without a continuance of it; for had I acted with the firmness—the duty of a parent, the son would never have dared to make such a remark, at such a time, or under such circumstances. Had I exacted the respect due to me when you were younger, I should not have been insulted in my old age."

"I certainly do believe," replied Walter, without the slightest hesitation, "that all my faults and follies are owing to your neglect of me. But what is the use of talking any more about it?—what is done cannot be undone. What do I care for the reverend gentleman's pen or for his expulsion? I shall be a soldier—I shall go into the cavalry; for I'm not inclined to use my own legs more than is requisite, and I'm very fond of riding; besides which, I shall have plenty of money; and therefore am not the lad to be placed on a high stool to dangle my legs, or to ink a desk: so that is settled, father; and now I may go, I suppose?"

"Stay, sir," replied the old man,—"stay; and since you have taught me my duty, I shall not hesitate to enforce it. Stay, sir, I repeat: and let me find that I have been mistaken, and that you are ready to follow my advice. True it is that your mother's kindness to her only child, whose wayward disposition was never checked, but each wish gratified almost before it was expressed, has led to this unfortunate end: but there is still a hope that you may be reclaimed,—that religion, affection, duty, may all be appealed to with effect. Walter, your conduct to me is more like that of an insolent, discharged servant, than of a son to his only parent! Your conduct is more like that of a hardened offender, than of a youth of fourteen who has received in his mind the germ of religion, although the flower was destroyed in its bud! I need not say how disreputable has been your conduct. Conscience must warn you that your behaviour cannot go unpunished, and I know that you bear about you the reproach which the last remaining spark of honour will still show to your debased mind. Come, my son, let me wean you by kindness from the sad path into which you have entered. For my sake, Walter—for the honour of our name, for your own reputation, cease this idleness of behaviour; devote your time to study, occupy your hours in some useful pursuit: that which has passed shall then be forgotten; and when you make the promise of amendment, you shall receive my pardon and my blessing."

The father paused, and fixed his eyes upon his son. The warm, affectionate tone in which he had couched the last remark had no visible effect upon this misguided youth, who seemed to consider the whole rebuke as very unseasonable after dinner, and who was most anxious it should come to a conclusion, and that he should be relcased from his parent's presence. In this he was mistaken: his father, as if awakened from a dream, had found, when nearly too late, the extent of his son's follies, and he resolved at once to use every effort to retrieve the boy's character and his own honour.

Walter answercd sullenly, that his father was never satisfied; that he was the head of his class; that whenever the reverend gentleman had written, he had never been punished for his lessons; and that no boy his junior in age was his senior at school. "What more do you want?" he continued. "I am sent to school to learn; if I am so taught that I retain my place, upon what ground can you censure me?"

"Upon the ground of dishonesty—dishonour. Walter," replied the father, "you are quick—you are clever: but you are idle; and 'idleness,' as you may have written—"

"'Is the root of all evil,'" continued Walter. "Who taught me to be idle?—my mother. When I was anxious to sit down and read, who told me not to mope the day over a book, but to go out to take exercise as other boys did?—my mother. Who used to complain of my pale face and sunken eye?—my mother. Well, I left off study and took to exercise; and now I am told that my idleness has occasioned my dishonour! As I said before, there is no satisfying some people."

The father during this speech had risen from his chair,

and walked quickly up and down the room, in evident agitation; and when his son had concluded this tirade of abuse against his mother, the old man stood before him. "Answer me, Walter," he began: "When your poor dear mother lay upon her bed of death,—when, as the last beams of the setting sun rested upon your face, she took from her bosom a locket and hung it round your neck,—did she not say, 'Walter, Walter, I fear I have been too blind a mother; but as you hope that my soul may rest in peace and quietness above, I implore you, every morning, when you have lifted your voice to heaven, to look at this last gift, and steadily to determine that throughout the day no error shall be committed which shall blanch the cheek with shame, or force the blood which shall arise as a witness on your face to give evidence against you?' You remember that, even at the last moment of her life, when I knelt beside the bed and moistened her cold hands with the burning tears which started from my eyes,—ay, after she had blessed *me*,—she blessed you, and bade you *remember* her last words. If now you have one spark of honour left in you, draw that locket from your breast, and say that one word, '*remember;*' then shall I have hopes that this current of lost affection may be turned into its proper channel, and the fountain which has been muddied by your faults may yet fall in clear drops upon the earth. I ask you—I command you, Walter, to take that locket in which is the miniature of your mother, painted after the hand of death had approached her, and as you look at those sunken eyes, promise me to amend."

A deep flush covered the face of Walter—a blush of shame and of regret. His father saw it and cherished it as a good omen—as a proof that he had at least touched the chord which would bring harmony and contentment to all—a proof, he thought, that every sentiment of honour had not been blasted by the withering breath of idleness. He stood before him, and as he watched the blush becoming more and more faint, he said, as he fondly took his hand, "Comfort me, dear Walter, by this one act of obedience, from which I argue the greatest good."

The boy remained silent and made no sign of compliance.

"Come, Walter, it is the only request I have made—and

which I now only make as conducive to your own happiness. I know you always wear it about you."

"I have not got it now about me," said the boy, feeling for it: "I know I have not got it on."

"I thought you promised your mother, Walter, as you knelt by her side, never to part with it, and that you would always wear it? Tell me," said the father, as a sudden thought seemed almost to check his speech, "what have you done with it, and where is it? Walter, do not tell me a falsehood, lest you make me hate as well as despise you. What have you done with it?"

"Sold it," answered Walter.

"Sold it!" ejaculated his father, with emotion: "speak, Walter, can that be possible?"

"Yes: one of the boys, a friend of mine, persuaded me to sell it, and I did sell it."

"Gracious God!" exclaimed the father, "do I hear rightly? or has some sudden visitation of Providence fallen on me—some affliction unparalleled overtaken me? Leave me, Walter,—leave me, that I may not curse you—that I may not by a hasty word render myself unhappy as you have made me to my last hour."

Walter, availed himself of the order, and, rising from his chair, walked hastily to the door; and before his father could summon back his natural affection to recall his child, he heard the street-door close violently, and was aware that the last spark of duty had been quenched in his son.

He threw himself on his chair, and thus allowed his thoughts to wander back to happier days, endeavouring to trace what errors he had committed that a gracious Providence should have cursed him with a disobedient child. "Let me see," be began: "from the time I left school, I was assiduous in my duties; I toiled for those who employed and who paid me—I never wasted an hour on myself which belonged to them—I gained their confidence, I was rewarded by being admitted into partnership with them. The wealth of other countries soon enriched me; I became a wealthy man. I did not niggardly hoard it; there is not a public charity in the metropolis to which I do not subscribe. I never injured the weak, or denied the poor; and as far as erring nature can control itself, I have controlled myself. I passed the chair as mayor of the metropolis; I was made a baronet by my sovereign.—This is the flattering side of the picture: let's see the reverse. Have I returned sufficiently grateful thanks for all the blessings I have received?—have I not at times been swollen with a purse-proud conviction of my wealth?—have I not envied others?—have I not forgotten my God in the remembrance of myself? Yet can I place my hand to my heart and declare that my principal sins must be those of omission, not of commission. My prayers have not been heard: for daily, nightly, have I prayed that my son might grow up in wisdom and in honour; that the finger of shame might never be pointed at him; that he might not squander his wealth; that he might remember the last moments of his mother. Perhaps," continued the old man, as he mused,—"perhaps my greatest error in life was my marriage; I was too old—I was fifty and more, and then I could not expect to see my son fairly launched in life. To whom can I now leave him? (for I feel this last blow has indeed done more to ruin my mind and my health than ten years of increasing age)—to an uncle who despises him—to a guardian he hates? My estates, the hard-won earnings of my youth and manhood,—my worldly treasures amassed with such toil,—will fill the pockets of the gamester, render the rogue prosperous, and the villain affluent! Ay, that was an error when my child was made independent of the parents! for tattling boobies are sure to teach a boy that he is independent, and that, come what may, he cannot be injured in his prospects. What can I do now? Alas! what charms has this once peaceful home to me? I dread to look upon the only human being who should regard me as his best friend, his protector, his parent. How my head throbs, how awfully cold I feel! Surely, surely, this last act of my son has stricken me with an arrow as poisoned as that of death. It must not be—I must rouse myself to my duty! Henceforth kindness is useless—I must be determined and resolute!"

He rose from his chair and rang the bell. It was answered by an old faithful servant, who had contributed his share in spoiling Walter, and who now stood before the master he had served for thirty years.

"Where is my son, Benjamin?" said old Murray, as if he listened for the echo; "where is my son?"

"I do not know, Sir Hector," replied Benjamin; "but I heard the door close about half an hour since. But perhaps he is in the drawing-room. Shall I see, Sir Hector?"

"Do. If he is there, tell him I *desire* to speak to him."

"Something in the wind," thought old Benjamin, as he closed the door. "Never heard master *desire* any man to do anything: another scrape, I'll be bound. How pale the old gentleman looked!"

"He is not there, nor in the house," said the servant, as he returned; and then observing Sir Hector wiping a tear from his eyes, he approached with the freedom of a faithful, long-tried servant, and said—

"I don't think you are well this evening, Sir Hector. Shall I send for the doctor?"

"What makes you think so?" asked Sir Hector, endeavouring to force a smile upon his countenance.

"You look so pale, sir, and you do not speak as you did. Lord defend us," continued Benjamin, starting, "if master has not fallen down dead in his chair!" He flew to the bell, and rang a peal which convinced the footman that something was wrong; for, in Sir Hector's summons for his servants, his hand never betrayed that eager haste, that sharp command, which may even be conveyed by a bell-pull.

The doctor was sent for, the house was alarmed, and perhaps Sir Hector might have died, verifying the old saying, "Too many cooks," &c., had not the old housekeeper declared it was only a faint, and soon restored animation. When, however, the doctor arrived, he found his patient in a strange, unusual state: there was no reason for the excitement under which he laboured, and which gradually increased; nor could the medical gentleman glean from Sir Hector one word of the cause of this sudden indisposition. The requisite medicines were prescribed; soothing draughts were administered; the lancet gleamed over his arm; and by midnight Sir Hector, watched by Benjamin, the most faithful and honest of attendants, was in a quiet slumber, his features pale but placid, his mind and his body apparently at rest.

In the meantime Walter had no sooner quitted his father's

house than he forgot the last words of his parent, or only remembered them with scorn, as if a curse was a matter of any consequence: indeed, he rather wished the idea would occur a little oftener, so that he might be dismissed from the long, prosing lecture which old heads think proper to inflict upon lads of right spirit, who only do what young men ought to do. As he walked to Drury Lane Theatre, where he had appointed to meet one or two of his companions, he turned over in his mind his future prospects. "My father," he began, "can't last long: and poor, good old soul, it will be a happy release *for him;* he is not fit for this world. Wealth is of no use to him, except to patch up an old cottage on the estate for some lazy, lurking scoundrels, who have persuaded him they are honest, and that circumstances have reduced them. By heavens! wait only until I'm of age, and I'll clear them out root and branch, every mother's son of them. I'll have no lazy vermin to fatten on the estate, and it *must* come to me. Then there's that old sanctified-looking hypocrite, Benjamin; thirty years has he been gleaning the rich fields of harvest, in both town and country. Out he goes, stock and fluke, as that young midshipman used to say. 'Faith, I'll have no old chronicler of my theft!—That's an awkward word, but it's not so bad as it sounds. I did not *steal,* I only borrowed the money without the owner's consent—and certainly with not much idea of repaying it: but who does pay? only your stupid fellows who talk about the pleasure of being out of debt merely because their credit's so bad that they cannot get into it. Now, if it only would please my father to have a sharp fit of the gout, I could get through a fortnight's fun without interruption. But frolics cost money, and with that I do not like to part, excepting when I have borrowed it as I did at school; and then perhaps the sooner the evidence of the fact is smothered the better. It's not the act, but the discovery of it which engenders shame. Holloa! here already! I must have walked fast. But I remember hearing my old father say that people in love or in thought always keep their heads down and go along at a quick pace."

"Half-price yet?" said Walter, as he neared the man in the box-office.

"Yes, sir," said he.

"Can't you let me in at the gallery price? for the play must be nearly over, and I have only two shillings about me."

"No, sir," replied the man, "quite impossible; for I should have to pay it myself, as the check-taker above would have the tally against me."

"It's very hard," replied Walter: "here am I, a boy from school, only twelve years old, and I shall have to walk back again."

"Very hard indeed, sir," said the man; "but much harder upon me if I was obliged to pay for your pleasure."

"Oh!" said Walter, finding he could not succeed by his falsehood, "I have the money: how odd I should have forgotten that I put it in my pocket!"

He paid, received the leaden check, and was not so quick in his departure but that he heard the box-office man say, "Well, he is young enough surely to have lied like a tooth-drawer."

This made no impression upon Walter—he was quite accustomed to such expressions applied to himself; and, fortunately enough, one would suppose, for the nursing of that talent the very development of which the money-taker had observed, the farce just begun was "The Liar," to which Walter lent a very attentive ear, and certainly profited by the example, although he scouted the moral. His companions, two young lads about sixteen or seventeen, had joined him, and seemed to cheer him on by hazarding an unfounded remark, that *Young Wilding* beat him hollow, and that it would require years for Walter to surpass his model.

"I think," said Gordon, the elder of the two, "Murray might give *Jeremy Diddler* a lesson in the art of filching."

"Yes," said Hammerton, who was a midshipman, "every finger in his hand is a fish-hook, and it will be a sharp craft that will turn to windward of him."

These remarks, and about a dozen others, were unnoticed by Walter, who watched the play with the greatest attention, and who smiled with satisfaction whenever the actor of *Young Wilding* came out successful from any of his monstrous untruths; but when at the close the liar was likely to be unmasked, he turned round to Gordon and said, "Dreadfully dull this! let's be off."

"Ah!" said Gordon, "I suppose you have profited all you can, and now for the practice!"

"Let's top our booms," said Hammerton, "and steer away for an oyster-house."

"No, no," said Murray, "let's take a turn in the saloon." This was agreed to, and they forthwith repaired to that rendezvous of vice, which, in the time of which we write, had no equal in England. All that could display a contempt of decency was here congregated and exhibited. The young midshipman, who had been three years afloat, and who had associated with these specimens of frail mortality at Portsmouth or Plymouth, and who had seen them by hundreds as they were mustered into the ship to which he belonged, looked carelessly on the scene. Gordon was afraid to be thought less manly than his inferior in age but superior in worldly knowledge; Hammerton re-echoed his sayings; whilst Walter, inspired as it were by the low wit and ribaldry of the cockpit, treasured each remark in his mind, and wondered how people could remain on shore when such a field for improvement was open for them afloat. Fortunately, however, an uncle of Gordon came into the saloon: the young man instantly declared that he must depart; and Walter and Hammerton being indisposed to part company with him, the three adjourned to an oyster-room, and there passed a jovial hour or two.

It is alarming how, with increased rapidity, the novice in guilt falls from the insecure pinnacle of virtue to the lowest depths of crime! Few, if any, fly from top to bottom without touching the steps; but some, and many there are, who take long strides, and hardly rest for a moment on any one of the different gradations. Walter, from one false step at school (a falsehood, backed up by circumstances all equally false), made his first descent. His lie was believed; he saw he might escape detection; he descended to meanness, selfishness, and finally to theft. His only chance of restoration to any character was in the navy, for there the smallest prevarication, the slightest meanness, is instantly discovered and punished; the active scenes of life, the daily perils, the constant employment, the ever-watchful eye over the youngster's conduct, may reclaim the most vicious. In Hammerton, for instance, all that was noble and generous could be traced; in Walter there was nothing but selfishness and deceit; whilst in Gordon might be seen the eagerness of youth to catch at anything, however trivial, which emanated from the straightforward seaman, and even to relinquish his classical dictionary for the more questionable vocabulary of the cockpit. The straightforward manner of a youngster who has been in a well-disciplined ship, saving always that the language is not the most polished, would be aped by half the boys of the public schools who were his superiors in every accomplishment as well as in age.

Before leaving the theatre, Walter fixed upon the oyster-room they were to visit. It was agreed to, and he was seen moody for a moment; he then resumed his gaiety. It was a drizzling rainy night: the young companions called a hackney-coach, and it was remarked by Hammerton how excessively civil Murray had grown, for he insisted upon handing his friends in. Their astonishment, however, soon gave way to a cheer of disgust, when, on the coach stopping, Walter, who was nearest the door which was opened, jumped out exclaiming, "The last out pays for the coach!" and he rushed into the house, leaving Hammerton to pay. He was a generous lad, and merely remarked, when they were seated, that Murray had taken advantage of a start of wind and made a stretch to windward of him.

CHAPTER II.

HOW TO OBTAIN A PARENT'S BLESSING AND A PARENT'S CASH.—A MIDSHIPMAN'S FIRST DEPARTURE FROM HOME.

It is needless to comment upon the neglect of Sir Hector in regard to his son. From the single fact that a boy of his age should have been allowed to visit the theatres unprotected, it will be easily conceived by the reader how completely Walter had assumed a right to be his own master, and how scornfully he rejected any advice. The assumed gravity of the parent was now useless; and it would have required more firmness of character, more energy of mind than Sir Hector possessed, to repossess himself of his lost authority.

The hopeful youths mentioned in the last chapter, after

having enjoyed some few dozens of that living nutriment which the bravery of men has converted into food without first sentencing it to death,—and thereby in this instance confuting the definition of man, that he cooks his victuals, —and having imbibed long and deep potations of that bitter, muddy mixture called porter, and finished by some more congenial beverage in the shape of grog, they separated for their respective homes.

Walter attempted to shirk his portion of the payment by proposing the alternative of heads or tails—the money being under his hand, and artfully kept on the exact balance, so that it might be turned against his adversary, whichever he happened to call. Foiled in this—for both his friends seemed to know his propensities—he walked home, although it rained, and called to his remembrance all the lively anecdotes of Hammerton, who had not only read the title-page of life, but had turned over some of its pages. In his idea, the sea offered the best profession for a boy of desperate character: for with all Walter's faults, he was no coward; he was a contradiction to the received notion that guilty people are always timid, as the Swedes are a living lie upon the wisdom of the world, who, ever since the first tippler was known, have declared that all drunkards are dishonest—the inhabitants of Dalecarlia being proverbially the greatest habitual drunkards and the most honest race in Europe. Walter's idea of a hussar dress gave way in his opinion before the white patch of a midshipman's collar, and the long swaggering sword lost in comparison with the neat dirk.

On his arrival at home, Benjamin opened the door; a very unusual circumstance, for Benjamin was no night-watcher, —his toil ceased when Sir Hector retired to rest, and the baronet was a great lover of early hours and beauty sleep.

"What keeps you out of bed, Benjamin?" said Walter; "is it the praiseworthy employment of watching my return and of tattling to my father?"

The old servant looked with an eye of astonishment at the question, and answered that he was not accustomed to such mean acts, but that he was up in consequence of the severe illness of Sir Hector, who, he said—and this he added with that peculiar voice which real fear eauses—"will, I apprehend, never recover."

"Nonsense!" said Walter; but it was expressed as if the news was much too good to be true.

"No nonsense, sir, I assure you," replied the servant; "when you left him, he was seized with a giddiness, and fainted."

"Was he drunk?" asked the unfeeling boy.

"Not so much," replied Benjamin, "as you appear to be. I think, Master Walter, you had better go as quietly to bed as possible. Master has fallen asleep, and the doctors have desired him to be kept quiet. As your room is over his, perhaps you will pull your boots off here, and I will get you your slippers?"

"I shall do no such thing—give me a light;" and upstairs walked the hopeful boy, purposely making a noise, in order, as he said, that his father might know when he returned, without asking his spy; and there, forgetful of those duties his mother had inculcated, he threw himself upon his bed, unmindful of the thanks he owed his Creator for the life of the day past, and which he had so unprofitably—so disgracefully spent.

The morning dawned; Sir Hector was better, and desired to see his son. He was slow in attendance, and then appeared like a boy who knew he deserved a rebuke, and expected it. He found his father better than he even believed, and was agreeably surprised to find that so far from a rebuke, his kind-hearted parent extended his hand, and seemed rather by his manner to ask forgiveness than to censure a fault.

"Come close to me, my boy," said Sir Hector, "for I am not strong enough for any great exertion: a night's sickness does more to weaken this old frame than a month's indisposition does to yours. I am very anxious about you, Walter. I should like, since—now your character——But I will not say a word about that; I shall forgive you the instant you amend, and which, for your own comfort and respectability, will, I know, be shortly done. Remember, Walter, you inherit my title—my fortune—my name. I would not have that disgraced by the son which has been respected in the father. I must place you in more stirring scenes; and this war, I think, offers a prospect of employment. You are too young for the army, to which last night you seemed to give the preference. It requires long study and much steadiness," continued Sir Hector, a slight smile passing his lips, "to make either a clergyman or a lawyer; and your disposition does not much fit you for the former, and the latter requires too much mental labour. Now, the sea, I think—although, Heaven knows, I shall part with you with much sorrow!—would suit you better than any other; and if you are so inclined, I think I could get you into a comfortable ship with an old friend of mine, who will be as considerate as the service permits, and who will be kind and attentive to you. I have selected a man of mild, gentlemanly manners, to whom I will write by to-night's post; his ship is at Portsmouth, and before a week you may be afloat. It is no small trial for a father to part with his only son when he has the means of making him comfortable and respectable without a profession; but I never liked idle men—they are always pests, and mostly vicious. Think of it, Walter, and give me your answer."

"I am ever willing," replied the artful boy, "to follow your advice; I admit I have done wrong, and I am willing to retrieve my character."

Sir Hector grasped his son's hand: "God bless you, boy! the acknowledgment of an error is the first step towards sincere repentance; and from the admission you have just made, I argue that your day of dishonour is past: henceforth I shall see a son who will add honour to my name; and I trust that the profession into which he is about to enter will know nothing of the past, and have reason to be proud of the conduct of Sir Hector Murray's boy. Enough of this for the present. You were late last night, Walter; where did you go?"

"To the theatre, my dear father: I hardly knew where I was going when I left the house, but decided upon the play to cheer me up."

"Did you meet anyone you knew?" asked Sir Hector.

"Yes, father; I met Hammerton, a midshipman, and Gordon, an old schoolfellow of mine."

"Hammerton?" said Sir Hector, musing; "is he a Somersetshire man? for an elderly gentleman of that name who has seen better days resides on my estate in that county. I think I remember that, when he became suddenly impoverished, one of his sons was sent to sea, on board the *Tribune*, Captain Barker. In that ship I intend to place you: Barker is an old friend of mine, and I shall write to him this evening. Before you leave me, Walter, in order that I may get a little repose, let me again tell you how you comfort me by your promise to amend. I shall earnestly pray to God to strengthen the laudable resolution. Good-bye for the present."

Sir Hector had no occasion to say good-bye twice. Out came Walter, saying, "A precious good businecss this!—got my own way once in my life without opposition, and a blessing to boot. If I thought blessings accompanied by some money were so easily obtained, I should be more liberal of my promises. By-the-bye, it's not a bad time to reap a little harvest." As he said this, he re-opened the door and asked his father, who had fallen back on his pillow much exhausted, if he could give him a little pecuniary assistance.

"There is my purse, Walter," said the kind old man; you have made me so happy that I cannot be niggardly in regard to anything which contributes to your comfort. Take what you want."

Walter was very quiet in his lightening of the purse; he merely took two or three guineas, he hardly knew which: but twice after he had opened the purse and replaced it, he weighed it in his hand, and squinted round at his father. He again left the room; and before the father was asleep, the son, like all idlers in cities, was hunting for pleasure, with a whole day before him, and without the smallest notion as to how he could kill the long hours between ten o'clock in the morning and six o'clock in the evening. Homc was the most hateful of all placcs to him; he never could feel comfortable near his father, although it has been seen that no parent was ever more indulgent than Sir Hector: yet the miniature of his mother was not entirely forgottcn, and he felt every now and then, that if he could repurchase it at a moderate price, he would part with the money to obtain it. Now indced, as he was about to try the most dangerous of all professions excepting that of a powder manufacturer, some few boyish superstitions crossed his mind, and he began to sum up all he had read about parents' blessings and parents' curses. The excitement of the town —the thoughts of the uniform—the belief that he would shortly be his own master—(an error he had time afterwards sufficiently to acknowledge)—changed a little the general evil current of his thoughts, and on his return he was gratified beyond measure to hear that the letter to Captain Barker had been written and sent.

The recovery of Sir Hector was owing to the pleasure he received from the hope implanted in him that his son was not entirely lost, that the seeds of virtue were not entirely choked by vice, or that his heart was not the barren rock from which nothing good could emanate. The fond belief that Walter might retrieve himself, and the advice of all his friends to send him to sea to be tamed and taught, gave him a gleam of satisfaction through the dark mist of obscurity and gloom. The answer arrived on the third day; the *Tribune* would be ready in a week, but a fit-out could be obtained in a day Walter became more anxious as his friendship increased for Hammerton, who gave such a spirited account of battles and prizes, that now it would have been impossible to restrain his curiosity from being gratified. Hammerton had been ordered to return immediately, and Walter thought this a good opportunity of forwarding his own views; he therefore took him to Grosvenor Square, introduced him to his father, and it was soon settled and arranged that they were to start together (Sir Hector not being sufficiently recovered to accompany them) in Sir Hector's travelling carriage—for he was particularly anxious that his son should be known as the offspring of a man of fortune, and not a needy adventurer, in the wooden walls of Old England.

The morning for their departure came, how eagerly hoped by Walter, how bitterly regretted by his father! The last advice—the last lecture, was nearly as follows:—

"Walter," he began, "it is a duty a parent owes his child to give him as far as he is able the wisdom of his experience; but well I know this is a commodity often offered as a gift, but strangely enough never accepted, but always purchased. It is the only thing I know which people young or old will buy; and they generally pay a very exorbitant price for the article, useless to all but themselves. From the time you embark, you will find yourself one of many, and yet so cautiously watched that you might fancy yourself the only object on board. Lay aside all pride of fortune, otherwisc your equals will despise you, your inferiors will envy you. Envy, Walter, is another word for unquenchable hatred: a man who envies you, will gladly see you ruined, and will not be over nice as to the mode. There is nothing in which poor weak human nature more exults than in trampling on the person it once envied; there is no news more gratifying than the ruin of such a man. Therefore, conduct yourself in such a manner, that whilst you do not debasc yourself to the level of those below you, you do not exalt yourself so much above them as to excite their jealousy. Be generous to all to whom you have the power of being generous. Avoid all low, coarse expressions: any one may be vulgar,—the difficulty is to excel in suavity of manners; in this your profession have not as yet produced a model which we prefer to ourselves. On no account be quarrelsome: you are young, and if defeated in your first battle with a boy of your own size, but who from exercise had become stronger, you might become fearful of your strength, lose confidence, and become timid. Be foremost in any danger; but remember, if you have wronged a man, it shows more couragc to apologize than to fight. Every one has a certain proportion of brute courage, but that which is the result of cool determination is bravery; that which is done under the sudden impulse of revenge, or when heated by wine or madness, is not courage, but temerity. I remember once in early life seeing a Spanish bull-fight. It was impossible not to admire the cool dexterity and courage of the picadores; but on a sudden, when the animal was infuriated from the fireworks which were struck into it, a half-drunken mule-driver rushed into the arena, imitated the brute in putting his head down, and ran unarmed towards the bull. His head went exactly between the horns: he was thrown, of course, and would have been trampled on but for the interposition of one of the metadores, who coolly walked up and killed the animal. In this anecdote, Walter, you can distinguish between courage and temerity.

"Never be guilty of falsehood—the slightest deviation from truth is to be censured. I speak not of *embellishing* an anecdote, in invention to convey a moral, in wit to excite gaiety: I speak of the careful abstraction of a part in order to disguise the whole, or the making addition to a circumstance to give it more weight than it deserves. Falsehood which is wilful has no name sufficiently strong in the English language to express its shame; it is the refuge of the coward, the resource of the mean and the pitiful. I know as you grow up you will be exposed to temptations, to which we weak mortals are subject: against these the constant restraint of religion is your best defence. Remember, Walter, the difference of prayer related by an old author. A soldier before a battle made the following appeal to heaven: 'O God, if there be a God, have mercy upon my soul, if I have a soul.' When this was related to the Bishop of Rochester, that prelate remarked, that so far from its being excusable on the score of its brevity, it was every way objectionable, and better for the soldier would it have been to say: 'O God, if in the day of peace I have forgotten thee, forsake me not in the hour of peril.' The groundwork of religion, I trust, is still within you; a year or two will convince you of your faults and your follies, and the reaction will, I hope, be the stronger. But mistake me not: I would not have you fall into the opposite extreme. 'Be not righteous overmuch,' and never let your pride overstep common sense. Some people tell you that they feel they are of the number of the elect, and that those who are not exactly of their creed cannot be saved. They thus condemn seven hundred and ninety-nine millions, nine hundred and ninety-nine thousand, who dare to dispute the orthodoxy of one thousand fanatics. When you have performed an action which your conscience tells you is a good one—when you have neither transgressed the laws of God nor those of your country (and for the latter the punishment is summary), I tell you not to believe that you cannot be saved unless on any peculiar tenet of faith; for if you do, you are as unjust to yourself as the one thousand blockheads who have felt their election sure, and thus become prouder than the proud, and more ambitious than the fallen angels.

"The good things of this life have been given you with a

generous hand: you are not subject to the misfortunes which press heavily on some who labour for existence. You are neither deformed in person nor deficient in intellect; you are neither stunted of stature nor short of strength. Be not, therefore, ungrateful for the kindness you have received; but rather strive by the cheerful discharge of your duty here, to merit a reward hereafter.

"The time now grows short, Walter, before we part, and perhaps for ever. The distinguished bravery of the man under whose command I have placed you will lead you into dangers and difficulties, and no man can say that *you* are certain to return. On the other hand, old age and perhaps some regret at what lately happened have sapped my health; but, by the blessing of God, to whom I confidently hold up up hands in earnest hope that my prayer may be granted, we shall meet again.

"Now, Walter, before we part, I have a present to make you; and let me implore you on no account to part with it. The attention you now pay to me warrants the belief that the words have not been uttered in vain. I have mentioned all on the score of advice excepting the avoidance of drunkenness. It is so ungentlemanly, so filthy, to degrade the man to the level of the beast, that I need not recommend you to avoid a moment's exhilaration, which is most amply paid for in the sickness, the lassitude of the morrow. I have, at a considerable expense, but which I do not grudge, recovered your mother's locket for you; how I traced, what I paid for it, I need not say. Here it is, Walter; and as I place it round your neck, I implore heaven to protect you, and that whenever, through the levity of youth, you should be inclined to swerve from the proper course, this locket may attract your attention.

"I am certain, after all that has happened, that you will feel for me as I feel for you, with all the attachment which ought to subsist between parent and child. You will write frequently—indeed, whenever an opportunity occurs,—and do not plead as an excuse the having nothing to say: every act of your life will interest me—every friend you make will be acceptable to me; and nothing will give me greater satisfaction than the assurance of your captain that you have diligently performed your duty. To my diligence in early life you owe your future prospects; and those who come after you should have the same excitement to imitate a good example.

"And now, Walter, as I hear your friend's knock, and as the carriage is ready, I shall wish you good-bye. Benjamin will accompany you; I have given him the money which is requisite; your own purse is well filled; and here is a letter to Captain Barker, begging him to endorse any bill he may think you require. God bless you, my boy, and may heaven restore you to me!"

CHAPTER III.

AN OLDSTER AND A YOUNGSTER.—TEMPTING SKETCH OF LIFE AFLOAT.—A SENIOR IN COMMAND.—A POST-CAPTAIN'S AUTHORITY.

WALTER hurried from the library, inwardly rejoicing that his father's admonitions had terminated. The lecture was over, the purse was stored, the letters of credit were pocketed, and Hammerton was waiting for him. It required no persuasion on his part to quicken the pace of Walter: he jumped into the carriage, threw himself back with the ease of one accustomed to such luxuries, and very unlike a thriving apothecary, who sits in the middle of his vehicle in order that he may be seen by every one who passes.

Benjamin was in the rumble, the carriage drove off, and never once did Walter look towards the home of his infancy, although his poor sick old father had crawled from his sofa to catch the last glance of his son's eye, or watch the carriage which contained him: his heart sank as he saw that no last look was bestowed either upon him or his house, and he inwardly ejaculated as he retraced his steps to the sofa, and swallowed one of those delectable draughts to be taken every four hours: "Show me the man who has no local attachment, and I will show you a selfish, heartless creature."

Hammerton, who, in consequence of the marriage of one of his sisters, had obtained leave of absence, and had been somewhat suddenly recalled to join his ship, was a straightforward, open-hearted fellow. The fun and frolic of a midshipman's berth were to him the greatest joys of life—he was up to anything, alive to every enjoyment, steady in the performance of his duty, friendly to those in distress, ever willing to assist the less fortunate than himself. He sat by the side of his contrast;—a contrast indeed! for Walter was penurious, tyrannical by nature, proud—purse-proud, haughty. But he had three times the talent of Hammerton, and could, when his surliness was softened, be a very agreeable, lively, witty companion. He had all the boyish levity of fourteen, as he felt that at last he was a man, his own master, free from a school, an emancipated slave. No sooner was he clear of Grosvenor Square than he rubbed his hands and exclaimed, "Now I begin life."

"Which has been the death of many. a man," replied Hammerton; and then he continued: "Pray, Murray, is that your trunk in front, with all those brass nails jammed in, like the ornamental part of a nobleman's coffin?"

"Yes," replied the new-fledged midshipman.

"I don't think you'll know it again," continued Hammerton, "after it has been shaken in the hold, or tumbled in the wings: the carpenter's yeoman will soon have those to decorate his store-room. Why, you must have clothes enough to fit out the mess!"

"I have no more," replied Murray, "than any other gentleman ought to have."

"If all the gentlemen, as you are pleased to call midshipmen, had as many traps as you have got, the ship would never be large enough to hold them. Midshipmen are called young gentlemen, but at present the system is not altogether quite so elegant as might be found in Grosvenor Square. By-the-bye, Murray—excuse my freedom—we sailors are rough knots, easily untied, and leaving the naked rope visible—do you know, I think you are a confounded fool!"

"That's pleasant," replied Walter; "but perhaps you will explain?"

"Certainly," continued Hammerton. "If you saw a man who was walking through a sheltered shrubbery, where he was amused, happy, contented, dry, and comfortable, would not you think him a precious donkey to leave the shrubbery and its sheltered walks, to come out upon an open terrace where the wind and the rain came pouring down—where he was exposed to cold and every evil under the clouds, when he could have continued his quiet walk in warmth and comfort?"

"Certainly," said Walter.

"Well then, you are exactly in that position. You have had at your command every luxury in life, and yet you give them all up to follow the worst profession ever dreamt of for anything better than a Malay or a chimney-sweep. Instead of comfort, be prepared for every discomfort; instead of rich dishes at seven o'clock, make friends with your stomach, to digest salted horse at noon; instead of a comfortable bed to snore in for ten hours, with your head supported by down pillows, with curtains to draw round your face lest a breath of cold air should disturb your slumbers, what think you of walking up and down some miserable planks for four hours;—the harder it rains and blows, the more requisite is it that you should be in it;—and when tired—ay, even to hinder sleep, for over-fatigue is as fatal to slumber as inaction—to turn into a wet hammock to swing about like a monkey in a fair—to go to bed hungry, and to rise hungry—to bc obedient to every call—to be uncertain of the smallest moment of time as your own—to go when you are bidden, and to come when you are commanded—to eat and drink out of the coarsest materials—to have bread swarming with insects, and water dirtier and more stinking than would disgrace a ditch in Devonshire? These are but the fewest of all the miseries to which you will find a midshipman's life is heir."

"But," said Walter, with much animation, "the midshipman is free; he is not the slave of a taskmaker; he is not under the eye of a misdoubting parent; he is not watched in his out-goings or in-comings."

"No," replied Hammerton, chuckling at the joke; "but he is *watched*, as you will find, rather too regularly to be pleasant. The captain watches him; the first lieutenant gives him a watch; and the officer of the watch takes care that he keeps his watch, or else it's watch and watch for him. You'll understand more of this before you are a week older; but now I'm thinking how differently people feel under different circumstances. I dare say you like this easy affair in which we are boxed up until we get to our journey's end, but I would a hundred to one sooner be in a stage-coach; for in that there's always some fun and frolic. I remember once, when travelling in this kind of vehicle, we received among us the most disagreeable old woman that ever shipped a petticoat—and that is saying a great deal for her talent of tormenting. I was a passenger with another mid, whose acquaintance you will make before to-morrow evening. We tried to please this old lady; but she kicked out one leg here, elbowed another there; would have her window up, although it was July; and whilst Smith and myself were reeking at every pore, this old creature *would* keep fidgeting about; and although I knew that in the Black Hole at Calcutta it had been represented to those unfortunate sufferers that their chance of keeping themselves cool was to keep quiet, and I recommended the same precaution to the old lady, hinting that heat was a very desirable thing during the winter at the North Pole; but that in July in England a cool breeze and a cool body were luxuries of which we debarred ourselves by our incessant motion, it was of no use—the old lady would continue her art of tormenting, playing with her fat poodle-dog, nursing it one moment, and sending it adrift between our legs the next. We were both too much of sailors to ill-treat a dumb animal; and although we lifted it carefully off our feet, yet we never hurt the poor thing, excepting that it never was allowed to be still for a second. Smith proposed putting his elbow through the glass, and there establishing a current of air and of abuse; but I whispered to him—(I knew the road well, for I had been on it only the day before)—to begin making all possible grimaces when I should give him the signal, and leave the rest to me, taking care to bark like a dog and exhibit other canine accomplishments. We then introduced the subject of hydrophobia; and certainly the horror of this malady was much, if possible, enhanced, each of us telling some wonderful stories of what we had ourselves seen in foreign parts. 'Ah!' said Smith, who saw the game I was playing, 'I never have felt easy since I was bitten by that curly cur at Lisbon; and every now and then I fancy myself with a shaggy skin, and twist round to look for my tail. I'm sure I shall go mad before long; for it was about this time three years that it happened, and every July since I have never passed a dog's-meat barrow without whiffing a little, and clapping my nose nearer than the seller admired.

"'Good heavens!' remarked the old woman, 'I hope you won't go mad in the coach, sir. Here—Muff, Muff!' and she nursed her bloated beast like a baby; 'and don't, sir—pray don't bite my dog!'

"'I won't, ma'am,' said Smith, with the most coaxing countenance in the world, 'not if I can help it; but I like the smell of it a little. No, no, ma'am; if I bite anybody, it shan't be the *dog*. I suppose, under such circumstances, I shall feel too much interest in my species, and revenge myself upon their tyrants.'

"'Oh, sir!' said the old woman, who kept watching Smith, who every now and then made a wry face, and got up a gentle snarl, 'I never ill-used the poor creature in my life—did I, Muff? Do tell the gentleman, who perhaps understands you—do tell him how kind I have been!'

"Muff snarled, and Smith repeated it, as well as a signal-man in a repeating-ship. We were now fast nearing a small stream. The bridge over which we ought to have passed was broken and under repair; and as the water was not deep, the coaches passed through it a little to the left of the bridge. I kept my eyes about me, and when we came close to the place, I gave Smith the signal; he began to howl and bark, to the infinite horror of the old woman; he seized the dog, and pretended to bite its tail, and then looked with an eye of anger at the woman.

"'Hillo! coachman!' she began, letting down the window; 'murder!—stop!—a madman!—I'm eaten—my dog's tail is off!' and here she was stopped, for Smith clapped his left hand out as he seized her with his right and opened the door; splash went the horses into the stream—the noise made him worse—the old lady made a struggle to escape, Smith having fixed his teeth upon her dress; when out she bounced, dog and all—smack she went in the middle of the stream, and lay kicking about like a harpooned porpoise. There was, of course, a halt; but we refused to have the washerwoman inside, which to be sure she did not insist upon, and she was taken on the roof to dry—Smith every moment clapping his hand out of the window, pinching her heel, and barking like a dog. Believe my yarn, if you can,

That's one way of getting a cool coach with lots of room in it: now, what can we do in this grand concern, but *tell* yarns and get sleepy?"

Walter smiled, and although much amused with Hammerton's manner of relating the anecdote, thought that in all probability he should find himself rather overmatched than otherwise in mischief, if all the midshipmen were as frolicsome as Hammerton and Smith. He responded, however, to the last question, remarking that, "Gentlemen travelled in their own carriages," for upon this point he had imbibed all the parvenu pride of his father, and that "every person should maintain by outward appearance his rank and his station in life."

Hammerton looked at him, and with a sneer that he could not control, remarked, "We shall soon take the starch out of you, my hero. I dare say you want your carriage and horses shipped, and will pay a morning visit to the captain according to your station in life? If you do, Master Murray, it will be on a gun-carriage. But as to your station, the first lieutenant will consider your lofty birth and give you an exalted one. I have no doubt you will be able to look down with the most sovereign contempt on all below you; and if you should fail a little from some trifling misconduct, to which I hear you have a little propensity, we will trice you up again: but take care you don't fall in love with the gunner's daughter and marry her, or you will have a scratch from her cat, who has nine tails."

Walter never condescended to answer Hammerton, but bit his lip in silent disdain, nursing his wrath, and inwardly wishing that such a vulgar fellow had never been placed so near himself. Hammerton, on the contrary, considered himself as an oldster, and consequently as having the youngster under his care, to be delivered like a mail-coach parcel to the person to whom he was directed. He had already become commanding officer, and it was evident that he felt his authority, from the manner in which he spoke; for he said to Walter, with an expression of sorrow, "Poor fellow! why, you are like a young bear—all your sorrows are to come, and to-morrow you will be as much out of your element as a mosquito in a squall of wind."

This rather roused the wrath of Walter, who replied in a

measured tone of voice, "Pray, *sir*, do you take me for a baby?"

"No, *sir*," replied Hammerton, "but I take you for an impertinent brat, and advise you to keep a civil tongue in your head, or——"

"Or what?" said Walter, bristling up like a boar in a breeze.

"Or I'll make you! There—don't answer—hold your tongue, without you want your ears a little longer than nature has made them."

"By heavens!" said Walter, "I'll stand this no longer!—Benjamin, open the door and let Mr. Hammerton out, and desire the postilions to turn back again."

"*Go on*," said Hammerton out of the window, "and drive to 'the George.' The peacock," said he, as he resumed his place, "is envied for its gaudy plumage; but the strength of the eagle is a better safeguard than feathers. Your father put you under my care, and I do not relinquish my office until I introduce you to Captain Barker. You may then go back, or elsewhere, if you like, for me: but I have got my sailing instructions, and I shall obey them to the letter."

"Do you pretend to say," said the petulant boy, "that I can't do as I like in my father's carriage. I *will* go back, and the devil shall never force me to live in the same ship with you."

"Your father put me in command of his son and his carriage; I'm commanding officer here, and will be obeyed. And as for your not going on board, why your name is on the books of the *Tribune*—go you *must*: there's a word for pride to swallow—you *must* go. But don't fancy you will be detained against your will: one volunteer is worth two pressed men, and we have not come to pressing midshipmen as yet."

Murray sat back biting his lips and inwardly vowing vengeance against Hammerton: he even turned over in his mind the best mode of annoying his parents in the event of Sir Hector's death, for Hammerton's relations were tenants of his father; and in the worst passion of Murray's mind, he vowed he would extirpate such weeds, root and branch. Weeds they were in his eyes—loathsome weeds which sprang up and poisoned all around. What right, indeed, had such parish paupers to send their sons to serve in the navy; and by what right did these upstarts domineer over their betters? Walter was ignorant that in the noble—the honourable profession in which he had entered, the daring courage, the ready zeal, the active mind, the quick in resources, the fearless in danger—weeds or not weeds—soon became the highest flowers; and had he at that moment taken the trouble to think, his own good sense would have told him that if all the world were on one day born, and all equal, long before noon it would be settled which half were to make the beds of the other half. The lazy, the passionate, the idle, the thoughtless, the timid, the weak, the sickly, must give place to the active, the temperate, the studious, the thoughtful, the brave, the strong, the healthy; and the more wealth a man inherits, the more activity of mind it requires to regulate it. He who is indolent must become subservient; he who is blindly generous must become involved; and he who trusts to another to do that which he *ought* to do himself, can have no cause of complaint if the undertaking fails.

Walter was not indolent; but his pride, his overbearing pride, scarcely allowed him to think, lest he should be thought to work. The last remark of Hammerton stung him to the quick, *must!*—there's a word for pride to swallow; —it nearly choked him; and when his throat relaxed its efforts to keep down its rage, he said with a slow voice and a most malignant sneer, as he turned his eyes towards his companion, "Set a beggar on horseback and he'll ride to the devil."

Hammerton looked at him in anger; but his generous heart soon made allowance for the petulance of youth, and he merely replied: 'When you have done mourning over the loss of your parent, and eaten the cake and jam which your old servant has crammed into the corner of that gingerbread trunk, then such remarks might meet their deserts. But come, Murray, no more of this; you are endeavouring to make an enemy of the man who can be—nay, and in spite of yourself, will be—your friend. You must drop your pride; you must remember you are going amongst young men liberal by profession, and although as poor as Job, as proud as Lucifer. Take heed of the stubborn disposition of your nature. The donkey gets terrific blows on its crupper, and as it lifts its sluggard legs to resent the injury, merely kicks the air. The noble horse goes on without whip or spur—distances all animals of less active motion; but the sulky horse which refuses to go, although the same animal,—nay, perhaps of the same breed,—is beaten, and spurred, and driven in spite of itself; and, thus goaded on with bleeding sides, is not a bad picture of the youth who can do anything, but, from stubborn pride, will do nothing, until force, actual force, compels him.

"We are now drawing towards Portsmouth; in a quarter of an hour you will stand before your captain. Remember, he is more absolute than his king; for he can make it whatever time of the day he likes, and we must set our watches to his will and caprice. Do as others have done before you, —swim with the tide, which it is useless to oppose. When you speak, answer 'Yes, *sir*,' and 'No, *sir*;' for if you were a Quaker, you would find that without you added the 'sir,' their creed, 'Let your communications be yea, yea—nay, nay,' would get you a mastheading. If you *come the Quaker over the captain* or any of the lieutenants, you will have time to correct your answer as you sit for four hours at the masthead, blowing your fingers like a Norway bear, and thinking of Grosvenor Square which you are leaving behind."

In justice to Hammerton, it must be remarked, that Sir Hector had urged him to disgust his son as much as possible with the service in which he had embarked; and as all men are rather partial to exaggerating either their wealth or their woes to strangers, Hammerton took especial care to finish the picture in his best style. His manner would have damped the courage of many a youngster; but Murray was not a lad to be frightened at a shadow—the very difficulties to be overcome gave him a relish for the undertaking; for he was just that kind of lad who would not have married the Venus de' Medicis with ten thousand a year, if there was no opposition to the match, but would have eloped with a poor parson's ugly daughter, if the parent merely exercised his right in the shape of a negative.

"Very well, Hammerton," said he: "I take all but the hint about my ears as it was meant, kindly. I shall do my best to be civil and discreet; and as I have nothing to fear from a captain, I may approach him without any apprehension. I wish I had stopped to dine at that last stage; I think eating a capital foundation for courage, and everybody fights better when well fed. Can't we stop now?"

"It is too late," replied the companion, "for we are close to the lines, and that gateway ahead is the entrance into Portsmouth."

At this moment the postilions looked at each other—smack went the whip, the wheels turned round faster, and they entered the town in proper style. Every one, from the sentry to the sweep—every soul, from the pensive marine, to the jolly tar—every Jew, tailor, draper—apothecaries, with all their household goddesses, ran to the door to see the dashing equipage; and never before did two midshipmen make a greater sensation in Portsmouth. Hammerton had his quick eye at work; but Murray looked back. The bell at "the George" rang for the waiters, the postilions having given the signal; and before the carriage drove up, twenty or thirty people had assembled to see the unlading of the valuable cargo.

It happened that three or four captains had agreed to dine together that evening, and who, between the numerous enterings of the waiters, who brought first a salt-cellar, then a spoon, then the bread-basket,—noodling out the time in order to keep hope alive in the hungry sons of the sea,—had huddled together by the window, wasting life by watching how others idled it away, when the noise of the approaching carriage, with the ring at the gate-bell, gave a little turn to their conversation.

"Faith," began one, "this must be the First Lord of the Admiralty, or the Secretary for Foreign Affairs. What a row these great fellows kick up! I think, Barker, we had better remind the waiters that we are waiting, or the bigwigs will take the *Tribune's* share of the dinner. I wish we could get the soup up before the cook splices it."

"I'll ring directly I see who comes out of this gingerbread affair," replied Barker: "I should be more inclined to think it contains some lucky son of an Indian director, whose careful mamma had sent him down comfortably, in order that he might not feel annoyance until he takes a head-sea, which will turn his head."

"And his stomach!" said another: "what a lucky thing it is to have one's father born before one, and to be sent out to have money put into one's pockets in spite of oneself! He is young enough at any rate," continued the same speaker;—"why, he has a midshipman's uniform! Oh! it must be some youngster come to join his ship; and here appears the unhappy father about to part with his fond son. Look how the old servant bobs his arm out! Why, d—n it, if it's not another youngster! Well, now then for the venerable parent!—Holloa! what's this? Why, they have shut the door, and there goes the carriage to the stable. If those two youngsters belonged to my ship, I think I would teach them not to make such a noise in the streets. Who the devil can they be?"

"Do you sleep here to-night, sir?" said the waiter.

"Yes," said Murray.

"Chambermaid, show this gentleman his room. Porter, take that trunk up into No. 4. Do you take dinner, sir?"

"Yes," said Murray, surlily, for he could not understand why a gentleman could not arrive in his carriage without being so over-pestered by civility.

"A private room, sir; or the coffee-room, sir?"

"A private room, sir!" replied Murray, his upper lip turning in arrogant disdain. "Do you think I am going to dine at an ordinary?"

"No *ordinary* fellow that," said a waiter, in an undertone; "I never saw so young a lad with such a look. I wonder what his name is. Oh! here it is large enough on the trunk—"Walter Murray." Now, I should like to know who Mr. Walter Murray may be, that he drives about in a carriage and four horses, and not more than fifteen years old. The other chap has nothing to do with the carriage, that's certain, for he's in the coffee-room, and pecking away at the cold round-o'-beef like a midshipman from a long cruise."

The captains had now got to work,—the soup had not been spliced, and all were in high good-humour, when the master of the inn brought in the first course.

"Who came in that carriage, landlord," said one of the true blues, "which came rattling on as if it would pound the stones into powder?"

"Two young gentlemen, sir," replied Boniface.

"Young gentlemen!" said the captain,—"young gentlemen with four horses! Why, who are they?"

"One is a Mr. Walter Murray, who, I understand, is going to join one of the ships at Spithead, sir."

"Tell him," said Captain Barker, "to come here to me directly. Has he dined?"

"No, sir; but he has ordered dinner in the next room."

"Well done!" said the first speaker; "a midshipman, or a boy of the second class, in a private room!—and turtle soup, I suppose?"

"He desired his servant to order dinner," quoth the landlord; "and certainly," he added, with a smile, "it is rather an expensive one."

"Tell him to come here," said Captain Barker; "he belongs to my ship,—and," he continued, as the landlord withdrew, "is a neat nut for the devil to crack!"

"I must confess," said the first speaker, "that I have some curiosity to see this youngster, who comes down to join his ship in such style. Who is he?"

"A son of Sir Hector Murray—a man of great wealth and of sterling worth: he has given me a line by the post, mentioning his son's pride and folly, and I'll begin with him as I intend to go on: he is a kind of youth who must be brought up with a round turn, or he'll get such headway that he'll be wrecked before he can heave about."

"Mr. Murray says, sir, he'll come after he has dined."

"Oh!" ejaculated Barker, "much obliged to him for his civility. Have the kindness to tell the youngster who came down with him—a Mr. Hammerton—to come to me."

"He is in the coffee-room, sir—I will send to him directly."

Hammerton seemed to enter almost as soon as the landlord had shut the door. He was hard at work at the beef and pickles when the messenger arrived, and he dropped his knife and fork and ran up stairs, knowing full well that his captain would ask him to dinner, and that, if he delayed to appear, he would be bundled on board in the first boat. As he entered the room, he bowed respectfully to the captains.

"Come here, Hammerton, and sit down.—Waiter, get a plate and knife and fork, and bring the soup here again." Hammerton did as he was desired. "Now," continued

Barker, "tell me what kind of a lad was your companion in Sir Hector's carriage, and how it is you have separated from him."

Hammerton spoke like the straightforward gentleman he was, not too boldly, not too timidly, but with a modest deference, such as inferiors in rank should bear towards those above them. "He is, sir, a very curious young lad: he is older at fifteen than many at twenty: he is a bold, daring youngster; but he has never been accustomed to be controlled. I left him because I could not afford to pay my share of a dinner such as he ordered: he did not invite me to partake of it, and I was too proud to hint my poverty."

"Well said, Hammerton," remarked the first speaker, whilst Barker patted him on the shoulder, and looked at him with the pride a man feels when those who have been under his orders are praised by others. "Has he begun dinner yet?"

"No, sir," replied Hammerton, "I should think not; for I heard one of the waiters say that his servant had ordered enough for a mayor and corporation."

"Then while they are bringing up the soup for you, go and *bring* him here."

Away went Hammerton, and without any preface opened the door and began—"The captain wants you, Murray: come along as quick as you can."

"I have sent once to him," replied Murray, "that I should come after dinner."

At this Hammerton burst out laughing and said, "You'll know better before half an hour is over your head than to send such a message to the captain: but come, he has sent me for you—don't stand gaping there like a stuck pig: come along, I say."

"You may say what you like," said Murray, "but I don't care any more for the captain than I do for that sweeper in the street, and go I shall not until I have had my dinner."

"Don't make an ass of yourself," continued Hammerton, getting a little on towards an angry expression; "but come along, or I must take you by force."

"By force!" said the petulant boy; "I should like to see you use force!"

"Oh," said Hammerton, "you will not be long in being gratified;" and forthwith he seized his victim by the cuff of the coat with the left hand, and taking hold of a certain part of his unmentionables, he forced Murray's head forward with one hand, whilst he kept back his stern with the other, and thus navigated him, in spite of all kieks and starts, through the passage. Meeting a waiter who was near the captain's door, he desired him to open it, and in walked Mr. Murray in spite of himself. He seemed rather startled at finding himself in the presence of five captains, all in uniform, and all men not very likely to be frightened by a youngster.

"Come here, sir," said Barker, in a quarter-deck voice, which, in spite of the independent air and bearing of Murray, who had drawn himself up for impertinence directly Hammerton relinquished his grasp and allowed him to be perpendicular, went through him, and he felt, to use a common expression, cowed. "Come here, sir," repeated his captain: "did you hear me speak to you? Pray, sir, why did you not come when I sent for you, without obliging Mr. Hammerton to execute his orders in the manner he has donc—and done properly?"

"I thought——" began Murray.

"Thought, sir!" interrupted the captain; "who gave you leave to think, sir? A midshipman think!—d—n it, we are come to a pretty pass now! I *ordered* you, sir, to come to me; and take care you never disobey my orders. And now, sir, that you have received the reprimand you have deserved, sit down and dine here."

Murray, astonished at this welcome of his captain, crept like a frightened dog to the chair, which was placed by the side of his commander, and began the operation of eating without much appetite. This being remarked by another captain, one who afterwards enjoyed the title of a most magnificent tyrant, led to the following observation by him: "It's well for you, youngster, that you don't belong to my ship; for, by all that's sacred, if you did, you should be flogged this evening and starved to-morrow. This comes of sending midshipmen down in carriages; whereas, if they were packed up like fish in baskets and bundled into carts or waggons, they would get a kind of hint as to what they might expect afterwards."

Murray's pride gave way to this uncalled-for remark, and he burst out into a flood of tears. His captain, with that consideration and kindness for which he was throughout life so respected, immediately endeavoured to reassure Murray; but the great step had been taken, his pride had given way, and all attempts to place him at his ease were ineffectual. At that moment he would have given worlds to retire and retrace his steps, and, since his feelings were hurt, he resolved to rely on his cunning. In a moment his resolution was taken: he dissembled his real sentiments under a smile; he ate without tasting, and drank without thinking.

"Pretty well that, youngster," said one,—"five glasses of wine in as many minutes! I dare say your old father, although he sent you down here like a nabob, did not give you more than a glass of port when you came down with the children to dessert."

Murray never answered; but the sneer which curled his lip could not be mistaken.

"Hammerton," said Captain Barker, "it is now getting high time to go on board, and I don't like my youngsters to sleep on shore at Portsmouth: so, do you hear, take Murray with you on board, and make him as snug and as comfortable as you can. Tell the first lieutenant to send the gig for me at eight o'clock to-morrow morning—we shall sail about noon. And here—stop—the blue peter must be hoisted at eight. And tell Mr. Garnet to turn all the women out of the ship, and to unmoor at daylight. Take my gig, and see this youngster's traps safe: he'll be as much adrift as a wreck in a tideway. Good night.'"

Murray, glad to escape, bolted out of the door; but he was recalled in the instant by his captain. "Mr. Murray, when gentlemen leave a room where they have been invited to dine, it is customary to wish their companions good night, or to bow to them: it is a mark of respect which I beg you will now manifest, and of which I trust I shall never again have occasion to remind you."

"I wish you a very good night, sir," said the captain who had made the remark relative to the wine, at the same time bowing his head and continuing, "It's pretty lucky for you, you unlicked cub, that you do not belong to my ship!" Murray heard it all, bowed, and retired.

No sooner was he clear of his tormentors than he ran into

his own room: the cloth was laid, the wax-lights flaring: he rang the bell and sent for Benjamin. Hammerton told him to get his traps ready, jumped down to the coxswain and ordered him to bring up some of the gig's crew to take his own and Murray's trunk on board, inwardly cursing the sulky cur who had thus deprived him of his cruise on shore; for Hammerton, smart as he was, had no intention of going on board before the following morning.

"Benjamin," said Murray, as the old servant came into the room, "we must go back to town directly. Be as quick as possible—get horses—never mind packing up, but be round in a moment. Not all the devils alive should get me on board a ship—I have had quite enough already; and my father will be pleased to see me return. Run, good Benjamin."

Benjamin was no runner—he was no footman; he stood a second in thought, and then said "Master Walter, your father will be so pleased!"

"There—there—no long speeches; run like a lamplighter—round with the carriage—pay the bill—look sharp! Why, you move like a snail—there—quick! quick!" and he shoved the old servant out of the room. "I don't think," he mused to himself, "that there is necessity to leave anything behind me. I'll get my ornamented coffin, as Hammerton called it, packed; I had better work myself than lose the contents." And away he went to pack up; whilst Hammerton, who had given the requisite orders, had started off to 'the Fountain,' to see if any of the mids of the *Tribune* were on shore, and wished a passage on board without paying the heavy fare which some of those eager boatmen demand who ply either from Common Hard or the Point. Murray, for once, was active both in mind and body; he was turning in his brain how fortunate it was that he should escape paying for his dinner, which honour he intended for his new captain. He shoved in his linen, which Benjamin had placed ready for next morning, inwardly cursing the officious fellow who thus rendered his escape subject to delay; and then came across him the certainty that if the carriage was brought round, his captain would hear the noise, and detection follow. He knew he was clear of Hammerton; so, jumping down stairs, he desired that the carriage might not be brought round, and himself urged the postilions to their exertions.

In the meantime one or two seamen belonging to the gig had arrived at "the George;" and having inquired for the trunk belonging to the new young gentlemen, were shown into his room, handled the future ornaments for the carpenter's storeroom, and trudged merrily along to the boat, the coxswain remaining to show Murray the way to "the Fountain," where Hammerton awaited his arrival.

Things were in this train, the trunk on one tack and the owner on the other, when the bell of the captain's room rang. When the servant entered, he was asked if the young gentlemen had gone on board. The waiter answered, that one had left the hotel and sent some of the gig's crew up; but that the other was waiting for his carriage, to which he had ordered four horses.

"This," said the tyrant captain, "is some trick of your other youngster, Barker: he has persuaded this young colt that he must drive to your *gig* in his *carriage*, and some fun will come out of this."

"Yes," said Barker, "likely enough; but I think it rather unfair on his father, who will have to pay for the frolic; and although I like frolics as much as any one, yet I think they might break in the youngster at a more reasonable expense. I must put a stop to this. Tell the landlord to come here."

Up came Boniface, who had been arguing a point on which there was much difference; the landlord desiring to be paid for the dinner ordered, though not consumed; the others—for Benjamin and Murray both agreed in saving the money—holding that people never paid for things of which they had not partaken. Whilst this was in dispute, the waiter came and told his master he was wanted. Without, therefore, coming to a conclusion, the landlord desired his auditors to await his return, and attended the summons of the captains, whom he knew to be impatient gentlemen, and men who liked to see all orders promptly obeyed. If Murray's love of money had not been uppermost for the moment, he would have had a clear start: the moments he lost in disputing with the waiter proved fatal to his scheme.

Barker asked about the horses; and, to his astonishment, he learnt that the young gentleman was about to return to town. He desired the carriage might not be allowed to leave, and that the young wanderer should be sent to him. Down came Boniface just in time to meet the waiter. "All right, sir," said the latter; "here's the money: gentleman's gone, horses paid, and all settled." Barker had followed the landlord, and hearing this, ran without his hat, at once steering for the gate, Boniface puffing and blowing behind him like a broken-winded horse.

CHAPTER IV

THE MID'S FIRST NIGHT AFLOAT.

There was scarcely time for the captain to recover his breath, before the clatter of the carriage was heard, and the landlord stood ready to prevent the progress of the postilions. "Stop, Thomas!" he bawled out, directly they were within hail; but Murray, fearful of some recovery of his person, called out, "Don't stop for anything or anybody, and I'll pay you handsomely." But Thomas knew the voice and the portly figure of his master, and pulled up in obedience to the order. Out popped Murray's head; and the first thing he saw was his captain. In one moment he was handed out; the captain took charge of the truant midshipman, and without saying a word to the servant, or taking the least notice of the capers of the postilions, he walked off with the youngster, got his hat at the inn, and, calling his coxswain, saw Murray into the gig, desired the crew to shove off, and merely said, "Tiller, tell Mr. Garnet to see that young gentleman made comfortable." At this moment, Hammerton came running down to Sally-Port: seeing the captain, he turned short round, ran down to the Point, popped into a boat, and away he went on board. The gig's crew took it easily, talking as they pulled; to them time was indifferent. A light flaw of wind coming off, they shipped the mast, hoisted the sail, and then lolled on the thwarts. Murray was in a sea of wonder: they took no more notice of him than they would of a dog; the only object they had in view was to spin out the time until all duty was done on board and the hammocks piped down.

Old Benjamin having paid for the four horses, went in that dignified manner the first stage, and then lazily continued his route, arriving in London the next morning. Hammerton concluded something was wrong, and was anxious to repair it; his chance was to overtake the gig; and the two boatmen pulled heartily on the promise of extra pay, and a glass of that villanous stuff which, whilst it exhilarates, poisons the blood. They soon got sight of the white lug-sail, and it was not long before the coxswain heard "Gig ahoy!" In a moment every man was upright in his place; the oars were out in a second, the sail lowered, the mast unshipped, and the boat's head pulled round. Hammerton jumped on board; and, taking no notice of Murray, sat down, seized hold of the yoke-lines and said, "Give way, my lads." Even Murray, who was brooding over his capture, was sensible of a great difference: the increased labour of the men, the silence which was observed, the steady manner in which they plied the oars, was sufficient to show him the respect which was paid to his companion, and which had been neglected towards him. "Boat ahoy!" was now heard. "No, no," was answered. "Are you coming here?"—"Yes."

The men now pulled harder, the bow-oar was laid in, and Murray was alongside the *Tribune.* Hammerton sprang up the side, saying, "Hand up that youngster, Tiller," as if he had been a pig or a box; but Murray, active by nature, caught hold of the side-ropes, and, much to the astonishment of Tiller, who was ready to assist him, was on deck much quicker than almost any other youngster who thus made his first step on board a man-of-war. Hammerton, who knew that when the captain came on board he should in all probability get a lecture for allowing Murray to give him the slip, and for losing sight of his convoy, began to tame his refractory messmate before he could recover his astonishment at the first sight of a frigate.

"Take your hat off when you come on his Majesty's quarter-deck," he began; and suiting his action to the word, he knocked it off; and then the natural goodness of his heart returning, he told one of the side-boys to pick it up, and said in a mild manner, "I only did that, Murray, to remind you that for the future you must never come on the quarter-deck without that mark of respect. You will remember my way of giving the hint until you get so used to do it, that when you come on deck in the middle of the night, your finger will go up to your hat as mechanically as a watch goes. But I must be off to the first lieutenant. Here, Weazel," continued he, calling another youngster, who was supposed to be keeping watch, which means dozing over the gangway, "look after Mr. Murray until I come back, and take care he does not fall down the hatchway."

Weazel was one of those sly young gentlemen who sleep with one eye open, and, like all youngsters of that day, was fond of tormenting a Johnny Newcome. The very idea of having something to do was pleasant to him; for there is no greater difficulty than keeping one's eyes open when there is no duty to perform. Weazel made a kind of bob of the head, which was not noticed by Murray; for Weazel's dress, a round dirty jacket, a large pair of Flushing trousers, and a glazed hat, were not very likely to strike Murray with admiration.

"Come to join the ship?" said Weazel.

"I am," replied Murray.

"Are your traps on board?"

Murray answered, that he had no traps that he knew of.

"No traps!" re-echoed Weazel: "what! are you one of the wash-and-wear boys—is all your kit in a worsted stocking? or are you like the marine who had only two shirts and made six of them?"

"I dare say," replied Murray, "that I have shirts enough, but should have no objection to know the secret how to make two into six."

"You are a precious greenhorn, I see," continued Weazel. "Why, this way to be sure:—If you have two shirts, you have one on and one off, one dirty and one clean, one wet and one dry,—and there are six of them. Did you bring your bed with you?"

Murray looked at him with surprise, and said, "I suppose I have money enough to pay for my bed and my room also."

"That's true enough," replied Weazel; "but you must know where to buy them. Here, quarter-master, take this gentleman to the gunner's yeoman," (and he conveyed his meaning to the old sailor by a sly look,) "and ask him if he has a bed to spare, and show this gentleman into a decent room, with white curtains and a mahogany wash-hand-stand."

"Ay, ay, sir," said the quarter-master. "This way, sir, if you please;" and he was directing Murray forward when Hammerton came on deck and called him.

"Where are you bound to, Murray?" asked Hammerton.

"I was going with this gentleman," said Murray, with great simplicity, "in order to see my room and my bed."

"What, Weazel," said Hammerton, "getting him into a line before he has been five minutes on board!" and he burst out laughing at the answer of Murray, who evidently considered a ship as a floating inn, where accommodations might be had by paying for the same.

"Follow me, Murray," said Hammerton; and forthwith he led the way down the companion, saying to Weazel, "Let him rest to-night, and to-morrow we will give him such a run that we will break the neck of his pride and make a jolly fellow of him."

"Holloa!" said Weazel, who was quite a youngster; "what, pass the officer of the watch without saluting him! I tell you what it is, young gentleman," continued the little scamp, "if you are guilty of such disrespectful behaviour, I shall perch you at the masthead to look for the wind. Go down, sir,—follow that gentleman, sir, and take care to behave better in future."

Even the old quarter-master could not help laughing, and Hammerton's titter was plainly heard below. Weazel had drawn himself up as straight as a boarding-pike, and imitated one of the lieutenants in repeating the very words which had been applied to himself not a fortnight before. Hammerton led the dejected Murray to the steerage: his visions of liberty had flown—Hammerton's words in the carriage had already been verified, and instead of one tyrant he saw himself surrounded by dozens.

"Here's a youngster come to join the ship," said Hammerton, as he entered the starboard berth of the *Tribune*: "the first lieutenant has told me he is to mess with us, and the captain says we are to make him comfortable."

All eyes, even those which had been directed to a cribbage-board where two of the elder midshipmen were playing, were raised towards him: one midshipman, who was busy in playing over some wretched air on a still more wretched flute, just lifted his glance from the old thumbed music before him; and three or four who were playing blind hookey gave a squint and continued the game. A miserable candle, something between a dip and a rushlight, barely sufficed to show him, who had left all luxury behind, the nature of his dreary abode, and Murray almost wished himself again on deck with Weazel to go in search of the dimity-curtained bedroom.

"Sit down, Murray, and we'll have some supper."

"Avaust there, boy," said the caterer; "supper's done; and it's against the rules of the mess for those who've been on leave to have any when they return. But stop, as Mr. Murray's a stranger, we will break through the rule."

In a few minutes there was placed on the table a japanned basket, rather the worse for wear, in which was some biscuit; and close by its side was a piece of cheese, which looked as if all the rats in the ship had been pecking at it: and a black-jack of swipes completed the display, and the fastidious Mr. Murray was told to fall to with what appetite he had. Hammerton gave directions as to a hammock, and then it was ascertained that the good man to whom Sir Hector had intrusted the outfit had omitted the bed. A mattrass and some purser's blankets were spread upon the deck, and this delightful retreat from care was voted ready for its tenant. In the meantime Murray's mind was undergoing a rapid change: he saw his position; he knew it was useless to swim against the stream, and swallowing his pride, although he could not screw up his courage to swallow the swipes, he assumed a look of more contentment, and when Hammerton returned, he entered into some conversation, giving an account of his attempted escape, with the unexpected interposition of the captain. This was not altogether very pleasant to Hammerton, for he knew that Murray had been placed under his care, and that it was needless to conjure up excuses when no excuse in the least degree satisfactory could be made: like a wise young man, he was convinced it was of no use to annoy himself about the past, and as he could not dive into futurity, he made a compromise with his memory not to bother him, and he began to ask all the news since he had left—mentioned the orders he had brought on board—and thus the time crept on until the master-at-arms popped his unwelcome head in the berth, saying, "Nine o'clock, gentlemen; please put the light out."

The lantern was borrowed, and Murray was conducted to his bed. He looked at it with no small surprise: it was impossible for him to disguise his disgust, and it was not until then that the pride of the haughty boy gave way. He who could have brooked anything rather than show himself conquered, was now completely subdued; and as he lay down, without undressing, on the bed, more than one tear started from his eyes. Hammerton saw this, promised to make him more comfortable the next night, advised him to turn in regularly, and finding that his presence only made the matter worse, wished him good night, and, like a mule-driver in South America, rolled himself up in his scanty bed, and was soon in a sound sleep.

Mr. Weazel's love of mischief now began to show itself. "It would be capital fun just to cut down the Johnny Newcome by the feet," said this urchin; "that would not hurt him, and in all probability would do him much good, as he would get accustomed to tricing up his own hammock, and thus receive one salutary lesson before the ship sailed."

The officer of the watch, the ship being moored and all boats hoisted up, considered himself entitled to a nap; so, looking round to see that all was right and quiet, he desired the mate of the watch to call him at six bells, at which time the tide changed, to keep a good look-out and not allow any shore-boats to come near the ship, after which directions he went below. When he was supposed to be asleep the mate called Weazel, who had been stretched out on the signal-lockers, one eye shut and the other star-gazing, and repeating the words of the lieutenant, he also went below out of the cold, rolled himself up in a cloak, and closed his eyes in forgetfulness. Weazel, who did not care about sleep, but preferred fun, now called the quarter-master; the same orders were given to him, with directions that if he (Weazel) should not come up before five bells, to take care and give him a hail; upon which he went below, leaving the rough old sailor to look out for the ship, which he did by going to the signal-lockers and bringing himself to an anchor on them.

As the bell struck four, the "All's well" went round the ship, the sentries walked the gangways, and the old quarter-master, who had been in Howe's action, began running up the log of his memory, every now and then humming a bit of a stave which grew less and less in sound and in length, until it subsided into something very like a snore; and thus his Majesty's ship the *Tribune* floated on the waters at Spithead with only four or five marines awake, all the rest, with the exception of Weazel, being snug enough below, fast asleep, and likely so to remain.

Weazel now got down to the steerage, the sentry was leaning against the after-bulkhead so nearly asleep as not to heed him, and whilst the young scamp was groping his way to find out his victim's berth, he fell over something on the deck and tumbled alongside of Murray. The proud boy had just dozed off, and fallen into incoherent dreams. The tawdry servants of Grosvenor Square were standing ready to receive their young master; the warm hall was a welcome from the cold without; the rich repast tempted even the half-cloyed appetite of the spoilt boy; the spacious bedroom, the clean furniture, the comforts of life—all won him to repose. Anon came the rumbling of carriages—Hammerton's figure—the captain's sudden appearance—a faint glimpse of the features of Boniface and his waiters; and then the wit, even in sleep, which prompted the thought—"Curse your chattering waiters! no waiters are worth a straw but tide-waiters and dumb-waiters: had this rascal been dumb, I should have been back again." The tyrant captain's words and proposed works came across his recollection with a cold shiver; he had mentioned flogging—pride turned away at the word;—he was on the waters, the boat lazily pursuing its way; then came the shudder as the bread-basket and black-jack darkly pictured themselves in the foreground; and as the ideas got more confused, the black-jack mixed itself up with the captain's face. At the moment when the bread-basket seemed to dance a well-bred caper with Hammerton, Weazel's toes came in contact with the pillow, and he rolled over the fallen boy, himself falling with his nose against Murray's thick shoes, the one rousing up at the sudden intrusion, the latter letting out a few words more frequently in the mouths of midshipmen than in the pages offered to the public. When the first volley of exclamations had escaped Weazel, he thought of his fallen dignity, and assumed the officer, forgetting that he had been left on deck to look after the ship. "Halloa! sentry, bring your light here. Who is this fellow lying about the decks with his clothes on?—send for the master-at-arms. Who the devil are you?—rouse up. Why, you are as hard to weigh as the best bower, and rigged in dock too like a Liverpool ship!"

Poor Murray, unused to such ungentle intrusions, remained flat, for he still thought himself in a bed; then, having the intention of getting *out*, he found he had only to get *up*. He rubbed his eyes, astounded at finding a lantern poked into his face, and was so much surprised at seeing a soldier close alongside of him, that he could only say, "Where am I?"

"Where are you?" replied Weazel: "why, where you have no business to be! Don't you know the orders, that no person is to lie about the decks, and no one to turn in all standing like a trooper's horse?—Oh," continued the young scamp, who pretended just to discover the mistake, "it's you, is it, Mr. Murray? Hammerton ought to have mentioned this. But go to bed; I hope you may not be disturbed again: but you must take your clothes off; why, to-morrow you'll look like a walking blanket! Sentry, lend Mr. Murray a hand to unrig himself, and take care how you lift his stays—good night!" and away went this urchin on deck again, full of mischief as an egg is of meat. He knew from his own practice that the quarter-master would take a calk, and being baulked in his cruise below, he was resolved to make it up upon some one. Very gingerly he stepped on deck. Not a sound was to be heard: the sentries thought it better to be posts than to walk their posts, so they were on each side lolling over the gangways. The quarter-master's nose announced his situation, and forthwith Weazel stepped towards him. The old fellow seemed to know that he had no right to sleep, and talked a little in his dreams, as if to prove that he was not quite in slumber, and thus he betrayed his thoughts, and perhaps what he remembered with most pride:—"29th May, 1794," he began, then came a slight snore—"starboard tack—double-reefed topsails"—snore again—"led through the French line—touching up the *Montague*, and I think I hear the admiral now giving orders to set the top-gallant sails—signal up for close action"—snore—"slapped at it—saw Polly Jones handing the powder, gallant creature!—fire away, lads"—snore. At this moment, when the old fellow was in the middle of the action, Mr. Weazel lifted up the quarter-master's legs, gave him a haul, and down slipped the warrior from the signal-lockers, making sundry most uncomfortable noises with his head against the brim, and landing on his stern on the quarter-deck. "Run aboard of us, by the piper!" said he; and up he jumped like a lamp-lighter.

"Fast asleep, eh!" began Weazel: "a very pretty fellow you are to be trusted!"

The old fellow rubbed his head, got his hat on again, and coolly answered, "Why, Mr. Weazel, if you had been on deck, I should not have shut my eyes in order to rub up that battle."

In the meantime the sentries were all walking about again, and his Majesty's ship had a watch.

"Hold your tongue, if you please," continued Weazel, "and don't speak until you are spoken to. Get me a small fish-hook somewhere: trot, and look sharp."

"Ay, ay, sir," said the old fellow, who took the joke in good part, although he was none the better for the stern-board he had made—or, as Weazel said, "for having gone down by the stern so fast." And jumping below to his berth, he soon returned with a mackerel-hook which he happened to have in his bag.

"Here's one, Mr. Weazel," said he, on his return, "that will hold any fish you'll catch to-night."

"Ay," said Weazel, "that's a good one: run and get a long, stout ropeyarn." This was soon managed; and the gentleman, who had studied the art of tormenting thoroughly, fastened the yarn to the hook, and saying, "Now see if you can't forget Lord Howe for once, and keep your eyes open," down went the youngster to carry on his fun.

He had now got the bearings and distance of his victim,

and went to work quite sure of success; whilst Hammerton, who had roused up in consequence of the noise occasioned by Weazel's fall over Murray, had waited until the mischievous elf had returned on deck, and knowing that he would pursue his frolic, told Murray to change beds with him; and with much care and kindness he put the youngster into his hammock, tucked him up, and not minding the want of sheets himself, for he was used to all rough work, he lay down on the deck, and imitated the precaution of Mr. Weazel, which was to keep one eye open, twisting up his handkerchief, and keeping all ready for action. Weazel was soon at work, and Hammerton saw him fasten the hook to the blanket. Weazel then retired the length of the rope-yarn, and in a minute afterwards away went the blanket, and away went Weazel; he was up the hatchway, on the main-deck, blanket and all, in a second.

"Well done, Master Weazel!" said Hammerton: "but I'll pay you off in your own coin!" So he leisurely walked to Weazel's hammock, and taking therefrom a blanket, rolled himself up in another, leaving Weazel's all loose for another haul. Weazel was soon down again and up again, having made another successful cruise, and stowed both blankets away in the stern-boat. Hammerton took another from the same place, and five bells having struck, the mate of the watch was roused, and all offensive operations stopped. At six bells, with the change of the tide, came two very unwished-for companions,—the officer of the watch and a heavy fall of rain. The wind came off the land, veering about; and the officer of the watch, the mate, and Weazel, all took shelter under the heavy canopy of heaven. When the lieutenant was on deck, all eyes were open; he asked the mate what weather they had had since four bells, and the mate responded as if he had been watching in reality.

The breeze and the rain freshened towards midnight: and when Weazel was relieved and went below, there were too many eyes open for any more of his frolics. A minute was ample time for him to get into his hammock, and a sixtieth part of that time was sufficient to convince him that his blankets were on a cruise. Out he turned, and directed his operations towards his supposed victim. Hammerton was on the look out for this, and when Mr. Weazel began to uncover him, he started up and administered such a flagellation as kept him warm for some time; and when Weazel was nearly asleep—for it was doubtful if he ever was so much off his guard as to shut both eyes at once—he was welcomed by the arrival of the two soaking blankets, thrown over him, and mingling their dewy drops with the before dry bedding.

This little anecdote is related principally as it was the means of bringing Murray forward in a prominent manner next morning.

CHAPTER V

A PUGILISTIC ENCOUNTER.—THE "TRIBUNE" UNDER WEIGH.

The morning of the 16th of September was ushered in by a sweet squall from the south-west; the rain fell in torrents, and his Majesty's ship *Tribune* presented about as miserable a picture of happiness as the imagination of a man beaten down by blue-devils, and under the infernal torments of a headache, could fancy. The thick haze of the morning—the dirt, which in newly-fitted out ships is excessive—the wet—the dreary dulness of that morning struck a chill upon Walter. Glad to escape from his wretchedness below, for the gratings had been placed on the hatchways to prevent the wet from reaching the lower deck, and two hundred and fifty men had, until five o'clock in the morning, if not totally exhausted, rendered the air below very unlike the cool breeze which blows pure over a snowy mountain—he tumbled out of his swinging bed upon a wet swab which the prudent solicitude of Mr. Weazel had provided in case any accident might occur to his victim during his first night's uncomfortable slumber on board. It was placed as a convenient mat, and fortunately was used before his feet were covered with stockings. To this succeeded the horrors of a first toilette in the steerage of a frigate, and the mortification of a wilful boy who suddenly finds that by his own folly he has relinquished the comforts for the miseries of life. It is in vain to paint this picture; no one can express how severely the mind may be wounded, and what an effort it requires to conceal the sufferings. Walter was no boy to cry amongst boys: his pride forbade it. He had felt abashed in the presence of his captain, and he could have cheerfully stood the rebuke which occasioned it, had he been prepared: taken unawares, he was unable to resist the first impulse of Nature, and she was victorious. Now he was on his guard; and when Weazel, in kindly offering to place his basin in a better position, capsized it over the half-clad son of Sir Hector, the midshipman of one night showed himself capable of revenging an insult by striking his tormentor a most undeniable blow on the nose. The basin was dropped in a moment, Weazel was stripped for a fight, and the first round had been fought before Hammerton had time to interpose.

"Murray," Hammerton began, "this must not be; it's against all regulations."

"He struck me," said Weazel, "and I will have satisfaction."

"Certainly, certainly," said half a dozen youngsters, who were always ready for some fun. "A ring! fair play's a jewel! Mr. Long Togs is not going to come Captain Grand over Weazel; and if Hammerton interferes, we will soon get an oldster on our side to see fair play. At him, Weazel!"

Weazel went at him directly; and Murray, who was by no means averse to the fight—more especially when he learnt all his antagonist's projected annoyance against him—received him warmly: he stood head up boldly, and returned more than blow for blow. The youngsters generally sided with their old messmate; but, like gallant little fellows, they cheered on Walter, and kept calling out, "Bravo, Greenhorn!" "Now, Long Togs!" "Hurrah, young Hector!" And whatever might be the probable result, either for or against their inclination, it was a regular stand-up fight—fair play and no favour. Walter was soon discovered to be not only the most scientific, but the strongest; and Weazel, after a visible change had come over his features, hauled down his colours and surrendered. Murray immediately stepped forward and offered him his hand, which Weazel accepted, saying, "I did my best; but, confound your school exercises! you have more knowledge." At once all angry feeling passed away: it was decided that Murray was the best man; and although Weazel looked forward for another more prosperous result, he in reality became the friend of his antagonist, and lent him all the assistance in his power.

The very circumstance of a youngster not fourteen hours on board the ship having fought his first battle, and having bravely stood forward against one who, to use a familiar expression, "fought like a cock on his own dunghill," served to exalt the victor much in the eyes of his new messmates, and a more kindly feeling was instantly shown towards him. Those who knew Weazel as their better man at once seemed to acknowledge Murray as a superior; whilst those who were beyond his reach were not backward in their praises. Walter soon found that to begin well is a great point; and he shrewdly enough considered that it was easy to maintain a position carried against an inferior force, and that the best way to calm the anger of an opponent was by a generous behaviour after the victory.

He dressed and went on deck.

"Holloa!" said the first lieutenant, who was as busy as first lieutenants like to be, "who have we here with a swelled face and black eye, out of uniform, and strutting about like a peacock? Who the devil are you, sir?"

"I am Mr. Walter Murray, sir."

"Walter Murray, sir?" reiterated the first lieutenant; "and how came you on deck in that dress? Come here, sir: pray what is the matter with your face?—you seem as if you had been fighting."

"It was last night," replied Murray: "a boy attacked me in the street, and I punished him."

"'Faith, youngster," replied Mr. Garnet, "he seems to have punished you! Where was Mr. Hammerton when this happened?"

"He was not with me, sir; it was before he met us in the boat, when he came off in the other boat."

"Why, what nonsense is this," said the first lieutenant. "Quarter-master, tell Mr. Hammerton I want him."

Murray now found that, from a generous wish to save Mr. Weazel, he had involved his friend and told his first falsehood. And he was right. Hammerton got a serious rebuke for having lost sight of his charge, and having thus allowed him to be attacked, and perhaps plundered, by any dirty vagabond of a boy, or a more likely prowler in the shape of a female pirate. In saving himself by telling the truth, he implicated Murray; the whole affair came out, and Mr. Garnet read Murray a lecture which accorded well with the advice of Sir Hector. Whilst he gave him credit for a proper spirit, he rebuked him for the ungentlemanly rencontre; and whilst he remarked upon the generosity of feeling which prompted him to save his beaten antagonist, he deprecated the falsehood by which it was done; and gave Walter clearly to understand that the next lie, white or black, in which he detected him, should be followed by a punishment as disgraceful as it should be severe.

"Take him below, Mr. Hammerton," he continued; "put him in his uniform: mind, he is in your watch—to be stationed in the mizentop—one of the captain's aides-de-camp at quarters—in the third division—and to have charge of the jolly-boat. Look after him, Hammerton, and tell him in a kind manner that I shall teach him to ride on the cross-trees if ever his tongue gets the better of his heart. Pass the messenger below—turn the hands up—unmoor ship. Carpenters, ship the bars! There—get out of the way, youngster!"

In a minute Mr. Walter Murray found himself stationed and quartered; the orders given for the first step towards removing him from his native country; himself already despised; his talent at lying made evident; in a scrape with his captain for having attempted to run away without even facing the danger which he fancied awaited him; in awful subjection to those in authority above him—in a hornet's nest with his equals, and as yet unheeded by his inferiors.

He was soon in harness, and again on deck. Walter's mind was naturally active, and had it not prompted him to use his curiosity, the close smell below would have driven him on deck. Here he found himself always in the way, as intruders generally are—called youngster by the first lieutenant, and shoved about right and left by all who approached him. "Pride will have a fall," as the copy says, and Murray, like a sensible lad, allowed his pride to fall without hurting himself. He seemed to shake off all remembrance of home; and when the men stepped out, as they leant their weights against the capstan-bars, to the tune of a fife and drum, his heart beat lighter—his mind felt casier.

No sooner was one anchor weighed, than thc messenger was shifted, and the ship hove short upon the other cable; and at this moment, when the bars were unshipped, the gig returned on board without the captain. A note was handed to the first lieutenant, who immediately called out. "Get a gun ready forward;—quarter-master, convoy signal at the mast-head." The gun was reported ready, and was fired as the stop of the signal was broken. Walter watched the harmless smoke as it curled over the ship, and kept his eye fixed upon a ring which retained its form although blown far away to leeward, and which was occasioned by some grease having been placed round the muzzle of the gun. Weazel, who was stationed abaft, saw what Murray's eye was directed to, and approaching him, said, "That is curious, Murray."

"It is," replied Murray, "and I was puzzling my head to think how that ring is formed of one part of the smoke, when the rest is unattached and is blown away."

"God bless you," said Weazel, "nothing so easy to explain. That ring is where the shot went through; and if you want to see how it is made, you have only to look into the gun when they fire it off. The shot comes out so quick, that it jams all the smoke together, through which it passes and blows away the rest. You have heard of the wind of a shot; I've known it upset a jolly-boat at a quarter of a mile; and last year, when we fired a salute as the port-admiral passed the ship, the old boy's wig was blown off, and the little hair he had left on his head was turned black with the smoke."

"It must be very dangerous," replied Murray, still watching the ring, "to fire a shot amidst such crowds of shipping. I wonder no one is hurt."

"Wonder indeed!" replied Weazel: "you'll see by-and-by how nicely our gunner can fire a gun. What a family of daughters that man has, to be sure! If you want to see them, only go and ask him for an introduction. Tell him 'the first lieutenant desires him to fire another gun, that you may see the shot come out.' Here, quarter-master, just introduce Mr. Murray to the gunner: he wishes to see his daughters.

"Shall I show him the one in the cabin which you married the last cruise, Mr. Weazel?" said the knowing old sailor.

"Yes," said Weazel, with indifference; "and I make no doubt Mr. Murray will soon be as well acquainted with her as I am, and cut me out in that quarter."

The design of the mischievous Mr. Weazel was, however, again frustrated, in consequence of the appearance of Hammerton, who came abaft in order to take Murray below, the first lieutenant having given the order to pipe to breakfast. In the meantime the captains from the different merchant-ships came on board for convoy instructions, and reported their vessels ready for sea, receiving in reply an order to unmoor; for which purpose a general signal was afterwards given by the fore-topsail of the *Tribune* being loosed and another gun fired. Active preparations were now going forward: the women were all turned out of the ship; the shore-boats desired to shove off, although many lingered round the frigate; there was a constant intercourse with the other ships; and about eleven o'clock the young gentlemen were summoned to attend on deck, as the captain was coming on board.

It has often been remarked, and with great truth, that there is no respect more conspicuous than that which is shown to a captain when he is received on board his own ship; neither can any stranger witness a scene more likely to impress him with the absolute power of the little monarch afloat, than in the very proper manifestations of respect so readily offered. It was not lost upon Murray: it filled his mind with an ambition to have equal devotion paid to himself—the hope of youth, which manhood so seldom realizes, broke upon him, and all the Weazels in the world, with all the miseries of the midshipmen of the time to which we refer, could not at that moment have weaned him from the Navy.

"Where is Mr. Murray?" said the captain, as soon as he had returned the salute of his officers, and had spoken some words concerning the outward appearance of the ship to the first lieutenant. "Hoity toity!" said the captain, "what is this I see! Pray, sir, with whom have you been fighting?"

"With Mr. Weazel," replied Murray.

"Where is that little scamp Weazel?"

Mr. Weazel, who had heard the captain ask for Murray, and who well knew the probable consequence of having fought him below, instantly ran over to another midshipman, who was ordered to go on board one of the convoy to give some instructions, and said, "Thompson, the first lieutenant desires you will attend below to the stowing away of the boatswain's stores just come on board, and I am to go round the convoy." Whereupon Thompson dived below, glad enough to escape a drizzling rain, and Weazel got out of the ship in order to let the captain's rage subside a little before he faced him.

"Mr. Weazel, sir," replied the midshipman of the watch, "is just gone in the jolly-boat on duty."

"That is a little scamp, that Weazel!" continued the captain; "but I'll make an officer and a gentleman of him yet. Mr. Murray, I am cxcessively displeased with you, because I had hoped that from your situation in life you would have been above such low conduct. A gentleman, indeed, who drives up to 'the George' with four horses to his carriage, twelve hours afterwards to be fighting like a common chimney-sweep! For shame, sir, for shame! Where's Mr. Hammerton?"

"Here, sir," replied Hammerton.

"How came you, sir, last night to disobey my orders? Did I not tell you to take care of this youngster—not to lose sight of him, to take him on board, and to deliver certain messages to the first lieutenant?"

"Yes, sir," replied Hammerton, "you certainly did; and I only left Mr. Murray whilst he prepared his unpacked trunks to go on board; and thinking some of the midshipmen might want a passage, I went to 'the Fountain.'"

"I am very much obliged to you, Mr. Hammerton," interrupted the captain, "to make my gig the midshipmen's passage-boat: I hope this will not happen again. Take this youngster under your charge. You know his failings; mind! I look to you for their correction. If I find him at any of his school-tricks here, he shall not escape the proper punishment, nor you my severest reproof. Why did you allow this battle to take place?"

"Mr. Murray struck Mr. Weazel, the blow was returned, and the mischief was done before I could interfere."

"And pray who had the best of it?" continued the captain.

"Mr. Murray, sir," replied Hammerton.

"Let me hear no more of it.—Mr. Rackum, turn the hands up!—up anchor!"

Mr. Rackum, the boatswain, wound his call, and the tramp of the men followed the command. Immediately the bars were shipped, the cable brought to the messenger, the order to heave round given; then the fife again struck up, and in five minutes the *Tribune* was lying at a short stay peak, and the signal was up for the convoy to weigh. During this time Mr. Weazel had got on board, and crept to his station abaft the mizen-mast, where he kept dodging the captain so as to keep out of sight. "Loose sails!" was no sooner given as an order, before Weazel made a run at the mizen rigging, and got safely housed in the top before the captain had seen him.

"Ready forward!" said the first lieutenant; "ready on the main-topsail yard! ready abaft!"

"All ready!" squeaked Weazel.

The captain looked aloft directly he heard the voice: "Let fall the sheet home!" The topsails were shortly at the mast-head; the yards braced for canting the ship to port; the bars again shipped; the anchor aweigh, catted, fished; and his Majesty's ship *Tribune*, under her three topsails and jib, stood out towards St. Helen's, her ensign and pendant blowing proudly out. When clear of Spithead, the *Tribune* hove to. By this time every rope was in its place, flemished down—except the clue garnets, which were kept ready for running; the watch called, and only one boat alongside—that boat was retained by the captain, in order to send some letter by the night's post.

"Mr. Murray," he said, as he descended the companion, "have you written to your father?"

"No, sir," replied Murray.

"No, sir!" repeated the captain: "is it possible that you have already forgotten his injunctions? Come into my cabin, sir, and write to him directly."

Murray went down; and when the paper and ink were

placed before him, he kept biting the end of the pen, not knowing how to begin.

"Have you done?" said the captain, as he took his eye off his own letter, yet continuing to write.

"I don't know, sir, what to say"

"You are not such a fool as that, Mr. Murray," replied the captain. "Tell him that you have joined your ship—that your captain has overlooked your first fault—that the ship is under weigh for Halifax; and give him some general idea of your feelings since you have been on board. Why, you have enough to say to fill a ship's muster-book. Come, look sharp—I shall not keep the boat for you; and mind, sir, I expect you to be ready when I am."

The idea once given, Murray's own talent supplied the rest, and he gave vent to his feelings in the following letter, almost the first he had ever written to his father, beyond the half-yearly announcement of when the holidays were to commence—a kind of up-and-down pleasurable toil, in which more paper is wasted and more pens nibbed than in one day's hard work in any office in London.

"My dear Father,—I suppose Benjamin, if he did not forget it on the road, told you that I got safe to Portsmouth, and very nearly got safe back again: the fact is, if that old blockhead had moved his stumps properly, I should now have been in Grosvenor Square, wishing to be where I now am. The captain has desired me to write to you; so I do it, although I have nothing to say, excepting that I have already been in two rows—fought one battle and got a dark eye,—but I beat my adversary. I can't help telling you that I think you have behaved very badly to me, and you must have written all about the business to the captain; for this morning, when he put me under the care of that yellow-faced fellow Hammerton, he said, 'If I find him at any of his school-tricks here, he shall not escape the proper punishment.' I think it very ill-natured of you, who told me how much you had my interest at heart, to have written this to the captain; and certainly, if you continue to write like this, I know I shall never get over it. I hope you are better, and that you will not forget me. You had better direct your letters to Halifax—that is the place the captain's are to be sent to. As to him, I think he is the worst-looking man I ever saw: he speaks always as if he were going to swallow one up; and when he comes on board, we are all obliged to go up stairs in the wet and take our hats off whilst he comes up the side. He found fault with me, Mr. Weazel, the boy I fought with, and Hammerton, and then turned his hands up with the boatswain: I don't like him at all. He is now sitting opposite to me, every two minutes looking up to see that I am writing, and he watches me as if I was going to rob him. The boat is waiting for this, and the captain has done his letter, therefore I cannot tell you any more news, because he won't let me: he says the boat shan't wait for any midshipman's scrawls. If all your friends are like him and Hammerton, I don't want to extend my acquaintance. I am determined to do all I can to get sent back again; although I should like to be able to find fault with everybody, and have everybody take their hats off when they speak to me.

"Your dutiful son,

"WALTER MURRAY."

"Have you finished your letter?" said the captain.

"Yes, sir," said Walter, as he folded it up.

"What have you told your father?" continued the captain.

"Just what you told me, sir;—that I was on board, and that we were going to Nova Scotia, and that he had better direct his letters to Halifax."

"What did you say about me, sir?"

Murray looked like a criminal as he answered, "Nothing very particular, sir."

"Let me see the letter." Murray hesitated. "Why, I don't want to read your rubbish, you young suspicious monkey! I want to add one word to your old father, and tell him what *I* think of *you*; which, from what has happened, will not be the most flattering portrait that I hope I shall be able to make of you; and if I fail, I can hand you over to Captain C., that gentleman you had the pleasure of meeting at dinner: if he cannot tame you, by the powers! you must be worse than a hyæna." The captain took the letter, turned it back, and added,

"Your son is a boy of high spirit, which he has already proved; he will do well enough after the sea-sickness has moderated his bile. I will take every care of him, and rest assured he shall write to you often. I have no doubt, from Hammerton's account, that he will like the life you have chosen for him: there are always a few rough steps at first, but when we get upon the level, the surface is smooth enough. We are now under sail. I trust to hear better accounts of your health, and to return, after a prosperous trip, about the latter end of January."

The letter was folded, sealed, and sent; Captain Barker read his additions to Murray, saying, "I have written just what I think of you. Now, sir, take yourself off! Ask Mr. Hammerton about your station, and mind you are always to be found in it. And here—stop a minute—I have heard you are rather addicted to telling lies. Now, as sure as I catch you out in one—ay, of the most trivial kind,—I will have you married before your father's consent can arrive; and you may ask Mr. Weazel to introduce you to one of the gunner's daughters."

"He offered," replied Murray, with the most innocent face in the world, "to do it this morning, and sent one of the men to the gunner, sir, to tell him that I should be happy to make her acquaintance."

The captain could not resist smiling, and replied, "His introduction will not signify so much as mine. You will dine with me to-day. Mind, I have forgiven your first fault: beware of the second. Be off!"

CHAPTER VI.

DEPARTURE OF THE FLEET.—THE FIRST DINNER AT THE CAPTAIN'S TABLE.

"WELL," thought Murray, as he got clear of the cabin-door, "this is a strange kind of life I have embarked in! I hardly dare open my mouth for fear of saying something wrong, and I always appear to be in somebody's way. There,—thank you, sir,—I am very much obliged to you for that!" said he, as a sailor banged a wet swab across his stockings: the fact is that Robert Dunlap was swabbing the larboard side of the waist with his back to the cabin-door, and as he lashed the swab from side to side of him, he stepped backwards, of course not seeing those behind him, who ought to have kept clear of him.

"Begs your pardon, *sir*," said the sailor, as he touched his hair with his right hand; "I did not see you, *sir.*"

Somehow this little event was consolatory to Murray; there was evidently great respect in the manner with which the man addressed him; and if his pride had been mortified before, it received some soothing from the words of the sailor. Shortly afterwards Murray went on deck. The last boat had left, the main-topsail was filled, and the ship, about two points off the wind, was standing out from the land. The convoy were crowding all sail, and the *Tribune* resembled the schoolmistress of a country village, who sees all her little ones walking before she herself moves. Murray was standing abaft the lee-side by the taffrail, watching the town of Portsmouth, which every moment grew less and less to the eye. Before him was one large world of water, into which he was rushing apparently blindfolded; whilst behind him grew less and less in the distance all he knew of life—of home—of happiness. Yet Walter shed no tear; nor did he, boy as he was, look forward with any fear as to the result; he felt assured from what he had seen below that he would always have fair play shown him,—that Hammerton, whom he hated most cordially, would not allow him to be ill-treated by those stronger than himself, and for those who were his equal in size and strength he was a match. Still, however, he kept his eye upon the lessening shore, lost in a kind of pleasant meditation which even the trifling motion of the ship had not disturbed, until at last objects grew less distinct and were forming themselves into one long loom of land,—the town—the ships,—the shore, alike undistinguishable to the naked eye; and Murray had no telescope to bring objects closer.

"Don't you dine with the Captain to-day?" said Weazel, as he tapped Murray on the shoulder.

"Yes," said Murray, starting from his reverie. "Why?"

"I only wanted to know if I could be of any use to you: I mean, if you haven't got your proper dress, I might be able to assist you?"

"I have got everything, I believe," said Murray: "I suppose I have only to walk in as I am."

"And then you will walk out again immediately.

Why, you must go in full uniform! A dinner on board ship is a kind of state affair: in merchant ships they call it the state cabin; and in a frigate the captain is a king, and always has proper respect shown him. I suppose you have got your knee-breeches and buckles?"

Murray looked at his own legs, and smiled as he said, "Why, Weazel, I fancy it would be no common tailor to make knee-breeches fit me!"

"Why, to be sure," said Weazel, "it would puzzle a shore-going snip; but we have one who will do it for you quickly enough. Let's see,—there's four bells striking now."

"I only hear one bell," replied Murray.

"It is striking four times, and that means two o'clock. At six bells the captain dines; you will hear the drum beat: you must be dressed in knee-breeches, silk stockings, buckles, a long coat, your cocked hat and sword, your hair powdered and dressed, and with ruffles to your sleeves. Have you got all those things?"

"Not one but the cocked hat and sword; I may have a pair of silk stockings: but as to the rest, I have seen them, to be sure, when my father went to the Lord Mayor's feast; but for one of my age to have such things, it never entered my head."

"Well, Murray, it's no use thinking about it; you must remedy the omission by using a little despatch. Let me see,—there's Strop, the ship's barber, he, of course, has hair-powder; if not, you can buy some—Scales always has plenty of that. Then your confounded long trousers, we had better look after that first; I'll send one of the mizen-top-men with you, for I can't leave the deck—it is my watch: do you go below, get out your best pantaloons, and give them to the lad; I'll tell him to take them to the tailor, and get you fitted out at once."

"Why," said Murray, "can't you lend me a pair without altering mine? Yours would fit me—you are just about the size."

"Very true," replied Weazel; "I have a pair,—I will send them to you: but now, look sharp. Here, you Maxwell, show this gentleman to Mr. Rackum's cabin; and tell the ship's barber he wants his hair curled and powdered.

Look sharp—down you go, Murray: attend to him, Maxwell, do you hear?"

Away went the unconscious Murray down the after-companion; whilst Maxwell, who had received his lesson from Weazel when in the mizen-top, jumped down the main-hatchway and lodged Murray in Rackum's cabin; the boatswain being on deck, and not very likely to leave it until they piped to supper. When Murray was shut in, away went Maxwell for Strop: but Weazel, always active when any of his own fun was in the wind, had already told the barber what he was to do, and the man, like all seamen who enjoy the frolic of having a greenhorn *in a line*, jumped down in the steerage, and appeared with an old comb, a pair of gaping scissors, and two pieces of rusty ramrods lashed together to represent curling-tongs. Murray told him to dress his hair in the manner the other midshipmen wore theirs when they dined with the captain.

"Ay, ay, sir," said Strop, "Have you your powder-box and a puff, sir?"

"No," said Murray, not willing to appear ignorant of customs: "my foolish servant forgot to send them. I suppose you have some in your shop for sale?"

"Plenty, for the matter of that, sir, of puffs; but you must buy the powder at another place."

"Oh yes," interrupted Murray, "at Mr. Scales's; Mr. Weazel told me he sold powder: can you show me the way?"

"Certainly, sir," said Jack Strop, who managed to keep his countenance and act his part uncommonly well: "this way, if you please, sir,—down this ladder, sir; you will find him in his shop." And forthwith Mr. Murray descended the after-ladder into the cockpit; and there he saw Mr. Scales sitting apparently at his shop with a book in which he was writing, and to all intents and purposes apparently a shopkeeper; his store presenting, to the astonishment of Murray, candles, sugar, raisins, and divers other useful articles and *comestibles*.

"Have you any hair-powder for sale?" said Murray.

"Yes, sir," replied Scales (he had been tutored by Weazel) "how much do you want?"

"Only a small quantity," replied Murray, "to dress my hair to-day."

"I always keep it in small parcels; here is a paper quite sufficient, sir, and by your leave I will enter your name on my books—we can settle the account another time."

Murray took the flour, thanked Mr. Scales for his obliging attention, and returned to Rackum's cabin. Here he found Weazel, who had brought in a pair of knee-breeches, and had affixed two large sailor's silver buckles into the shoes.

"Get your silk stockings, Murray," said Weazel, "and get your lower rigging up before you deck your mast-head. That's your sort—what a leg for a boot! it's lucky green is not in fashion, or the pigs might mistake them for cabbage-stalks! Now then, Strop, set to work: why your curling-tongs are cold! five bells has gone this quarter of an hour, and the roll has beat for the servants. Well done, Murray, clap your legs well through the breeches: now then for the shoes! Why, you look like an admiral!—are you any relation to Lord Howe? That's well done, Strop; you have made his head for all the world like an overgrown cauliflower;—that will do. Mr. Murray will call at your shop and pay you to-morrow. You live in Tier-street, No. 20, I believe;—we won't forget. Now then for your waistcoat;—that's beautiful! Your coat?"

"I have got no coat, I have only got a *coatee*."

"Well, on with that. There now, pull your ruffles down. Here's your sword: why, it's long enough to toast cheese at the galley fire without burning your fingers. And as a topper over all, here's your three-cornered scraper: you must carry that under your arm. Let's see," continued Weazel, talking to allow the time to creep on:—"mind how you behave at dinner! I know you are a man of high family, but it's not every man who dines with kings. You must never answer the captain, only bow, and whatever he offers you must take. How do you feel in your full dress?"

"Why, I feel very much like a fool," said Murray; "and all I want to make myself more ridiculous is a large nosegay, and then I should be as much like one of the gilded donkeys which dance round a jack-in-the-green on May-day as needs be."

"I forgot the nosegay, Murray, or we might have got

one from the captain's garden in the mizen-top. There's *The Roast Beef!* Now run in the cabin, and never mind the men looking at you; go right in, for sometimes the midshipmen turn out to see how a new-comer looks in full uniform. Now then, skim up the after-hatchway, and mind what I told you."

Murray, who had witnessed the great respect paid by the first lieutenant, of whom he stood in considerable awe, to the captain, and had seen with his own eyes how all bowed to the king afloat, had never allowed it to enter his mind that a boy like himself could be too absurdly dressed; and few can imagine, who have not themselves seen, how very ridiculous anyone looks in knee-breeches and buckles, and with a short coat. He bustled up the after hatch-way, and never heeded the shout of laughter by which he was assailed. The sentinel opened the door with a wonderful grin upon his countenance, and Mr. Murray stood in the fore-cabin, the captain being in the after one waiting for his guests. Hammerton was likewise invited, and was at that time inquiring for Murray, when Weazel said, in the most innocent manner, "I believe he is gone up—I think I saw him go up the after-hatchway just now."

"Did you tell him," said Hammerton, "to wait for the first lieutenant?"

"No," said Weazel, "I think he is too great a nob to wait for anyonc; but I suppose he will smooth down like the rest of us. "It's quite astonishing," said the young mid, "how being elevated high above the quarter-deck makes a man wish for a more lowly situation. There goes the first lieutenant."

Hammerton followed his senior officer, taking it for granted that Murray had gone before, and arrived at the fore-cabin just as the captain opened his door, and beheld the unfortunate victim of Weazel's malice, his first lieutenant, and Hammerton, all at the same moment. He immediately —although he could not entirely command his countenance—turned his eye towards Hammerton in order to ask how this could be, and he privy to it. Hammerton, seeing his *protégé* dressed in so ludicrous a style, could not restrain his laughter or conceal his mortification: he merely said' "I assure you, sir, I know nothing whatever of this foolish business." The first lieutenant gave a look of reproach at the three servants, who very soon saw it was possible to laugh the wrong side of a face; and the captain, with that kindness which marked him through life, taking no notice whatever of Hammerton's remark, said, "Sit here, Mr. Murray," placing him on his right hand.

Murray knew something was wrong, for he was quick enough to perceive the almost suppressed titter, and to remark that Hammerton and the first lieutenant neither had powdered heads nor knee-breeches. The captain's manner soon overcame his first shyness, and Murray began to feel more at ease; although, whenever he caught the eye of any present, he saw the broad grin which was over the countenance. By degrees the captain wormed out of Murray the author of the trick, and the manner in which it had been carried on: nor could they exactly blame Weazel, for the joke was well-conceived and happily executed; the manner in which it had been conducted—the privacy of the boatswain's cabin so as to keep others out of the secret, was a happy thought; but the simultaneous roar, which even the captain's presence could not control, and in which he joined, when Murray said that the hairdresser lived at No. 20, Tier-street, and that Mr. Scales had provided him with the hair-powder, opened Murray's eyes to the tricks which had been played him.

CHAPTER VII.

NIGHT AT SEA.—A SQUALL.—A SCHOONER UPSET, AND THE CONSEQUENCES.

THE captain was really not sorry for the trick played upon his young midshipman; he knew his character well, and foresaw that the laugh this would occasion would humble the pride of the boy, and perhaps ultimately do him more real service than Murray himself was aware of. Hammerton knew that the play was only begun, and that Mr. Weazel would certainly be kind enough to have a full attendance of midshipmen and men to welcome the young courtier when he came out of the cabin, that minute being pretty well known. But here he was overreached by the captain, who, when the first lieutenant retired, took Murray into his after-cabin, told him the trick which had been played upon him, and recommended him to take no notice whatever of it, but to run below and change his dress when the hands were turned up—"reef topsails;" and thus frustrated Mr. Weazel's kind intentions. The first lieutenant reported all present and sober at quarters: the order was given for the signal to be hoisted for the convoy to close round the commodore, and to take one reef in the topsails.

"And now," said the captain, as he heard the men rush up the ladders when the boatswain turned the hands up, "do you run below, and be quick: beat that flour out of your head, put on the clothes you wore this morning, and join in the laugh against yourself."

Down dived Mr. Murray: but he soon found that Weazel never slept over fun. The captain's kindness was almost frustrated, by the boy; he was resolved to have a good laugh, even if it finished in a good thrashing, and he took care to stow away Murray's dress. This, however, was soon remedied; and as Weazel was desired to remain at the mizen-topmast-head to count the convoy, although they were close alongside the frigate, he had not the satisfaction of seeing the consummation of his plan; and one hour before he was called down from his elevation, Murray was rigged according to orders, and was busy in making himself a sailor.

The night was nearly calm; the frigate, under easy sail, crept silently through the water at the rate of a knot and a half, and the convoy as silently followed the commodore. No sea ran to sicken Murray with his new profession—the stars were forth, and the moon shone beautifully on the smooth water. In such moments there are thoughts which steal over us and win us from ourselves; and those who have braved longest the perils of a sailor's life, feel most exquisitely the glory of the calm night, when the stars are reflected in the vast deep, and when the sea takes "the moods, and wears the colours of her mistress—the sky." He who first perils his existence on this mighty and immense mass of waters,—for, as Campbell says,

"The eagle's vision cannot take it in;
The lightning's wing, too weak to sweep its space,
Sinks half-way o'er it like a wearied bird;"—

experiences a solemn feeling of awe, of wonder—nay, oftentimes of fear. And yet, lost in the very magnificence of this image of eternity—this throne of the Invisible, man feels himself a prouder being, in the knowledge that the science of his fellow-creatures has taught him to explore its wondrous depths,—to steer uninjured by rocks or islands through its pathless desert, and to draw a higher and a better notion of the glory and divinity of his Maker by the never-ending wonders which are presented to him. The poor in pocket and in mind, condemned from youth to age to toil, perhaps in the darkness of a mine excavating the ore, and returning when oppressed with fatigue to the shed which serves him for a shelter: the mechanic, who from daylight to dark continues his labour in one city; the husbandman, who ploughs the field and sows the seed, who reaps the harvest and who stacks the hay,—can never have that exalted notion of man, and of man's works, as he whose whole life is one scene of continued change; who is associated to-day with the dark, sulky negro of the Gold Coast,—with the gay Frenchman to-morrow; who sees the pigmy race of Mexico or the giants of Patagonia,—much less can he form a just estimate of the power of the Divinity. The wonders of creation are to be seen in the ocean, and in the stupendous mountains of the Andes, or the still prouder Himalayas. It is in sights like these that man is convinced of his own insignificance, and yet of his own power: it is when standing on the Andes, and seeing a city like a speck, that he feels his vast inferiority. But he becomes conscious of the greatness of his intellect when he measures the heights above him with mathematical exactness, or looks for the moment — the well-calculated moment, when a comet shall return and be visible. Oh! the delight — the calm delight of pondering on such sublimity, supported by the still ocean! when the mind, in harmony with the scene, calmly surveys the greatness of the works of God.

The *Tribune* was a thirty-six gun frigate,—a small, compact, trim vessel. Her commander was a man of sterling worth and tried experience; and he was on the present occasion entrusted with the protection of a valuable convoy, bound, some to Quebec, and others to Newfoundland. Her orders were comprised in a few words,—"to see the convoy safe to its destination, and to await further orders from the admiral in Halifax."

There is no service so much detested by active officers in command of frigates, as that of counting every night and morning a certain number of merchant vessels in which they have no personal interest. The vigilance required is excessive; the drudgery of eternal signals to the slower sailers—the constant reproof to the inattentive masters, who, directly darkness allows an opportunity, edge away to make a run, not liking to be detained by their heavier companions, and anxious to avail themselves of the first of the market to which they are consigned—are everlasting. The forecastle gun is always in requisition, and the flags for the convoy to make more sail might always be kept bent and ready for hoisting. In war—and convoy frigates are useless except during a war—that which is the constant wish and thought of all must be relinquished. No suspicious sail must entice the frigate from her convoy: the sneaking schooner, edging perhaps towards the vessel farthest from the commodore, may be chased but not pursued; she may be scared away—not followed: and even the rich Bataviaman—the ship nearly sinking with wealth, must pass without obstruction, if in seeking her detention the convoy are likely to be run out of sight. Talk of patience! place a keen cruiser of a captain in a fast frigate with a slow convoy, and if he keeps his temper more than twenty-four hours, he will die of the effort the minute afterwards.

Murray from day to day grew in seamanship; he liked it wonderfully. It is true his never-sleeping annoyer had played him another trick by sending him to Mr. Scales to buy a quadrant. Mr. Scales had none in his shop, but recommended him to Ropeyarn, the boatswain's yeoman, who was unfortunately out of the article, but believed that the gentleman could be supplied by Mr. Chips, who kept a large carpenter's store and shop near the fore-hold. Again, however, was he to be disappointed: Mr. Chips had sold his last to Mr. Weazel, but knew that Mr. Handspike next door retained one. This, however, could not be sold without the consent of the captain of the foretop, Daniel Munroe, who was to be found in his house, of which his rank was the name, or in the garden which surrounded the huge *Agave America* which grew from its centre. To mount the fore-rigging was no easy undertaking, but Murray persevered; and as he nearly reached the abode of the gentleman to whom he was despatched, he found himself lashed to the rigging, only to be released by paying a certain sum, which was to entitle him to free ingress and egress to and from the above-named garden, and give him the right of plucking and eating any fruit he might find therein. The first step made aloft soon prompted Murray, under the encouragement of Hammerton, to use his best endeavours to reach the mast-head. The difficulty once overcome, was succeeded by the pleasurable sensation of surmounting a difficulty and of getting forward in the service;—nay, in spite of all the tricks of the youngsters, the hardship of the life, the discomforts to which the spoilt boy was subjected, he grew fonder and fonder of the service, and before the first breeze and sea-sickness were over, he had laughed at the prejudices of his youth, and was always to be seen where the greatest danger was to be encountered.

Boys of this stamp, however much addicted to pecuniary meanness, always do well on board a ship: they soon get the rough husk rubbed off, and by associating with lads of spirit and enterprise, partake a little of their companions' feelings, and soon become well disposed towards each other, and often establish friendships which last through life. There was one person, however, who, kind and obliging as he was, Murray hated: this was Hammerton. The feeling was engendered when he struck him, and became rooted in his mind when he heard himself placed under his control;—nay, the very patronizing manner which Murray imagined to be practised by Hammerton when he interfered to stop a quarrel, or to thrust himself into it in order to keep Murray out of it, was wormwood to the proud boy, who considered this officious intermeddler as a man supported by his father, and whose family might be reduced to beggary at the whim or caprice of Sir Hector.

Murray controlled his feelings; but the hatred increased—the blow was never to be forgotten; and although others of the oldsters pulled his ears or slapped his face, the injury was forgotten when the pain was over: but towards Hammerton he had quite a different feeling. Time, instead of obliterating, only strengthened his hatred;—kindness, instead of soothing this unfortunate disgust, only rendered it more lasting, and rooted it more deeply. Hammerton perceived it through the disguise by which Murray attempted to conceal it; and not feeling any animosity against Murray, and being well aware that Sir Hector was his best friend,—for from him alone had he any hopes of advancement, whilst his father, mother, and sisters subsisted upon the bounty of the baronet,—he would not allow himself to be deterred in his endeavours to teach Murray his duty, or slacken his kindness even when that kindness was refused. Murray was in Hammerton's watch. If it rained, Hammerton would ask the lieutenant to allow Murray to go below; but the latter, with determined spite, would rather stand on the lee gangway, and catch every drop which fell from the mainsail, than go below. If the officer of the watch was solicited, and gave him a hint to be off, he was in his hammock a minute afterwards. Such was his dislike to Hammerton, that he would sacrifice personal comfort even when the favour granted was one which was commonly accorded to every youngster in the ship, rather than accept it from him who was in reality his truest friend. Such are the contradictions of human nature, that in many cases we would rather receive the poisoned cup from an enemy than the most delicious nectar from our friend: it is a blindness of heart from which we may well earnestly desire to be delivered.

The *Tribune* had now been about a fortnight at sea, when the morning of the 2nd of November dawned upon her. During these fifteen days the convoy had nearly reached the Western Islands. Murray had overcome all disposition to sea-sickness, and was as much of a sailor as his short apprenticeship would allow. The clouds which at daylight began to rise suddenly from the north-west soon banked up heavily to leeward. At this time the wind was in the south-east quarter, and the convoy were going nearly before the wind; the frigate, under her topsails and foresail, making and shortening sail occasionally to keep close to her convoy. About seven o'clock the officer of the watch apprised Captain Barker that the wind showed every disposition to shift—that the scud aloft was going at a very considerable rate towards the south-east, and that a heavy squall was brewing ahead. The signal was instantly made for the convoy to shorten sail. The foresail of the *Tribune* was hauled up and a reef taken in the topsails. Every preparation was made for the coming squall, and finally the ship was brought to the wind and hove to. Several of the sternmost ships—for in spite of the vigilance and attention of the different officers of the watches, the convoy was much separated, and many ships far astern—disregarded the signal, and still kept their studding sails set in order to close the commodore. Some who must have seen the approaching breeze waited until it should arrive before they set seriously to work to reef their topsails; thus giving their crews about eight times the labour they otherwise would have had, and ultimately paying severely for their want of attention and discretion. About nine it fell a dead calm. In the south-east the sky was clear and cloudless; whilst in the opposite direction, dark, heavy purple masses rolled over each other, more unnatural in appearance owing to a lighter cloud covering the curling fluid as if with a veil. Shooting from this dark heap of clouds, some few were separated, and rose to a higher region of the air, in which they were dissipated and blown out like mares' tails, passing rapidly over the convoy: whilst on the water, and about a mile from the ships, the sea appeared as if covered with a thick white haze, before which seemed a dark line of black. As this was evidently no common squall, the hands were turned up, the topsails lowered and made as secure as possible, the yards were squared, the jib hauled down, and the fore-topmast staysail set—the *Tribune* lying at this time with her starboard broadside to the approaching storm. Murray had never seen a sight like this; and much as he had read in books of fiction, of waves rolling mountains high—of storms, of dangers, of perils encountered by seamen, yet he was by no means prepared for the silent approach of the enemy. There was evidently much apprehension on the countenances of several of the old seamen, and the first lieutenant was overheard to say that he was apprehensive the convoy were too close together, fearing that if a thick haze came on with the squall many ships would run on board of each other. It was in vain now to attempt to remedy this oversight: it was a calm, with the squall coming gradually up as if to burst upon them; and from the manner in which the dark cloud had blown over them—the immense rapidity with which it swept aloft, it was most evident that it would be a serious storm.

About half-past nine it burst upon the ships, and no pen can describe—no words give the most faint outline of the tremendous force with which it assailed the convoy. The *Tribune*, although so well prepared, suffered much: her main-topsail was shaken to ribands, the fore-topmast stay-sail disappeared in a moment, and the fore-top-gallant mast was carried away; the ship heeled over to port, and lay like a wreck upon the waters. Her loss, however, was trifling, compared to that suffered by those around her.

There was in the convoy a smart-looking schooner—a vessel always in her station, and one frequently sent astern to whip up the idle and the inattentive. This schooner was the *Jane*. Before the squall burst, her commander tried all in his power to creep a little ahead of the frigate, in order to avoid falling on board of her: indeed, so close was she, that she had been hailed to that effect by Captain Barker. When the first effect, which was momentary, had passed off, the schooner was seen close to the *Tribune* on her beam-ends and sinking. A cry louder than the wind reached the frigate, and the echo of "The schooner is upset!" was repeated fore and aft the frigate. Instantly some daring hands leapt into the small cutter on the larboard quarter. Hammerton was seen casting off the after-stopper; whilst, in the bow of the boat, Weazel, who was quite a boy, was observed using his utmost efforts to cast off the foremost stopper. Four or five men had got into the cutter, some casting off the gripes, others getting the stretchers clear to fend her off from the ship's side; and at this busy moment it was in vain that the master, a good seaman, declared that it was inevitable ruin to lower the boat—that she would be blown away to leeward and be of no service whatever: his voice was lost amidst the whistling hiss of the wind, as it surged through the rigging. At this instant Murray had got upon the hammocks and scrambled outside the mizen rigging, intending to reach the boat, unequal as he was to cope with such danger; for a fortnight's apprenticeship in light breezes will not enable a seaman to dare every peril in a gale. He still persevered; but at the moment when he reached over to touch the gunwale of the boat in order to throw himself into her, where he would have been useless, the gripes were cut off, and owing to the laying over of the frigate, the boat immediately swung away from the chains, and Murray dropped overboard between the space.

On occasions like these there are hundreds to give assistance, and all ready to bear witness of exertions either successfully or fruitlessly made. The deep-sea lead-line, which had been kept on the reel, was hanging in its beckets under the cleat of the larboard main-brace. The end was thrown into the cutter by Mr. Chubb, the master, before Murray fell overboard, and it was in Hammerton's hand when he saw the accident. The stopper was off; but owing to some confusion in the coil of the boat's fall, they would not lower her: or perhaps the man at the foremost fall had perceived that Weazel was not so quick, not being so strong as his messmate; and whilst another hand stronger than the youngster's took his place, Weazel was bundled very unceremoniously on board again. He had beckoned, for it was useless calling, to the man at the after-fall to hold on. There was not a minute's time—nay, nor half a minute's, in the performance of a duty which it takes much time to describe. Hammerton, finding that his order to "lower away" was unheeded, if not unheard, grasped the lead-line firmly, and was overboard in a second. Murray could swim a little; but the ship was drifting to leeward fast, and he was under the larboard counter, when Hammerton caught hold of him, and passing the rope under his arms, made it fast. Strange as it may seem, Murray actually tried to disengage himself from the rope; and even in that struggle, when his life was far from secure, he actually shook off the hold of Hammerton, and saw the brave fellow who had risked his own life to save his, drift round the stern without once stretching out his hand to proffer assistance. Murray was saved: a bowline knot was passed down by the lead-line, which fell over his shoulders, and he was hauled on board; but such was his hatred of Hammerton, that he never even inquired if he was saved, or spoke one word of encouragement to others, who, more ready and willing than himself, would have thrown a grating or an oar to save their favourite. The boat was now in the water; but all efforts were ineffectual to keep her head to wind; the spray blown from the ocean covered her as a tropical rain, and it was hard to say, if by the means attempted to rescue the men belonging to the *Jane*, the *Tribune* had not wilfully sacrificed her own. Hammerton was now far away on the weather quarter, evidently getting much exhausted, for the spray was so heavy, that if he had attempted to swim head to wind he must have been drowned. The boat's crew, regardless of the distance, which now became great, still plied their oars, and bent their backs to save Hammerton, the schooner being in the same direction, but a little to windward of him. She of course did not drift so fast to leeward as the frigate; and the last time either boat or Hammerton were seen, the one was pulling in a right line to save the other. Murray had watched the exertion with intense interest, nor did he turn away from the last gaze of the man he hated until the increased distance and the thickness of spray hid him from his sight.

The different ships of the convoy were much injured: more than four fell foul of each other; but the squall came on so fast, that one dismasted, and another with a signal of distress flying, were the only two which were observed on board the *Tribune*. Vain and useless were it to attempt to depict the scene. In vain was the shriek for assistance uttered, the uplifted hand of terror as a signal: in vain did those who still clung to the wreck of the *Jane* scream to those who risked their lives to save them—in vain was the eager supplication to heaven—the hasty repetition of the too long neglected prayer! And, oh! the bitter moment of memory, when even Hope withdrew her last light, and the *Jane* and her crew were immersed below the water! There sunk the father, the husband, the friend, the brave seaman, the beloved of many! and no imaginary tablet can be upraised amidst the rolling waves to point the grave of that gallant crew! When the sun dawned on that morning, and whilst the crew were engaged in the usual avocations of the seaman's life, little did they, in the full vigour of health, imagine that before the noonday sun should shine to guide the vessel on the pathless deep, that vessel should be a wreck! her sails scattered, her hull sunk, themselves drowned! cut off in a moment when danger was unthought of, and preparation deemed useless!

The crew of the cutter saw the schooner disappear. Hammerton, for the minute, had been rescued from the danger which assailed him; but his situation in the boat was apparently a mere prolongation of very uncertain existence—for when he recovered himself from the giddy effect of unusual exertion, no ship could be discovered as a welcome home to the wearied crew—not a speck on the now contracted horizon could point a way for escape. Although the gallant fellows still plied their oars and kept the boat's head towards the part where they imagined their frigate to be, yet gradually they grew weary of the ineffectual labour, boated their oars, and looked at each other with despairing countenances.

On board the *Tribune* all was exertion to recover the boat. The fury of the first squall being past, it was now possible to carry a little sail; but, owing to the fog which had thickened with the squall, all was uncertainty as to what was best to be done. To wear and make sail might be to cross the boat, pulling in an opposite direction, besides the fear of running on board some of the convoy. It was useless to continue firing guns: the wind was so high that the noise of the explosion scarcely reached the taffrail, and it was evident that one hundred yards astern the sound could never reach. In the meantime the sea had begun to run, and the danger grew more imminent. After a consultation with the first lieutenant and the master, it was resolved to keep the frigate as near her present position as possible, and if in half an hour's time no appearance of the boat became visible, to wear under a close-reefed main-topsail and foresail, and endeavour to preserve not an improbable distance from the scene of the calamity. This was no time for inactivity: the sails were reefed, and not an order was given without being followed by the continued disheartening question of, "Can you see the boat?" Men were stationed in every part of the ship: but those aloft could not see so far as those on deck. The captain strained his eyes; glasses were used, and as quickly laid aside. The guns were still fired, however: the whole crew were on the alert. There was but one person below—it was Murray.

CHAPTER VIII.

SIR HECTOR MURRAY'S VISIT TO OLD HAMMERTON.—A MELANCHOLY TALE.

NEAR one of the prettiest towns in England, Taunton, in Somersetshire, there *was*—for Time has not spared it—a neat white cottage. It stood near the high-road, almost opposite to a splendid lodge, which was the entrance to the estate of Sir Hector Murray. On one side was all the economical neatness of good taste reduced to circumscribed limits; on the other, all the display of riches. The small, neatly gravelled pathway to the cottage was but the ghost of the broad road which led to the mansion of Sir Hector: still, however, the nicely trained plants which grew in great luxuriance on the fertile ground gave rather an elegant appearance to the smaller abode, and comfort was evidently to be found where riches could not command it. The leaves were now falling before the last of the autumnal gales; the blossoms had long since forsaken the plants; the azalea, which brightened in summer and spread its thick yellow blossoms, was now a leafless shrub; the gaudy peony, whose thick, deep flower had beautified the little gardens cut with scrupulous exactness from a small grass plat dignified as a lawn, was divested of its summer grandeur; the lively lilac, the golden, showery laburnum, and all those millions of Nature's fairest ornaments, were fast assuming the cold deadness of winter; and even Somersetshire wore a certain periodical dulness which three months previously had been unknown.

It is strange that at this season of the year, when Nature puts on her richest dress, as if to entice the intelligent and the curious to examine her, many human beings seem to shun the beauties which a bountiful Providence has spread over the land, and congregate in cities, to revel in crowded assemblies; but when, as if to warn man that he should seek the companionship of his own fellow-mortals, the earth is covered with snow, or when the wintry showers descend in such torrents that exercise is debarred,—then, instead of seeking the warm cheerfulness of society, and enjoying the luxury which is concentrated in large communities, as if in contradiction to the law of nature, the towns are deserted, and the country swarms with the tide of human beings.

This is neither the first nor the hundredth time that a similar remark has been made; and on this subject, without derogating much from the stubborn opposition which characterises the English people, they might borrow a little wisdom from their long-hated neighbours the French. With us legislators pant in oppressive heat, instead of deliberating coolly on the measure before them; and the best effort of eloquence falls dully upon the ear when oppressive heat relaxes the body and unstrings the mind.

It was about noon, as we have said, towards the close of autumn, that an old gentleman, dressed in deep mourning, and with a countenance mânifesting woe and heaviness of heart, stood leaning over the cottage gate, looking at a travelling-carriage which was approaching, and which stopped while the great gates of Sir Hector's estate opened to receive their master. Sir Hector, who saw old Mr. Hammerton, made him a bow of recognition, which was answered with much form by the old gentleman. As he lifted his hat, the long gray hairs, thin enough to be moved by any breeze, fell upon his shoulders; and a finer specimen of beneficence and benevolence never brightened the human countenance more than in the features of Mr. Hammerton.

Struck by the unusual figure before him, Sir Hector desired his servant to open the carriage-door; and descending with a proper slow and stately step, he bade his servants take the carriage home whilst he crossed the road; and extending his hand with much cordiality, he began, "It is many years, Mr. Hammerton, since I have had the pleasure of seeing you: I trust your health continues unimpaired, and that your wife and family are well."

Sir Hector paused for a reply, and was much disconcerted when he saw the old gentleman turn away and commence beating with his stick against the door. Almost immediately a beautiful little girl about ten years of age came running towards Mr. Hammerton; and after looking with an inquisitive glance, she turned to Sir Hector and said, "Papa, sir, is quite deaf: *I* can make him understand if you mention to me what you desire."

Sir Hector repeated his former question; the child by her

fingers and signs made the old gentleman understand, and he answered—for he was not dumb—that he believed it was now twenty years since he had *seen* Sir Hector,—he therefore apologised for not having recognized him at first, but now gladly seized the opportunity of expressing his sincere thanks for the many kind and liberal proofs of friendship he had given him. Here he was interrupted by the baronet, who took the old man's hand and pressed it warmly in his own. The little girl stood interpreter to the following conversation :—

"I have," said Sir Hector, "renewed our acquaintance, Mr. Hammerton, in order, if possible, to convince you that, notwithstanding the little bickerings and acrimonious feeling which separated us, and which I am willing to believe originated in myself, the good wishes of my heart were ever warm towards you. Your son is on board the same ship as my son ; and I have placed Walter under the direction of your Frederick, thus bringing them together, in the hope that a permanent friendship may exist ; and further that, should I be suddenly cut off, this cottage and these grounds may be your undisturbed possession ; for I hear you have grown to this spot, and regard it with more than common affection."

"When I was in distress, Sir Hector," answered the old man, "you stepped forward : when greedy creditors would neither allow me time to repair the mischief, nor even give me a place in which to lay my head, you came forward and lent me this : when my wife,"—and here the old man became much affected,—"who now is an angel in heaven,—brought me this dear little child into the world, your liberality supplied her with medical advice, and the dainties which affluence only can afford. From the first moment of my entering this abode—now sacred to me, since it is but a month since she who had contributed to my happiness, and bore without a murmur the increased infirmities and troubles of life, was taken from me, you, although you concealed the donation, have regularly remitted me one hundred pounds a-year. I was a stranger to you—had no tie, no relationship, no claim upon you ; I was relieved by you when even my own family turned their backs upon me. Can you be surprised, then, that I should desire to end my days in this abode? I would be a beggar for that favour; and when I am gone, Frederick must be a father and protector to this dear little child; and may the God of mercy shield her from the sufferings her parents have experienced!"

"Fear not for her, my old friend, nor for your son: if I live, he shall be advanced in the service, and placed beyond the chance of want; he who is now a guide to my son shall not find me unmindful of his services, and I will this evening add a codicil to my will, leaving in it an earnest request to my son that you and your family shall never be disturbed in this dwelling. You know they both have sailed—their destination is to Halifax."

"I know it," replied Mr. Hammerton; "for Frederick has written twice since he sailed. I suppose your son has not omitted to avail himself of the same opportunities?"

"I have not heard," replied Sir Hector, "since the day they sailed;" and here the mortification of Sir Hector was visible.

"I dare say," interrupted Mr. Hammerton, "that the poor fellow was sea-sick; but of this you may rest assured, that he was going on well in his profession: my son particularly mentions that he was active and intelligent, and very careful to do all that he desired. Besides, sir, when a youngster first enters the service, he generally has so much to do in his own ideas that some excuse will readily be made for him."

"How old are you, my pretty little girl?" asked Sir Hector, willing to change a conversation which did not exalt his son in his estimation.

"I am just ten, sir," replied the little dark-eyed beauty.

"Just ten?" replied the baronet; "does that mean you are past ten, or nearly ten?"

"I shall be ten on the 2nd of November," lisped Amelia.

"I shall not forget your birthday, I dare say," said the baronet, as he took a book from his pocket and made a memorandum; "we shall be better friends and neighbours, I trust, for the future, And now, Mr. Hammerton, you must walk over with little Amelia and dine with me. I am a poor lone trunk now; the prop which might have supported me has left me, and I find that wealth and large estates do not necessarily give either comfort or happiness; for, although I confess it is selfish to say so, I would relinquish nearly all, to have my son near me to the end of my life. It is true I walk through large halls and splendid rooms, but the voice of my child is wanting; and you, Mr. Hammerton, have twice the satisfaction in life, by having by your side one who must love and respect you, and whose little winning and affectionate look would chase away any gloom. But I must get out of this moody manner, and I doubt not your kindness will bestow a few moments on a man who has long respected you."

"I should be ungrateful, Sir Hector, if I did not acknowledge at all times your kindness to me."

"Then let me beg of you to acknowledge it by your silence upon that subject. Come, my little interpreter:—why, your fingers and your eyes would make any man understand a speech in parliament. Take my arm, Mr. Hammerton: I think I am strongest upon my legs, although the gout every now and then does all the mischief in its power, and whilst it makes them thicker makes them weaker. How long has your son been at sea, Mr. Hammerton?"

"Five years," replied the old gentleman; "and during that time I have only seen him once. He has seen some service: he was in Howe's action, and escaped untouched. I put him with Barker, because that kind man, whom I knew under different circumstances, did not forget a former kindness, and was anxious to requite it."

"If, Mr. Hammerton, the subject is not too painful to you, let me ask you how you became deaf? for when I knew you before, you heard as well as any man, and your age is not sufficient—without some sickness or some great nervous excitement—to have caused this infirmity."

"It is a melancholy tale, but it is soon told, Sir Hector. I had another son: you may remember him, for he was alive when I last saw you. His name was Charles, and he was my eldest boy. During the period of my affluence, I had not withheld the benefits of education from him, and I saw the seeds of a refined mind gradually developing themselves in him. He was studious; I intended him for the church, in which I had some little interest; and looked forward with some hope that one day my son would become a distinguished minister of peace. I often pictured to myself the pleasure I should experience in hearing the congregation, as they crowded through the porch of the church, express their admiration of the discourse, and from the poorer classes hear my son called as good as he was wise. His early habits of charity—his ceaseless regard for the poor—his solicitude for the sick—his mildness—his benevolence—all qualified him for the sacred profession he himself had chosen, and which should never be ventured on by the thoughtless lover of pleasure. I own to you, Sir Hector, I have a sovereign contempt for your sporting parson—a man who crams his horse at a fence to keep pace with yelping dogs which run the faster the nearer they are to a death; nor can I think it consistent with the character of a minister of Christianity—one who should spare, not slay—to occupy his mornings in shooting. When the winter with all its rigour cramps the aged and the infirm, it is little consistent with the character of a minister of God to gallop over fields and waste his time in pursuing a poor and hunted creature: rather should he then be striving to warm the hearts of his parishioners."

"Surely," said Sir Hector, "you would not debar the clergyman from all recreation?"

"Assuredly not. There is recreation for the mind in the solacing of others. I would not have him a weed to choke the exertions of the flowers around him, or by too much austerity rebuke the innocent gaieties of others. Those who think it a sin to smile on the Sabbath, I hold to be fanatics. Could we find one amongst all the fanatical preachers who would lie down for years upon a bed of spikes for the love of God? I have always remarked that your over-pious person has generally been the greatest sinner; and as a racket-ball rebounds the farthest the harder it is propelled, so the reaction is the greater in proportion to the extent of crime. No man has a greater regard for the proper performance of religious duties than I have—no one a more thorough contempt for those who arrogate to themselves a superiority from the nonsensical belief in an inward light, or who proudly, impiously,—nay, blasphemously, sit in judgment upon others, and denounce them as the children of Satan—the infants of the devil."

"I confess myself much of your opinion, Mr. Hammerton,"

remarked Sir Hector; "and I think the parents who allow their children to enter the Church, knowing that from their manner of life they are unfit to uphold its sacred character, are more to blame than the eager young man who is anxious to hear his own voice in public and to read his own production to his attentive congregation. But you have been led from your subject in your zeal for the Church."

"True, Sir Hector,—apparently so; but, in reality, it was done on purpose to save myself the repetition of anguish. You have a right to know all, however, which concerns myself; and as I am now somewhat prepared for the task, you must bear the infliction of its recital:—

"My son was about eighteen, as handsome as ever a mother could wish; and, as if preparing himself for the honourable profession he had chosen, he had relinquished all the sportsman's pursuits, and would for hours walk in the fields studying. Frequently, such was the enthusiasm of his mind, when darkness stopped his studies, he would find himself far from home. The poor all knew him, and knew his circumstances. At that time I had very little to give him; but the little I could spare, he gave to others more in want of it than himself. The blessings of the poor followed his steps, and his security was in the affections of all around him.

"It was in December, 1780, that we heard of a family, about ten miles distant, which had been swept away, with the exception of the widow, by that fearful disease the small-pox. My children all had it when young, excepting Charles; and although many of the gentlemen in the neighbourhood sent money, as I know you did, Sir Hector, yet few would venture within the poisoned walls of the wretched and lonely widow. Charles, when he heard of it, instantly prepared for his long walk; and, although his mother and myself warned him of the danger he ran, yet he was resolved to see the poor woman, and to return home to get whatever she most required. He promised us not to go into the house, and he kept his word. The old woman received the small pittance we were able to collect for her, and with outstretched hands to heaven she prayed that he who thus relieved the miserable, might never want the protecting arm of God in any adversity! Vain prayer unheeded! Who dares to direct the will of the Omnipotent? His ways are inscrutable! Who can avert the evil when the hour is arrived? My boy's goodness led to his death. That evening he returned home in high spirits at having gained his point. Finding the poor woman in much distress, he had taken a circuitous route to regain his home; had called on several gentlemen, and by his warmth and eloquence,—for in England the ears of the affluent are seldom closed against the tale of misery,—he had obtained from one some wine, from another some medicine, from a third money. Tired and jaded as he was, he could not restrain the generous feelings which animated him. He proposed—it was then eight o'clock—to rest a little and to return that night. Against this I interposed my authority; for the snow fell fast, and drifted so as to conceal the path, and it was not a time for a solitary boy to venture on a walk of ten miles. But the next morning, although the severity of winter was at its height, he started at the first dawn of day, delivered the comforts he had gathered, promised a visit on the following day, and returned home. The third day the rain fell so fast that I kept him from his wishes. That very restraint, the offspring of parental affection, blighted all my hopes. By three in the afternoon the storm subsided: Charles was instantly on the alert. From that moment to this all is conjecture. He reached the poor woman's cottage,—that we have ascertained, and that he proceeded on his return home. We hardly expected him before ten o'clock, and all the little comforts we could command were in preparation for our son. Well I remember the shoes which were placed before the fire, and the change of linen; all that a mother's care could suggest to render her son happy—all that could show an anxious parent's love of her child was then displayed. The swift hand of time!—for time never lingers when anxiety commences—when an object is expected and yet comes not to the moment. Eleven o'clock, and no sound of the wicket-latch had preceded the footstep of my son. I told his mother to go to bed; but that order was useless. We sat in silence, only interrupted by remarking how quickly the hour flew. Midnight came on: the murmuring breeze had swelled into a gusty, riotous noise; the little rain, which before feebly reached our shutters, now came with quick force upon our dwelling; and as the morning wind, the herald of misfortune, died for a moment in order to resume a greater strength, we heard the voices of men—we heard our wicket open—we ran to open the door, which common prudence had left barred and bolted. Oh! gracious Heaven! I received my dead son, my murdered boy into my house! The knife of the assassin had nearly severed his head! his eyes seemed started from their sockets! whilst his firm hands were closed beyond our strength to open them. I stood like a statue; I scarcely could credit the awful truth before me. I never spoke; but with eyes fixed and riveted on my Charles, I heeded not those around me. They tell me my wife's scream might have been heard above the storm: she was as close to me as you are. I never heard it—I never caught one sound of it; but, lifting my eyes on those who had brought him to me, I saw their lips move, I saw the eager description of the dreadful crime; but from that hour to this I have never heard a human voice. I pray that at the great day, when the secrets of all hearts shall be disclosed, I may stand before my Maker with the same hope of redemption as my son—for I have a belief that he will be numbered among the blessed."

The poor old man, overcome by the effort he had made, fell back upon a sofa, for they had reached the room long before the painful recital began. The little child leaned over and kissed him, and then sat upon a cushion near him, holding his hand; whilst Sir Hector felt for him as a man, and consoled him as a Christian. After a pause of some moments, Sir Hector remarked that from one expression which escaped Mr. Hammerton, there was a slight allusion to the cause of this murder.

"By signs and by having the sad account written," replied Mr. Hammerton, "I only gleaned that three labourers passing the road, observed a body lying by the side of the ditch. As the weather was bitterly cold and rainy, they imagined it must either have been a man intoxicated, who had fallen down and slept in spite of the elements, or that sickness had overtaken the traveller.

On lifting it, their horror may be better imagined than described, when they saw that it was a murdered man. They took it instantly to a house not far distant, and my son was recognized by a poor old man he had often relieved. No trace, no tidings of those who did this savage deed have ever been discovered: years have passed away, the crime has gone unrevenged, and perhaps the murderers prosper. But it was so ordained, and it is not for us to arraign the decrees of Providence; rather let us bow with all submission to His will."

"Surely, Mr. Hammerton, you do not believe that it was destiny,—that it was ordained above that this murder should be committed on earth?"

"You put the question strongly, Sir Hector, and I am embarrassed how to answer. The belief that it was predestined is my only solace. If I discredited that, I should consider myself the direct cause of my son's death."

"There are few men, Mr. Hammerton, who argue this great question with coolness and with reason. Men embrace the creed readily which yields the most comfort. It is evident that if we are not left to our own guidance here, we cannot be responsible hereafter. The belief in predestination shakes to the dust the free agency of man, and renders him nothing more than a mere puppet at a show, the strings being worked by other hands. To what use shall we turn conscience? It ceases to be an inward monitor, to forewarn us of the commission of a crime, and must be considered only as a part of memory which most vividly retains the picture. Is it not more consistent with reason to argue that certain men who existed by plunder, and who nightly prowled about for prey, met your son: they saw by his dress and manner that he was a gentleman; they imagined that money was always to be found upon such a person; they demanded it; he resisted; they, to be rid of a man who held the thread of their lives in his power, rushed upon him, and finding him powerful and likely to escape, murdered him? Is it not, I say, more consistent with reason to argue thus, than to consider that it was predestined before the formation of the world,—for you must go so far back as that—that those men should be at a certain public-house at such a time, and leave it to a minute; that the old widow should be ill, and that your son should leave home exactly at three o'clock to relieve her? And all—what for? why, that a murder should be committed."

"I own, Sir Hector, it does look like desperation of thought; but the belief that it was so ordained gives me great—nay, my only comfort; for I cease to weep when I think that I could not avert it; I cease to mourn when I ought to rejoice. It is this thought which comes as a consolation in my affliction, and strengthens me now to bear up against my accumulated misfortune in the loss of my wife. How could you, Sir Hector, bear to have a child fair and lovely like that little angel, to see others catch the quick remarks she made; to see the joyful smile play over the countenances of strangers as her childish wit suggested the ready reply, and yet never to hear her, never to have heard one word she uttered? If you, like me, should stand in the church deaf, stone deaf, and murmur your prayers in silence; if you feel what it is to see the preacher exhorting his Christian brethren to repentance; or whilst you saw others with eager ears catching every sound, and bearing witness of the truth by the flushed cheek, the quivering lip, and not unfrequently the tearful eye; then would you feel as I feel, a great, an only consolation in believing that my present affliction was an evil ordained, which I could neither fly from nor avert."

"I believe," continued Sir Hector, "that great misfortunes are likely to lead to the extraordinary belief we have just argued. Yours are great, and you bear them like a man; as far as human power can alleviate them, I will alleviate yours. We must consider this question again under other circumstances. I own, at this time, when newfangled opinions on the awful subject are bandied at every table; and when, I grieve to say, many learned men employ their time and their talents to undermine the belief of their neighbours, and to take from them their greatest consolation by shaking their faith,—that I feel much inclined to be, as far as my poor abilities will permit, a more than silent upholder of our Church. Our neighbours the French have given us sad examples what brutes men become when they have shaken off the restraint of religion; and I, as a father, would strive to inculcate that doctrine from which I have received so much comfort. My son, Mr. Hammerton, is not exactly a Charles or a Frederick Hammerton."

"I would to heaven, Sir Hector, he were like one or the other. In my children I have been blessed; Charles was all a father could wish, Frederick is the stay and prop of my house, and that dear little affectionate Amelia, my consolation, my hope! Although Providence has afflicted me in some respects, the balance is still in my favour. But who would have riches for a disobedient boy to inherit? or what affluence could compensate for the dreadful calamity of seeing one's own blood turning against one? Thus, Sir Hector, do I borrow consolation from the ills of others, and verify an old saying, 'There is something in the misfortunes of our best friends which alleviates our own.' Your boy, like mine, will do well. Perhaps from over-indulgence—for an only child, Sir Hector, is always a little spoilt—he may be a little refractory; but the benefit of example and discipline will soon restore him to rectitude of conduct. He must be brave to be a Murray, and to be a Murray he must be good."

"I hope," said Sir Hector, with a smile, "you were predestined to be a prophet; but that boy has given me much uneasiness, and the fact of your having received two letters while I have not received one since they sailed, does not contribute to make me feel more satisfied with his conduct. Come, Mr. Hammerton, dinner waits."

CHAPTER IX.

THE BOAT AT SEA.—A SHIP IN SIGHT.—MUTINY AND DISAPPOINTMENT.

It has been said that friendships contracted early, or those formed late in life, are generally of a more lasting nature than friendship formed in the intermediate time. Sir Hector, now without his boy, experienced much pleasure in the society and conversation of Mr. Hammerton. Every morning some little comforts of life were sent to the cottage; and the quiet gentlemanly manner in which these comforts were conveyed, rendered Mr. Hammerton less averse to accepting them, and softened his pride, if one so humbled could be proud.

The 2nd of November, the day on which the *Tribune* experienced that heavy gale, and on which Hammerton was so miserably separated from his ship, was a day of great rejoicing at the cottage. Amelia received a handsome present from Sir Hector in the shape of a workbox; and it was whilst with childish eagerness she removed the reels for cottons that she discovered a small piece of paper, on which was written a cheque for one hundred pounds. Mr. Hammerton was at once aware of the delicate manner in which Sir Hector had conveyed this timely present, and the tears started from his eyes as he pressed his benefactor's hand. But Sir Hector had not stopped here; he had written a letter, dating it on Amelia's birthday, to Frederick, directed to Halifax, in which he had enclosed fifty pounds, with a desire that if Mr. Frederick Hammerton should at any time require pecuniary assistance, he would draw for the amount upon Sir Hector Murray. In this letter he desired his affectionate remembrance to his son, mentioning that he had heard of him twice from Mr. Hammerton, but that he had not received a line from himself.

Sir Hector now resolved to remain in Somersetshire for five or six months; and scarcely a day passed without Mr. Hammerton being an inmate for some hours at the hall. Thus time glided on agreeably to both the old gentlemen until the middle of December.

We must now return to Frederick Hammerton and his few companions in their frail boat. When he had sufficiently recovered from the stupor occasioned by his great exertions in maintaining himself above water, Hammerton became much alarmed for the situation of those who had thus generously risked their lives to save his own. He was the only officer in the boat; for Weazel, who was ever ready for any dangerous enterprise, as well as for any practical joke, had been called out of the boat before she was lowered;—in fact, he rather delayed than expedited the movement, for his strength was unequal to the casting off the stopper; but his generous disposition had been shown, and was not overlooked by either his officers or messmates.

No sooner had Hammerton surveyed the danger by which he was surrounded, than he took the command with as much coolness as if he had been sailing up Portsmouth harbour. He was sensible that he was rescued from one peril only to face a greater.

The different ships of the convoy, finding they had made but bad work of shortening sail, bore up before the squall, and were soon far, far distant from the boat. The frigate wore at the appointed time, and crossed the boat out of sight; and when, towards evening, as the sun was going down, the haze cleared off and the wind abated, not a speck was to be seen in any direction. The cutter of the *Tribune*, with six men and Hammerton, all hungry, faint, exhausted, with two breakers of water, but no provisions of any kind, was alone on the wide waters.

The setting sun, which blazed in all its glory before it sank below the western horizon, was the first object which recalled to Hammerton's mind that the boat was standing to the southward—or rather, that her head was in that direction; for Hammerton had considered it the best plan to keep only one oar at work to leeward, in order to keep the cutter's bow to the sea, and with this view had made the other men take spell and spell about; his object, like that of the captain, being to remain as near his first situation as possible. To look for the frigate was hopeless; and as the wind had so far moderated as to allow him to carry sail, he put her head towards the north-east, stepped the mast, and set the close-reefed sail.

Here at once is an instance of the prudence of first lieutenants in well-disciplined ships: the oars, mast, and sails of the boat had been lashed amidships in her. Fortunately that which is often done—the removing the masts and sails out of the quarter-boats in order to lighten the weight upon the davits,—was no plan on board the *Tribune*. Captain Barker always kept every boat ready for service, and the two breakers of water now in her proved how necessary such precautions were: many lives have been sacrificed in the Navy from covering the boats on the quarter, and many are imprudent enough to remove the masts and sails.

This was a trying situation to one so young as Hammerton; and it was when the sun's upper rim was but for a moment visible before it sank below the horizon, that Hammerton's busy memory recalled to him that this unfortunate day was the birthday of his only sister Amelia. Little did Sir Hector think, and Mr. Hammerton know, when they drank Frederick's health after dinner, and when his father added, "May God bless and prosper him!" how necessary were their prayers. Little did they think he was then sitting half-drowned in a lonely boat with six other gallant fellows, their only hope of salvation being their safe arrival at one of the Western Islands.

In the cutter there was an awful silence: the near approach of darkness, although the weather moderated gradually, brought with it much apprehension to the minds of all; but as yet discipline maintained its place, and none spoke aloud of either dangers or difficulties. Hammerton, whose thoughts took a homeward range, looked into futurity with a dreadful fear. In the event of his death, he beheld his sister an unprotected orphan; his father he knew could not last long; his mother he believed alive, but upon the verge of the grave—for in comforting her husband she had ruined her own health: and thus did an hour fly in thoughts of home—of former happiness, and of trembling apprehension for the future. He was awakened from this dream of reality by one of the seamen asking "what he intended to do?"

"To reach the Western Islands," replied Hammerton. "We have only about two hundred and fifty miles to go, and I think they ought to bear about north-north-east of us. We look up nearly our course, for there is the north star; the weather is moderating, and with another reef out of the sail and keeping her full, we may force the boat along five or six miles an hour. But we have another hope almost greater than our success in reaching either Corvo or Flores,—which is the possibility of meeting some of our convoy: they will push for the Western Islands to repair damages, and some which were dismasted may yet supply us with a home. One thing, my lads, we must all join in—that is, a resolution not to waste the water in the breakers. We are all in the same perilous condition—any chance may save us; but we must not oppose ourselves to the possibility of chance rendering that assistance: each man must now be a sentinel over us all. With the water and our shoes, or what chance may throw in our way—sea-weed—a turtle perhaps,—we may manage to hold up well and strongly for three or four days; in that time, if no gale of wind comes to mar our hopes, we may be safe and snug on shore. At any rate, it is no use looking on the worst side of the picture. We are, it is true, in a sad situation, and nothing but forbearance, prudence, and courage can extricate us. I thank Heaven, although I am the innocent cause of this calamity, that it was in endeavouring to save others I became that cause; you in endeavouring to savc me have now need of the assistance of others: but as long as I live, my brave fellows, I trust you will neither want an example nor a guide. From me you must learn to bear without a murmur the privation of food, and from me you must learn to hold up against difficulties and dangers. I speak to men—men who have already volunteered to sacrifice their livcs for the crew of a strange vessel, not one of whom was known to any of you; and I now call upon you to keep steady and resolute of purpose, in ordcr that each may assist thc other—that each may contribute to keep up the spirits of the rest."

"I wish," said an old fellow who was sitting on the afterthwart, "that we had the purser's steward and some grog here to keep our spirits in the natural way."

"We'll do all that's right, Mr. Hammerton," said a second; "but I should like a drop of water just now."

"Well, my lad," replied Hammerton, "you can have it. I think it would be better now to begin as we are to go on, —to serve out the small quantity we must allow each other, to arrange the watchet, and to make the best of this bad business. So now, Jones, hand up that breaker, and let us start the bung."

"Ay, ay, sir," said the gallant fellow, as he reached his hand towards the object; and then he looked up with a face that showed the sincerity of his words, whilc hc said, "It's half, if not quite empty."

A thrill of horror ran through Hammerton: here at once half his hope was destroyed. The crew seemed instinctively to catch the rising fear, and a movement was made towards the other, when Hammerton said with great coolness, "Never mind; the other is full, and we shall be safe long before that is finished." But no imagination can picture his feeling of horror lest thc same words of distress should arise when the other breaker was lifted.

"It's full!" said the sailor who lifted it.

"Thank God! thank God!" said Hammerton, as he raised his hands to heaven. "How grateful, my lads, ought we to be that the man whose duty it was to have secured this breaker has done it more effectually than the idle fellow from whose carelessness we might have lost our lives. Is there nothing in the first breaker?"

"Why, it rattles a bit, sir," replied M'Donald, a hardy, fearless Scotchman, who had learned in his younger days to think a handful of oatmeal a luxurious feast; "and I think it must have a quart or two in it."

"Then let us begin with that first: hand it here."

A small pannikin, which had been used to bail the boat, was likewise handed aft; and Hammerton, with steady exactness, measured the allowance to each. When this was done, he poured out for himself, taking about half what he had given to the others.

"No, no, sir," said M'Donald; "fair play's a jewel. Molly, let go my hair, and I'll fight till I die! We won't have a drop more than you, and you must take your allowance. You served it out to us, and now I will stand mate of the tub, and give you your portion."

Hammerton, who had controlled his desire, could not resist this generous display of feeling in his comrades; and the last drop in the breaker hardly gave him his full and fair allowance. "And now, my lads," said he, "I think from the feeling you have just manifested, that we shall all face this danger like men. We must not, however, leave ourselves blindly to chance. We are in the hands of Him who made us; but we must exert all our powers to retain the life He has been pleased to bestow. This, in our case, will be best effected by regularity. We will divide ourselves into three watches. M'Donald and Jones, you are in the first watch; Wilson and Barrow, you are in the second; and Henderson and Williamson, you are in the third. I am in all your watches, to be on the alert continually! And now we must pipe the hammocks down: but, before we go to sleep, let me implore you, my lads, to kneel down with me, offer up thanks for our deliverance until now, and earnestly pray that God's mercy may still be extended towards us."

The six men then, with the exception of the steersman, joined Hammerton, who knelt in the stern-sheets, in a short but heartfelt prayer for deliverance.

As Hammerton ceased, a simultaneous Amen responded from all; and "they rose," as M'Donald said, "better men, with better courage."

The cutter was a lugger-rigged boat, with a fore and mizen sail. Both were now set without any reefs; and those who were appointed to keep the first watch came aft into the stern-sheets; the other four went forward, or in the midships of the boat; and Hammerton lay down with his head on the breaker of water. Young as he was, he knew that when hunger or thirst assailed, reflection never interposed her authority to check the desire. He had read of shipwrecks, and of the crews on rafts, even during the first night, having seized the provisions, and in one moment rendered starvation a certainty; but in these acts of insubordination, the mischief had generally arisen from bad characters, who were only to be controlled by the fear of punishment; and as that restraint had been withdrawn, the wild disposition had broken adrift to the prejudice of all.

Amongst the six men there was but one who bore a suspicious character—and this was Jones. Hammerton had placed him under the eye of M'Donald, one of the finest specimens of a British sailor—a man known for his rigid adherence to truth—a petty officer, a good seaman, a brave and a generous man; and when Hammerton placed Jones in his watch, he conveyed by a glance of his eye what his tongue would have said had he been on board the *Tribune*. It may be supposed that Jones could not be a very bad man, as he risked his life for others; but history affords many instances of the most doubtful characters not unfrequently proffering generous assistance.

It was not without a suspicion that Jones might attempt to purloin a draught of water that Hammerton made the breaker his pillow. The calm tranquillity of a good conscience assisted him to sleep; and in a situation which would have kept most people awake, did five out of the seven find refreshing repose. Hammerton was frequently on the alert during the night, in order to see that the boat's head was kept as much towards the north star as possible; and when the approaching daylight hid that guide from their eyes, he steered the boat himself, making a due allowance from the rising of the sun.

At daylight each anxious eye was somewhat saddened, from the conviction that not a vessel was in sight,—no fog-bank even gave a hope, a momentary hope, that land was in view;—and many of them would willingly have been deceived;—but on this occasion, the eager eye, which scanned with expressive care every second of the degrees by which they were encircled, turned sickened by the useless effort, and the tongue bore witness to the fact as it repeated, "Nothing in sight! nothing in sight!" The wind, however, continued fair, and the little cutter slipped along. This was some consolation; although now the appeal of human nature in the shape of hunger came rather strongly, as if determined to draw its proper attention.

For two days their condition remained much the same, saving that the wind shifted to the north; and Hammerton saw the first approach of insubordination on the evening of the third day in Jones's careless levity, and in his many expressions, approaching even to taunting Hammerton with having been the occasion of their misery. M'Donald sat quietly on the after-thwart, making as much out of a shoe as would suffice for breakfast; and the even-tempered Scotchman, as he returned it to his foot, after he had taken his allowance of water, said, "Aweel—aweel, I'm just thinking it's no very great hardship, after all, to have soles for breakfast: and an idle mon might rather like the business of being obliged to do nothing, just as well as hollystoning the lower deck during his watch below."

Jones, however, soon began to show a worse spirit; he could neither control his hunger nor his tongue, and he vented his abuse against all the creation at a breath, finishing by making an attempt to tear the leather hat from Wilson's head. Wilson defended that which was not only a defence for his head, but his all for his stomach, and a serious affray took place. Hammerton immediately rushed at Jones, who now boldly disobeyed his orders, refused to acknowledge his control, and in the fury of his passion struck him more than once; the others took their officer's part, and the business finished by Jones being rendered incapable of more mischief, from the exhaustion his exertions had occasioned.

This was, however, a sad harbinger of that which was to follow. The line of discipline had been cut through, the officer had sunk to the level of his men, an open defiance had been manifested, and it was evident that each person was too much occupied with himself to pay any attention to Hammerton's directions. The many long hours of daylight, —long, for no occupation but that of thought could interfere to divert hunger,—wore slowly away. Jones refused to take his turn to steer: he lay forward with his face in his hands, cursing and swearing, and calling loudly to the others to seize the breaker and have a good hearty draught at once. It was evident that he had not a very inattentive audience—Barrow and Williamson seemed much inclined to join him; and although the evil was postponed, yet the thought had been engendered. Towards noon the wind died away, and the idle and useless sail flapped against the mast as the boat rolled from side to side.

Hammerton, who knew that every minute was precious, suggested the necessity of using the oars: and one or two, such as M'Donald and Wilson, immediately took their places. But when they found that Jones, Barrow, and Williamson refused to lend a hand, they remained inactive; and quite unavailing was the example set by Hammerton, who seized an oar, and worked away until fatigue and annoyance overcame him. He addressed his men again; but it was useless, —they were clamorous for water, and they resolved to have it. In this they were opposed by M'Donald, Wilson, and Hammerton, who in vain kept saying, "Fools that you are! you only hasten what you wish to prolong. Should you gratify your desire now, how are you to wet your parched lips five hours hence? Is it not better to bear a little suffering, than wilfully to increase it? The more you drink, the more you will require; whilst on the contrary, the less you accustom yourselves to, the less will be requisite to sustain life. And now,—while the calm prevents the approach of any vessel—now is the time to endeavour by the oars to alter our position, that, should any vessel be near, we may approach her."

"All very fine," said Jones: "but I'd rather die outright than feel what I do."

"If you'd just keep yoursel quiet," said M'Donald, "you'd nae have the fever upon you as you have now."

"Keep the devil quiet!" rcturned Jones. "I tell you I'm thirsty, and I would rather jump overboard five hours hence than live until to-morrow evening and be saved as I feel now."

"Oh," said Barrow, "no gammon, M'Donald: it's now every man for himself, and God for us all; and I say, let's have a good drink, and never mind to-morrow."

At this instant, Hammerton saw, or fancied he saw a vessel; it turned all thoughts immediately to the mutual safety, and with one accord they agreed to take to the oars if an extra allowance was served out; but without this, three of the crew positively refused to work. This was a moment of intense anxiety. The quick sight of M'Donald had confirmed Hammerton's report; whilst Jones, desperate from fever almost to madness, and blinded from eagerness, immediately caught hold of the halyards of the yard, and in a moment was at the mast-head. The boat had rolled heavily before from the swell; and as miseries and misfortunes always assail those in distress, so were they now true to their usual current: the boat surged over on the larboard side; the halyards had been belayed on that side, and made the only security to the mast—it snapped just above the thwart, and mast, sail, and Jones fell overboard. It would have been well for the rest had this man met his fate: but although he was the cause of all the confusion which had prevailed, for he alone had commenced insubordination, and the chance of escape might also be sacrificed if he was saved, yet such is the inherent generosity of British seamen, that cach stretched out his hand to his assistance; and as M'Donald said, "Here, Jones, just seize this, my mon," he continued, drily enough, "I'm just thinking that we might spare his company, for all the good he'll do us."

The wreck being saved, the sail was rolled up, and even Jones, having seen the vessel, thought it was as well to take an oar; but not one of the three would pull a stroke until some water had been given them, and Hammerton, knowing that every minute became more and more precious, persuaded M'Donald to yield to the desire of the three men, and give them an extra allowance. The small quantity only gave an additional desire without quenching the thirst, and Hammerton discovered his error when it was too late; for the three discontented men, after pulling about twenty strokes, laid their oars athwart, resting their arms upon them, and in sullen determination expressed their resolution not to pull another stroke until they had more water. The haze which the calm occasioned was going off as the sun declined, and the stranger was plainly visible; it appeared as if they had already neared her considerably, and Hammerton was not without hope that, could he near her a little more, she might distinguish the mizen of the boat, which still remained hoisted. It was this apparent closing with the stranger that made the refractory more clamorous, and the reasoning of the disaffected reached all but M'Donald.

"We shall be saved in an hour," they said, "and therefore, why suffer what we do suffer, when at the end of that time we shall not need it? Give us the water now, and we will work like men; but we are not horses, to work first and be fed afterwards."

Time now was not like the tortoise—every moment was of value; the slightest breeze might fill the sail of yonder ship—the setting sun and coming darkness might shut her from the sight of those already fatigued with watching her; and who was to inspire the wearied and the hungry with courage when the object which was to relieve both should be invisible? Whilst the finger could point, the eye bear witness, and the tongue assert, "There she is," there was hope.

"My men," said Hammerton, "why throw a chance away? It is true there is the vessel, and we have neared her; but we are not yet on board. A breeze may spring up: our mast is gone—rendered useless. How, then, are we to keep sight of her but by the oars? Consider the valuable time we are losing: for if before sunset she does not see us, the evening's breeze may take her from us; and then what are we to do without water, without provisions, without mast or sail, our strength exhausted—our hope gone? Take example by me and M'Donald, my lads;

work as we work; every struggle brings us nearer our salvation—every moment lost renders our chance more desperate."

It was quite useless: the three men refused to pull a stroke, and the fourth and fifth men now followed their example, leaving M'Donald and Hammerton, the only two who still plied the oar and kept the boat nearing the stranger. At last M'Donald said—

"I'm thinking, Mr. Hammerton, there is but one thing to do, and that nae so pleasant to you and me, who are not such down-hearted curs as those vagabonds without courage forward. I'll just propose to you one thing which will make them work,—and that's the only thing that will, since we've no boatswain's mate among us. Give them the breaker, and let them drink their fill; then start the rest overboard. It's a desperate measure, sir, but we have to deal with desperate men, and every minute now is worth an hour hence."

"Good God!" said Hammerton, still pulling away; "what do you propose, M'Donald? Suppose we do not reach her, what is to become of us?"

"Die like men, Mr. Hammerton," replied the cool Scotchman; "and if we don't do it, we shall die like a pack of cowards, as those fellows are there. I'm thinking I've half a mind to see if one of the stretchers might not get a little life into them."

"I'd just advise you, you Scotch rascal," said Jones, "to put a little life into us that way, and we'll put a little death into you."

"That's the mon, Mr. Hammerton," replied M'Donald, "whose life we saved half an hour ago! You see, there's nae use in piping to people who canna dance."

"It is one and all," said Hammerton, laying in his oar; "and now then for the water."

At this intimation all hands made a rush aft; two of the oars went overboard, and drifted astern, none making an effort to save them; and Hammerton and M'Donald not seeing them, the others took care not to say a word about that which might keep them lingering even a moment. With greedy lips each applied his mouth to the pannikin, which was filled and refilled until every one was satisfied.

Hammerton, as he took his last draught, shook the breaker, which did not contain more than half a gallon, and proposed to save it.

"Nay, nay," said M'Donald, "that is of nae use even for twa of us. Look here, you Jones—there's the ship: do you see her?" Jones nodded. "And here," said he, as he started the rest overboard—"here is no more water—not a drop; and now the oars and your own labour is your only chance."

This desperate act recalled every man to his senses: they took their seats, and bitter were their curses as the boat's head was turned from the ship in order to recover the oars. Some time was lost in agreeing to do so; but Hammerton was resolute, and as even hunger was satiated for the moment by the large quantity of water swallowed, the last spark of subordination gave its twinkling light before it was extinguished for ever. The crew now became sensible that their only chance was hard work and no flinching. The stranger must have been about eight or nine miles distant, and Hammerton, as he cheered them on, said, "Two hours at the farthest, and we shall be safe. Give way, my lads; don't keep looking behind you! And then think how much dearer life will be when by our exertions we shall have saved it. Stretch out, my lads!"

The men pulled, and pulled their strongest; M'Donald was the only one who responded "Pull away, boys!" the rest used their utmost strength and in silence did their work. In about half an hour they had neared the vessel considerably, and in an hour, had the vessel been as eager to discover vessels as merchant ships generally were during the war time, the boat's mizen might have been seen; but the captain was more intent upon trimming his sails to a light breeze springing up from the westward. With dismay Hammerton saw the studding-sail set to catch the wind, and imagination pictured the ship increasing her distance. Now came the fact, that the time lost in disputing about the water had been the most precious in their lives; now was the truth confirmed, that had they stuck to their oars when they first used them, they would have been nearly, if not quite, alongside of that ship which, beginning to feel the influence of the breeze, was no longer lying becalmed upon the waters, but with her head in the same direction as the boat, was evidently, from the steady course she maintained, under the influence of the helm.

Every man saw this, and every man felt that now or never was the moment. The moment had passed: in vain did the man steering the boat stand up and wave his handkerchief; in vain he bawled his loudest—his voice never reached one hundredth part of the distance; in vain the more and more wearied men used their efforts to near her. The palpable truth admitted of no doubt: the vessel was increasing her distance, the boat was unseen, the sun was about to set, and further exertion was unavailing. One by one the oars were laid in; the breeze had not as yet reached the boat; and although a cat's-paw or two appeared broad on the bow, and perhaps aloft there was a breeze, yet they who needed it most never felt it.

"It's nae use, I'm a-thinking, Mr. Hammerton, to pull onesel to death after this manner," said M'Donald: "we had better see if we can get the foresail up, and they might see that."

This last chance, desperate as it was, was tried: the broken part of the mast was placed on the step, and two of the crew kept it upright, whilst others lashed it to the thwart and hoisted the wet sail. Then might have been seen the last effort of human beings, whose reason was half estranged by despair, endcavouring by every act to catch attention. One placed his jacket on an oar, and held it above the sail; another had fastened his handkerchief to the boat-hook, and was waving it to and fro; a third, who could not relinquish hope entirely, still pulled an oar; whilst he who had steered relinquished thc tiller, and standing up, supporting himself by the mizen-mast, still hailed the more distant ship, as the tears of disappointment ran down his chceks. Joncs had applied the breaker to his mouth, and had perhaps succeeded in squeezing one drop from the bung-holc, when Williamson snatched it from him and in vain attempted to be equally successful: enraged at the disappointment, he threw the breaker overboard, and fell exhausted on the stern-sheets.

In the mean time the light breeze had reached the boat—a mere prolongation of agony; the end of the halyards was passed round the mast, and secured it pretty firmly to its thwart; M'Donald and Hammerton tied up a hasty reef; and the boat thus placed under canvas, made some progress to the southward, in which direction the ship was still plainly visible, and even then hope would not be entirely defeated. Few were the words spoken: Hammerton steered, keeping his eyes fixed upon the ship; but shortly the sun, in one unclouded blaze of light, touched the horizon, sank, and was invisible.

It were useless to picture the last efforts of the nearly exhausted crew. Again the oars were tried; again was the cheering voice heard; again the falsehood which hope had pictured as a truth, that they neared the ship fast, was declared; again even the little jest was heard; again the "Give way, boys!" resounded, until the fast-coming clouds of night gathered over the clear sky above them; and as the obscurity increased, the darkness of despair became more intense; but when the vessel was ultimately lost sight of, more than one groan reached the ears of all. All was over—every effort was now unavailing; no star would direct them in their pursuit, no compass point the right bearings; the resolute and robust sank fatigued and overcome; the oars were once more boated; and had not Hammerton still remained faithful to the tiller, not another man would have given himself the trouble even to steer the boat.

It was at this dreadful crisis that the thirst, satiated for the moment, had now been recalled by the exertions which had been made; but all knew that no remedy remained. After venting their curses upon Jones, who had been the cause of their sufferings, some extending them to Hammerton, who, had he acted at first as he acted ultimately, would have saved them, the voices, even in cursings and blasphemings, grew more and more indistinct, until nature was entirely overcome, and all but two sank into a kind of stupor, remaining for some time insensible to the peril which surrounded them. Two of them, however, mastered even exhaustion; and in the stern-sheets of the boat Hammerton and M'Donald knelt down, and again implored the divine support during the miseries which impended.

CHAPTER X.

DESPAIR, MURDER, AND PUNISHMENT.—HOPE TO THE LAST.—A SAIL APPEARS.—RESCUE.

NOT long did the pleasure of forgetfulness remain—not long could those lulled in the stupor which over-exhaustion had occasioned continue in comparative blessedness. The last hour of life will not come for the miserable and the afflicted, however eagerly it may be desired; and although the strongest are sometimes laid low by the most trivial event, yet the spark is not always quenched without the fierce struggle which hope to the last moment never fails to inspire. It is well that it is so; else the faint of heart would, when the bright colours became a little dim, sink into dejection. But strange—passing strange it is, that those who are nearest to death cling with the greatest tenacity to hope! In atrophy, does not the poor, emaciated, exhausted skeleton propose schemes the fulfilment of which would require the longest life; and when the winter is at hand, and death at the door, plan parties of amusement for the coming spring, when Nature shall revive, and Fashion give new laws?

The light breeze which had sprung up during the latter part of the day freshened sufficiently to blow the mast over the side, the lashing having been insufficient to maintain it erect, more particularly as the broken part only rested on the step. Hammerton and M'Donald retained sufficient energy to save both, and the wet sail was hauled carefully into the boat, and the mast placed in security. It was now evident that starvation was near at hand, and that within the small space of a few hours one must die for the rest. M'Donald remarked,—

"I'm just thinking, Mr. Hammerton, that we are in a doleful situation,—we're without water, and without a morsel to eat; and it's nae use being frightened to death, and still less use putting one of us above the rest. Misfortunes humble us alike, and now we are all equal. It's nae use calling a mon an officer when he has nae authority: and the captain himsel would not get much attended to by yon Jones there, who's already as mad as a real Bedlamite, and has been drinking the salt water for the last quarter of an hour. You and I, Mr. Hammerton, have more strength left in us than all the rest put together; and I'm thinking that if any stranger hove in sight now, we should have to save the others. There's poor Henderson, a child who has seen better days than these,—for none of us has ever seen worse,—he has been singing away as if he were under the forecastle bulwark in a gale of wind.

"And as for that child of the devil," continued M'Donald, "that Wilson, he has been amusing himsel wi' getting the pannikin and pouring it over Henderson's face to whet his whistle. I'm thinking, Mr. Hammerton, that they're all mad together: for there's Barrow swearing he's captain of the frigate, and ordering Williamson to be flogged. I've laid my head down whilst you slept, and I have heard it all. Now, Mr. Hammerton, you and I, by the blessing of God, are not mad yet; and I'm just a-thinking that nothing shows a man's mind more than his preservation of himsel and his body. We must stick close together and protect one another; we must keep close."

"God of all mercies!" said Hammerton, in a feeble voice, for the last business of the mast and sail had almost rendered him speechless from exhaustion, "save and protect us in this awful moment."

"Amen, amen!" repeated M'Donald. "I say amen, sir, but I'm thinking it's the first law of nature to save yoursel. And of what use is a mon to himsel when he is not himsel? It's nae doubt very bad to commit a murder; but I'm thinking, Mr. Hammerton, that it's nae sin to kill one to save five."

"For Heaven's sake, M'Donald," said Hammerton, "do not think of it! Better to die as we are, than to die with blood upon our hands."

"It's very right what you say, nae doubt," said M'Donald; "and as long as this piece of biscuit lasts, which I have kept pretty much to mysel, I'm thinking, since we got into this scrape, and which, with the half of my shoes, has kept me more alive than the rest, I may think so too; but if we get mad, there will be murder enough, and perhaps all will perish then."

"Oh," said Hammerton, as he lifted his hands, "that I could die this instant! And yet, my little sister, I would live for you!—who will protect you when I am gone—who will be a father to the fatherless?"

"Now, Mr. Hammerton, you are talking just for all the world like a madman and not like a wise man. It's bad enough for the best of us all to die when we are summoned; but for any man to wish to die who is not absolutely mad, is a cowardice which I'm thinking was never born in that fine heart of yours. I've a child too in Aberdeen awa, and I must try to live to feed her."

M'Donald, who with his usual foresight and prudence, had still kept a small piece of biscuit, because circumstances requiring it might occur either aloft or in a boat, was, as might be seen, the man best calculated to survive a desperate event like this. His coolness of temper, his general methodical manner of setting to work about anything, had all calculated him to sustain hunger or thirst better than his more irascible neighbours. Now, however, that he saw starvation inevitable, his mind became busy with horrid thoughts. At this instant Jones, infuriated to madness, cursing, swearing, and blaspheming, rushed with an open knife upon Henderson, who was singing a sailor's song, but not with a seaman's voice; and as he reached the part—

> "There's a sweet little cherub sits perched up aloft
> To look out for the life of poor Jack,"

Jones caught the words, and rushing with maniacal fury upon his comrade, exclaimed, "I'm the cherub, my lad!" and plunged the greedy blade into his heart.

M'Donald saw the deed, and his goodness of heart overcame every other feeling; he staggered forward,—for Henderson lay on the second thwart from forward,—and wresting the knife from Jones's hand, whilst he in vain attempted to clutch it more closely, threw it overboard and instantly seized upon Jones. The confusion and scuffle awoke the others, who, recovered a little from their sleepless drowsiness, joined in the uproar with their maniac companion. By the united force of M'Donald, Williamson, and Barrow, Jones was removed from the exhausted Henderson. The stream of life flowed fast away from the murdered man, and soon reduced him to so weak a state, that he died without an effort to save himself; and, with a calmness and composure only known in deaths like these, surrendered up his spirit without a groan or a sigh.

Jones, with the violence of a maniac, now seized upon M'Donald; but the wary Scotchman, in order to shake off the murderous nip of the madman, vibrated the boat from side to side, until, watching an opportunity when she surged over on the starboard side, he shook Jones from his hold. The murderer fell overboard and was drowned.

Far different was it now from that day when he fell with the mast!—no friendly hand was now stretched out to proffer assistance—no eager voice cheered him to exertion—no rope, no oar, no boat-hook was thrown or held towards him—not a man but Hammerton heeded the feeble cries of the poor wretch, and he sank within a foot of the boat, unable to assist himself, and without exciting either the pity or the compassion of his shipmates.

"I would I were you!" said Hammerton to himself, as he watched the extended circles caused by Jones's fall. "Far better to be as you are now, than to linger a few hours more; to see reason blighted in others—to hear murder defended—perhaps to live upon the unnatural food forbidden by God, and only countenanced by the savage,—and to feel the gradual approaches of idiotcy pushing reason from her throne. O God!" he added, "in the coming catastrophe may I glorify Thee to the last moment, blessed with the reason with which I am endowed, and surrender my soul to Thee as patiently as my poor comrade!"

It is certain that man is capable of receiving the greatest consolation from prayer—nay, that from the lull of disturbed nature which calms his mind, he may even control for a time the very hunger which has dictated the appeal; and it was whilst Hammerton received this kind of momentary peace—for it is but an effort of the mind in the belief of the efficacy of the appeal, as hunger must still do its ravage, thirst must dry up the mouth, swell the tongue, inflame the throat, and fever and fury do their worst—that M'Donald staggered towards him and sank down at his feet.

"I could nae help it, Mr. Hammerton," he said: "the Lord forgive me for the act! I saw him murder Henderson; and although I was half inclined to do some dreadful act, yet somehow when I saw the deed I could nae keep my hands from the ruffian's throat. He's dead, poor fellow, and I'm thinking, Mr. Hammerton, after all, that he's better off than the rest of us. I'm very hungry, sir—very thirsty; and before daylight, which seems as if it never would arrive, we may be starved!"

"Wait, wait, M'Donald," replied Hammerton; "there may still be some consolation in store for us, and mayhap we may yet be rescued from this dreadful situation by some vessel. I can survive another day on this leather, and if we could but manage to bathe we might alleviate our thirst; but though the water is very near, yet we are too weak to try the experiment; if we got overboard, we never should have strength left to get on board again. Wait, and until daylight, M'Donald."

"I'm just thinking, Mr. Hammerton," replied M'Donald, "that I'm getting mad very fast myself."

There came over Hammerton a dizzy giddiness—nay, the perspiration started upon him in large drops; he lay down and became sensible of his situation by the intervals of reason, between his wandering thoughts. Whenever a trifling reaction brought him to himself, a vision of home, his aged parents, his darling sister Amelia, floated before him; and when he could command his reason, he always had recourse to prayer for them more than for himself.

At length the long-wished-for day dawned. M'Donald, a little relieved by an hour's slumber, was the first who caught a glimpse of returning light; he did not speak, but resting his chin upon his hands, which were placed upon the larboard gunwale of the boat, he watched the increasing light, which gradually appeared more palpable, until the sun itself, rising as it were from the bosom of the ocean, shone unclouded upon the miserable men, and showed their eyes the dreadful scene. The crew, now reduced to four, were disposed of in different parts of the boat; three were in a stupor, the fourth watching, and Hammerton praying; the daylight showed the latter the situation of himself and his companions. A light breeze still blew, the mizen was still set, and the boat's head would occasionally fly up towards the wind, and then fall off, drifting away to leeward.

The first thing which Hammerton perceived was some of the Florida weed close to him. He reached out his languid hand and caught it. Aware that it would only make his thirst the more intense, and yet unable to resist this glutinous sustenance, he carefully squeezed as much of the water as possible from it, and was busily engaged doing so, when Barrow saw the prize. A ray of reason returning, he watched the languid hand of Hammerton feebly retaining the weed. He was on the after-thwart; and as all restraint had long since been removed, hunger levelling all superiority, he sprang towards his officer and seized it. Hammerton held on; and M'Donald turning round and seeing the scuffle, was not behindhand in securing his share. As they tore the welcome food from their officer, they crammed it eagerly into their mouths: the more they ate the more they required. In this dilemma Hammerton managed to save for himself a thick piece of the stalk, by allowing both to get a good hold of some of the small branches and then slipping them off. His assailants now turned upon and attacked each other, leaving him free to secure a small piece in his pocket whilst he hastily swallowed the rest. This welcome assistance, and the still greater benefit derived that evening from the fall of a small shower, restored M'Donald and Hammerton a little; but Barrow before noon went raving mad, and he and his two comrades were in no condition to avail themselves of the blessings bestowed upon them.

It was about three o'clock in the afternoon, the forenoon having passed away without the smallest hope of relief from the appearance of any strange sail, that Hammerton perceived a growing wildness in M'Donald's manner. "He was thinking," he said, "that he should like to go mad, for then all his sufferings would be over." Hammerton endeavoured to use his own former reasoning against himself.

Another and another day passed: the breeze still continued. Whether the three men forward were dead or not, he was in ignorance. M'Donald had lain down to die. Hammerton had stretched himself along the seat of the stern-sheet, and the boat floated and drifted as the wind blew or the current ran. No motion was visible in any of the crew, save in Hammerton, who occasionally varied his posture: all of thought—all of memory was extinct. A boat of more wretched spectres never floated on the high seas. No words were exchanged; indeed two only could speak. Ten days of hunger and thirst had worn out even the strongest; and Hammerton, when he saw his stanchest adherent M'Donald lay himself down leisurely to die, felt the last chord of his own existence snap asunder.

How long they remained in this forlorn situation, not one of the number knew; but when the breeze died into a light flow of wind, and before utter exhaustion had prostrated all, a vessel which had passed about five miles from them had been seen by two; but the rest were not even to be roused by the words that a stranger was near them. A slight effort to attract attention was fruitlessly attempted, and when the sun went down the last hope disappeared with it.

It happened that the *Jonathan*, of New York, in her return to her port, crossed the track of this devoted boat. The wind being light, and the merchant ship hardly steering through the water, she might have been seen to alter her course. A lug-sail had been observed by one of the seamen who had crawled aloft to repair the foot of the fore-top-gallant sail; the glass confirmed her as a boat apparently untenanted; the ship neared the unusual stranger, and objects became more visible—still not a soul was seen. The sea was smooth, the boat rode upon the water without rolling, and in that manner she was approached by the *Jonathan* until the ship was steered alongside of her. The horrid stench was enough to frighten the American from his first intention of appropriating his prize to his own use; and when he ran alongside, and securing the boat, saw the five people motionless, the captain had determined to sink her in order to avoid any fever which contagion might spread in his vessel. The mate's observation that one might be alive induced the captain to risk a closer observation before he proceeded to put his intention in execution; and then it was, as the boat touched the side of the ship, that Hammerton lifted one hand, and murmured out loud enough for intense attention to overhear, "My God! my God! we are saved!" It required nothing more than the indication of life to prompt the most generous efforts of the American. Hammerton was brought on deck by means of a rope fastened round him. The buttons on his waistcoat, for his jacket had been lost, confirmed the captain in the knowledge of his rank, and he was instantly taken to the cabin, stripped, and laid in a cot. M'Donald was alive—a hammock was ready for him; the rest were dead, not one showing the smallest symptom of animation. The horror of the scene appalled the bravest mind. The men were afraid to touch them; the loathsome smell still clung to the boat; and to shorten as much as to alleviate the symptoms of growing discontent in those who were *ordered* to assist—for when the men who retained symptoms of life had been removed, even the boldest of the crew shrunk from the scene which by turning over the bodies of the dead was made visible to them—the order was given to scuttle her.

The boat which had been true to them whilst living, became their coffin when dead. The oars and sails were handed out, and when scuttled she was cast adrift from the ship. She sank gradually as the water rushed in and filled her. In her sank the remains of Barrow, Williamson, and Wilson; they died without knowing that death was near; and the element which they had chosen for the theatre of their services rolled over them, and swallowed them in its fathomless abyss. The crew of the *Jonathan* watched the last inch of the gunwale as it gradually sank below the surface, and the waters of oblivion and eternity covered the dead.

CHAPTER XI.

THE "TRIBUNE" ASHORE AT HALIFAX.—AWFUL NIGHT.

On board the *Tribune* of course the greatest anxiety prevailed as to the fate of Hammerton and his comrades. From the time the haze cleared off, a most vigilant look-out was kept for the boat; as the wind subsided, guns were again fired, men were placed aloft with glasses, and not an officer in the ship went below until darkness came on, and it was beyond question that no boat was in sight.

To leeward were two of the convoy, one dismasted, and

the other all in the confusion of a merchant ship whose sails had been split by the squall. They were a considerable distance off; and one of them showing a whiff as a signal to speak to the commodore, it was surmised that Hammerton with the boat might have reached the vessel. The *Tribune* therefore bore up, edging away to the south-east. This, as the boat had stood to the northward directly the north star was visible, made the distance so great between them, that the dawn of next day only confirmed the apprehension of the last evening. Still, however, there was hope. When the boat was last seen she was near some of the ships; and although the vessel which had shown the whiff in order to get some assistance had not seen her, yet others might have picked her up: and thus those who really liked Hammerton, and who knew the value of men ever ready to risk their own lives for others, kept up their spirits under the delusion that they should meet again at Halifax. Captain Barker being unable to persuade the captains of the two merchant ships to continue their course,—one having sprung a leak and the other being a complete wreck,—he lent every assistance to the former; and having rigged jury-masts for the latter, they stood away to the northward, made the island of St. Mary's, and then parted company from the frigate, which ship continued her course to her destination without one of her convoy.

On the 16th of November the harbour of Halifax was discovered; the wind being from the east-south-east, blowing fresh, and the ship nearing the land fast. Murray, whom Captain Barker had noticed from his exertions to be of service in the boat, and from his conduct since on every occasion, was ordered to get ready to go ashore in the gig. Released from the surveillance of Hammerton, he had joined Weazel in all his frolics; and the messmates of both, regarding them as youngsters likely to rise high to honour in their profession, as they had so gallantly come forward on the before-mentioned occurrence, overlooked most of their practical jokes or laughed at the frolics of the boys.

The harbour's mouth being visible, and the dangers of the navigation known, Captain Barker desired the signal for a pilot to be hoisted, and the ship to be hove to. The master, Mr. Clubb, a man of known worth, and yet not worth much, seeing that if the pilot came on board, the money allowed for that service would pass into other hands, remarked to Captain Barker, when he gave the above order, that he had before beaten a forty-four gun frigate into the harbour; that every rock and shoal was as well known to him as the dead-eyes in the main-chains; that as the captain was anxious to anchor without delay, he would take charge of the ship; and as the wind was fair, there could be no danger.

To such a statement what captain could advance an objection? The signal was countermanded. "Never mind the gun—forward," was heard; the sails were filled; and the commander of the frigate, in the full assurance of the perfect security of his ship, having ordered leadsmen into the chains, went below to his cabin in order to collect his papers, prepare his report, sign his log, and finish his letters. In the meantime the *Tribune* approached the Thrum-cap; and Mr. Clubb, having consulted a negro who had formerly belonged to Halifax, but whose character was sufficiently bad to have subjected him several times to punishment, felt convinced the ship was standing in free from all danger. To his question to this effect he might have remarked the malignant, sinister look of the black, as he replied, "Him steer good course, sar,—no ab fear, Massa Clubb—him shoal out there; and really for true, the man wid um lead no more use than rum to catch Jamaica-fly."

Mr. Clubb in reality knew nothing at all about the pilotage; and in those days the Admiralty charts were not on the splendid scale of the present time. Not overflowing with the golden current, he thought that, under the directions of the negro, and with the assistance of Mr. Galvin, one of the master's mates, a man conversant with the difficulties and dangers, the harbour might be entered in safety without the pilot-money going to a stranger. In all cases like the present, a certain timidity may be observed in any man undertaking what he knows he cannot perform; and to such a nervous degree of excitement had Mr. Clubb arrived, that he took fisherman's turns, called out to know the soundings, looked over the side, and exhibited feelings very contrary to the calm disdain of danger arising from accurate local knowledge.

About noon the ship had approached so close to the Thrum-cap that Mr. Clubb could no longer command his fears: he seut down instantly for Mr. Galvin, who followed the messenger on deck at the moment that the man in the chains called out, with the long, careless notes by which the soundings are invariably accompanied, "By the mark five!" The negro, who considered himself the pilot, and who was quite pleased with the confidence reposed in him, remarked, "Berry good leadsman; teddy boy at de helm;" but Mr. Galvin's look of horror when, on jumping upon one of the carronade slides, he beheld the situation of the ship, convinced Mr. Clubb of the danger she was in; and as he seized the wheel with the inteution of wearing off shore, the ship struck with tremendous forcc, and remained fixed upon the rocks.

Mr. Weazel, who was below, instantly called out to Murray, "By Heavens, Murray, the ship's fallen overboard, and you'll have to walk on shore on the iron ballast!' Murray had no time to heed the fun. The confusion occasioned by this event baffles all description. The men had been sent below to clean themselves for going into harbour, the ship being considered by the first lieutenant as perfectly safe under the master's charge, with a leading wind and all marks plainly visible. The noise of the crew as they rushed upon deck, and the horror apparent in all, bewildered Murray, who found himself quietly seated on the deck. Weazel availed himself of the confusion to run against his enemy unawares, saying, "Out of the way, Johnny Newcome! don't you know the ship's on shore, and every man ought to be on deck?" Murray was not slow to follow his tormentor; and if the squall mentioned in the preceding chapters had blanched the cheek of some of the oldcst seamen, this calamity produced a greater extremity of fear, for the men ran to and fro without any order or regularity; and it required the cool command of the captain more than ouce when he called, "Every man to his station—shorten sail!" before order could be restored. The order repeated soon enforced obedience; but few can tell how hard it is to maintain discipline when fear predominates.

As the sea rolled on, heedless of the danger it created, the *Tribune* felt every shock the more severely; the mainmast as she struck amidships slackened the stay, and as she recovered herself, flew back to its original position with such force as to render it dangerous to be near; the masts and yards shook—nay, rattled, and it was useless to attempt to send men aloft to furl the sails, for they would inevitably have been shaken from their holds and have lost their lives. The signal of distress was hoisted—and that signal is not made on board a man-of-war until the danger is imminent. It was answered instantly by the ships in the harbour, whilst at the military stations they conveyed the intelligence inland. Then was to be seen all the generous ardour with which men court danger to save their countrymen; boats from the dockyard, under the boatswain of that establishment, and even some of the boats at the military stations, unawed by the high sea and increasing wind, succeeded, after enormous labour and unremitting struggles, in reaching the ship; but others, equally zealous in the cause, in vain toiled and toiled—the sea drove them back into the harbour; and although many more volunteered, and again and again tried to render service by being in readiness to land the crew, all labour was ineffectual, and they were as often forced back, until the increasing wind rendered the attempt abortive.

In the meantime Murray was learning a great lesson in his profession. It is in danger that British seamen are most conspicuous; the boldest soldiers have been seized with a panic and have fled—the English sailors have frequently at a sudden disaster lost all courage for the moment; but both rally, and as they look with more calmness at the accumulating danger, so they brave it more steadfastly and oppose it more manfully. Murray soon exhibited symptoms of his daring character, and he even distanced Weazel, who was, like himself, a novice in shipwrecks. Murray quitted the captain's side only to convey an order—he knew in that alone he could be useful,—the order delivered, he was back again; and young as he was, it was observed that when the ship struck the hardest, he betrayed no symptoms of fear, but kept his eyes steadily on his captain as if to anticipate his commands.

In the mean time the perilous situation of the ship became obvious: the gale was fast increasing; the night—a long night of November—was closing in upon them; already had the haze of the evening dimmed the welcome shore, and the thick mist of the gale gradually spread around. The crew, assisted by those from the shore, were busy in lightening the ship: the guns were thrown overboard; every shot that could be reached was thrown clear of the ship; the sails were backed so as to assist in clearing the shoal should she float; the stores were given to the sea, —everything which could assist in the object, with the exception of cutting away the masts or the boats, was thrown overboard, and exhausted nature almost sank under the continued exertions.

It was now dark—the night had closed in: the rolling sea with its white heads came rushing on higher and higher: above no moon shone to cheer them, or exhibited the lamp of night to point out a place of refuge should she float; but the heavy clouds seemed to fly over the devoted ship, while as the sea increased she was lifted the higher to fall the more heavily. Ay, and well each seaman knew that the hard sides which had rolled over many a sea must shortly yield to the harder rock on which they struck, and that the worst danger now was her floating clear of the shoal. No bell marked the hour—no watch was called to relieve the tired—no hammocks were hung to welcome the sleepy; nor could all the exertions of the crew avail against the storm: the ropes were flying about unbelayed: the whole scene on board was indescribable confusion, and no pen—no, not of those who have witnessed such scenes the most frequently, can draw any adequate picture of the dismay, the apprehension—the almost abandonment of hope on board the frigate. The long night had but begun, and who was to survive to see the sun rise? The gale came howling through the rigging, whilst the sea as it dashed against the ship surged by her with a deafening roar or broke right over her.

It was at half-past eight that Daniel Munroe, a fore-topman, who was then in the starboard main-chains, called out that the ship was afloat: a sea which had threatened destruction swept her off the rock, tearing the rudder from the stern-post. The well was instantly sounded, and the cry of "Seven feet water in the hold!" told the dismayed and wearied crew that all escape was impossible. Still, however, they did not throw a chance away: the chain-pumps were instantly rigged, and little Murray might be seen endeavouring to turn the heavy winch. His voice as he cheered the men seemed to recall them to themselves; and that boy by his example kept them to their work. They could not despair when a boy so young seemed ignorant of the danger; and as the carpenter reported that the pumps gained upon the leak, their efforts were redoubled. Hope gleamed for a moment: it was possible that the anchor might hold—that the carpenter's report might be true, and that the ship might be kept above water until the long-wished-for dawn should appear. The lights which blazed upon the hills only convinced the crew that those on shore knew their danger; and as they stood high above the beach, they were no guides to lead them to the best place on which to run the ship. How many an eye was turned to those beacons! how many a heart panted to be there! and how often did the weary seamen look towards them!

The best bower was let go—that was an anxious moment; the cable flew through the hawse-hole, setting fire to the bits, and running out to the clinch, snapped. Vain was every effort to stopper the cable or to choke the hawse-hole: the sea was running too high for any cable to have checked her; and hope, justly painted as an anchor, had parted. The jib and fore-top-mast staystail were now set: the former sail was split, but the latter answered the intention of keeping the ship off the wind; and in this might be traced the wavering disposition which clung to the hope of yet saving the ship, and still running her nearer the shore, on which she must inevitably be wrecked.

The south-east gale still increased, and the shore bore north-west: no sail like a topsail could have been carried: and even if the reefed courses and close-reefed topsails could have been carried, the ship was too far to leeward to weather the points which embayed her; and now that heavy deadening sound which follows the roaring waves as they split upon the shore might be heard. The leak evidently gained upon the pumps; the approaching shipwreck was more manifest, when again the last effort of seamanship was tried. Soundings in thirteen fathoms had been called, when the small bower was let go, the fore-top-mast staysail hauled down, the mizenmast and all the topmasts were cut away, and for a minute even the least sanguine hoped. It was but for a minute: the ship, which had rode to her anchor, gave a tremendous pitch—the cable snapped like a rotten stick, and the *Tribune* fell broadside to the wind. The catastrophe was now at hand; the roar of the sea as it ebbed from the shore became more and more distinct; the surf—(for at that time, as if to mock the prayers of the weary crew, the moon shone to point out the horrid death which awaited them)—became visible, towering up the black steep rocks, obscuring them in its midst and then whitening the waters as they fell below. All order was gone. The crew crowded towards the gangway, from which the horrid view was most perceptible: some, knowing that death was close, resolved to gratify their appetites by breaking into the spirit-room, for that as yet remained untouched; some hastily reviewed their lives, and seemed to live again in scenes far, far away; whilst others knelt down and prayed. A few had been below and dressed themselves in their best clothes. But Captain Barker still remained on deck, watching the near approach to the shore. Beside him, holding on by the capstan in order to steady himself, stood Murray: he appeared the only one unmoved by the danger; he had wound himself up to face anything; and when Barker took his hand and pitied him and his father, the resolute lad replied, "We have yet a good struggle for life: I can swim, and I shall do my best."

It was about ten o'clock. The ship rolled over the waves, but there was an unsteadiness in the roll; each time as she recovered herself she seemed to stagger like a drunken man; she did not rise quickly to the sea, and she fell with a more sullen lurch. The pumps were now deserted: the continued report that the water gained upon them had been made through Murray to the captain; and knowing that seamen may be disheartened, he kept the secret to himself. But the warning came from those who went below to have one long draught before they died: the after-hold was afloat.

the cock-pit was impassable, and they returned on deck shouting, "The ship is sinking! the ship is sinking!" Then indeed rose the cry of a loud farewell; then some ran up the rigging, others jumped in the quarter-boats to cut them away, whilst others held on an oar or a spare spar. The order to cut away the lashings of the booms was quickly obeyed, each saw a chance of safety from some floating spar; but whilst almost all were engaged in the work of self-preservation, Murray thought not of himself, but of others. In the ship were a few women and one or two children: they had come aft to the stump of the mizen-mast. The horror of the night, had the ship been whole, was sufficient to scare the weaker sex; but now that they comprehended the extent of the danger, kneeling down with clasped hands round their children, they vainly lifted up their prayers in all the incoherency of madness. But not for themselves did these women implore assistance: it was for their helpless children—for their daring husbands. This scene attracted Murray's attention; and, even at that moment, he endeavoured to comfort them. He persuaded them to run forward, as there they might cling to the rigging; he actually caught one of the children from the mother, tore it from her arms, and with it reached the forecastle. The mother followed, screaming for her lost child, and mingling curses upon Murray with the cry for mercy from above.

Captain Barker knew, and so did his officers, that every chance was over, and that the ship would never float to reach the shore. He hurriedly took leave of all near him; whilst the women, believing that a captain can save, rushed towards him and knelt down, seizing him by the legs. It was at this distressing moment that the ship gave two heavy lurches, shook as if overpowered, and sank. A loud shriek arose that seemed the parting farewell of the brave crew; and two hundred and forty men, besides the gallant few who had reached the ship in boats, and the women, were in a moment plunged in the angry element.

Murray was at the instant when the ship foundered in conversation with Mr. Galvin, who was still urging the men below to try the pumps: both were washed clear from the ship, which as she sank soon touched the ground, for she had shoaled her water to about ten fathoms, leaving her upper works under the water, whilst her main rigging half-way up was above the surface. Each struck out to regain the ship and reached the rigging, although Mr. Galvin had managed to evade the grasp of three of the drowning crew, who had endeavoured to clutch him in their dying efforts. Murray got into the maintop, supporting himself against the arm-chest, which had been secured to the mast.

About one hundred men still kept above water, holding on by the shrouds: the rest had perished—the sea had washed them far away, and their bodies rolled upon shore, breathless, dead. The foretop had been reached by ten men, who endeavoured to secure themselves there in the hope of surviving the night. No assistance was possible—no boat could have lived in that raging surf; the south-east gale was at its highest, and the iron-bound coast, as seamen call that part which presents nothing but abrupt hills or cliffs rising perpendicularly from the high-water mark, threatened that, should one more fortunate than the rest reach the shore, it could be only to be there dashed in pieces. Thus, deprived of all chance of succour, did these hundred men, worn out with fatigue and cold, make preparations to pass the night. For an hour the numbers scarcely diminished; but now, as the sea dashed over them, their grasp became more and more feeble. Then was the horror of the night at its highest; for sudden death, when the corpse is removed from sight, shocks not imagination like the gradual ebb of life, as wave after wave diminishes the strength, enfeebles the mind, and deadens the little remaining energy. Then was heard, as the wind appeared to lull under the approach of a roaring sea, the feeble cry for help; and when it passed rolling higher and higher, and boiling in its savage fury, one or two who called aloud for mercy were swept from the wreck.

CHAPTER XII.

PERILOUS SITUATION OF MURRAY.—BRAVERY OF A BOY.—COWARDICE OF LANDSMEN.

THE storm continued with unabated fury—midnight was advancing. At first one by one of the men were swept away; towards morning the number had been reduced to fifty.

Despair soon rendered others desperate—more than one slackened his hold and dropped into the sure death beneath. In vain those higher up the rigging called out to their comrades below them to hold on;—few know the resistless power of the sea as it sweeps towards a shore—the utter uselessness of prolonged opposition;—but above all other voices those of Galvin and Murray were heard, still exhorting the men to pass their bodies between the ratlines, keeping their legs on the other side, and to hold on "like grim death."

Towards two o'clock almost the whole had disappeared;—some calling upon their more fortunate shipmates to bear home their last farewell and remembrances: others, with a levity ill-befitting the scene, died cursing everything, upbraiding those in the top for not changing places with them, promising to return to the post of danger when their strength was recruited; and while they thus taunted them with the coward disposition which kept them aloof from the greater danger, the mainmast fell and everyone had a struggle.

Before this happened, Murray, being aware that in the event of an accident his clothes would much impede him, had stripped off his jacket and trousers, and although thrown off the maintop, he endeavoured to regain it; for, as if destined to be a haven of security to some, the top rested on the mainyard, that being held to the wreck by a portion of the rigging. Galvin reached it in safety; but Murray was yet struggling for life. His feeble efforts would never have availed against the sea which was now fast approaching, had not Galvin reached out his hand to his aid; and catching firm hold of his hair, placed Murray in comparative security.

Still many hours were left to face death in its worst approach. How long—how very long—will the strength of man last, though wearied, when life, wretched life, is the object of preservation! and after, perhaps, having surmounted the dangers—having avoided that which has been called "of all dreadful things the most dreadful"—how frequently does he linger on in poverty and wretchedness, toiling and labouring only that he may live, although life be a burden to himself!

In this scene of desolation, when the angry waves burst against the shores, shivered like mighty artillery into minutest drops, uniting again as they fell, and sweeping in their recoil the poor strugglers, who imagined themselves in safety from their grasp, how loud was the call to Him who had been until then forgotten! Then would the insatiate wave sweep by and over them; and as they recovered their breath with frequent gaspings, they would see one of their number gone—the gap left where a human being had lived not a moment before, and another wave rolling on appearing to them higher than the last, or perhaps ready to burst upon them.

So passed the night—a night of horrors never to be effaced from the memory of Murray; and he—for justice bids us state it—was the boy (man he could not be called) who evinced the most generous courage of them all.

It was soon evident that the fore was a much more secure haven than the maintop: the latter, resting on the mainyard, was more liable to be swept to atoms than the one which was only passed over by the surf, and which remained stationary as long as the foremast would stand; whereas the maintop occasionally shifted, and from that insecure abode already two had been washed away. Murray, who was wise enough, if not sailor enough, to know that a few seas more—or only one if it burst upon them, would sweep them all to destruction, proposed to Galvin the dangerous expedient of reaching the foretop. Galvin was quite aware of the insecure position which they held; but he feared being swept away to leeward even from the hold of the rope by which he proposed to pass, and which was ascertained to be fast to some part of the rigging forward: he would not allow Murray to make the experiment alone, and he was fearful himself to be the first to try it.

"We never shall get there safe," said the brave fellow; "and as I've saved you once, I'm not inclined to lose you now. It is to be done; but you are too weak, and I cannot spare one hand if I have to haul myself along the rope."

"Then I'll go first," said Murray; "my life is of no more value than yours: I cannot make myself stronger, and by delay I shall become weaker. Give me the rope; I'll wait until this sea has passed, and then I'll start directly."

"I would rather," replied Galvin, "take my chance where I am. The top has held on, and may still; and I'm not sure but by changing we may be worse."

"That may be," said Murray; "but I think otherwise: you will do as you like."

The sea swept along as before—another and another had gone; and almost before it had passed, Murray swung himself upon the rope, and contrived to reach the foretop in safety. Here, however, was no place of security: in the top three men were dead. They had clambered up the fore-rigging, as their shipmates had been swept away, until, from the crowds which had clung to the ratlines, ten only remained. These three, exhausted and half-drowned, laid down and died at the moment they were apparently safe; and Murray, when he reached the top and threw himself down, fell upon the lifeless bodies. Here, however, was a repose. The seas, as they towered along, swept, it is true, occasionally as high as the top; but, generally speaking, they passed below it, the surf or spray alone flying into it. A short time restored Murray;—he was not a lad to be killed easily—his mind would have supported him where almost any others would have failed;—and hc began instantly to see who were his new comrades. They were only four in all,—Dunlap, Munroe, Weazel, and another. The two first-named seamen considered themselves safe as long as the foremast stood—the last lay panting and almost dead; and after some conversation as to the probability of assistance at daylight, a feeble voice was heard in lubber's hole, and Weazel was recognized. Assuming the command, Murray desired Munroe and Dunlap to assist him in throwing the dead bodies overboard; and this was done without a murmur. He then got Weazel into the top and lashed him securely to the larboard side: he took the same precaution with the exhausted seamen, and sat down to wait for day.

Far along the eastern horizon already had streaks of light heralded the approach of the sun; the thick masses of clouds, as they rose from the horizon to discharge themselves in heavy showers or to feed the wind, began to assume a lighter hue; the shore became more distinct; and the eye of hope could discern some few on the cliffs watching the wreck, and waiting as if to tender assistance.

Murray told his shipmates to fasten a pocket-handkerchief, or any article of dress which could be distinguished, to the broken part of the toprail; for he well knew that nothing would tend more to stimulate those on shore to render assistance than the proof that some were yet alive. It was useless to stand up and attempt to wave it, as Munroe did, for that was wasting strength; and sanguine indeed must that man have been who expected assistance, when he cast his eyes towards the shore and witnessed the tremendous roll of the surf.

Daylight came: Galvin was in the maintop—every man was gone but himself and four others, and he seemed faint and exhausted. One by one they had dropped off—human nature could not support itself longer: the hands, so firmly fixed upon the shrouds, at last opened, and the body fell; there, rolling over and over, it was dashed against the shore without a sign of life, a mangled and breathless corpse.

With the sun came a trifling decrease of the gale; the wind somewhat abated its force; but the sea rolled on, the surf looked more horrible than darkness, and Murray found it advisable to quench a little of that hope which evidently was nurtured by the seamen. As for Weazel, he was insensible: he lay stretched out, and Murray's kind attention to him, by rubbing his heart and his feet, alone appeared to keep in the little portion of life which seemed to flutter before it expired.

Long did the time appear between daylight and eight o'clock, and yet it was only half an hour. The conspicuous signal was answered from the shore, and hundreds were seen waving their hats, as if to animate the sufferers to a longer exertion; but no boat came—there was, apparently, no haven from which a boat could come; all seemed an iron-bound coast, now whitened by the surf and spray.

"It is impossible," said Murray to Dunlap, who kept his eyes fixed upon one part of the coast, "that any boat could live in such a sea as this. We had better keep quiet; we shall have need enough of all our patience and energy before we walk upon that cliff."

"I'd give a trifle just now," said Munroe, "for a piece of salt junk and a glass of grog; and I think I could hold out four-and-twenty hours longer."

"The gale is breaking to windward," said Dunlap; "and I think, if I were there, I would try if I could not get out of Herring Cove, which lies round that point. But it's not any of those men who are walking up and down like a marine before the cabin door who'll get into a boat to save us: we had better do as Mr. Murray says, for we may have to swim for it."

"There goes another," said Munroe; and each eye was directed to the maintop. Another had been swept away; in vain the poor wretch held out his eager hands—no one could assist him, although for some short time he wrestled strongly against his fate. They saw him gradually grow more and more faint and faint, until at length a sea lifted him on its surge, and dashed him against the rocks. Those on shore saw and watched him approaching to the verge of the beetling cliff; but assistance was vain, and curiosity was soon satisfied.

It was now near eleven o'clock, when Dunlap called out the glad tidings that a boat was endeavouring to round the point.

"I see her! I see her!" was spoken by all.

"Here, Weazel, my boy," said Murray, "here's a boat coming off—cheer up! cheer up!"

"Leave me! leave me!" said the poor fellow; "let me die or sleep!"

"Neither one nor the other," said Murray, "if I can help it; we must all be awake now, for now comes the trial. She'll never reach us in this sea, I fear; and what a skiff it looks!"

"There's only one man in her," said Dunlap; "and how he is to get her through this sea I don't know; but he must be a right good one to venture it alone. They say it's sweet to be hung in company; and drowning alone is cold work."

"Ay," said Murray, as he looked towards the maintop; "cold enough. Thank God, however, Galvin yet holds on; and if one boat reaches us, fifty may come. I don't think she nears us—do you, Munroe?"

"Yes, sir, yes; he's farther out from the land than he was; but I'm blessed if I ever saw such escapes! There! he rides over it, and he's safe! There! he bends his back! If ever that man lives to reach us, he shall have all my back-pay; which, now as the purser's gone, and his books are destroyed, will be a pound or two more than I reckoned upon."

"Hold on in the maintop!" roared Murray, as he saw a sea higher than those which had rolled for the last quarter of an hour. It came; it passed; four only remained: but he that was gone was not watched; every eye was turned towards the boat.

It neared the ship, and then wonder, astonishment, exclamation, and gratitude were at its highest pitch. The boat was a mere skiff, pulled by a boy not more than thirteen years of age. With immense perseverance he toiled at his oars; as the sea approached him he slackened his exertion, and the boat rose gradually to the swell. It passed; and the youngster again, as if inspired with supernatural strength, strove to gain his object. Nearer and nearer the little frail skiff approached the wreck, when Murray stood forward and waved for it to pull to the maintop. The boy never heeded the signal, but was pulling towards the foretop; and even those nearest to him, although they thought how sweet was life, and how near the chance of saving it, never contradicted the order, as Murray screamed out to save the men in the maintop, and to leave him and his companions to another chance. There stood those weather-beaten seamen, their hair blowing out in the gale,—wet, soaked, hungry, jaded, nearly exhausted; but they never opposed the generous offer; on the contrary, Dunlap said, "Galvin's a brave man, and he cannot last much longer. We are safe—or, at least, safer than he is."

The lad who had thus nobly risked his own life was in no situation to pull about from mast to mast; and having got under the lee of the foretop, he turned his boat round and backed her towards it.

"Quick! quick!" he said; "I can only carry two, and I'm already nearly swamped."

"Jump in, sir," said Monroe to Murray.

"I jump in?" replied the youngster; "never! I was the one who proposed the boat should go to the maintop, and I will not avail myself of its having come here."

"Well said, sir," ejaculated Dunlap; "by G—d you will be the greatest man in the navy: I won't go—I won't leave you!"

"And I hope I may drown if I do!" said Munroe. "No man shall say Daniel Munroe looked to save himself when his officer refused to leave the wreck. He may go ashore again for me."

"Let us put Mr. Weazel and this poor fellow in the boat," said Murray.

"Ay, ay, sir," both responded; and with the greatest care (for it was ticklish work, and as the boat could only touch the top brim, or rather come below it for a second, and one instant's unsteadiness, and the people they endeavoured to save would have been drowned) did these brave fellows lift up Weazel and Waller, and landing them safely in the boat, gave the gallant youngster three cheers as he pulled towards the shore, and left them exposed to all the perils they might have escaped.*

Those were no common-hearted men who could have cheered the boy as the boat left them again, exhausted and and in imminent peril. Neither should the increased blackness of the clouds be altogether overlooked, for at noon on this day the weather again indicated a continuance of the gale. The eyes which one moment watched the skiff as it rose in security over the wave, and surged along to its haven, turned with a saddened apprehension to the squalls settling to windward, the dark mass of clouds resting, as it were, upon the horizon, whilst the higher roll of the sea indicated that farther off to windward the gale had increased.

* This is no fiction—no conjuring up a hero to dress a novel; the whole is true—every name, with the exception of two, real—every circumstance occurred which has been mentioned; and the only regret now experienced is, that the name of the boy, who was worth a legion of men, should have escaped unknown. The historian of this calamitous wreck, James, in his "Naval History," toiled with all his known perseverance (and if ever a man persevered in the cause of historic truth, James was that man; his unremitted research is perfectly wonderful), to rescue the name of this young hero from oblivion; but in the greater excitement which followed the loss of the *Tribune*, the poor little fellow's gallantry was forgotten: for those who looked on were ashamed of their own cowardice, and therefore did not come forward to attest the truth, when they must have been censured for withholding their aid; and thus he who ought to have been pensioned for life, who should have been held up as one worthy to be emulated, probably died in obscurity, and the fame of all his daring feats may have been usurped by another, who, whispering his own bravery, has risen upon the valour of the boy.

Each man waved his hand as the boat darted round the headland and was in security. Murray felt an elevation of mind as he retraced what he had done. What would his father have said to this noble conduct? and how would all the faults of the boy be lost in the blaze of an action which the proudest man who ever lived might have rejoiced to have numbered amongst his greatest feats!

"They are safe," said Munroe, "and long before this are piping to dinner; but Mr. Weazel won't go to sleep without thinking of us. I recollect when you slipped overboard, Mr. Murray,—that day when Mr. Hammerton went adrift—he was one of the first in the boat to assist you, and now you've saved him, and like a man too; and this is it, sir, I must say I should like to shake hands with you."

"Here, my fine fellow," said Murray, holding out a hand; "and here's the other for you, Dunlap; and if I could reach Galvin, he should have them both. Cheer up, lads!" he continued, "the worst is over. Those idle vagabonds will be ashamed to wander up and down there, looking on doing nothing, when that boy gets ashore and tells them that we are here. We must keep up our spirits."

"I wish I had some of the purser's spirits, I know," said Munroe; "and if ever I do get on shore, I'm mistaken if I don't bowse my jib up in memory of this escape."

"You had better be thinking of something else, Munroe," said Dunlap; "for the wind's getting up, and I see no one coming out to lend us a hand."

"But I do," said Murray; "for there is the youngster again, or his boat."

Again, sure enough, came the same boat and the same boy. Tired as he was, the shout of applause which greeted him as he landed the nearly dead persons, prompted him again to brave the perils he had escaped. "What! can't I get any one to lend me a hand?" said he. Not an answer was made. Some, it is true, were anxious to carry away Weazel and Waller, and all volunteered to take them to the nearest house: but amongst all the people there assembled, and there were plenty of seafaring men amongst them, not one volunteered; not one threw off his coat and offered to stand by a boy of thirteen; not one proposed to launch a larger boat, nor even offered a reward for others to go!

"What! not one out of such a batch as you be?" said the boy. "Then here's try it again by myself; and if I'm capsized, I hope some of you will look to mother, and take care she don't starve or come to mischief. They call me a boy in the village," said the daring lad, as he sat down in his little boat and got his oars out; "but there is many a man of six foot high, and I see plenty of them, who is afraid to pull round Herring Cove Head; although, if it was calm it would be, 'Youngster! get out of the way and make room for a stronger hand.' Give us a launch there, Bob, will you?" said he to a lad of ten years old; "and don't let any one else but a boy touch the boat. I'm very tired," continued the youngster; "but I won't leave those to die who might have saved themselves, but gave up their chance to those poor helpless fellows I landed, and one of them is only a boy."

"Stop," said an old fellow of about eighty; "I will go with you."

"No, no, daddy," replied the boy; "you may as well stay at home and keep warm. There," said he, as he winded his boat, "look at that grey-headed man, and be ashamed! There you stand, hale and hearty, by scores, and you let an old infirm man volunteer, and leave a boy to pull against a gale of wind! Well, here goes!" and he forced his little skiff ahead in the smooth water; "one can but try."

It seemed at first quite evident, even to those who felt a little inclined to a personal risk, that the boy would never reach the wreck; but those who saw what he had accomplished had yet some hopes; for the goodness of human nature at that moment overbalanced the slight satisfaction which would have been felt by all had the brave youngster perished: then indeed they might have found a trifling excuse in the circulation of the anecdote, while they heightened the danger and ridiculed the temerity of the action. The youngster, when he landed his half-dead cargo, was so fatigued as to be unable to render any assistance; but the buoyancy of youth rose superior even to physical exhaustion; and, reanimated by the cheers which even these heartless cravens had given, he felt what he had accomplished, and nobly dared it again.

In Halifax harbour every exertion had been made and failed: the jolly-boat of the *Tribune*, which had left the ship with one or two officers who had witnessed the wreck, and who volunteered assistance in the first instance, and before indeed such a calamitous termination had been anticipated, had tried and tried again; but all in vain,—the sea ran so high near the entrance of the harbour that the boat was washed back, and more than three times nearly swamped. All that gallantry and a noble disdain of life could effect had been done in that quarter; but it was from Herring Cove alone that any assistance could be given, for it was a kind of soldier's wind, "there and back again," from that point; the greatest danger was in first rounding the headland—and from this Cove only a boy could be found to face the danger.

It was, as may be conceived, a time of intense anxiety to those in the fore, and the very few left in the main-top. The rest had all perished; each sea had taken its victim—each minute had rendered life more precarious. Hunger and thirst, fatigue, anxiety, hope, fear, had all contributed to waste energy, until at last one or two preferred an instant death to the lingering uncertainty and pain which assailed them. More than one feebly cried, "God bless you, boys; if you live to weather this gale, remember me;" others lifted up their dying voices in prayer, and as if inspired with a courage to overcome the fear of death, dropped designedly into the foaming waters below, and were swept in the boiling surf far, far away.

"He does not get much ahead," said Munroe. "Poor fellow! I wish I was at that oar now. If he gets into the surf once ——"

"Then amen," interrupted Murray. "We must hope for a better end to such a gallant spirit as that. I fear he does not near us at all; and to windward it looks very angry."

"I'm in hopes the gale is broken," said Dunlap; "for the clouds have risen considerably, and they don't hang together as much as they did."

"I wish," said Munroe, who in the height of danger

could still find time for a bad joke,—"I wish all those fellows on shore were hanging together to those clouds with only slippery fingers to hold on by. A lazy, cowardly set of curs, to be airing their heels on the top of the cliff, when it's down below they ought to be washing them! I wish I had the mustering of those rogues by divisions, and leave to freshen their ways according to my notion!"

"Good God!" said Murray, "he is swamped!"

"No, sir," said Dunlap, who had watched the boat with almost breathless anxiety; "thank God! not so bad as that! He has given it up, and has turned back—he must be tired indeed. He's getting nearer and nearer to the surf—ay, he does not meet it now as he did. There! thank God! he rises again over it! I thought that last sea must have swamped him. He's getting close; he'll do it yet!"

"Hurrah!" they all cried at once; "he has rounded the point, and is safe."

CHAPTER XIII.

MURRAY'S ESCAPE FROM THE WRECK.—HIS TEMPTATION AND FALL.—NEW YEAR'S EVE IN SOMERSETSHIRE.

THAT hurrah was sincere—the brave always feel for the brave. Murray, Dunlap, and Munroe felt a secret pleasure in believing the little hero safe, although it might leave them yet without a prospect of relief. Munroe, whose spirits were better and higher than those of his comrades in affliction, was the most vehement in praise of the youngster; and as they sat down in the top to rest themselves after the painful exertion, he said, "There's many a man been worse off than we are, and yet got saved. I have seen the weather fore-topsail brace give way in a squall, and the lad who was rigging in the top-gallant studding-boom went overboard, the ship going about ten knots, on a dark night, and yet he has been saved. Something will be done from Halifax,—although, to be sure, it's getting towards dark again, and here we are like so many purser's shirts on a scrubbing-day hung out to dry, after being pretty well seasoned with salt water."

"It's quite impossible," said Murray," "that Galvin can

hold out during the night; and who knows that the foremast may not go, and we be all sent adrift?"

"Then it will be fair play and no favour—we should all have a swim for it," replied Munroe. "Why, Dunlap," continued he, "you seem to have got your figure-head a fixture—why, you keep your eyes on the same bracings, and brighten up like a chap when it's 'Grog ahoy!'"

"There's a boat coming out of Halifax," cried the seaman, with delight: "I saw her just now. There! there! she is again rising over the sea to the left of that bluff point."

"I don't see her," said Murray.

"Let's take a squint, sir," said Munroe: "I'm more accustomed to a masthead-lookout. There she rises sure enough! Well, we've time enough to dive below, and get our chest and bags out of the lower deck before she arrives. She'll get here!—they are not like those Herring Cove cowards. There! she rides over it like a duck!—Hold on, Galvin!" said he; "there's liberty for shore coming along. Cheer up! cheer up! we'll turn into a snug berth to-night yet."

"I pray that you may prove a good prophet, Munroe," said Galvin. "How cold and wretched I feel! and yet that boat keeps me in hope—she rides over it famously. I see her now; and she closes us fast! Why, there's another just astern of her!"

"Yes," said Dunlap, who had never taken his eyes from her, "I see three more: if the mast and top but keep together for another hour, we shall have a fair chance of being saved. When three or four boats pull together, one cheers the other, and no one likes to be first to give up: they are sure to be good ones, or they would not be there."

The foretop was the nearest to the boat now fast advancing, and every time she rose upon the sea, Murray turned his eyes to see if Galvin was safe: he appeared quite insensible, and lay stretched upon the maintop, his head apparently jammed in the rigging, which mainly constituted his support. The boat came within hail, and Murray stood forward.

"Pull first," he began, "to the maintop: we can hold on a little longer. But there they are quite exhausted."

The boat, however, still maintained its course for the foretop; the man who was steering the boat kept waving his hat, as if to cheer the sufferers to hold on longer; and seeing more people in the foretop, he directed his attention first to them.

"Not one of us," said Murray, "will get into the boat until those in the maintop are saved."

"This is no time for talking," said the steersman; "stand by to jump in as the boat rises." A sea came and washed them to leeward; the boat was again backed, and again all three declared they would not get into the boat unless she went first to the maintop. Seeing all persuasion useless, and having three times narrowly escaped, the boat went to the maintop, and by dint of great perseverance and most excellent management they succeeded in saving Galvin and two other men, all insensible: they were lifted into the boats by those who availed themselves of a second's lull, to jump into the top, when the rare opportunity occurred. By this time another boat had reached the foretop, and the three gallant fellows, the only three who had maintained their senses, jumped into her, Murray insisting on being the last. Some cloaks had been brought out, and the almost naked, shivering son of Sir Hector Murray was the last who would accept of a covering, although from his appearance, and the eagerness of the two seamen to pay him respect, it was evident he the officer was the one who had most nobly behaved himself.

Out of a crew of two hundred and fifty people, twelve only had been saved; two by the youngster, six by the boats, as just related, and four in the jolly-boat before the ship struck the second time. Amongst those who perished were the captain, and all the lieutenants and midshipmen, with the exception of Weazel and Murray. The master, who was the sad cause of this wholesale calamity, and two hundred and fifteen seamen and marines perished; but no blame whatever could attach to the captain.

It is unfair to deny an officer the small remuneration to which he is entitled—nay, it is a stimulus to make masters become pilots,—it is the hope of this reward which makes them toil whilst others sleep, to weary themselves in sounding shoals, and fathoming rocks and difficulties, when their duty on board is done. For one ship which has been lost by their cupidity and ignorance, to use no harsher language (for in this case it is evident, that when the master said he knew the pilotage, he was not speaking the truth), hundreds of ships and thousands of lives have been saved. How often does it happen that ships in gales of wind are obliged to run for a harbour out of which, it being a lee-shore, no pilot can come! It is the knowledge of the pilotage by the master which saves the ship, and which, under his assertion that he is acquainted with the port, warrants the captain in seeking the security of a haven. But no words can be sufficiently strong to censure the conduct of those people of Herring Cove who refused to render any assistance, although stimulated by the successful exertions of a mere boy. Had this wreck occurred on the Goodwin Sands, *thousands* of those gallant fellows, the Deal boatmen, would have come forward. No surf would have stopped *their* endeavours; they would have tried (although we are quite aware they might not have succeeded), and those who clung to the wreck would have found that their countrymen keenly felt their danger, and did not hesitate to risk their own lives to avert it.

How imminent was the peril to the few who survived, may be conceived from the fact that, as the boats pulled towards the shore, the maintop was observed to have been washed away; and long before they entered the harbour, the foremast had disappeared! In one half-hour longer, and all but two must have perished.

The generosity of the people of Halifax is well known to all officers of his Majesty's navy: on this occasion two of the principal merchants received the seamen into their houses. Murray was removed to the house of the commissioner, and every attention which experience could prompt and liberality supply was generously afforded. Two, however, died; but Murray, at the expiration of a week, was seen walking about quite recovered.

Strange it was, that he who felt so much for the life of the youngster as he turned his boat and left him almost without hope—he who could then cheer him and speak in raptures of his conduct, had now grown proud with his security, and left till to-morrow the duty of inquiring after the boy. Not once even did Murray take the trouble of visiting Herring Cove. But the two seamen who, with Murray, had witnessed the boy's exertions, were no sooner recovered, than they walked over to the Cove; and having found the youngster, each gave him some trifle which they had saved when wrecked; however, they saw him only once, for men were much wanted in the different ships, and a week after they reached the shore, they were drafted on board different vessels, and were soon separated, perhaps for ever.

It now became a duty, which the commissioner urged upon Murray, to write a letter to his father. The reports of the loss of the frigate had gone to England without the names of those who had been saved. When such a destruction of life was circulated, a parent would feel most anxious to ascertain from his own child the proof beyond contradiction that he had been saved. The little energy which a sailor's life had instilled into Walter was fast ebbing, and day after day he was sinking into his former state. At last the packet arrived; and as the letters for the *Tribune* were directed to that port, Murray mustered up energy enough to inquire if there were any letters for him, or for the other midshipmen of the *Tribune*: he particularly asking for those which might be directed to Hammerton. He received two; one for himself, and one directed to his unfortunate and still-hated messmate. The blow given by the latter had never been forgotten; and even now, when he thought him dead, or far beyond his vengeance, he regretted the event, not in sorrow for the supposed sufferer, but because it deprived him of some of that pleasurable feeling arising from meditated revenge.

"I shall take charge of these two letters," said he; "and as both are in the handwriting of my father, I can mention to him my having received them."

Had there been any impropriety in giving up Hammerton's letter, the character which Munroe and Dunlap had spread of Murray would, in all probability, be considered by the postmaster a guarantee that the letter would reach its proper destination. The letter was given and quietly placed in his pocket, whilst that of his father to himself was opened and read. It was a letter of advice, not of credit: it urged Murray to be attentive to the advice of Hammerton, mentioned Sir Hector's close intimacy with the father, spoke in the highest terms of the little girl, and was very affectionate and very admonitory throughout. The curiosity of the boy soon mastered any honourable feeling he might once have been taught; and when he got into his own room, he began looking at his father's letter to Hammerton.

"I wonder," he commenced, "what that old respectable gray-headed papa of mine can be writing to this lout; of course it is all about me—he can have nothing else to write about; and as Hammerton, by the blessing of heaven, has long since paid an unexpected visit to the sharks, I may as well learn all that he would have told me from my father himself. There can't be any harm in opening the letter, because if it does contain advice I ought to have the benefit of it,—and if it does not, why I have only shown a laudable desire to be instructed. Then if Hammerton is dead, which in spite of all the captain said, is likely enough, he never can see the letter; and if he is not dead, I can remember the contents much better than I can send the original. So that, upon all points of principle and interest,—and money matters rule the world,—I think I had better just take a peep."

The harbouring of a dishonourable thought is the first step towards the committal of a crime. He who is convinced that he is treading upon slippery ground seeks the surer steps of the bank; but he who is heedless plunges at once into the mire. The more he then struggles to extricate himself, the deeper he generally sinks: like a man in debt, unless he can give up all at first, it is a hundred to one if he ever retrieves himself—as he pays off with the left hand, he runs in debt with the right; as a cheque is given for present payment, a bill at six months is drawn for trifling contingencies. The safest way then is to avoid all temptation.

Hammerton's letter was very unceremoniously opened; from the envelope fell an enclosure in the handwriting of Hammerton's father; and although the commissioner had given what money he thought requisite, yet the sight of the fifty pounds in his father's letter to Hammerton was irresistible. It was the easiest thing in life to say that it came in his own letter,—indeed, why mention Hammerton's at all? It was read, wondered at, skimmed again, concealed. The one from Hammerton's father was retained: in the event of being asked for a letter, there it was. Sir Hector had never written to Hammerton before, why should he now? It is the easiest thing in the world to imagine an excuse, but the most difficult thing in life to lie with consistency. The fifty pounds had cleared away all obstacles; the letter of Hammerton's father was returned to the post-office; but Murray slept not quite so soundly that night as after he had landed and saved Weazel.

In the mean time, the last-named gentleman having recovered from his fatigue, began some of his boyish tricks; and his room being preferred to his company, he was despatched to England to join some other ship, where we propose leaving him, to follow the fortunes of our more prominent friends.

New Year's Eve, 1799, was kept in all due form by Sir Hector Murray: the ash and faggot ball, a Somersetshire piece of antiquity, was held at Taunton, and the worthy baronet, who was always partial to old customs, made a point of attending it. In those days, when the hour of midnight of the 31st of December was close at hand, large faggots bound round with ash bindings were placed upon the fire; the company generally sat round this blazing hearth, and at every crack occasioned by the bursting of the bands, the merry guests gave loud hurrahs and quaffed their generous ale: the old year thus departed under a fire of satisfaction, and the new year was ushered in by merry faces and grateful hearts. It was a sort of thanksgiving for favours received—an acknowledgment to Providence with a cheerful countenance of all the blessings which had been bestowed; and far, far better is it thus cheerfully to offer up thanks than, with long, lank, straight hair, to *whine* over the calamities and miseries of existence—to believe merriment a sin and recreation a misdemeanour. Sir Hector was in high force that night; he had persuaded old Mr. Hammerton to allow Amelia to join in the amusement. The worthy old man never quitted his young charge for a moment, and as the various groups passed and remarked the beauty of the little affectionate girl, Sir Hector felt an inward satisfaction, and looked upon her as he would have done upon a daughter. The evening passed, the baronet returned, and the next morning at breakfast he found seated at his table old Mr. Hammerton and his silent interpreter Amelia. The common salutation having been performed, Mr. Hammerton at once began—

"I have received a letter from Frederick, Sir Hector, and it contains a description of his miraculous escape from the dangers and difficulties by which he was surrounded."

"What!" interrupted Sir Hector, "an action, I suppose? Victorious, of course? the navy, thank heaven, are seldom defeated."

"Not so, Sir Hector,—worse, ten thousand-fold worse."

"Is my son safe?" interrupted the baronet; for there was a rumour of the loss of the *Tribune* afloat, but so garbled and so contradictory that no one believed it.

"Yes; he is safe. But in saving his life, Frederick nearly lost his own. You had better hear the letter."

Sir Hector manifested a little impatience; and old Hammerton read the account of the boat, with the danger and deprivations neither heightened nor abbreviated, but a plain straightforward narrative of that which has already been related, and it terminated thus—

"In all my sufferings, dearest father, I thought of you and of Amelia: I knew that my death would rob you of your only prop, and Amelia of her only safeguard. I never lifted up my prayers for my own safety without eagerly soliciting that God would endow you with sufficient fortitude to bear up against the calamity, should it please Him to shorten my days. My prayer has been heard; I am yet alive and able, I trust, to work for your maintenance. The first money I can gain shall be transmitted to you; although I confess at this moment I see but little chance of earning more than is absolutely necessary for my subsistence. For the present I must remain in this small village, situated on the banks of St. James's River, in the Chesapeake. I had anticipated landing at New York, but we were driven off the coast in a gale, and ultimately reached this place. Do not grieve that I am without money, or indeed without raiment; I am spared to you, and I am grateful that I am thus enabled to hope that I may contribute to lighten the load under which you have so long groaned. I shall work my way to England if I can fall in with some English man-of-war and find some unexpected assistance. I am grateful for the misfortunes I have undergone, as they will teach me hereafter, should chance plunge me into difficulties, not to despair when danger looks the most dreadful, or give up life without a struggle to preserve it. The hand—the bountiful hand of Providence, which has sustained me in this trial, may yet guide and direct me safely to you; and that I may one day be blessed with your blessing, and again see my own dear affectionate mother and sister, is the unceasing prayer of your ever-dutiful son.

"P.S.—I hope young Murray will continue to do and to improve as he did before he slipped overboard. He is a bold, daring, desperate youngster, with one or two little failings which time and a midshipman's berth will rub off: he is a rough diamond; but rely upon it he will never disgrace his name if chance should throw the *Tribune* alongside of a force double her strength. I forgot to mention that it was in endeavouring to save the lives of others that he fell overboard himself. It happened on my dear little Amelia's birthday."

"Strange are the ways of Providence, and short-sighted indeed is man! You remember, Hammerton," continued Sir Hector, "that on that very day when your son was thus left to the winds and the waves, we were drinking his health and imploring God to protect him."

"You may rely upon it, Sir Hector," answered Hammerton, "that this meeting of the American ship was the means predestined to save him."

"A fiddlestick, Hammerton!—predestined, indeed! Then why did not the first ship save them?"

"Because it was ordained," replied the staunch old man, "that the crew were to be starved and die. You may laugh, Sir Hector, but nothing can shake my faith: I am certain in my own mind that nothing is the effect of chance—everything is ordained, and we walk blindly into the snare we cannot avoid."

"I wonder, Hammerton, would you think so if a man was busily employed cutting your throat with a blunt knife?"

"Certainly I should, Sir Hector; and I should hope that the man enjoying the high situation of finisher of the law would have been predestined to exercise his art upon the murderer. But tell me, sir, have you any tidings of the *Tribune?*"

"There are reports by hundreds: one, that she was wrecked in Halifax; another, that she was blown in the gale off Bermuda and there signalled; others, that she was seen going into harbour with her number flying; another, that she had fallen in with a French frigate, and having been dismasted and left a wreck, was seen under jury-mast standing towards the Azores; but as no two accounts agree, I am quite prepared to believe that the ship is safe enough, and only wish the accident-manufacturers of the newspapers would find some other vessel to lose besides the only one in the navy in which I am personally interested. I was about to remark upon your son's letter. He seems inclined to come home; I think it is a pity he did not endeavour to get to Halifax; he might work his way up to New York, and thence he might reach his own ship."

"His poverty, and not his will, consents to the steps he is about to take;—it certainly would have been the wisest plan, one would have supposed, to have done so."

"I wrote to your son, Hammerton," continued Sir Hector, "and I took care not to make the letter merely one of advice. Now, indeed, I could have wished him to have received that letter; for, to tell you the truth, I wrote it on little Amelia's birthday, and I sent him a trifling present to let him know the interest I took in my little favourite, and that he participated in my best wishes."

"You have, my dear Sir Hector, placed us all under a load of obligations which we can never return, excepting by a grateful remembrance of them: and now I leave you Frederick's letter to scan over at your leisure, and by the aid of charts and newspapers to make out the situation of the *Tribune.*"

CHAPTER XIV

LETTERS HOME.—PRANKS AT HALIFAX.—LOVE AND PREDESTINATION.

THE post arrived at Sir Hector Murray's country mansion about half-past one in the day, bringing him two letters;

and with the post came always that provision for half-starved garrisons—that comfort of each man's life—that cheapest of luxuries—the newspaper. Sir Hector was seated by his library fire waiting for the tide of novelty which sweeps through the long columns of the papers, taking us from times past to time present, filling the noddles of noodles with conversation to be drawn forth at that day's dinner, circulating scandal, reviling political opponents, and giving the true history of the times, its bearings, opinions, and changes. While Beujamin, who was much too good a servant to hand his old master a rheumatism in a wet newspaper, aired the sheet, Sir Hector opened one letter. This was from the person in charge of his house in Grosvenor Square, merely mentioning that two or three unknown individuals had mistaken Sir Hector's house for their own, and had, with all the right of the master, appropriated sundry pieces of furniture to their own use; had examined the cellar, and relieved one or two of the chimney-pieces from the weight of candelabras aud clocks; and, in fact, had taken the very questionable liberty of converting the property of Sir Hector to their own uses.

Benjamin shrugged up his old shoulders and congratulated his master upon the good fortune of having removed the most valuable articles; and, upon the principle of a clumsy nursery-maid who lets all the crockery of the little people down stairs by the run, only saving a cracked slop-basin, and then declares that "*for* a breakage it was a most fortunate affair," Benjamin argued that *for* a robbery it was the very best which could have occurred, and that Sir Hector ought, under the circumstances of the case, to consider himself uucommonly fortunate. Sir Hector rather differed from his old servant; and as, with a little more petulance than he usually exhibited, he snatched the paper, he said, "Misfortunes never come alone, Benjamin."

"No, sir," replied the old fellow, "that's true enough; for when I married my second wife, who was a lady's *maid*, I found that I had three daughters to provide for."

"Ah," replied Sir Hector, "in that case you were not singular. See if you can make out this wretched scrawl, and give an intelligible list of the loss." Saying which, he placed his spectacles on their proper resting-place, for previously they had been pointed to heaven like a pair of Herschel's telescopes, and he ran his eye over the leading articles of the *Times*. A larger type attracted him, and there he read "Melancholy Loss of the *Tribune*—Authentic Account." Sir Hector gazed almost breathlessly at the paper, and read the following narrative:—

"It is this day our melancholy duty to detail to our readers one of the most frightful shipwrecks which it has been our painful lot ever to circulate. The public are aware that some vague accounts of such an event have reached this country; but so very confused was the statement, and so serious might have been the consequences to the numerous friends of the unhappy ship's company, that we merely adverted to the report, and mentioned it as wanting confirmation. We sincerely wish we could now say that the present information required the same attestation; the fact is beyond dispute, and the public will read the horrid narrative with feelings of sympathy and regret which we have felt in thus giving it publicity."

Sir Hector drew breath feebly, the blood had left his lips, and his whole frame was seriously agitated; but he read it all—hurriedly, yet not a word escaped him. The paragraph finished thus:—

"Of all the officers and crew of this unfortunate vessel only eight have been saved, two midshipmen and six seamen; and we sincerely regret, for the consolation of those who are most interested in this awful calamity, that we are unable to give the names of the survivors. The report was brought by a schooner from Halifax, which, in consequence of the sudden change of wind, was enabled to put to sea on the evening of the 17th, the wreck having taken place on the night previously. The whole account is past a doubt; for the captain of the schooner has assured us that he saw the vessel himself, and beheld the survivors brought from the fore and maintops; and that when he weighed, every vestige of the ship had disappeared,—that the coast was literally thronged with people, all anxious and eager to afford every assistance to those who might have been washed on shore alive; but that, from the violence of the surf, and the particularly steep and rugged rocks along that part of the coast, not the slightest hope remained that another human being could be saved."

The bell was rung violently, and Benjamin ordered to send the quickest person in the house for Mr. Hammerton.

"I'll go myself, Sir Hector, and then I'm sure it will bc quickly done."

Sir Hector motioned him away, and his friend having soon reached the house, again read the account. There was no consolation to be gleaned—Hope itself sickened over the graphic description. Only two saved! how could he expect his son—unused to scenes of this description, raw, ignorant—to be saved? And all Hammerton's kind condolence and vivid painting of the possibility of such an event could not reconcile him even to the most distant idea that his son might be saved. Inva in was all Hammerton's persuasion that the old baronet would reconcile himself to the will of heaven; he who had smiled at predestination would now perhaps have gladly availed himself of its false creed to borrow consolation or repose. In vain did his friend again break open the wounds of his own heart, and let them bleed afresh, as he pointed to what he had suffered in life; and equally vain was it to use the best argument that, "sufficient for the day was the evil thereof,"—that hope always gave some spark until the light was irrevocably quenched,—that out of the two saved his son *might* be one,—that it was useless being borne down with woe before the actual knowledge of the fact, and that even then religion and a strong mind should bear up against that which would crush the sceptic and the timid.

Sir Hector hcld both hands before his face, for hc felt there was some truth—some reason in Hammerton's words, and he did not wish the torrent which gushcd from his eyes, and which was as plainly visible while it oosed through his fingers as the fingers themselves, to be seen.

"Miserable, wretched man that I am," he began, "to have partcd with him! Why should I have let the prop of my house, the inheritor of my name, run into dangers which might have been averted!"

"Stop, stop! my good sir," said Hammerton; "be assured they could not be averted. Gather comfort from that: nations credit that creed—millions of men believe in it; and out of the eight hundred millions who exist upon this earth, more than half acknowledge it. Turn your mind, my dear sir, for the present, to some other object; allow, if you can, your friend to divert your attention. Here is a letter unopened. Amelia shall sing to you. Come, my dear Sir Hector, when the blow falls, you may bow your head; as yet it is suspended. Do, sir, read this letter; perhaps it requires an answer."

"It can give me no comfort—no consolation. It refers, I suppose, to the robbery in my house; and would to heaven I could forget such griefs as easily as I can bear such trifling mishaps!"

Hammerton caught at the idea of leading him to relate the robbery. It had the effect desired; but as Sir Hector was about to relapse,—for he wandered a little and showed evident symptoms that grief was likely to master his intellect—the letter was again placed in his hand. Smiling through his tears at the kind intentions of Hammerton, and willing to alleviate the sorrows of poor little Amelia, who cried as most children cry when their seniors set the example, he opened the letter, gave a kind of shriek, and fell back fainting in his chair. Whilst the elders in the room assisted the unfortunate man, the eye of female curiosity was directed to the letter which fell from the baronet's hand. It required no time to be possessed of its contents. It ran thus—

Halifax, 17th November.

"SIR,—A schooner being about to sail for England, I hasten to remove all fears from your mind. Your son is this instant brought to my house alive, although much exhausted: depend upon all care and attention being given to him; he is not in the slightest danger, nor is he the least hurt. He shall write to you himself by the packet; and as a proof of his being here I shall make him place his name to this. I am, sir,

"Your obedient servant,

"THOMAS STYLES."

At the bottom of this was written "Walter;" the "M" had been begun, but Murray had been too exhausted to finish it.

Strange that the excess of joy should have more effect upon the mind than that of grief! Strange that men can bear calamities, cruelties, tortures, death, with unflinching eye and scarcely quivering lip,—that under the most aggravated circumstances the mind may be brought to fortify the man—that poverty succeeding to affluence can be looked upon with calmness and sometimes with contentment; but that the opposite extreme—that which we most wanted and least anticipated, the sudden acquisition of enormous wealth, the means whereby we are rescued from grovelling penury and lifted into ease and comfort—that which gives the power of gratifying revenge, exciting envy, causing jealousy—that any sudden flow of good fortune should paralyse the brain, and but too frequently turn the sensible into maniacs! Sir Hector slowly recovered from his fainting, and eagerly asked for the letter. Amelia had forced her father to read it, and as he returned the welcome epistle, warmly congratulated the baronet upon the fortunate event; as the agitated old man read the letter again coolly and calmly, he soon became restored to his wonted energy; and after giving a striking illustration even in old age of the excessive folly of imagining evils before they are in sight, and of giving way to an enemy before he has made his attack, the friends parted, and the overjoyed old man nearly danced round his own table, to all intents and purposes mad with joy.

More strongly to contrast the character of Walter Murray with those of his protector and him who risked his life to save him, perhaps the publication of his letter to his father would be the best document. It was received a few days after the arrival of that which removed the doubts and fears of the father; and it ran thus:—

"Halifax, 26th November.

"MY DEAR FATHER,—As Mr. Styles wrote to you the other day and told you I was safe, it's no use my entering into any details more than to confirm it. I was a little done, as they say; but I soon recovered when I got hold of the old gentleman's port wine. I am without clothes or money, and must get a refit upon tick; for I have no idea of being the son of a baronet and naked as a savage. Hammerton went adrift in a boat some time ago, and in all probability is drowned; and no great loss either to us or to him; he had no money, and was as poor as a piper. The captain thought he might be saved by some of the convoy, but I think with the others, that the boat was capsized, if ever he reached it, and that all hands are snug enough in Davy Jones's locker. The last time I saw him, he was striking out hard for the boat, which was a long way to windward of him, and when the fog came on he must have been drowned. I am in the commissioner's house here; he is a good fellow enough, and draws his corks freely. He had me rubbed down with rough towels as if I had been a horse; and no sooner was I a little recovered than he talked of getting rid of me, and I am to join the *Surprise*, commanded by Captain Edward Hamilton: she is on the West India station, and as I rather like the service, having weathered the last gale, I shall be off to my new ship in the first vessel that sails.

"I received your letter and have pocketed the advice. Weazel was the only midshipman saved besides myself: the devil always takes care of his own, and a neater nut for Old Nick to crack never got into a shell than Weazel. He was taken to a house where there were four women,—an old one and her three daughters: they were all very kind to him, and he pretended to be very much obliged to them. He soon got well: the salt water, as he said, 'preserved' him, for he was a nice pickle. Well, there he remained for about a week, eating and drinking, and spending all the money these fools gave him; and there he might have remained until now, if his godfather, the devil, had not got to work at him and put him up to some of his usual tricks. The two youngest daughters, girls about sixteen or seventeen, all made up of combs and curls, both fell in love with this weed taken off the rocks, and he thought he would repay their love after his fashion; so the first thing he does is to dress up a bolster with a black mask and nightcap on its head, and clap it up in the young ladies' bed; and before they went to roost he told them long yarns about murders in the West Indies, and of the strange look of a negro who had that day been near the house asking for charity. The old woman was in a dreadful fright, and believed that the poor black was likely to walk off with one of her daughters and murder herself, and she went to bed shaking all over like a chicken in a shower. The young girls undressed in their mother's room, while Weazel was watching for the result. No sooner had the little loves got into their own apartment, than they proceeded to take a last look at their pretty faces in the glass which stood opposite the bed; and in that they beheld the face of the negro very comfortably ensconced in their bed. They could not stir, but with one consent gave a tremendous scream. The old lady ran to see what was the matter, rushing in very thinly clad; and seeing her daughters as pale as death, looking in the glass, she ran to it and beheld the horrid blackamoor staring at them; and such a scream as they all set up together! Weazel crept into the room, and pinching the old lady by the heel, began to bark like a dog. The scene which followed baffles all description: the old lady fainted, the girls went into hysterics, and Weazel was found endeavouring to restore animation to the little curly-pated Rosette, laughing and giggling at the mischief he had created. He was told to depart the next day. This annoyed him; so, after placing a broom upright with a basin of water on the top of it against the drawing-room door, he gave a rap. 'Come in,' said one of the girls. No answer, but another rap followed; up jumped the eldest girl to open the door, when smack came basin and broom on her head, drenching her with water, spoiling the carpet, and frightening the old lady. Before he left the house and got despatched to join the *Arethusa*, he cut off the best ringlet of Rosette's hair, clapped some cobbler's wax in the shoes of the old lady, pinned the eldest and number two together, tied a squib to the cat's tail, and set the dog adrift with a bundle of crackers to his stern. He was worth a hundred Hammertons—lazy fellows who do nothing but their duty, without any fun or frolic about them.

"I must conclude this long letter, as I have to get my new rigging over my mast-head. I have drawn a bill upon you, and once more I am quite recovered and well. And I am,

"Your dutiful son,

"WALTER MURRAY."

Not one word throughout this long rambling letter was there of grateful acknowledgment to a parent for all his former kindness—not one syllable of filial affection—not one sentence praying that the good old baronet might not have received the intelligence of the shipwreck before Styles's letter removed any fear of apprehension he might have entertained concerning his son's safety. There was nothing but unfeeling egotism, ungrateful remarks, hatred and rancour, against the man who tried to save him, and a chuckling satisfaction at the mischievous pranks of Weazel.

And yet there was a good point, one rather of omission than commission: it made no mention whatever of the gallant conduct of Walter when he refused to be saved, placing his nearly-dying messmate in the boat; it launched into no self-commendation; nor did it convey to his father one idca of the manner in which Walter had been received in Halifax in consequence of the circulation of the intelligence of his gallant and exemplary behaviour. Still the worst part of his character, ingratitude, was fully developed: he had never tried to ascertain the boy's name who first pushed off to save him—he never mentioned the brave act which would have placed the lad for ever on the pension-list of Sir Hector. If the bad parts were developed, the good were concealed; and had all been known, the father might have found a balance in favour of his son, instead of contrasting it with the former letter of Hammerton, so little filled with himself, and so much—so kindly warmed by the affectionate spirit which breathed throughout it.

Frequent conversations passed between the two parents on this head; the one groaning over the calamity of having a son (whom he yet tenderly loved) with such an ill-regulated mind to inherit great wealth; and the other, convinced that in whatever station of life Frederick might be placed, his steady adherence to his duty, his untiring spirit, his religion, would support him through all difficulties, and ultimately obtain for him the respect of the world, even if they failed to give him its riches. Over and over again did old Hammerton recapitulate his doctrine of predestination; and just as often did Sir Hector overthrow the flimsy creed, by reasoning upon its fallacy. In the mean time, the friendship became gradually more closely cemented: Amelia was more caressed—even called an adopted daughter; and bright and sparkling were the young eyes of this little beauty as she listened to the arguments of the old people, her little fingers, lips, and eyes all moving together as she conveyed Sir Hector's meaning without a mistake, and listened to her father's answers. She of course believed as did her father; and had already been heard to say, "If it's predestined that Frederick is to return, return he will: or if it was arranged that I am to marry old Sir Hector, why I suppose I should do it, although I am only twelve and he nearly seventy." If beauty could increase like a flower, to blossom and to fade in a year, perhaps Amelia might have been the unenvied plant; but she grew more gradually, not hastening into bud to fade in its bloom, but slowly progressing towards a perfection of feature in which talent and vivacity embellished the rose and the lily.

CHAPTER XV

PROMOTION AT JAMAICA.—A DOCTOR DOCTORED.—DEBAUCH ON BOARD, AND DEATH ON SHORE.

The commissioner of Halifax soon discovered all the bad propensities of Walter; he well knew that there was no school to correct or tame a wild boy like a midshipman's berth; and that where bravery was known, or where a reckless disregard for danger existed, it was on board a man-of-war they were most esteemed, and properly watched and rewarded. Having in his early life been acquainted slightly with Sir Hector Murray, and having been very favourably impressed with the character of Walter, he resolved to serve him according to his power; for all his little failings were lost in the blaze of his splendid behaviour in the *Tribune*, which lost none of its colour from the circumstance that Galvin, Munroe, and Dunlap came and requested the favour of shaking hands with him once more before they were drafted into different ships, and expressed a hope that at some future time they might again be under the command of one who, in the greatest danger, and with hope actually fast to the side, cut adrift the painter, and remained to die in order to save his messmate.

Sailors never forget these things. Trifling errors they call "being a little scampish;" but the word scamp on board a ship, either in the cockpit or before the mast, does not carry with it the same bad meaning extended to it on shore. Let but a brave scamp beat up for volunteers, and every man in the ship will soon respond to the call; they care very little for some ungentlemanly debauchery,—the leader is brave and determined, and will never return them on board the subject of ridicule and contempt.

In the year 1799, the *Surprise*, a small frigate, was under the command of Captain Hamilton, an officer well known in those days for his daring exploits; and it was on board of this frigate that Mr. Walter Murray was in future to exhibit his bravery. He was packed off in a gun-brig bound to Jamaica, having in his pocket the best part of Hammerton's fifty pounds, and a supply from the commissioner of all requisite articles; nor did he sail without some advice better than he occasionally got from home.

"You have done nobly, generously, manfully, Murray," said the commissioner, as he extended his hand to him for the last time, "act always so—risk your own to save a messmate's life, and in the hour of danger you will find dozens by to protect you. A brave seaman never quits a brave officer, and mayhap you may experience *that* under your new commander. You go to him with a character that all your messmates will envy: young as you are, you will soon be placed in danger. I have no fear for the result; you will never disgrace your name before an enemy. Remember, I have written to Hamilton: he will expect much of you; he will watch you narrowly—he will censure you privately, and reward you publicly. God bless you! let me hear from you occasionally; but if you, like some youngsters, are afraid of writing to old captains, I will get a remembrance of you through another channel. I see the blue peter up, so away with you; and whenever you come back to Halifax, here you will find a home and a welcome as long as you uphold the credit of what I know of Walter Murray."

Murray parted from his kind friend with real regret. In his society he had heard of daring deeds done in days gone by; he had seen the battle of the Nile fought upon a mahogany table: he had heard how enthusiastically, how generously, one naval officer could praise another, without the little bickerings of envy and jealousy; he had heard

Nelson called "Britannia's watchword:" and as these stories were recounted, he vowed, if chance but offered, that he himself would emulate the fame of the hero of the Nile. If ever a heart beat high with hope—if ever a heart throbbed with determination, Walter Murray's was that heart; but he was true to his character to the last: although he had remained six weeks at the commissioner's, he never gave one of the servants a farthing; and quite unintentionally, as the commissioner said afterwards, when telling the anecdote—the dismal anecdote of the *Tribune's* loss—he left Halifax, having forgotten to pay for his washing, and leaving one or two bills to be presented for payment.

No sooner had the gun-brig cleared the harbour, than Murray saw the cliffs on which the lazy vermin crawled when the boy pulled from Herring Cove; and then for the first time he thought he might have endeavoured, at least once, by the sacrifice of a trifling pleasure, to find out the lad who had saved Weazel. But he soon rather rejoiced over his neglect, for he argued thus: "If I had found him, I should have mentioned him to my father; he is so confoundedly foolish about money, that he would have pensioned the boy: and when I came to the property, I should have a great deal of trouble to get rid of him. Better as it is. I have not been ungrateful, for he never saved *me*, and Weazel, I dare say, has sent the lad's boat adrift with his favourite dog in it, or broken both his oars to prop up some shed in which he proposed to cut off the dog's tail by way of a joke."

Here he was interrupted in his sweet thoughts and gentle reminiscences by the officers of the brig asking him to point out the place where the frigate drifted and ultimately went to pieces. His memory was correct as to all particulars; it must have been a more dunderheaded lad than Murray to have forgotten what was so unpleasantly engraven on his mind: his account was vivid—and his eye sparkled as he told the tale. "There it was we struck, close to that bluff point: and there, just by that sharp projecting hill, she fixed herself. There is Herring Cove, from which we first got assistance;—ay, and well I know that small round knob; there it was we saw many looking, but none offering aid."

Murray was a favourite in a moment; he volunteered to be placed in a watch; and when stationed on the forecastle at reefing topsails, he said respectfully, "I should prefer the foretop, if you please, sir."

"I wish we were going to keep you in the brig, youngster," replied the first lieutenant: "you are just the lad we want."

"I should have no objection to stay, if I were not already fixed for the *Surprise*."

Fifteen days saw him in the vilest hole on earth—Port Royal at Jamaica—of all places the most dreary, the most desolate. It is built (that is, the town) upon a low, sandy point, projecting into the sea, the water being so deep that a lead line may be dropped from the thin projection into seven fathoms water. It is here that a poor boy, the son of a negrô, was washing his feet, when a shark rushed at him, and before he could gather his legs up, one was carried away by the voracious creature, the blood which followed the bite bringing about twenty more in pursuit of a similar treat. Beset on the sea-side by sharks, it has its rear adorned by the Palisades, a place *on* which—for it cannot be said *in* which—the victims of yellow fever are ultimately laid: the sandy soil being so near the limits of the water, that after digging a two-feet-deep grave, the water rushes in, and the place is shortly filled up: the coffins, therefore, are sometimes uncovered, and when, as is the case, putridity succeeds to life, and the cool land-breeze comes wafting the odours over the miserable remnants of a town, the inhabitants have no particular need to hail that breeze which in other parts of the island is most eagerly welcomed. Let no man say his life is safe for a day at Port Royal; the wholesale murderer, yellow fever, even as he walks, is stealthily sapping his best health, until it has fixed itself steadily and strongly upon its victim. A shivering fit at rising in the morning is the signal for the coming assault; and if the razor and the lancet, calomel, and other vile means, be not speedily called in to aid the garrison, the outworks will be carried by noon, by sunset the mind will have surrendered, the victory will be secure, and by the dawn,—and here, as if in mockery of the human race, who toil to live, and live to toil, the opening day is more splendid than in any other part of the globe,—the poor beaten creature, once a man, but now a maniac, is at the last gasp; by noon on the second day he will be laid in his shell on the Palisades; and when the sun goes down, and the land-breeze comes on, his remembrance may be recalled in the vile miasma he has already contributed to generate. Here the young and the old, the sickly and the healthy, the rich and the poor, the sober and the drunken, are on a par; there is no premium upon good conduct: the tippler, the glutton, and the gambler,—he who walks out at noonday's heat, or lies exposed to the rays of the moon, is very nearly as secure as the careful, the prudent, the reserved,—he who walks only in the cool of the morning or evening, shuts out the cold air of night, and more carefully avoids the moon than the daylight.

"Beware of the evening dews," said the doctor of the brig to Murray, as they approached this most beautiful island; "trust not to appearances—this is the fatal beauty which beams forth in all its attractions to entrap you; and like the eager fly which approaches the rich treat before it —disregarding the thin and almost imperceptible web which has been spun for its capture, it rushes into the mesh and the spider appears,—so is it here: lured by the great beauty of the island, young and inexperienced men walk in the noonday heat to partake of the great feast Nature has prepared for them; they sit down to view the glorious sight, they rest after fatigues in apparent security; and the next day—there, there," said he, as he pointed to the thousand wooden remembrances of lost friendship, "behold the result! Where you see those negroes laying down their load—their daily load, there will the rash youth lie and be forgotten in a moment—for death is no rarity here. Be prudent, Mr. Murray; avoid young rum, which is old poison; live temperately, moderately; rise early, go to bed early; and you may weather the Palisades."

Three days after this good and wholesome advice, Murray being in want of some more linen, purchased the stock of the doctor, who, while adopting his own advice, proved the fallacy of human precautions,—for, before that time, he was carried by the negroes he had pointed out to the Palisades.

"A good medico, in truth," said Murray to himself; "he pointed out the danger he could not avoid; and since temperance is thus rewarded, perhaps the other extrme might be as bad. I shall walk in the middle path—live as usual, fatigue myself only when my duty requires it—live neither too riotously nor too abstemiously—take the good things when they are offered,—one may drink any *given* quantity. I shall never think of the fever, and shall say with some truth, 'Sufficient for the day be the evil thereof.' Half the dead have frightened themselves into the fever, and the other half have starved or drank themselves into it. Precaution is better than cure; but here precaution appears useless, and I shall swim with the tide in the best manner I can."

It happened that his new ship, the *Surprise*, was at sea when the brig anchored, and Murray was drafted on board the *Shark*, the guard-ship, (and never was there a more appropriate name for such a reservoir as that,) to await her arrival. He was welcomed, for he could not displace any of the older midshipmen, who were feeding upon rum, vegetable marrow, and hope. The cup which held the last was too often dashed from their lips when it appeared brimming with the sparkles of life. Some, after years and years of active service, had been placed upon the commander-in-chief's list, and kept in the *Shark* to leap into a commission; but before death could take a lieutenant or a captain, Sir Hyde Parker had a cargo of young sprigs of nobility sent out to fill the first vacancies; and thus year after year would pass, the commission always apparently within grasp, yet invariably eluding the touch. These men, soured by disappointment, formed the laudable design of killing every lieutenant they could catch, not with a dagger, but with a poisoned bowl. The victim was asked to dinner—new rum, strong unhealthy port, villanous rubbish called claret, heavy porter from the store of one John Ferrong, of most notorious memory; whilst smoking, raw nips, punch, wine, milk, beer, sangaree, lemonade, and cup filled up the stomach of iniquity, and the yellow fever stepped in conveniently to prevent inquiries.

It was amongst a host of such men that Walter Murray, bearing the stamp and impress of a gentleman, was welcomed as he mounted the sides of the *Shark*. It was four o'clock in the afternoon, and the midshipmen, the oldsters, had obtained leave to dine at five, when the heat of the day would have somewhat passed, in order to welcome a young lieutenant just come out on the station, with red hair, a thin skin, and every circumstance favourable to the impression of the sun, or its equal in heat and fire—new rum. He had been at sea under one of the oldsters; at which time the new lieutenant was thirteen, and the oldster twenty. Now the ages had advanced; the one being nineteen, the other twenty-six; the one having risen in the service, the other having suffered from "hope deferred:" the one all elated with his prospects, the other soured by past events, having been wounded three times, mentioned in the "Gazette" twice, but still a midshipman; whilst the lad who came to sea under his guidance had passed him, and now heard this very oldster order the boatswain's mate to attend the side for him.

This is one of the many miseries a man may experience in the navy, and be saved in the marines. In the latter no slip of a noble stock can jump over his head, no wealth purchase above him; each man takes his turn at dangers and difficulties, and rises slowly but surely when his time arrives;—there is some consolation, but very little hope, in the Royal Marines.

The young lieutenant and his old shipmate shook hands cordially; the one evidently extending his with a little condescension, the other receiving it with a slight diffidence. This always occurs in a difference of rank in the navy, and may be traced even in the admiral and old captain.

The stranger was taken below into the gun-room of the *Shark*: and Murray witnessed the eager looks of the other midshipmen, who were calculating how long it would be before they entombed their victim and stepped into the death vacancy.

"He will be soon done," said one.

"I think so," replied one of the name of Douglas; "but we must not make him drunk too soon, we must let him take a good quantity—and an unwholesome mixture."

"Old Oliver," said another, "has got him nicely in tow there, about some '*glorious fun*' they had in Portsmouth.

If we can but get him to lie out upon the logs, just leave the moon and the dew to do the rest."

"Let's do it like gentlemen," said the first speaker, who was the oldest of the party, and, according to all accounts, the second on the admiral's list. "That cursed packet will be in before the week's out, and then we shall have some other honourable villain to rob us of our due."

"If he weathers the Palisades between this and Friday I'm a Dutchman, and the devil's a beggar."

"Come, lads," said Oliver, "dinner's ready. Let me introduce you to Mr. Abbot, a luckier dog than any of us, but a right good fellow, and therefore we can bear having the 'go-by' given us by him. Sit the larboard side, Abbot; when this sea breeze they call 'the doctor' dies away, the ship will ride with her stern to the Palisades, and you will get the land-breeze in your face. You always know a Johnny Newcome by his getting his back to the breeze. Sit down, youngster; what's your name?"

"Walter Murray," replied the boy.

"D—n it! you answer as if you were a lord. Walter Murray, indeed! service is come to a pretty pass when a youngster has such a mouthful of names as that! Bring yourself to anchor!—sit over the starboard side!—there's no breeze which blows that can blow any good out of you just yet! Boy, take this soup to Mr. Abbot!—make a long arm, youngster!—you must learn to sit on your thumb, and think that a broad seat! What kind of a craft is that old ship you came out in?"

"Good enough," replied Abbot.

"Are there any of the officers sick on board of her?" asked the impatient Douglas.

"No," replied Abbot; "the captain looked rather bilious the other day, but he is all right again."

"Is he a young man?" asked Oliver; I mean a man about thirty?"

"No," was the answer; "I should judge him a lucky fellow of about five-and-twenty."

"I wonder if he knows any of the lieutenants," said the oldest bird of this raven's nest of destroyers. "Abbot, take a glass of wine: here's some sherry—hand here your glass!—No half-laughs and purser's grins here; fill it up with the rose in the middle for old acquaintance' sake. Here's your health, and next step to you soon! It's devilish hot; let's douse our jackets and take to it comfortably."

"Mr. Abbot," said Douglas, "may I have the pleasure of drinking wine with you? Here's some claret, not so hot and fiery as that sherry."

Abbot swallowed the newly-imported stuff from St. Jago de Cuba, bought at Johnny Ferrong's,—or rather borrowed, under the solemn asseveration that it was taken out of a vessel from Bordeaux, which had been captured, and her cargo sold at Kingston.

"Pray, sir," said Murray, with all the pertness of a spoiled boy, and all the manner of one who felt himself likely to give the "go-by" to all present, addressing himself to Mr. Abbot, "have you a good stock of linen?"

The question astonished all hands; but Abbot, who with his coat had dropped his rank, looked at his shirt-sleeves, and answered, "Pretty well for that, I think, youngster; but why do you ask?"

"Because if you go on as you are going on now, you will be by the day after to-morrow alongside of the doctor of the brig, who came in here a week ago in health, and is now *there;*" (as he said this, he pointed out of the stern windows, the ship having swung, and the Palisades being close on board of her) "and I bought his shirts."

This produced a shout of laughter, and its proportionate ridicule from Abbot, who declared the doctor must have predisposed himself to fever from the fright he was in when he rounded the low point, and then added, "By Jove, it's too hot to laugh in this climate! What have you got to drink, Oliver?"

"Capital ale—right good wholesome stuff,—none of your negro-boiled porter, or your stewed donkeys fermented, but right good Fermoy, made the better by keeping down the bubbles by a glass of brandy. I'll show you how we manage it here—Boy! bring the bottle here! Why, you cuckoo! you have not drawn the cork. Now, Abbot," said he, "pop this glass of brandy into the tumbler, and drink it off at once.—That's well done!—don't you think the brandy improves it?"

"I think it does," said the foolish young man; "but it tastes very much like rum, and very strong too."

"Why, you spalpeen of the devil!" said Douglas, looking at the boy, "you have put the old Jamaica on the table!—take it off and bring the brandy."

Abbot was now reeking at every pore, thirsty of course, and was persuaded by Douglas to try some cider with some sherry in it, just to correct the acidity. The dinner was done, the cloth removed—conversation all alive, principally about promotions, cuttings out, dashing actions, and comfortable stations. In the mean time the land-breeze began slightly to stir the surface of the water: Abbot had thrown his waistcoat open, and the cold damp struck back upon his chest, delightful to feel, but fatal to experience.

In the *Shark* the midshipmen might smoke or do anything else they pleased,—and they did please to smoke and drink—both. The wine was now put aside for grog; and although Abbot manifested some signs of coming inebriation in the thickness of his utterance, and the devil-may-care manner in which he handled the bottle, yet some of the more knowing ones saw that if he went on at the pace he was going, he would soon be rather too hazy to undertake a quiet excursion on shore, this being the *coup de grâce.* The victim, after being walked or reeled about until he can no longer stand, is left without a hat on one of the logs near the shore, and "the moon and the dew do their duty."

Murray saw what was going on, and he guessed that the doctor's advice was well worth following: he took only water, and this enabled him to see the end of the tragedy; for had he drunk brandy, the fork would have been stuck in the table, and he bundled off to his hammock. Oliver proposed a song: he sang a good one himself, and therefore having proposed it, and being able to do it, he set the example, and sang the following, all hands joining in respectable chorus, while Douglas occasionally poured a few drops of new rum—the bottle stood by him—into the sangaree of Abbot.

"When the world was first made, all was order, we know,
Until Admiral Noah took a cruise in the ark:
He had a strange crew to trim sails in a blow,
But he sailed without compass to steer in the dark.

If to north, south, or west, 'twas no moment to him;
For who could make land when of land there was none?
He drifted about as it suited his whim,
And the jolly old admiral revell'd in fun.

"When he turn'd out at daylight—he never slept late—
His daughters and sons took the scrub-brooms in hand;
And they fagg'd and they toil'd, but they never once ate
Of the pairs of provisions which came from the land.
They had ducks, geese, and sheep, with a lion or two;
Cameleopards, with other large drones;
An elephant also, to clap in a stew,
With a rather thin donkey to make some broiled bones.

"Now we are much wiser than Noah, my boys,
We eat and we drink of the good things on board;
Not a duck or a goose his existence enjoys,
But a savoury stew he may also afford.
Let us live whilst we can, let us love whilst we may,
For the slight breath of life in a moment is past;
Seize the hour which is *now*, make the best of the day,
And a fig for the cloud which may evening o'ercast."

"Bravo!" said Douglas, "Hurrah for the present time, and the devil run a-hunting with the future! Fill up, Mr. Abbot; here's Oliver's good health and song, and it's

"A very good song, and it's very well sung,
Jolly companions every one.
Put on your hats, and keep your heads warm,
A little more liquor will do us no harm."

"Ah!" sighed Murray, for he had got a little of his own good sense for his guide, "that chorus is not like Parr's maxim of health, 'Keep your head cool by temperance, your feet warm by exercise; never eat but when hungry, nor drink but when dry.'"

"Holloa!" said Douglas, "why, we have got a parson on board, rigged out like a boy of the first class. I dare say you know all about Noah and his Ark: now, can you tell where he made the land?"

"I know," replied Murray, as he looked Abbot full in the face, "where he will make the land."

"Do you think so really?" said Douglas, his face sparkling with animation and rum, as he heard the youngster predict what he most wished realized. And so it is,—words which would have been regarded with contempt from one so young, if differing from his wishes, were treasured up as a prophecy by Douglas, who looked at that evening's work as his release from the heavy burthen he had so many years carried.

"I call," said Oliver, "upon Douglas for a song."

"Bravo! bravo!" resounded. "Come, Douglas, clear your whistle, get the huskiness of the Kingston sand out of your throat, and give us 'The Shark's Prayer.'"

If anything could have startled Abbot, it would have been this song; but he was wound up to meet all the evils which flesh is heir to without flinching: his face was crimson with heat, and he mopped away the perspiration, whilst those long inured to the villanous climate scarcely (to use a familiar expression) "turned a hair." The cry was "Douglas!" the president beat the table, and this lieutenant in expectation gave forth the following song, in a deep, clear voice, his spirit warming with the subject, and his voice gradually increasing in the chorus:—

"Saturday night was the sailors' delight,
When they sang of their love, or described the fierce fight.
It's in England, or far, far away from this spot,
That this song of the seaman is never forgot.
But who in this climate of sickness and sorrow
Shall dare to look forth for the light of to-morrow?
Hark! hark! to the prayer of the *Shark*:
Promotion's uncertain, our prospects are dark;
Our toast shall be DEATH, though it savours of treason;
And this is the prayer of the mids of the *Shark*—
For a bloody war, and a sickly season.
Hurrah! hurrah!
Near and far,
For a bloody war and a sickly season.

"What's life but an ocean of strife,
For ambition, promotion, another man's wife!
Who cares for the living placed over our head?
'Tis a world full of cares, and the bless'd are the dead.
The captain's last sigh, though in madness it be,
Or his groans, would make music the sweetest to me.
Hark! hark, &c.

"What's death but the stoppage of breath,
And a rather damp bed in the ground underneath?
The best friend we have is the quick yellow fever,
And the first toast we drink is 'Promotion for ever!'

Let them die who're above us, and, bless'd in repose,
Their troubles all ended, we'll step in their shoes.
Hark! hark, &c."*

It is needless to add, that the toast was drunk even by Abbot in a brimmer, for although it was partially directed at him, yet he had to move up the ladder, and in his delirium of drunkenness he would not have cried if the man on the step above him slipped off in a hurry.

Again was the glass filled and emptied; and now the red eye of drunkenness was fixed in stupid gaze, then came indecent songs, revellings, cursings, complaints of prospects blighted, in almost inarticulate language; and as the relater of his woes dashed his hand on the table, the tears rolled down his face, the glasses danced before and around him.

There sat systematic drunkenness, a kind of unmeaning smile upon his lips, his eyes scarcely human, muttering to himself the last words of the song, they being what he really most wished and best remembered. By his side was sullen indifference rolling upon his chair: if brandy or water went into his mouth, he could not distinguish the difference. By him again was delicate sensibility moistened in tears,—a man crying drunk, his mouth unable to contain the fluid which, like an infant's dribbles, oozed through his lips. On his right was frantic intemperance, quarrelling with all, but noticed by none; and as he rose higher and higher in his blasphemy, his laughing-drunk companion was pouring the grog intended for his victim's mouth down the collar of his shirt.

Murray eyed it all; and the lesson—the Spartan lesson of making their slaves drunk—was not lost upon him; he became an attentive witness of the danger of drunkenness. The man who had treasured the secret in his breast with religious caution, now blabbed it forth; he who was rigid in his duty, now scoffed at discipline; the silent found an incoherent tongue, the coward became the bravest of the brave, the mildest and most modest was now the fiercest and the most indecent. In the midst of all this, the

* This toast was drunk every day by the midshipmen of the *Shark;* and I remember a certain officer saying, when he heard that the man was dead whose vacancy he got, "His dying groans would have been music to my ear."

principal object was not to be neglected: Abbot was considered sufficiently primed—it was proposed to go on shore, the party having prudently got permission beforehand. The boat was manned, and Murray saw the victim wreathed, filleted, and ready for slaughter. They landed; the billiard-room was lighted, Johnny's store was assailed, doors were forced open, the poor negro as he hurried past was abused or pelted, and Abbot, after a dreary and tiresome walk round that precious sink of iniquity, was left by his guide Oliver without his hat to sleep upon the damp logs, whilst the others, accustomed to such scenes, traversed the dirty town without a guide, reached the boat, returned on board, and tumbling into their hammocks, wallowed in their sleep.

The morning sun rose upon Abbot; the cold creeping shiver attacked him, his head was nearly splitting with that dreadful ache which is one of the penalties of debauchery. He walked towards Ferrong's to get a hat; he reached the door, and again attacked by his fierce enemy the fever, he became giddy and fell down. Assistance was soon at hand; he was removed to the hospital, bled, blistered, physicked.

On the other hand, the jovial companions of his last night's frolics rose with unsteady hands, and with perhaps that settled red of the tippler on their cheeks which ignorance might pronounce emblematic of health, and *they* felt but little annoyed by their intemperance. The news was quickly conveyed on board of Abbot's fate: he was raving mad in the hospital. In his lucid intervals he called frequently and loudly upon Oliver, his best—his earliest friend; and now feeling that his fate was approaching, the secret which he had hoarded in his bosom struggled to get loose. He implored to see his old messmate; and as he refused to take any medicine until he had been gratified, a request was sent to Oliver to repair to the hospital; and that worthy, as he stepped with Murray over the side, said in a laughing tone, "You may buy his shirts after to-morrow"

CHAPTER XVI.

ABBOT'S DEATH SCENE.—CONFESSION OF LOVE AND SEDUCTION.

"Now," said Oliver, as Murray and himself landed at Port Royal—"Now you shall see a scene which snivelling cowards call dreadful, but which custom has reconciled to me. It's only the death of another man; and perhaps, as you are on this station, you may as well see all its horrors at once and get reconciled to them: you may yet live to hear 'the Shark's Prayer' with more glee than you seemed to relish it last night."

"I never wish to hear it again," said Murray: "I knew how certainly it would finish your victim. Why, I saw you—you need not start, for *I* was sober—I saw you fill his glass to the brim with the raw new rum, whilst you helped yourself from a bottle which had brandy and water in it."

"Stuff, youngster, stuff! I am perhaps more seasoned to it than he was; but as to drinking, you know, especially when we run a tilt against death, that is always done fairly and above-board; besides, we consider 'the Shark's Prayer' as a bond of honour—we never flinch from that toast."

"It's a villanous toast," replied Murray, with much animation, "and the wretch who composed the song is only rivalled by the barbarian who gave the toast."

"I will take the liberty, Mr. Walter Murray, to tell you that your ears are in sad jeopardy, and that a donkey's will be shorter than yours by two inches, if you do not take a reef in your tongue and let one out in your manners."

"I am not much afraid of my ears, Mr. Oliver," replied the lad. "I have seen enough of men to know that those who talk most do least; and if that poor fellow dies—."

"Die!" interrupted Oliver; "why, is there any doubt of it? He had black vomit this morning; and, by Jupiter! in spite of all the Spanish nonsense of lemon and oil as a cure, no man ever yet digested in his waistcoat when the coats of his stomach were mortified. He is off to a dead certainty; and if the sea-breeze, which, confound it! is freshening fast, would only take breath to-day in the shape of a calm, to-morrow I should be a lieutenant in a death vacancy, and others might sing 'the Shark's Prayer' for me—unless indeed, some captain was inclined to dine with me after I had served my time."

"This poor fellow has sent for you, as his best friend, to bear some tidings of his fate to his poor old father or mother; and how can you sit by his sick-bed and hear his last wishes without feeling that you are the author of his misfortunes?"

"What a young ass you are, Murray! I am his best friend. This world is a world of woe, as the song says, and he is the happiest man who is freed from woe.

"Now," interrupted Murray, "are you going to this poor fellow's bedside actually wishing to see, if possible, his last shiver, or to hear his last word?"

"I should be better pleased," said Oliver, "to hear that he was dead already; for all these long-winded yarns of dying men are very troublesome, especially where no swizel is allowed, and where one is interrupted by continued ravings of other people who take a sad long time to die."

By this time they had arrived at the hospital; and Oliver, who mentioned his name, said he came in consequence of Mr. Abbot wishing to see him before he died. He told Murray to follow him, and the youngster, as if determined to face any scene, however dreadful, wound up his courage to the sticking-post and entered the ward in which lay Abbot. He was not the only patient, for a bed nearly opposite to his was also tenanted.

Oliver said, as he pointed to it, "It is only a purser who is going to pass muster aloft. No one cares a fig about him afloat: some of the clerks at the Admiral's office will get the vacancy. He ought to have been dead a week past; but the devil is certain of him, and therefore is in no particular hurry."

"Ah, Oliver," said Abbot, "that is a good fellow; come near me: you are not afraid of this cursed fever, I know."

Murray, as he looked, could hardly recognize the man to whom he had given the friendly hint. Abbot saw him and turned away his head as he looked at Oliver, and pointing at Murray, said, "He is come for my shirts."

Murray sat down at some distance, and was not an idle spectator of the scene which followed.

"You look ill," said Oliver, "my dear fellow. I see they have shaved your head and bled you down to weakness; but I hear you are better than you were in the morning."

"Better, Oliver," replied the desponding Abbot; "I fear I never shall be better! This morning I was ill—very ill, and am now so weak that I can scarcely hold my head up; and that poor fellow opposite has been dreadfully raving all day: the black nurse says he is sure to die, for he has had the black vomit: it is not a very comfortable idea to be stretched out by such creatures." Here Abbot stopped speaking, and his opposite neighbour commenced an incoherent speech: he was too weak to move, but his words came audibly enough.

"Then I won't stand it any longer!" began the purser. "If the youngsters amuse themselves kicking my lanterns about the tiers, I'll make it up in tobacco. What's the use of keeping books if we can't add a pound or two to a friend's account?—dead men eat just as much as we do, and they don't see quite so well.—Let's have a little more wine, Joe: prize-money will soon come in, and candle-boxes are cheap.—Those are queer chaps on board the *Shark;* they drink to *Death* every night when they can get a new-comer to dine with them. That old fellow Oliver has killed a score, and will have plenty more flats in his net: if the admiral would but promote him, the negroes would have a holiday at the Palisades, and a red-haired man have a fair chance."

Abbot, who was listening to this incoherent speech, seized Oliver by the hand and fixed his eyes upon him. "See, Oliver," he began, "how even in madness a man may be condemned! That toast last night—it frightens me now to drink as we did to Death!"

"Stuff, my dear fellow—don't think of it! As long as the *Shark* swims, the old custom will be kept up. Never mind the mad purser—you can tell me what you have to say *now.*"

"I suppose you think that shortly I shall be as bad as he is?"

"Not I; you are much too fine a fellow to yield to this rascally fever. I remember, when I had it, we had four midshipmen all raving mad,—you know you always go mad before you die,—and they kicked up as much row as if the devil had broken loose. Never mind the mad purser; he will be off soon, for I hear the rattles distinctly."

"O that I had never left England!" said Abbot: "I might have married her—I might have been a happy man! But here I thought promotion quicker, and am myself the most likely to forward it (Oliver looked towards the sea); here, more dreadful than the real thing, may I see what must be my fate. Madness—those rattles—left alone to die, or only watched by a negro; this is dreadful!—But all, Oliver—*all* do not die?"

"No," replied Oliver, "not *all*; but you know the chance is not considered favourable. I speak to you as a man, not like a youngster. Of course you know that when a man gets the black vomit it is all over,—he may linger a day, but can't recover; and therefore it behoves every one who is unfortunate enough to take the fever, to be prepared to cut and run. I have known many as bad as you are recover: but—"

"Stop!" interrupted Murray; "would you croak over your victim before you kill him? Speak to him kindly; and if you would have him behave like a man, behave to him like one. But if you continue thus, I will myself run and tell the doctor. You had better listen and let him speak."

"Thank you, youngster, for your kind feeling," said Abbot; "but the shirts, are you come for them?"

"Do quiet yourself, my dear sir," said Murray; "there are many happy days for you yet, I hope; and I have been told the best way to weather the storm is to show a fair front to it. Keep still a little—let me get you some barley-water. Now, if you have not anything you wish particularly to say, lie down and endeavour to go to sleep, and Mr. Oliver can come another day."

"Just mind your own business, Mr. Murray," said Oliver. "You fancy, I suppose, that a man can get leave to go on shore every day of the week. Shipwrecked boys always grow vain with their escape. Go and comfort the purser, he is just about as silly as yourself. Whilst you are able, Abbot, say your say: time and tide, you know."

"Listen, Oliver," began the sick man. "When I first entered the service, you may remember that I was placed under your charge. You were kind to me, and I do not forget it. A few years only had passed when you may recollect it was in my power to serve you. I don't mean to recall this act of common humanity to your mind with any other motive than to show that I risked my own life to save yours because I loved you; and I solemnly declare that when I rushed between the Frenchman's cutlass and your person, I would just as soon that it had pierced me as wounded you. From that moment, Oliver, I thought you hated me—I thought you felt like a man under a great obligation which it was almost impossible he could ever repay: and yet, if ever man tried to forget the debt you owed, it was myself. Now I come to the part which I would most willingly forget, and which touches you nearer still—your sister Louisa. Great heaven! I feel as if I was about to rave!—and yet well I know from yon poor fellow's rattles that death is nearer than I thought him when, with a foolish, impious word I toasted him. Don't hurry me, Oliver; I must wait a little, or I shall be unable to conclude my story."

Murray, who had listened with great attention, and who had felt a certain tingling of the conscience in regard to his conduct to Hammerton, ran to assist the almost exhausted Abbot; whilst Oliver sat by with unconcerned levity, keeping his eye to seaward, as if he feared an apparition likely to come from that quarter, while he broke through the ravings of the purser and his almost suffocating rattle with a part of the song,

"What's death but the stoppage of breath—"

Murray looked at him as if he could have eaten him; and, young as he was, he felt much inclined to measure his strength with the cowardly cur who could, in such a place, and with death within hail of him, dare to sing such a song. He offered some tamarind-water to Abbot, who had fallen back upon his pillow; and finding him too weak to be raised upright, he placed a quill in the glass and put it to Abbot's mouth. There was madness in the very eager manner in which the poor fellow drained it; and Murray was much hurt when he saw the purser sit bolt upright in his bed, and pointing to Abbot, say, "That man is mad! what is the use of giving him drink?—give it to me, or I'll claw your soul out, you lantern-jawed jackanapes!" The nurse ran to him and gave him some water: he swallowed it with fearful quickness, and then catching as it were an idea from Oliver's song, he took up the stave and continued,

"And a rather damp bed in the ground underneath?"

Abbot, after a heavy sigh, seemed recovered, and proceeded in a fainter tone, whilst the purser's song, at first fearfully loud, gradually grew fainter and fainter, until he fell back on his pillow and kept apparently endeavouring to pick from his counterpane some dirt which he imagined he saw.

"High for true," said the black girl, "now him go for die!—you no see how him pick um blanket! Poor Massa Buckra! me really t'ink it's odd that so many come here for die on Palisades."

"Stop your raven's croak," said Murray, "and don't frighten the living by your prophecy of death. Look there!" he continued, as he pointed to Abbot, "and keep that devil's tongue quiet. Faith! it's bad enough to die, without having a black woman to do the last office."

"Suppose massa get sick, him berry glad to have Nancy Bateson to cool um parched lip—him no call Nancy debil, and croaker, and raven; and when Massa Buckra come here wid um feber, him find his white friend look at um water and sing um song like him dere (pointing to Oliver), whilst poor nigger woman watch him all day and all night to give um drink."

Murray waved his hand, and the poor girl was silent. It was not long before he knew how true her words were; and had his fate condemned him to be sick at Jamaica, he would have experienced that kind solicitude and attention from the blacks which fear prevents the whites too often from administering.

"Oliver," continued Abbot, "I told you many years back I loved your sister Louisa, and that I never could relinquish the hope which she inspired, and you endeavoured to crush. I was then without money, a midshipman, and with, I admit, no very brilliant prospects, unless my uncle should return from India. I little thought ever to pass you in the service, and for Louisa's sake I would have given up my own for your promotion. In spite of all your watchfulness,

I often met your sister: the very opposition to the match increased our affection. When I was absent, she wrote, and you have oftentimes handed me the letters. What makes you look so earnestly from that window, Oliver? Do I weary you with a too oft-repeated tale? or is it ——"

"The packet!" interrupted Oliver, as he strained his eyes to make out a distant vessel.

"Oh that I could live," said Abbot, "to see her handwriting once more!—then, if I am to die, I could do so without a murmur! But it's hard—very hard, to go so young, before one has enjoyed the blessing of independence, and when one has lived envying all around, with plans projected never to be matured! Oliver, I tried to marry your sister, and now I tell you she consented. Here is her last gift round my neck: when I am gone, do you return it to her. I cannot outlive this!—See, see! how horrible! the only tenant of the ward is dead! And there! they take him away to bury him as unconcernedly as if custom had rendered it pleasant! Thank God, I shall be mad soon, for I feel it coming on!—Now, is it not horrible to think that the nurse who has just got rid of her patient must come to me, and then to another in turn? But she is a kind girl."

By this time the corpse was removed, and Nancy had taken her seat just opposite Abbot's bed: the bed-clothes of the purser had been removed, and a solemn stillness prevailed. Murray felt, and felt deeply; he even so far forgot himself as to put his hand in his pocket for some loose money to give Nancy, to insure greater attention to Abbot: but no sooner did he touch his heart's idol, than the silver slipped through his fingers and rattled against the rest which reposed in his pocket. Oliver's eyes continued turned towards the supposed packet: a little impatience might be traced in his countenance; and when he looked at Abbot, it was with a glance which almost seemed to say, "Why don't you die at once?"

"Here, Oliver," said the sick man, "give me your hand and forgive me. Whenever I could convey a letter to Louisa, I did it, and frequently we met by appointment. You know I was not like other midshipmen, revelling at 'the Blue Posts,' or wasting life in scenes of debauchery and riot: I never accustomed myself to drinking, and you know that I never had that blot upon my character. Can you forgive me, Oliver—can you forgive what in my sickness I avow, and for which, if I recover, I will give ample satisfaction—nay, all the satisfaction man can make to a poor injured woman?"

"Injured! Abbot," interrupted Oliver: "what can you mean?"

"It is for this that I have sent for you; and before I get worse, I may as well tell you how I intended to repair the injury. In the first place, after my own promotion, I urged my uncle, who is a man of considerable influence, to use his endeavours to forward you in the service. After much trouble, he succeeded in getting your name on the Admiralty list."

"Admiralty!" interrupted Oliver; I thought it was the *Admiral's.* Then I should, after all, not get a death-vacancy!"

"No," continued Abbot; "but it was my intention, and it is my intention when I recover, to invalid, and then your promotion will be sure."

"Invalid!" interrupted Oliver, as he bit his lip in vexation to find that his plans were at once frustrated,—"invalid!" continued he to himself: as if the admiral would let a man invalid who was just as certain of dying as he is of being mad! "I have no time, Abbot, to hear any more—my leave is expired, and I may see you again to-morrow."

"To-morrow!" replied the poor sick fellow. "To-morrow's sun may never reach my eyes! for, as you sang,

"'—Who in this climate of sickness and sorrow
Shall dare to look forth for the light of to-morrow?'

"Hah!—hah!" he continued, breaking into a little wandering; "it is a great song.

"'Hark! hark! to the prayer of the *Shark.*'

"Death—death! damnation! how I burn! I feel myself mad!—And there is that young harpy waiting for my death to buy my shirts. Curses on him! his eyes eat me up!—Come, Oliver, nearer to me. Louisa!—dear, dear, ruined Louisa!"

Oliver started from him, and gathering all his energy, he screamed rather than said, "What do you mean, you yellow-livered scoundrel? Speak! I say; or by the devil, who is now near you, I will shake you into reason!"

"For Gor A'mighty sake, massa, let um die quietly!" interrupted Nancy: "him really mad for true, or him no such fool to tell um brother that um sister ruined."

"Now," said Murray, who sat upon another bed near Abbot's,—"Now, Oliver, I think you have put in the new rum for some purpose; if ever a man got back evil for evil, you are that man—your very poison flows back in your own veins! I shall yet be a captain, and live to see you at that period a midshipman!"

"By heavens! you young devil, I will wring your neck as I would a turkey's if you interrupt me!—Get back, you black hag!—Now, Abbot, tell me of my sister and the truth, or by the Lord I will pray for your death as earnestly as I now pray for your living!"

Slowly the almost exhausted Abbot recovered his wandering senses. "I will tell you," he began. "It was about a year since—you were at home, and may remember the evening when your sister sang one song twice over. On that evening you retired early, not to bed, but to your old haunts with some of your messmates: I went out with you and joined in your frolics. Before that, Louisa and myself were engaged to be married; and how earnestly I hoped for that result no one can imagine. But temptations are seldom resisted: time and opportunity, when seized, make the hero a conqueror, the lover successful. I waited with you until I saw the punch and brandy had nearly done their duty. It was then, intoxicated as you were, you sallied forth with your companions to go to the theatre: I returned with a stealthy pace to South Sea Beach. A light glimmered in a room which I well knew to be Louisa's, and long did I walk under the window in hope that love might recognize a familiar footfall; at last, for the night was fine and the sea came noiselessly against the beach, the curtain was withdrawn, and your sister looked at the calm scene before her. How at that moment my heart palpitated!—how dizzily I saw—how sick I felt! I watched—I saw that I was observed, and yet I feared to make myself known, for I perceived the shadow of another person occasionally passing and repassing. It was your mother, to whom she had told the tale of our affection; she was urging her to cast off a hopeless and, as she thought, poor, destitute midshipman. She told her, for I was afterwards made acquainted with the secret, that none knew the fearful pinch of poverty but those who had endured it—none knew the misery of want when every luxury was denied, when children opened their little mouths for a day's sustenance and closed them with appetites unsatisfied, when the patient meekness of one sex was rebuked by the disappointments of the other; and she finished with the old saying, that "when Poverty camc in at the door, Love flew out of the window." She argued also that in all concerns of a daughter's life a mother had a voice; that a parent should seldom be disobeyed, even if the child thought the parent wrong, for it was more probable that youth should be mistaken, than that nature should war against herself, and urge a child to a guilty or a foolish action. Louisa cried much: it was to hide her tears that she opened the window. Her mother pressed her for an answer: she discarded me —she declared that henceforth I should be a stranger to her sight. Her mother kissed her—I saw it, and I guessed the cause in returned affection; I was not in error. I heard the door shut, and I gave a preconcerted signal, for we had often met clandestinely before. In a moment she was at the window. Oh, the force of woman's love is not easily turned aside!—promises may be made, the tongue may do violence to the heart; but few indeed can at once stop up the current of affection, or turn it like a drain into another channel. She came to the window and she whispered me to stop: I did—the lingering hour seemed a year. I should not have feared your return, for I knew you would, even if you slept on shore, be considered at home as having returned to your ship. Another light was visible through the shutters of your mother's room, and by eleven o'clock it was extinguished. I saw your sister again at the window, and she whispered to me the scene which had passed. I urged her at once to fly with me: she refused. I implored her to come down and join me in my midnight walk: she hesitated. At last I persuaded her, for all were in bed, to open the door and give me admittance: she did so. I urged my love again—I combated all your mother's arguments by the assurance that my uncle, just returned, would make me his heir—I told her of golden dreams of happiness which in her confined circumstances she could only expect in an alliance such as I offered her: she relented. Strange are the opposite extremes in women! she loved me the more —she hung upon my bosom; and now I tell you fearlessly, I seduced her. Don't start so!—hear me out, and then shake me back to madness, and I shall die as happily as the poor purser.

"It was about two o'clock that we heard your voice as you returned to sleep at your mother's house. Your sister, fearful of discovery, urged me to depart; with noiseless haste I prepared to do so,—I had reached the door and was opening it when you arrived. I knew that although you had threaded your way to the house, you were in no plight to follow me. I opened the door, rushed past you as you fell on the pavement—ran with all speed to the Point, awoke a slumbering boatman, and reached my own ship. The next morning we sailed to join the Channel fleet: my promotion overtook me—I was appointed to the *Ringdove*, which vessel was in company; and after writing a letter to your sister, mentioning my misfortune in this appointment, I sailed for Jamaica. Here I found you: it was my intention to have told you that your promotion was sure when I found myself a victim to this fever. Forgive me, Oliver! By God, I will marry her!"

"Marry her, you villain! already has Death his hand upon you!—and, by Heaven! my own brain turns! Can you hear me whilst I curse you?—backbiting hypocrite —infernal devil!"

"Hold, Oliver!" said Murray; "your revenge now is before you! never will he recover the death which you have produced! You have added to your sister's misery— you have ruined your own prospects—you have murdered him!"

Madness had now come in reality. The black girl ran for the doctor, whilst Abbot, raving, sang "the Shark's Prayer;" and as he vomited his last hope of life, he cried out, "Death! death! death!"

"He is gone!" said Murray.

"Not quite," replied Oliver, coolly: "but there is no

chance of his recovery. And hark!" he continued, "two guns! the signal for the packet!—My hope is as desperate as his—curse him!"

"Curse him!" said Murray: "rather despise yourself! His wish was to have invalided in order to have served you, and to return home to have married your sister. This is your own work, and even-handed justice has balked your malice: he was your best friend, and would have been your brother."

"Hold your infernal tongue, Murray, or I will place you by his side!—See! he recovers a little; but his voice is thick—yet the last symptoms have not appeared. I do not hear the rattles, and the packet draws closer and closer to the harbour. If the land-wind would but come on early, and the sea-breeze die away, it might be morning before she arrives, and there would still be a chancc."

"Oliver," said the dying man, "here!—nearer!—forgive me! I never intended what I did! I would have married her! Give her back the locket, and say that on the death-bed which my own intemperance made for me I thought of her.

"'Hurrah! hurrah!
Near and far,
For a bloody war and a sickly season.'

Death—death!—Poor, dear—lost—lost—lost Louisa!—No, no! he will never hear of it! I will invalid and serve him! My uncle got it done! Hah—hah! bravo! old Admiral Noah and his Ark! Don't let the youngster buy my shirts —he bought his own doctor's. The little devil! how his eyes shine! And see! there is the devil himself—all black!"

"Get away, Nancy," said Oliver: "you frighten me with your colour."

"Suppose massa ab white heart, him fear for debil; suppose him good, he no fear dead man."

"Look after him kindly," said Murray; "the sight is too horrible for me! "And here," he said, as his fingers again touched his money, which, however, again oozed through his fingers, "Mr. Oliver will reward you for your attention to his friend."

Murray left the hospital. The sound he heard was that of poor Abbot, who in his madness screamed out, "Death,

death!" The voice was heard: he died about sunset; the packet had anchored—the Honourable William Fairfield was at the Admiral's pen, and the next morning sold his midshipman's coat, and appeared as Lieutenant of his Majesty's ship *Ringdove.* Abbot was buried before noon; and Murray, as if to keep his promise and not offend the dead, refused to buy his shirts.

CHAPTER XVII.

THE WAR WITH SPAIN.—PREPARATIONS FOR CUTTING OUT "THE HERMIONE."

It was not until some time after the burial of Abbot,—who, poor fellow, had hardly lived long enough to see the blue mountains, or gaze on the beauties of Newcastle Hill, before he was carried off,—that Murray could efface from his mind the last scene of the life of the victim. It made a very wholesome impression upon him: he had heard that between the ages of thirteen and twenty-five life was a very uncertain tenure in the West Indies; and whilst he bravely resolved not to be frightened into fever, he likewise determined to live prudently, and not to court a contest with one so quick in his operations as the mower of human hay.

The *Surprise* arrived, and Murray, after being victualled on board the day she discharged, found himself a midshipman under Captain Hamilton. He was kindly received by all, and in spite of the sickness which was then committing sad havoc among her brave crew, he fell into his place on board the ship, and commenced his duty with becoming alacrity. The service was now everything to Murray: he had entered it to get rid of parental restraint—if such silken bondage could be called restraint; he was heartily sick of it before he had been an hour on board; but he had already faced some perils—he had seen the worst part of the service, and he now looked forward to deeds which would bring his name before the public.

His new ship had been one of the many captured from the French and now used against them; she had been the *Unité*, and was now the *Surprise*, mounting thirty-two guns, with a complement of two hundred men. He soon heard that his new captain was a keen cruiser; and that where-ever an enemy could be found, there would the *Surprise* be; that neither difficulties nor dangers stood in their way—the prize must be captured; in short, Walter was fortunate enough to be with an active officer, and in a ship where he would soon become familiar with the service in all its branches.

The West Indies at this time (1799) was not unfrequently visited by French frigates, which did immense damage to the trade, and the utmost vigilance was required in order to counteract, or rather prevent, this interruption to our commerce. The Spaniards added their share to the devastation: along the coast from Santa Martha to La Guayra pirates hoarded their ill-gotten wealth, and privateers lurked behind Punta Espada, or anchored under the protection of the Bajo Seco. There was no station more prolific in prizes than the West Indies: promotion, from more causes than shot and sabres, was rapid; the money easily made, circulated with rapidity; and for fun and frolic, death and disease, fighting and prize-money, it was the station most coveted by all who had not independent for tunes, or had every thing to gain from promotion.

The lamentable example of the crew of the *Hermione*, a frigate under the command of Captain Pigot, had fortunately not extended further than that ship. She was taken from her officers by her seamen, and conveyed in safety to a port in the Spanish Main; she was fitted out with a Spanish crew at Porto Cabello, and having treacherously abandoned the flag of his Britannic Majesty, now lay at anchor in the above harbour, with the Spanish ensign flying from her flagstaff, and with every indication of being ready for sea and as if about to sail.

If ever the recapture of a vessel was ardently wished for, it was in this case; the officers of our navy felt the stain upon the service inflicted by the mutiny on board that ship, and they viewed her a Spanish frigate, not taken in fair and manly fight—not run upon the coast by adverse winds in heavy gales, but conducted into the harbour by the people who ought to have defended her,—surrendered without a shot—captured in dishonour, disgrace and mutiny.

Every frigate on the station had stood close in to the harbour, and had seen the newly acquired ship of Spain;

every challenge had been given to provoke her to quit her secure harbour—blank cartridges had been fired as a signal of contempt—but still the *Hermione* remained at anchor ready for sea, but most unwilling to sail.

The year 1799 was drawing to a close, when Captain Hamilton, after a personal interview with Sir Hyde Parker, at which he mentioned his conviction that, with the assistance of a launch, he could cut out the frigate, notwithstanding the numerous batteries which protected her, despite the vast difficulties by which such an attempt would be met, and of the numerous crew with which she was provided.

The commander-in-chief listened attentively to the proposition; but it was one which it was perfectly impossible for him to sanction. For a small frigate like the *Surprise*, with many men sick on board, to attempt to cut out with her boats alone a frigate larger than herself, with a crew nearly double as numerous, savoured too much of temerity, —it was something quite new in the annals of naval warfare. Besides, several frigates had reported how securely the *Hermione* was protected, and a launch or a barge with twenty men (all that was asked for by Captain Hamilton) could never give sufficient aid for such an enterprise. Sir Hyde, therefore, after complimenting the man who ventured the proposition, refused the boat and dismissed the captain.

Next morning, at break of day, the *Surprise* was standing out of the leeward passage, favoured by the land wind, and shortly afterwards took up her station off Cape la Vela, a place about eighty leagues to leeward of Porto Cabello, with instructions to cruise off that part of the coast, in order to intercept the *Hermione*, should she put to sea and endeavour to run for the Havannah. She was likewise to be active in her endeavours to suppress piracy and privateering.

Murray's natural disposition was soon remarked by his captain: he never sauntered on the quarter-deck with his hands in his pockets, thinking of home and the comforts he had left; but his step was lively, his whole deportment active; and whenever a sail was reported, he was the first aloft to make her out, the last to lose sight of her. In squalls, and they are frequent on this part of the coast, the first lad in the foretop was Murray: he would be found on the yard whenever any danger was to be incurred; night or day he never skulked from his duty; and he was already known to his officers as a lad very far above the common; one who delighted in his profession, and one very likely to distinguish himself.

But time soon damped a little of his ardour. Day after day the *Surprise* kept her station, but no vessel wearing a suspicious look appeared; and although every creek and cove were examined, no small low schooner could be discovered sheltered by the thick trees, no indication of traffic; all was still along the coast, and the prize-money was talked about, but seldom touched.

The wood and water of the *Surprise* began to get low, and it was evident that before long she must return to Jamaica; but Captain Hamilton was by no means inclined to return without having seen the object of his search; he therefore made sail to windward, and after a few days' progress against adverse winds, he arrived off Porto Cabello, and there, with top-gallant yards across, and large Spanish ensign, lay the *Hermione.*

The *Surprise* stood within gun-shot of the harbour's mouth, and Murray for the first time in his life saw an enemy's frigate; the shot, which fell short of its mark as the *Surprise* tacked to stand out, was the first one he had ever seen fired in anger, and he caught the enthusiasm of the seamen who looked at her, and who, seamen-like, gave vent to their feelings as they d—d the lubberly rascal who fired a gun without a proper elevation.

In the meantime, Murray observed the captain particularly engaged in reconnoitering the position of the *Hermione.* The very narrow entrance was remarked: the frigate lay close to the battery, and on the other side large merchant ships were alongside the quay. The town, known to contain about eight thousand inhabitants, was disregarded: but the strong fort, the Castle of St. Philip, on the north side of the harbour, and the powerful defences on the southern side, consisting of batteries and fortified moles, were not overlooked; whilst on Punta Brava, to the north-north-east, another fort sufficient for the protection of the roadstead was visible. All who looked at the place shook their heads.

"She's snug enough," said one. "It is ealled Hair Harbour," said another, "because it is so close and narrow that a hair would ride a ship in security."—"She's too wise to get under weigh whilst we are off the port," said a fourth; whilst one of the lieutenants was heard to say, "he would take a kidney for breakfast in exchange for all the prize-money got out of her."

Very different were the thoughts of Captain Hamilton. Batteries he disregarded, because in a night attack they would become harmless directly his boats could get alongside of the frigate; and although they would not scruple to fire upon her should he succeed in cutting her out, yet they would make an indiscriminate murder of their own men, as well as of their enemies.

When the *Surprise* was well out of gun-shot, she shortened sail, made all snug for the night, and according to custom in that ship, where the fatigues of duty were relieved by amusement, the hands were turned up to skylark: the fiddler began to scrape his tune, and some three or four of the best dancers were doing the double shuffle and cut, and reeling away in high style; one fellow giving the real Highland fling, another toeing and heeling it after the most approved point of fashion; whilst the red raw Irishman kept hopping on one leg, and then on the other, which he called dancing.

On the forecastle were a dozen of the more active playing goose, a game easily learned by any one induced to go near the circle formed by the players; the great secret being to get a goose, whose curiosity leads him to listen to the nonsense sported on the occasion, when a good-natured poulterer, a man who supplies the tailors with geese, pushes the unsuspecting gazer into the ring, where he is kicked and cuffed to his heart's content; each man, as he applies his foot to either head or tail, proclaiming, "Goose! goose! goose!" "None of my child!" and so on. No sooner is the victim released, than away starts the leader of the fun up the rigging. "Follow the leader," is repeated; and if the leader be an active man, a stranger would be a little surprised to see the rapidity with which the whole batch of players will scud up to the mast-head, and with what speed they descend the backstays, taking up their seats on the deck as before, and waiting the arrival of another goose.

On the larboard side were a parcel of the younger lads playing "sling the monkey;" and at that moment the well-disciplined *Surprise* looked more like a booth at a fair than a man-of-war.

Fatigue superseded pleasure, and the night came forth in all the magnificence of the West Indies; for if a talented writer has dignified the North American night with the glories of the stars "as the angels' jewel-shop,"* what might not be added in praise of those beauties?—those sparkling worlds seen to such advantage in more southern climates! It is impossible to behold night robed in more dazzling splendour than in the West Indies; and all description, however poetical, must fall far short of the original.

On the starboard side of the forecastle, between the old foremost guns, sat a group of the good old breed of seamen,—fellows with tails half as long as themselves—rough, uncouth-looking men, ready for any danger and foremost in every adventure. These were "telling yarns" and singing songs. Various were the anecdotes—but not very moral in their conclusions—which they related: whilst ever and anon the call for a song varied the amusement; and Murray found that he was not the only officer or gentleman who derived pleasure from the fun of the sailor.

Although numerous voices joined in chorus over the many ditties of Dibdin, yet none had a better welcome, or received a louder and more spirited acknowledgment, than the following, which was intended for, and reached the ears of the captain, who remained a *little* before the gang-way-entrance, listening to the remarks of the men he commanded, and whom he himself had so often led into victory.

"When I first went afloat in a trim little boat,
   To the sea and its perils a stranger,
I never once thought that a man might be caught
   And be press'd into any great danger.
I thought on the sea, a large frigate might be
   A cradle to rock on the billows;
That tinkers or tailors would never make sailors,
   Or any such rough-looking fellows.

---

* Miss F. Kemble;—Journal, &c.

"Poll swabb'd out her eyes when she saw the *Surprise*,
A fine fancy frigate, at anchor;
Her captain and crew, to their king ever true,
And for sailing, my eyes! what a spanker!
Says I, 'Poll, my sweet witch, to the devil I'd pitch
Any shore-going snob in the nation:
I'll be one of her crew; so, dear Polly, adieu!
And hurrah for the West India station!'

"'Oh! Jack, avast heaving; you can't be for leaving,
And penniless leave your sweet beauty?'
'All gammon,' says I, 'is the tear in your eye!
Like a seaman I'm true to my duty:
Come, take all my money—now, don't look so funny—
Here's every note in my pocket.
I'm not on the wing yet; so cut off a ringlet,
And coil it in this pretty locket.'

"Poll pockets the rhino: says Jack, 'Now, good-bye, now;
I shan't shave my head for your fancy.'
She slaps her red elbow: says Jack, 'Now, to h— go,
And I'll go on board of the *Nancy*.'
The anchor was started, my love and I parted;—
Here's luck in my new situation;
Here's our captain and crew, and a slap at the foe,
In the frigate, the pride of the station."

"Well, that's a right good one, Jack! So Polly pocketed the Abraham Newlands, and left you to go on board the *Nancy*.—I wish we just had a glass of grog to drink success to the captain, and a touch at that Spaniard behind the Mole Head."

"Lord love you!" says one; "if I don't think we could take the shine out of those smoke and 'baccy chaps, with all their garlick and onions, with sixty of us in the boats. Spaniards, they say, stick for ever behind a wall, and are as hard to get out as an old rat from the purser's store-room; but if we once get on board, I'm mistaken if we don't start their anchors before they have time to say, '*Gracias à Dios*.'"

This speech chimed in well with the feelings of the captain, and before long his steward was seen giving the singer of the song a little of that generous stuff which makes life run away, and while it relieves care, is digging a furrow in the cheek for the tears of old age to run clear of the chin. Jack shared it out with his messmates, sang the last verse of his own song again, and then added, "Cut her out, Ben!

Why, for the matter of that, we could do that same thing, and board the governor's house through the front window, without ever mounting the hatchway."

"Place the look-out men forward," was heard from the officer of the watch.

"Ay, ay, sir," said Jack; and the whole party broke up.

The next day the *Surprise* was off the harbour's mouth. Captain Hamilton was at the mast-head, and by his side was Murray. As far as a calculation could be made of dangers and difficulties, it was done; and that evening every man was mustered at quarters with his arms, the cutlasses were inspected, beckets desired to be worked on the handles, the pistols were examined, and after the retreat had been beaten, the oars of all the boats were ordered to be muffled, the slide of the carronade in the launch was inspected, and all those minute preparations made which generally herald great and desperate undertakings.

CHAPTER XVIII.

A FIGHTING DOCTOR.—CUTTING OUT "THE HERMIONE."—MURRAY'S GALLANTRY.

It was certain on board the *Surprise* that something was about to be attempted; but not an officer had heard a word drop which led him to expect the affair was so near at hand. That day the first lieutenant, the surgeon, and Murray dined with Captain Hamilton; and the dinner passed off much as all dinners on board a ship generally do,—a certain condescension on one part, and a proper official reserve and respect on the other. Every man who has made the slightest observation on naval discipline is aware that no familiarity—no, not of the slightest kind, should take place at the captain's table: for the lieutenant to be respected, he must show a proper respect to his captain; the midshipman claims from his inferior that which he shows to his superior; and any innovation in the service which tends in the slightest degree to elevate any of the ranks to the prejudice of the one above tends to raze the pillar of subordination by which the naval service has been so pre-eminently upheld. It is the discipline of the navy which has led her fleets to conquest: and those who have read of the wreck of the *Alceste* and the wreck of the *Medusa* will be aware at once how much the personal safety of all is guarded and protected by subordination and discipline.

The cloth was removed, the steward had retired, the king's health had been drunk, when the conversation took a most sudden and unexpected turn—sudden and unexpected it might be called, for no soul but one on board of the *Surprise* had harboured the idea, and he had kept it to himself until this moment.

"I intend," began the captain, in a cool and measured tone of voice, looking at the first lieutenant, "to cut out the *Hermione* to-night."

Murray's face brightened with delight, the surgeon rubbed his hands, and Mr. Wilson, the first lieutenant, remained silent in order to allow his captain to unfold his plans.

"The fact is," continued Captain Hamilton, "that before long we must return to Jamaica, for the limit of my cruise is nearly expired. What will be the consequence? The *Hermione* will put to sea; she will either make good her run to the Havannah, or she will be the prize of some more fortunate ship. My plans are all arranged; and as I expect this will not be performed without some lost and some wounded, you must get your implements of torture ready, doctor, and be prepared to cut us up cautiously."

"Faith," replied the surgeon, Mr. M'Mullen, as brave a man as ever lived; "it's not myself, captain, you are going to leave on board such a night as this. Oh, sir, that same thing can't be, and I'm certain that somehow or other I shall be there touching the cigars."

"Why, doctor," replied the captain, much pleased with the enthusiastic manner in which his proposition had been received; "you must remember that you have no assistant, and that if you were killed, the wounded would suffer unaided."

"It's very little use, Captain Hamilton," replied the doctor, "making objections. I know all that's likely to happen, and I hope on such an occasion, when there must be real good hard work and a most glorious row, you will not refuse my aid, for I believe it's not the first time that I've stood by you on like occasions."

"I admire your readiness, doctor—I give you all due credit for your courage and your kindness; but in an affair like this we must take every precaution to have assistance at all points. There is no man alive in whose courage I have greater reliance than yours—no man would more readily face a desperate service than yourself; but should I allow you to share our dangers to-night, and some unfortunate shot take effect upon you, I should never cease reproaching myself when I saw the gallant fellows who had assisted in this affair writhing in pain, and no means left of alleviating their sufferings. It must not be, doctor; you really must stay on board."

Captain Hamilton had looked the doctor in the face when he made this handsome speech, and had closely watched his countenance and its changes; but when he concluded, he remarked a kind of desperation creep over his gallant friend, as much as to say, "I go there to-night, or curse me if I am here to-morrow."

"I hope, sir," said Murray, with a look of great anxiety, "that I may be permitted to go?"

"You are to be in my boat, Murray. I shall lead this business myself."

"And I, sir?" asked the first lieutenant.

"You will command the launch, Wilson. I have arranged all the plan, and after quarters I intend addressing the ship's company. I dare say, doctor, you will give me a cheer at the conclusion; you know how soon that electric spark is communicated, and how readily the seamen follow the example which a brave man sets them."

The compliment was lost upon the doctor, for he never heard it; he was working himself up for a speech as to his determination, and let out just enough to be heard. "Holy Father! here's a disgrace come upon us! asked to dinner to hear the plan, and then find that every blessed son amongst us is to be in the row except myself, and I am to cheer the very proposition I am not allowed to assist! Then by my faith, never one of the M'Mullens was treated that way before; and if I don't go, may the devil, after his own especial fancy, run a-hunting with me!"

The captain could not help smiling at the running base of the doctor's grief, and the nice hunting-party the devil and the doctor were to take together; but he continued his conversation upon a point so interesting, and so likely, one would suppose, to end in discomfiture.

"Whom do you intend, sir," asked Mr. Wilson, "to leave in charge of the ship?"

"Mr. Madge, the master," replied the captain; "he knows the reefs about this place, and he must keep the frigate as near as possible to the harbour. I hope I have made all arrangements for the best; and now I propose one bumper to the success of certainly the most desperate undertaking ever attempted."

He filled his glass, the surgeon filled his, Wilson his, and Murray let the drops fall until the glass was crowned.

"I will give you," said the captain, "Success to our enterprise, and little after-work to our friend the doctor."

Both the doctor and Wilson drank it; but Murray added, "And God bless the captain for putting me in his boat!"

This little deviation from the rigid behaviour at a captain's table was overlooked; the doctor adding, "Small blame to you, youngster, for the addition; and faith I'm mistaken if I wouldn't have said as much, and more besides, if I had been clapped in that boat, and sure of being hit the first shot."

"We had better not say a word about it before the servants," remarked Captain Hamilton: "these little surprises succeed best when the men have not long to wait between the intention and the deed."

"Faith, some of them," replied the surgcon, "had better let their wounds and their courage be cured by the *first intention*, for anything they'll get beyond plaster if they get on board again: it's not my advice they'll get, without I lend them some assistance this same blessed evening. I'm not particular, Captain Hamilton, about which boat you place me in: I'll take the jolly-boat if you like; or if you have given that to some one else, I'll just row myself in the dingay; and between you and me, Wilson, I don't think I shall be last on board either."

After the toast, according to immemorial custom in the navy, the white wine was handed round; the coffee followed, and within two minutes the drum beat to quarters. Wilson and Murray ran on deck; but the doctor followed the captain into his after-cabin, and in a very few words conveyed his intentions thus:

"Captain Hamilton, ——," began the doctor.

The captain started with astonishment at finding himself followed into his cabin, but instantly turned towards his guest and asked him what he required.

"Merely, sir, that you listen to me. I must go in this affray to-night; and I tell you plainly that if I am not allowed to do so, you will not find me alive when you return."

The tone and manner in which the intelligence was communicated, coupled with the known character of the man, decided Captain Hamilton in allowing him to go; and when this was communicated to him, he replied, "Now, by St. Patrick! let's hear if the cheer won't be heard half-way down to Jamaica;" and he walked on deck, to use the expression of a bystander, "as pleased as a piper."

Quarters were over, the men reported sober and steady, when Mr. Wilson desired the boatswain to send everybody aft on the quarter-deck; and as this is seldom done unless something is wrong, or something likely to be effected, the crew came aft like a flock of sheep all huddling together,—the most uneasy in their minds as to the result imitating the sick of the flock, and keeping somewhat aloof from their companions.

When the men were reported "all present," Captain Hamilton addressed them. "My men," he began (and his men instantly took off their hats, and began to plaster their hair down with the palms of their hands, as they edged up a little closer towards the combing on the skylight), "we have sailed together some time, and have seen a little service together. I know the value of every one of you; and, I trust, there is not a man in the ship who would be afraid to follow his captain even if he went to pull the devil himself out of his habitation." Here some of the men began to smile, others to hitch up their trousers, whilst others looked at their hats as they kept twirling them round. "Now, what I am going to propose to you is not quite so desperate, although we may have to go into as hot a fire to effect our object. You have seen that English frigate, the disgrace to our service, riding in a Spanish port with a

Spanish ensign; and if we remain here wishing her to come out, we might wish from the first day of January to the last day in December, and then begin again. Out she will not come whilst we are here, and to go to her in the frigate is impossible: in the first place, we should have to warp into the harbour, and I have counted quite a sufficient number of guns to believe that impracticable. We cannot leave her there, my lads, and return to Jamaica without having attempted anything: that is not like the *Surprise*, the fancy frigate of the station. She will not come to us, and we can't go to her; but we can cut her out with the boats," said the captain, as he raised his voice, "and we will do it this night, my lads!"

A burst of tremendous cheering followed the announcement, and far above all voices was heard the surgeon's: he had got on a carronade-slide, and as if not sufficiently conspicuous, jumped upon the gun, and last of all stood on the hammocks and bellowed himself hoarse.

"I see," continued the captain, "I need not ask for volunteers."

"I'll go, your honour," said an Irishman; and every man fore and aft called out, "And I, and I."

"Bravo, my lads! continued the captain; "you are the men to smooth difficulties—I knew you would all volunteer; and as it is impossible for all to go, I have selected some few of you to accompany *me*, for I will not send any man where I dare not go myself."

This met the wishes of the crew, and again and again they cheered their gallant commander.

"We have but little time," he continued, "for preparation; but we are always prepared. I shall therefore myself muster the men as they are to go, and tell them off in the numbers for each boat; so pay attention, my lads, and once for all understand that the men I have selected are not in any manner preferred to the rest, but are taken from different parts of the ship: so that she can be worked and handled like a man-of-war, without there being a deficiency in any one station. It's no use crowding the boats, when expedition and determination can do more than the creeping heaviness of crammed boats, in which there is hardly room for the men to pull, and where a single shot does immense mischief. As we seem to understand each other perfectly, there is no reason why I should say more than I have done; but, mind you, my lads, the first man who gets on board shall have three hundred dollars, and the man who places the Union Jack over the Spanish flag shall have three hundred dollars also. The rest shall not be without reward; and after what I have said, there is not a man amongst you but would give three cheers for the first on board, and success to the brave fellow who places the English flag once more upon that ship's signal-staff."

The speech was concluded, and again the ship's company cheered. The captain then took some papers from his pocket, and at the words, "Silence, fore and aft!" you might have heard a pin drop.

"The officers," he continued, "of the different boats will muster their men, and I shall afterwards inspect them. None of the blue-jackets are to have fire-arms, except pistols; and every man is to be dressed in blue, not showing the least white about him. The password is "Britannia;" the answer, "Ireland." The first division of boats, consisting of the pinnace, launch, and jolly-boat, are to board on the starboard or inside bow, gangway, and quarter; the second division, consisting of the gig, black and red cutter, to board on the larboard or outside bow, gangway, and quarter. I shall command in the pinnace, with Mr. Maxwell the gunner, Mr. Murray, and sixteen men, and lead; Mr. Wilson, with a midshipman, and twenty-four men, will be in the launch; and in the jolly-boat will be the carpenter, one midshipman, and eight men. In the pinnace, I shall board on the starboard gangway; the launch is to board on the bow, and instantly cut the bower cable. She will be provided with sharp axes, and a platform is to be run along the quarter: the jolly-boat is to board on the quarter, then to cut the stern-cable, and send two men in the mizen-top, to loose the mizen-topsail. And, remember! my lads, the men named to do these several duties are to think of nothing else but fulfiling their orders. I cannot sufficiently impress upon you how much depends on this; for if, for instance, we loose the sails, and the man has omitted to cut the stern-fast, she might be sunk by the batteries before the end was accomplished.

"The gig is to board on the larboard bow, and four men from her are to jump aloft to loose the fore-topsail; they will remember to foot it clear of the top, to cut all the gear away, so that we may sheet it home without any stoppage. She is to be under the direction of the surgeon, and will carry sixteen men. The black cutter, under Lieutenant Hamilton, with the marine officer, Mons. de la Tour du Pin, and some marines under him, are to board on the larboard gangway; the boatswain, Mr. Cook, will command the red cutter, and, with the sixteen men under his command, is to board on the larboard quarter.—Now, understand me well, my lads. In the event of our getting alongside unperceived, the boarders only are to board; the boats' crews are to remain in their boats, push ahead, and take the ship in tow: but in the event of our being discovered, and having to pull to the frigate in the face of her fire, then every man is to board, with the exception of the bowmen.—Remember," said Captain Hamilton to his officers, "our object is the *Hermione*. Turn not aside for boats or batteries—one only object is before you: let us but once gain a footing on her decks, and I know I can trust to my gallant ship's company to do the rest."

Here he concluded, saying to each officer as he gave him the paper in which were the names of the seamen selected to perform the several duties before mentioned, "I trust you will make your men understand you as clearly as, I hope, I have been understood. In half an hour we shall be off; and remember! our rendezvous is on the quarter-deck of the *Hermione*."

That was a busy half-hour; and out of the ninety-six men named for this desperate work, not one thought but of the certainty of success, so well and so carefully had all things been arranged. Murray knew that he would be in the hottest of the work, for the captain would be sure to be first alongside; and that as he planned, so would he be first to execute. He knew this would be a service of great danger—still his usual idleness could not be overcome—he could not sit down to write to his father; but from a superstitious feeling,—and the greatest minds are more or less tinged and darkened by it,—he placed the locket which had once saved his life round his neck, and even in the fervour of that superstition kissed it: he thought of her who was long since numbered with the dead; but though he might have thought of one who regarded him as the stay and prop of his house, he did not write to him. And that half-hour which others employed in sharpening weapons and in covering oars was passed by Murray in feverish excitement, thinking of the danger with which he had to cope, and taking some few precautions which the most indolent are apt to do when danger is at hand.

The *Surprise*, at dark, had stood in-shore under a crowd of sail; and when sufficiently close, the boats were hoisted out, and left the ship in two divisions, as indicated; the pinnace leading the first, and the gig leading the second, having the rest in tow. At the time of leaving the *Surprise*, the *Hermione* was visible through a night-glass; and such was the anxiety of the leader of this bold enterprise, that he never once lost sight of her, but stood with the night-glass in his hand until an event occurred which made the gallant captain look in another direction.

The boats had crept along silently and rather slowly towards the harbour's mouth; and now the lights were visible from the town: they were about two miles distant from the *Hermione*, and as yet apparently undiscovered. The oars, as they silently dipped in the water, were feathered close to its surface; no phosphoric brightness betrayed the approaching enemy—not a word was uttered, and even in the leading boat, so strictly was silence observed, and so well were the boats pulled, that the jolly-boat was scarcely discernible. Suddenly the boats were hailed; a volley of musketry succeeded, a long gun dashed its contents in the direction of the English crews, and it became evident that all was discovered. The *Hermione* was seen with lights on her main-deck and at quarters; a gun from the shore answered the gun previously fired, and it was plain that the only surprise which could have been effected was now destroyed.

Captain Hamilton trusted that his officers would have obeyed his directions, by disregarding every other object but the one in view; and when he cast off the tow and gave three cheers, he added, "Hurrah for the first on board!" Murray steered the pinnace, and her bow never varied in the least from the direction of the frigate. The gallant fellows now no longer dipped in their oars silently; but they dashed forward, cheering as they went, and giving the enemy ample time to make every preparation. It was now the first error was committed. The launch and the second division of boats, instead of dashing forwards, turned short round upon the gun-boats which had given the alarm, and thus Captain Hamilton, who kept his face towards his foe, reached the bow of the *Hermione* unsupported: not a boat was pulling in the same direction but the jolly-boat, and she was soon far astern.

As the pinnace passed the larboard bow of the *Hermione*, the forecastle gun was fired at her; but she was so close that the contents passed over her: and at that moment might be seen the extraordinary sight of a frigate's pinnace, with about twenty men in all, going unsupported alongside a frigate having at least three hundred men on board, to cut her out; that frigate being perfectly prepared and actually at quarters, with her main-deck properly lighted by fighting lanterns, and her captain and officers on the quarter-deck awaiting an attack, as was afterwards affirmed, from the *Surprise* herself, and not her boats.

In a work of this kind we only follow the hero. As the pinnace was crossing the hawse of the *Hermione*, her rudder caught a rope which went from the bows of the frigate to her boat moored at the buoy. Murray lifted the rudder, when the boat fell between the starboard forechains and the cathead. A rush was made to be the first man on board. Captain Hamilton, on jumping upon the bower anchor, which had that day been weighed and was still covered with mud, slipped off, and nearly fell into the boat: however, still keeping firm hold of the foremost lanyard of the fore-shroud, he recovered his footing, and leaped over the bulwark. He was not the first man, but he was the third. His gallant companions came close after him; Murray being foremost, and the gunner the next. The foresail of the frigate, ready for bending and hauling out to the yard-arms, was lying across the main-stay: this afforded a capital screen for the few men on board; and the Spaniards who had been stationed there being instantly dislodged, it was taken possession of, and breathing-time thereby afforded.

There was no time to be lost in thinking upon their deserted situation, and not a man of the party seemed to care much about it. The captain gave the order to advance, and the gunner, backed up by Murray, soon made a rush aft. At this moment the *Hermione's* crew opened their fire at the supposed frigate, and in the direction of their own gun-boats. In the confusion and the astonishment of the moment, the forecastle was soon cleared of the Spaniards, and the English party advanced to the starboard gangway, forcing the enemy before them until they reached the break of the quarter-deck. Here was a stop to all advance: in vain was Murray's voice heard—in vain his bright blade seen—in vain the rallying sound of the captain's exhilarating words, or the gunner's coarse appeal to the men:—the Spaniards, perceiving the few by whom they were attacked, rallied in their turn, advanced with overwhelming numbers, and the English, with their fronts to their foes and disputing every inch with uncommon firmness and determination, were forced back on the gangway, and beaten as far as the forecastle. It was in this scene of contention that the forethought of Captain Hamilton became conspicuous: he had armed his men principally with boarding-pikes and tomahawks; and the Spaniards, who had forgotten to fix their bayonets, were kept aloof from closer combat by the array of iron spikes. The Spaniards, as they fired, crowded together, and rendered it impossible for them to reload: they had advanced to the gangway; those behind forced on those in advance, and those in advance were met by the unflinching bravery of the *Surprise's* men, who were only to be beaten back by the press of numbers to whom they were opposed.

"At all risks," said Captain Hamilton, "defend the break of the forecastle until some assistance comes."

Murray called aloud, "Rally, rally—stand firm, my gallant fellows!"

The gunner seemed to gather fresh strength from the enemy's opposition; and although his blows fell thick and heavy, yet he continued them with unabated vigour, and boldly and bravely defended the place. Captain Hamilton at this moment saw that without assistance all was lost—it was otherwise impossible to hold out five minutes longer.

The Spaniards, elated at the retreat of their foes, cheered each other as they pressed forward; and for a moment the brilliant enterprise was on the point of being lost, owing to the different officers having disobeyed their captain's orders, and loitered behind with contemptible gun-boats.

A moment at such an hour was of value. The captain ran round the larboard side to the bow, and there found a man leaning over and giving vent to his feelings in most appropriate language. "The devil most particularly burn you all, you villanous, cowardly, craven curs!—here's a row, and you sit there cowering under the bows like a set of children under a shed in a squall of rain!"

At this moment Captain Hamilton, who mistook the gentleman for a Spaniard, touched him up in the rear with his dirk.

"Holy Father!" said the surgeon, turning round; "there's a prod that would start off a Galway post-horse! Is it you, Captain Hamilton? Bad luck to those brutes in the boat who refuse to board!"

"Come up, you scoundrels, this instant," said the captain, "or I'll fire right into you."

This brought the boat's crew up; and with this reinforcement, trifling as it was, hope began to brighten.

"Take these fourteen men, Mr. M'Mullen," said the captain; "push along the larboard gangway, and endeavour to occupy the quarter-deck. Quick, quick, my lads! never mind the fire on the main-deck: the confusion will favour you, and the Spaniards are crowding on the other gangway."

It required no second advice to the surgeon: ripe and ready for the row, he led his men as the captain directed, gained unopposed the quarter-deck, and seeing that the fighting was on the starboard gangway, he took the Spaniards in the rear—placing them between two fires. Murray rallied the men with his young voice; and the dispirited Spaniards, assailed fiercely by both parties, began to quail, and some to cry for quarter. Captain Hamilton was now alone on the quarter-deck—it was the rendezvous, and he awaited the surgeon's party; here he found himself vigorously assailed by four of the enemy; he had retreated near the mainmast, and, fearing lest his foot should get entangled in any of the ropes near the bits, he resolutely stood the attack, when one of the four swinging the butt-end of his musket round his head, struck the captain with all his force, and knocked him over the other side of the deck on the combings of the after-hatchway. This blow would have proved fatal, had not the captain received it on his arm. At this critical moment, the Spaniards having surrendered on the gangway, Murray advanced; and with him came some of the gunner's party:—they soon placed their commander in security, and armed him again with a tomahawk.

The Spaniards below had by this time become acquainted with the nature of the attack, and a rush was made from the main-deck by the after-hatchway; but the English, flushed with the success of the enterprise, and finding themselves in possession of the quarter-deck, soon repulsed the enemy. During this affair, the marine officer's party boarded on the larboard gangway. This welcome but tardy assistance,—for it appears they had tried to board on that gangway before, but were repulsed,—placed the success of the enterprise beyond a doubt, as far as the possession of the frigate was concerned, although from the main-deck a continued fire of musketry was still kept up. In the meantime the cables had been cut: the men appointed to perform that duty, as they got to their respective situations, made ample amends for their former neglect. The mizen-topsail was loose, the ship adrift, and creeping out of the harbour, when the marines made a rush on the main-deck, and the *Hermione* surrendered. Amongst the foremost men aloft on the fore-topsail-yard was Murray: he appeared the least fatigued of all the brave fellows concerned in this desperate act, and his voice was plainly heard calling aloud, "Hurrah! my lads, she's moving ahead from under the batteries!"

The gunner, who had been foremost in all dangers and difficulties, now took the helm, and steered the ship he had so mainly contributed to capture. He was assisted by two other men; though all three of them wounded, they were still sufficiently stout to stand to the wheel, and the *Hermione* was again under English colours.

It was still within the power of probable events that the frigate would not be cleared of all the difficulties by which she was surrounded: the batteries, being now convinced that the English held undisputed possession of the frigate, opened a tremendous, but, very fortunately, an ill-directed fire. Every precaution was taken to keep the men out of danger; and although the main and spring-stays were shot away, the gaff brought down, from the peak of which trailed the Union Jack over the Spanish flag, and several shot had taken effect below the water-line, to the no small discomfiture of the prisoners below, yet little actual damage was done.

The prisoners, finding themselves insecure, attempted, a few of them, to escape: the launch was called on board, and eighty of the Spaniards put therein and veered astern. The crew of the boat began, in spite of the fire, to secure the mainmast by the runners and tackles; the fore-topsail swelled with the land-breeze, which the firing that fortunate night did not put down; and five minutes after the cables had been cut, the frigate rose to the swell of the sea, at the mouth of the harbour.

This intimation that the ship was out of the harbour made the prisoners below desperate, and they resolved to fire the magazine, and blow up themselves and their conquerors. The plot was overheard by a Portuguese sailor, the coxswain of the gig, named Antonio. A discharge of musketry was immediately fired below, a general cry of "surrender" followed, and a guard was placed on the magazines to prevent the threatened catastrophe.

By half-past one, about an hour and a half after the first man had boarded, the batteries ceased firing; although the last discharge of grape reached the ship. One shot wounded the captain, and another fell spent against his leg. The surgeon, who all along had been in the thickest of the fight—who was one moment fighting on the main-deck, then down below securing the magazine—was at this time standing by the captain: he took the grape-shot in his hand, and remarked, "By J——, captain, had those Spaniards put five grains more of powder in the cartridge of the gun which fired this shot, my instruments and myself would have been wanted to cut off your leg."

In the mean time, Murray had seated himself on the taffrail, and never moved, in spite of the heavy fire. Very different thoughts occupied his mind. The deed was done, the excitement passed; but the reward remained to be claimed. The first man who boarded was killed; the second was Murray. A little of the devil of his former life was at work; and that avarice which had prompted him to purloin the fifty pounds from Hammerton, although checked, was by no means subdued:—the sneaking propensity to lying was also now on the ascendant. That he had done his duty he knew; for the captain had shaken him by the hand on the quarter-deck—the gunner had proclaimed him a devil at fighting—the man who loosed the foretopsail affirmed that he did more than the whole four put together—and the surgeon, who had seen him, young as he was, on the gangway heading his men, swore he was certain that Murray was from the Emerald Island, as he handled his sword with all the dexterity of a Patlander at Ballynasloe.

The little vanity which he might reasonably have felt when he considered that he placed the Union Jack over the Spanish flag never occupied him much; he was thinking of the money that might be got by the affair. If he failed in his claim to the first reward, he was certainly entitled to the second: if he could not establish that he was first on board—which in point of fact he was, for the man who had been foremost was killed on the shank of the anchor, and never actually got on board—yet he thought that he could claim to be so. The colours were a certainty: this so got hold of him, that when some one remarked "that those devils must have placed forty thousand grape-shot in one of their discharges," Murray remarked, "that he did not think she (meaning the prize) would sell for so much as forty thousand pounds."

Day dawned; the *Surprise* was in the offing; and no man who has not shared in an enterprise of this kind can tell the feelings—the proud feelings, which occupy the heart of him who, having achieved a considered impossibility, hears the first welcome of his shipmates in the cheers which they give him.

A schooner was observed to windward: the boats were manned by fresh crews—she was captured, brought alongside, the prisoners placed in her (with the exception of her captain and two men, who were necessary for her condemnation in the Admiralty Court); and by one o'clock, thirteen hours from the commencement of the attack, the *Hermione's* former crew were landed in Portobello—the two frigates had shaped their course for Jamaica—every damage aloft had been repaired, and the *Surprise* and her capture resembled two cruising frigates, rather than a capturer and the captured.*

It can hardly be necessary to point out the gallantry of this enterprise: it stands alone in the annals of naval warfare. We have had, it is true, numerous exploits of the most dashing and daring nature; but not one—no, not even Captain Coglen's—can be placed in competition with this. The *Hermione* was actually taken by, at the most, thirty men; seventeen held possession of her until the assistance of the surgeon and his party arrived, and it was at least twenty minutes from the commencement before the marine officer boarded. It was no surprise—every preparation had been made to resist even the frigate herself; and had the orders been punctually attended to, there cannot be a doubt but that the ship would have been carried in five minutes. In fact, it was the result of cool deliberation, well-organized crews, and of bravery as distinguished by the result, as by talent in the planning, and judgment in the execution.

On board of the *Hermione* were found eight thousand dollars. With this sum Captain Hamilton resolved to reward those who had been of the most assistance, and there was not a murmur heard when his determination was made known. The men were sent aft; the question was asked, "Who was the first on board?" The gunner answered, "Mr. Murray."—"Who next?" A man answered, "The captain."—"Who next?" "The gunner."—"Who next?" "John Watkins."—To John Watkins was given three hundred dollars.

"The officers," said Captain Hamilton, have other besides pecuniary rewards. Mr. Murray would be ill-satisfied indeed if his services, could they be adequately recompensed, were to be rewarded by money. No! let us

* The whole of this account is strictly true: it is taken from the papers of the gunner, and has been attested as strictly and impartially correct.

hope we have higher views; and he, I am convinced, feels more in the generous expression of the crew, than in receiving money he cannot want. I own properly it belongs to him; but I will convey to the crew what I know are his sentiments,—that both the money for placing the proud flag of Old England over the Spanish ensign, which he did, and that which is his by right for being the first man on board, are cheerfully given to other brave seamen, who, from the wounds they received, and the courage they exhibited, well merit this distinction. But Mr. Murray shall not go without a reward"—(here Murray's heart became a little elated); "before the crew now assembled, I present him with the sword I myself wore on that night, as well as the pistols taken from the first lieutenant; and I think no one will feel disposed to doubt his having richly deserved this public honour, when he was both the first on board, and the first to plant our flag aloft."

The crew here gave three hearty cheers, and many voices were heard praising the distinguished valour of our hero; but he very coldly received the honour: he thought it hard that his money should be thus handed over to others, and every chink of the silver, as the dollars were counted, jarred against his avaricious heart.

"The surgeon," said the captain, "will find an inadequate reward in sharing the prize-money with the lieutenants, to which, I presume, there will be no objection: the gunner we must get promoted to a larger ship, and we must reserve enough to fit him out as becomes so brave a man. And now, my lads, I think, when we enter Port Royal, we shall be welcomed by our admiral as men who have done good service to their country: and you shall not want liberty for a cruise on shore. For my own part, I attribute my success to the gallant manner in which I was supported; and whatever reward I may receive, I shall receive it as emanating from you. And in whatever situation I may be placed, the crew of the *Surprise*, the fancy frigate of the station, as I heard one of you sing the other night, shall never apply to me in vain. I have distributed the eight thousand dollars to the best of my judgment, and, I trust, to your satisfaction; and I have only once more to thank you for the support you gave me, and to congratulate you on our undertaking being crowned with success, and without, thank God! any very serious loss."

The crew cheered their brave captain; and four days afterwards, the *Surprise* and the *Hermione* rounded the low point of Port Royal harbour, the prize was anchored in security near the capturer, with the flag of Old England once more flying from her gaff-end.

CHAPTER XIX.

HAMMERTON'S COURTSHIP AND RETURN TO ENGLAND.—A SURPRISE AND A RECOGNITION.

THE honours and glories showered upon Captain Hamilton came more from men's tongues than from their purses. The freedom of the City of London was voted, and he was made a knight,—the one, indeed both, nominal honours; and if for the capture of a frigate men have been properly promoted to a baronetcy, one can hardly imagine why he who captured a frigate in a frigate's *boats* should have been so very insufficiently rewarded. Murray was rewarded as much as he could be—he was converted from a youngster into an oldster; and little as this may be in the eyes of the uninitiated, it is a prodigious advancement in the midshipman's berth. Bold and forward lads do well there—advance them once, and they never retreat. On the quarter-deck Murray found himself a mate of a watch, with the officers ready to instruct him; occasionally with the hands on deck he worked the ship; as far as practical seamanship could advance him, he made great progress, and before he had been three years at sea he was much better qualified to command than many men of four times the servitude. As such we leave him for the present, to record the adventures of Hammerton.

Hammerton, after some short repose in Virginia, and after having lost his heart to his benefactor's daughter, one Maria Corncob, departed for Halifax through the States. He had avoided or only partially partaken of the fogmatic or anti-fogmatic drams of peach-brandy which the settlers in these parts have recourse to in proportion or in quantity as the fog *is* or promises to be.

"I expect," said Jonathan Corncob, "that you've been a making of love to my daughter, and I calculate she loves you amazing*ly*. Now, before you go, I reckon you are going to say as much to her, because she expects it also and likewise."

"I do assure you," said Hammerton, "that I esteem your daughter very much."

"Oh, blow your esteem clean slick out of my pipe, Mr. Hammerton!—it's your love I'm a-talking about."

"I really do not know what to say, Mr. Corncob, after all your kindness to me: it would be worse than criminal if I were to engage your daughter's affections when I may never see her again, and if I did, I should be unable to marry her, for I have not a penny in the world."

"Well, Mr. Hammerton, and supposing you have not, I calculate I have though—and just as pretty a patch of ground as any man between the Capes. Now I—this is all about it; if you will let the old people on the other side of the water alone and marry my daughter, you shall live here whilst I live, and it shall be yours when I'm dead. I would not have made such an offer to any Britisher that ever stepped in shoe-leather, but boy and man have I lived for the last thirty-five years, and I am clear to confess I never saw the like of you before. Give us your hand upon it, and Maria's yours."

"I cannot," said Hammerton, "do justice to my feelings, Mr. Corncob, on this occasion; but when you have heard me out, I think you will not blame me for the step I am taking. I love your daughter, and I think she does not dislike me; but I have in England a father past seventy, struck deaf from grief: I am the only son he has now alive, and he is penniless. I have hitherto sent him all the money I made, and with this and the straggling charity of some old friends, he has managed to live and to educate my only sister. What would you think, Mr. Corncob, of me, if I could under any circumstances, however flattering, desert him, become an alien to my country, and leave my sister a prey to all the allurements of the world? I am a sailor, sir—a plain-spoken, upright sailor, and I cannot leave my duty although love might steer my inclination; but if you think that I have purposely striven to gain your daughter's affection and have been successful, trust to the honour of Frederick Hammerton that he will return when he has done his duty to his father and seen his sister in security."

"Give us your hand, for I calculate you are a Christian, although you don't like peach-brandy. There's not a man in the States who hates your country more than I do; but I expect Jonathan Corncob has got his heart in the right place. Go, and God bless you, young man! If ever the winds should blow you clean against our coast, ask for me; and as I know you are not troubled with many dollars to chink against each other as you shake in the cart between this and Philadelphia, here are a few; take them, and if your inclination and your love lead you back to Happy Hill and Maria's not married, I guess we will have a jollification, and old Corncob will have a son to take care of his old age. Maria won't bear this parting without a tear: but the time will come when you will find London is not paved with Spanish dollars, that you may feel contented to live and die amongst the freemen of America.

Hammerton took a lover's leave of Maria. She was not more than fifteen, but she was a woman grown: she loved him, for women mostly love the unfortunate,—the kindness, the natural inherent kindness of their dispositions prompts them to support the afflicted. The pity which is bestowed with a tearful eye upon the misfortunes of their fellow-creatures soon melts into love; and fortunate are they if, when that comes to pass, they find they have bestowed their affections upon such a heart as throbbed in the bosom of Frederick Hammerton.

"Farewell, farewell, my dear Maria!" said Hammerton, as the lovely girl wept upon his shoulder. "You will love me the more when you consider that the affection I owe my parent and my sister has separated me from you for a time; and I shall ever hold you dearer to my heart when I remember that you have urged me to the fulfilment of my duty. The good son will make the better husband, and he who has supported his father will never desert his wife: fear me not. I *may* return; but who shall say that the Atlantic can be passed in safety and security?—but if I live I will return."

"Never, never, Frederick!" replied Maria: "I feel this as our last parting—I know we shall never meet again! I do not think you will forget me, because I know you are incapable of an ungenerous act; but the busy, active life you have yet to lead will gently remove your love, and although we may be remembered with gratitude, we shall be forgotten in love. Good-bye! and if this will remind you of me, take it."

Hammerton's heart was full as he accepted the small portrait of Maria; and as he took his last kiss, she felt the tear upon her cheek which had flowed from the eyes of her lover.

With a heavy heart, yet with one which became lighter as he got farther from his late residence, Hammerton arrived at Philadelphia. He left the city of Quakers the day following, and got to New York; here he shipped himself on board of a small craft bound to Halifax, where he arrived one month exactly after he had left his Maria. Although he did occasionally think of her, yet the continued change of scene, the hurry and the bustle of the traveller's life, the hope of a return to his father, tended greatly to relieve his boyish affection: so true it is that idleness, although the parent of mischief, is very nearly connected with love. There is no fear of the studious or industrious man becoming love-sick, unless he sink under the first glance and become idle: once idle, he may run into any evil and court every temptation.

Arrived at Halifax, he soon learned the sad tale of the loss of the *Tribune.* With excessive gratification he heard of the character, the bravery, the generosity of Murray. This gave him real pleasure, and he looked forward with some degree of hope that the early misdoings of the boy might be forgotten in the gallant actions of the man. Hammerton thought like a sailor; but little did he know how careful Malevolence hoards up the errors—how meagre Jealousy and jaundiced Envy can treasure up the faults of youth to hurl them in the face of aspiring greatness—how the slightest blot in the escutcheon remains unimpaired, although the brilliancy of the colours on which it was fastened may fade by time or be lost in distance.

At the post-office Hammerton found three letters awaiting his arrival; they were all from his father. The first in order of date was that which had passed through Murray's hands; the second was on its road before the father received Frederick's letter from Virginia; and the third was written at the same time he answered the last, and was directed to Halifax; Sir Hector having persuaded old Mr. Hammerton, that as his son was no fool, he would in all probability endeavour to reach Halifax to rejoin his ship; and the old gentleman did not forget in this letter to mention how sincerely happy he was that Hammerton would find at the same time the fifty pounds which Sir Hector had sent by the same conveyance—nay, enclosed in the same envelope as his own. It was therefore evident that if Hammerton received the one, he must have received the other; and as Mr. Hammerton knew Sir Hector to have taken particular care to forward the letters to the Admiralty, so he knew that those letters were sure of being forwarded to their destination, barring capture or shipwreck.

It is needless to give the contents of the affectionate letters of Frederick's father: they were in that style which a religious and excellent man adopts to the boy of his heart—the prop of his house—and they were not hastily dismissed, but read and re-read often. The last letter puzzled him amazingly: after thanking Heaven that it had been predestined that his son should be saved, and after having poured out his very soul in thanksgiving for so great and merciful a favour, it proceeded to state the growing intimacy which daily increased between himself and Sir Hector, and then came this paragraph:—

"The timely assistance of the fifty pounds which Sir Hector Murray enclosed in his letter to you under the same cover as my own, written on Amelia's birthday, will in your case be particularly serviceable. I say nothing to you of economy; for from your economy, my dear boy, I have hitherto been much assisted. For the future, however, it is, I hope, unnecessary for you to forward me any money,—the kindness of Sir Hector has placed me beyond want. Therefore, do not stint yourself in order to send me any part of the fifty pounds; but, with the care of a man whose wants are numerous and whose means are small, so dispose of it that in the disposition there may be no present pang or future repentance."

Hammerton read the letter over and over again: he returned to the post-office to inquire if there was no other letter for him, but again considering his father's, and more particularly the part which referred to his letter having been sent by Sir Hector, he began to entertain some awkward suspicions. The letter said to have been enclosed by Sir Hector, and which was written on Amelia's birthday, was in his hand; but there was no direction further than his name, and it was evident from the clean state of the paper that it never had shaken hands with the villanous filth which is so often found in a ship's letter-bag.

It happened that Murray had often spoke to the commissioner concerning the sad loss of Hammerton, it being generally believed that he had been swamped during the squall, and all hands lost; and as his father made mention of the hospitable reception Murray had met with from him, Hammerton resolved to introduce himself to the old captain, and claim his advice and protection. He might have gone on board a frigate lying in the harbour, and this indeed was the proper step he should have taken; but from the tenor of his father's letter he thought there was no harm in trying the commissioner; for Corncob's dollars had vanished pretty considerably during his overland expedition, and he was now left with just sufficient to chink, and no more.

The commissioner, on hearing his name, although he had entirely forgotten it, gave him a cordial reception, and soon remembering the circumstances, inquired in what manner he could serve him. Hammerton placed the correspondence in his hands, and begged his advice how to proceed. The commissioner said that to all appearances the letter had come in the envelope of another; and he directed very particular inquiries to be made at the post-office. The result was far from satisfactory; for the only clue which could be obtained was very much to the detriment of Murray's character,—it being satisfactorily proved that he had taken a letter directed to Mr. Hammerton, and had afterwards returned one, which, as far as the postmaster could remember, was not the same.

With the generosity of character which had distinguished Hammerton in England, on board his ship, and in America, he refused to entertain the slightest suspicion against his gallant young friend, and induced the commissioner to see the case with his eyes;—namely, that as the letter had been sent to one of the Lords of the Admiralty, to be forwarded to Halifax in the bag made up for the *Tribune*, it required no direction beyond the name; and that the bag contained a better correspondence and a cleaner-handed set of letter-writers than are usually to be found about the Point, Sally-Port, or Plymouth Dock.

Hammerton was removed on board the *Diana*; and having refused all pecuniary assistance from the commissioner, he became a lower-deck passenger, in some of Corncob's clothing, and by no means disposed to meet the laughter of his more fortunate shipmates. This laughter, however, soon gave way to the generous feelings of young sailors, who are always disposed to assist their neighbours; and Hammerton, when he was rigged according to his rank, requested he might be allowed to do duty. His amiable manners—his frank, generous behaviour, soon procured him friends, and he found himself, when half-way across the Atlantic, with a very respectable show of clothes, and a chest of linen which would not have disgraced the son of Sir Hector Murray. In due time the *Diana* reached Plymouth; and Hammerton, having obtained his discharge, went on shore, intending to start that evening for Taunton, and thence to walk the few miles which would there separate him from his father's cottage.

Hammerton had left his father when the tide of prosperity was at its height; and although frequent letters had taught him to expect a great change in the appearance of his parent's habitation, yet he was very little prepared to find the once opulent merchant in the small cottage in which he resided. From the moment when Hammerton first heard of his father's failure, he instantly reduced all superfluous expenditure: he had known the full blessings of money, but instantly became prepared to resist all temptations. Out of the prize-money which fell to his lot, he carefully remitted the greater part home; and as misfortunes came faster upon his father, when his wife died and his elder son was murdered, then did Frederick labour to console him and to deprive himself of every luxury which the smallest expenditure may sometimes insure in a midshipman's berth. With a heart not much elated by the success of his early life, and with the full conviction that his future advancement would depend upon his own exertions—with the expectation of seeing his father weighed down by misfortune to the very verge of the grave, Frederick made the best of his way to Taunton.

The once opulent merchant was known more from his sudden change than from his large dealings in that town. The road which led to the cottage was pointed out, for the sailing directions were clear and distinct, although the language in which they were conveyed might have puzzled a less inquisitive head. Frederick was directed to follow the high Exeter road until he arrived at a large entrance-gate on the left hand: immediately opposite was a cottage—it was there the once great merchant resided.

As Hammerton approached the place, his generous heart beat quicker. He stopped to look at the superb entrance to Sir Hector Murray's house, and then turned his eye to the small wicket-gate which led to the cottage. Eight years had elapsed since he had seen his father: he had grown a man—his features were altered, his cheek was sunburnt—the heat of the American summer had altered his appearance; from a stripling he had become a well-set specimen of human nature, standing nearly five feet ten inches high. He knew he could pass and repass without being known: he feared to enter suddenly; and in order to collect his thoughts, he sat down nearly opposite the cottage, in the hope of seeing his father or catching one glance of Amelia. But this was not his only idea: it occurred to the generous fellow that he had arrived much about his father's dinner-time, and he was apprehensive that if he entered at once, he might deprive his parent of some of the food he could ill afford to lose. He too was hungry; but the very reflection of the mutability of all human affairs even cheated the hungry bowels of a midshipman: the man who had commanded thousands and thousands of pounds, now left to linger through the cold termination of life without a farthing but what some liberal friend might send him or what his son could earn for him!

It was about seven in the evening: the dark clouds of winter began to lower into night; the wind came with that surly sigh which proclaims to landsmen the approach of a storm; the leaves fell from the trees, their day of existence being passed; and as they flew by him, Hammerton cheated the time by watching how far they were carried, and moralised within himself upon the old subject of the passing away of generations of generations, and comparing the life of man to the leaf which fell by him.

Time flies when the mind is active; but rapidly does it hurry on when anxious expectation keeps the eye vigilant. The day soon closed, and darkness followed. It was strange that Hammerton was fearful to enter the house where he would have been most welcome: he even thought of returning to Taunton, dreading lest it should alarm his old father to demand an entrance at such an hour. No light had been seen at any window—no careful hand came to secure the frail barrier against intruders, and the cottage appeared untenanted.

"It is useless waiting," thought Hammerton; "and now I will enquire—I will ask at the great man's lodge: his porter looks better housed than the once richest merchant in England." Hammerton cared not to disturb one who held so good a situation, and who in reality did nothing but open a gate twice or three times during the day.

His appeal to the large bell was answered by a smart-looking girl, who, seeing a stranger, very wisely kept the gate fast as she held the light over her head so as to allow it to fall upon Hammerton's face without much showing her own.

"Is this Sir Hector Murray's?" said Hammerton.

"Yes, sir," was replied.

"Pray, may I ask if a gentleman of the name of Hammerton resides anyway hereabouts?"

"In that cottage, sir," replied the woman. "But he is not at home—he is at present with Sir Hector Murray."

"He has a daughter, I believe: is she with him?"

"Yes, sir; Miss Amelia, you mean. Shall I tell Mr. Hammerton you wish to see him?"

"No; I will wait for his return: it cannot be long."

"No, sir; this rain will soon make the old gentleman come home." Here Hammerton wished her a good-night, and taking a kind of quarter-deck walk, might be said to have closely blockaded the port.

It was not long before Hammerton saw a light moving

down the avenue, and with the impatience of a son naturally anxious to greet an aged and an unfortunate parent, he paeed the limits of his little walk, watching his father's exit from Sir Hector's gate. He saw how age had erept upon him—how the blows of an ungrateful world had nearly felled him to the earth: the step was unsteady, and he leant upon the slender support of his beautiful daughter. Carefully did he conceal himself, and attentively did hc listen to the woman's account of the tall, dark stranger who had made the enquiries, but refused to give his name, or see the person after whom he had enquired.

"Odd—very odd," replied old Hammerton, "that a man should eome to me at the dusk of evening, learn where I was, refuse to send me his name, and with as much concealment as he advanced, retired!—Which way did he go?"

"I really cannot say, sir," replied the woman; "but my little girl about a quarter of an hour ago heard footsteps opposite your gate."

"Let us go quickly, Minnie, my love; it might be some one inclined to deal another blow upon the helpless,—one, knowing my infirmity, eome to take by force that whieh I could not retain by opposition. Quick! quick!—open the gate!—There, go baek, Susan! keep cut of the rain and the wind; you must not take cold, you know."

The gate was closed, and Susan retired. Amelia held the light elose down to avoid any inequalities in the road, but did not speak, for that would have been useless. By her manner she conveyed what she would have said: shc led her fathcr with eare and caution; but being startled by a noise near her, she turned hastily round,—in her agitation for, shc was alrcady highly predisposed to fear, the lantern dropped from her hand, and poor old Hammerton, stumbling over a stone, fell down upon the road.

Susan, who considered it impossible, or at any rate highly improbable, that any aceident could occur in the crossing of the road, which, considering the situation of the cottage, could not be more than thirty yards, had shut up her door for the night, and the howl of the wind and thc pattering of the rain prevented her hearing the scream whieh escaped Amelia when her father fell. They were in total darkness, for they had not recovered from the glare of light inside the lodge; and therefore when their only guide, the lantern, was extinguished, they were unable to see one foot before them. Hammerton, on the contrary, had become accustomed to the darkness, and being close in the rear of his father, saw him stumble. At the very moment when prudence was the most requisite, he forgot himself; or perhaps it might be that his feelings were too highly excited when he saw his father fall, to allow him to refrain from proffering assistance. He made but one stride, and Amelia saw her father in the grasp of a stranger: she flew to defend him, and seizing her brother violently by the neck, found words enough to express her opinion of the act.

"Let go my father, you robber!—What! would you touch a man who cannot hear? Let go, I say!" And she made very excellent use of her nails, applying them to the cheek of her brother.

In the meantime, old Hammerton had been lifted on his legs before the son spoke.

"Amelia! Amelia!" he began, "is this the reward I deserve for assisting my father?"

"Who are you?" said the girl.

"Your brother Frederick," replied Hammerton; and no sooner had the words passed his lips, than the arms of his sister were entwined round his neck. Old Hammerton, who could not comprehend what was going on, and only aware that he had been assisted by the stranger, thanked him courteously, and asked him to take shelter in his cottage. Amelia left her father under Frederick's care, whilst she opened the gate, rang at the door, procured a light; and the three were ushered into the small room—which served for study, parlour, sitting, and receiving-room. No sooner had Amelia placed the light on the table, than without informing her father who the stranger was,—and all trace of whose boyish countenance had left him,—she hung round his neck and kissed him a hundred times.

Now, Mr. Hammerton in his early youth had known the ways of this sinful world; and although a man of very grateful heart, he was unable to comprehend directly what new frolic this was of the best of daughters, and what sudden fancy she could have taken for the dark-skinned stranger, that she could cling to him closer and closer, gazing with affectionate look upon the handsome man, and kissing him again and again.

"There," said he to Amelia, "that's quite enough, my dear; the gentleman was extremely kind in assisting me, but you need not kiss him for ever."

Amelia's glowing cheeks gave way to a smile, her fingers ran over the letters, and old Hammerton stood like a statue, his eyes fixed upon Frederick, tracing with scrupulous exactness the features, doubting the reality, and yet willing to believe that he beheld his son. Still was he so altered, that even his father could scarcely recognize him; but painful as the suspense was between doubt and conviction, it ended in a loud exclamation of "God bless you, boy!" and Frederick was in his father's arms.

The manner in which the sudden intelligence had been communicated, and the silence during the scrutiny, were superseded by young Hammerton's response to his father's blessing when he threw himself into his arms and said, "My father! my father!"

"I *heard* it," replied old Hammerton. "Gracious heavens! do I live to be so rewarded! I *heard* my son's voice, and what pain and misery deprived me of has been restored by unexpected pleasure. Speak, Amelia—let me hear your darling voice again!—speak, that I may kneel and thank God for this wonderful recovery."

"Oh! can it be true, Frederick?" said Amelia.

"I heard you, sweetest girl, and never can I forget that voice again! But kneel with me;—all ties of kindred must give way to duty—all feelings of affection, all filial attachment, all parental regard must be delayed until we have offered up our thanksgiving for this second life; for he is half dead whose remembrance is dulled by deafness, who cannot hear the voices of his children."

Giving an example in his manner, Hammerton lifted up his prayers to heaven, and sincerely did his children join in their thanksgivings; and although the most pious must have been gratified at this solemn sight, orthodoxy might have startled at the conclusion: "And if, O Lord, it is predestined that I may again be deprived of this thy greatest blessing, grant that it may be also predestined that with that loss I lose my existence."

Neither Frederick nor Amelia said "Amen" to it: the treasure so quickly found might be as quickly snatched away, and old Hammerton was a parent respected and loved.

The wild exuberance of the old man's joy seemed likely to occasion a delirium; his nerves were strangely agitated. Fearful that this might be a spark lighted up before its total extinction, he listened to all that was said with eager attention; and if he fancied some word fell not with the force of the others on his ear, his "*What?*" was horrible. To obviate any disaster from over-excitement, old Hammerton was sent to bed; Amelia retired to her room; and Frederick, regarding all the perils he had encountered as blessings now realized, threw himself upon the sofa, and, after again offering up prayers for his safe return and the results it had occasioned, he fell into a repose such as the poor can experience in fuller force than the affluent.

CHAPTER XX.

HOME SCENES.—A MIRACULOUS INTERPOSITION BEFORE DEATH.

Not long after daylight Sir Hector was awoke and a note placed in his hand. Mr. Hammerton, unable to sleep, had penned a hasty scrawl, apprising Sir Hector of all that had passed, and begging him to call as early as possible. Sir Hector was too true a friend not to participate in his friend's feelings, and when he made his appearance, although it was still early morning, he found Frederick ready to welcome his father's and his own benefactor, and the youth was not slow in making due acknowledgment.

"Strange alterations!" thought Frederick. "The man who was courted to be present at every sight and every party—who had thousands at his door imploring his support and assistance, solicitous for his interest—one whom the world looked upon as a giant of wealth—now to be mewed up in this cottage, hardly large enough to swing a cat in, and to be beholden for that to the man whom he scarcely knew, and who might have been considered a rival rather than a friend!"

Frederick could not complain of the cordial shake of the hand he met with from Sir Hector, but the latter asked no questions, being more than incredulous as to the sudden restoration of his friend's hearing. He found him alone—this was unusual, for heretofore his little interpreter was by his side; and if the pleasure of one was great when he held a conversation without the assistance of a third party, it was no less astonishing to the other, who could scarcely credit his own senses. As to any explanation of how it had occurred, none could be given; unaccountably as the sense had been lost, so was it restored. Old Hammerton, although suffering from a nervous excitement, was a new man; and, as he assured Sir Hector, perfectly satisfied that it was predestined it should be so, nothing could rivet him more firmly in the belief than that he had recovered in the manner he had.

Sir Hector now turned his attention to Frederick, and heard from his own lips of Walter's behaviour, and the good character he had left behind him at Halifax. Frederick was much too liberal to make any allusion to the fifty pounds, although he found himself awkwardly situated on that point; to return thanks for the money, which after all might never have been sent, would be a folly; and yet not to mention it savoured of ingratitude. This was a point which required some dexterity, and every time Frederick attempted to clear away the ground in order to lead to it, he was cut short by a fresh question from the baronet, who seemed resolved that no explanation should take place.

"Where is your sister, Frederick?" said Sir Hector. "This must be a happy day for her; I never remember to have entered this house before without seeing her."

"She is sitting upon that seat, sir," replied Frederick, "and is writing."

"Well, I must go to my little favourite, since she won't come to me;" and as lightly as a man of his age could hobble, Sir Hector approached the person whom he loved best in the world after his own son. So busy was Amelia at her task that she did not hear him approach; and he, with the freedom of a friend, as she concluded the last stanza, seemingly enamoured of her own performance, took up the paper and read as follows:—

"Some years of life have past and flown
Since last I heard a human sound:
My ear was dull, my spirits gone—
A dead cold silence all around.

I've known that others spoke and laughed—
I've *seen* wit kindle in the eye;
But when the generous wine was quaff'd,
I lost that cheerful wit's reply.

"When beauty touch'd the silv'ry lyre,
I tried to catch the stirring note:
How vain, alas! was that desire!
On ears like mine no raptures float.
I've watch'd the maid whose song was o'er,
Receive the homage of the rest;
And sylph-like would she tread the floor,
With flushing face and beating breast.

"Within that sacred, bless'd abode
Where I was early taught to pray,
I could not *hear* the word of God—
In silence pass'd the pray'rs away.
I saw the holy man pour forth
An inspiration of the word,
Whilst tears proclaim'd that preacher's worth,
Alas for me! *I* never *heard!*

"I had a child, a pretty child,
A darling only six years old:
The boy had eyes and features mild,
And yet he look'd both proud and bold;
And when he talk'd, I strain'd my ear,
Around me others laughed and smiled:
I could not hear—*I* could not *hear!*
My cares could never be beguiled.

"I've watch'd him play about the room,
I've seen his sister's laugh with joy,
His smile dispersed a mother's gloom—
It solaced mine, my darling boy!
I've danced him on a father's knee,
I've tried to guess what he might say—
Oh, pang unknown to all but me!—
I could not *hear* my infant pray.

"'Twas yesterday the morning air
Came with the balmy breath of spring:
I wander'd to dispel my care—
Great God! I heard a linnet sing!
I knew it, for though years had pass'd,
No other sound had that effaced;
Its cheerful note had been the last
Upon my dull'd remembrance placed.

"'Twas Sunday morn; I heard the bell—
I heard the organ's solemn sound;
I heard my children's voices swell,
Hymning thanksgivings all around.

I knelt to Him who thus restored
What He in wrath had snatched away:
Oh! how I fervently adored,
And own'd the blessings of the day!

"Let me not lift my pray'r in vain—
Still let me hear my child's dear voice!
No more, O Lord, will I complain—
My woe is past and I rejoice:
I bow my head, I rend my heart,
I lift my voice in hourly pray'r;—
Lord! let Thy servant now depart,
Lest I relapse—lest I despair!"

"You are a darling, kind-hearted, affectionate girl, Amelia," said Sir Hector, as he read the three last verses again: "it is under the influence of such a sun as yourself that virtue flourishes. Bad indeed must be the heart which cannot appreciate the merits of this juvenile production! Don't show it to your father; the last verse might engender thoughts which the blessing he has received ought to banish for ever."

"It was his own expression last night," replied Amelia, modestly, "when he knelt down and thanked God for his great goodness. I altered the first part and about the linnet, for fear it should recall the horrible sight which deprived him of hearing."

"It is a miraculous interposition, and I only know of one parallel to it recorded in history. But come, this must be a day of rejoicing, and we will not allow it to pass without acknowledging our gratitude to Him who has so signally manifested his power. Come, come to breakfast at my house. Now, Hammerton," he continued, as he took the father by the arm, "you will hear Frederick's story from his own mouth."

The narrative of the sailor's adventures was told with much earnestness: his escape from the perils with which he was surrounded in the boat—his own share, inasmuch as the directions given were his own, were related with becoming modesty; and when he drew towards the conclusion, and confessed his love for Maria Corncob, the faces of all began to alter from gloom to cheerfulness. The generosity of the American was properly commended: and Amelia added with a smile, that if the lovely Maria was as good in *grain* as the thing after which she appeared to be named, the Indian corn would be liked in any cob grown in Virginia or Maryland.

"The sooner, Hammerton," said Sir Hector, "that we ship off this sailor the better: a midshipman in love would be a fine subject for Amelia's poetical powers! I suppose you have no objection to his going to sea again?"

"On the contrary, Sir Hector," replied Hammerton, "as it is evident he is not predestined to be drowned."

"Not in that particular place and time," replied Sir Hector with a smile. "But who knows that, the next time he goes to Portsmouth from Gosport, he may not be run down by a dockyard lighter, the very one predestined before the foundation of the earth to founder him?"

"Pooh! pooh!—nonsense!" replied Mr. Hammerton; "I never carried it quite so far as that! But this I think—"

"Stop! stop!' said Sir Hector, good-humouredly; "we must leave argument to-day, in order to provide for him to-morrow. That shall be my charge; and in the mean time he must fit himself out, as Corncob's suit and the borrowed garments of his late messmates would ill become him now."

The day passed merrily. Amelia was unceasing in her questions as to Miss Corncob—she was particular in learning her dress, the manner of her pronunciation; and as time and distance had a little opened the eyes of Frederick, he gave a spirited caricature of the life, manners, and employments of a Virginia farmer, much to her amusement. They were interrupted only once by Sir Hector, who desired Frederick to write down Corncob's direction; and from an insight into his banker's book afterwards, the American's liberality and generosity were found not to have gone entirely unrewarded.

A very few days past before Hammerton was properly refitted—new rigging over his mast-head, his chest stocked, and his pockets lined. He was to go to Malta in a packet, and there to remain until the arrival of the *Leonidas*, the captain of which ship was a distant relation of Sir Hector's, and who, he had no doubt, would receive him.

A great difficulty had arisen in procuring a certificate as to Hammerton's servitude. The log of the *Tribune* had been lost with the ship: and as he had left her previously to the wreck, he was unnamed among those who were tried for her loss at Halifax. This placed an insuperable barrier against his passing for a lieutenant; for the whole of his time had been served in that unlucky vessel, and no officer could be ferreted out in England who could attest such servitude up to the period of her last sailing. It was true, in her pay and muster books there stood the name of Frederick Hammerton; but a certificate of good conduct was requisite. All these difficulties Sir Hector pledged himself to overcome, and Hammerton sailed for his destination.

It was a singular fact, that Hammerton's father appeared, as the day approached for his son's departure, to relapse gradually, and again to show trifling symptoms of becoming deaf: increased age might have done something, which his nervous agitation, whenever he allowed himself to think upon the subject, made still worse.

Why prolong this description? the last part of the old man's prayer had been heard. When his hearing entirely failed him he died; and she who had been to him as ears in his deafness—as the medium of understanding between him and the world, continued as a nurse, a daughter, a most unwearied attendant. She scarcely closed her eyes; the restless pillow of sickness was smoothed by her delicate hands; and when the old man would bless her, and lift a prayer to heaven that she might be protected from the world's ways, and die the angel she had lived, her gentle voice would sweetly rise to heaven in supplication for him who was her father and her friend—who had been unfortunate in life, and who was resigned in death.

"Think not of me, father," she would say; "the protecting hand of Providence will guide and direct me;—think only of yourself: your race is run, and your account must be rendered. We who have known you have little fear for the awful trial; for he who never injured his neighbour—who in his affluence assisted the distressed—whose charity was unostentatious, whose integrity was undoubted—who was kind as a parent, affectionate as a husband, beloved as a friend, and sincere as a Christian, may justly hope for that inheritance which his life has merited."

"I care not for myself, dear girl," he would say; "my

days of misfortune and trial are over. I am not such a hypocrite as to believe that a life of error can be atoned for at the last minute: if I am predestined to be saved, so will it be done; if not, I must abide the chance. I do not know that at this awful hour I have any great sin with which I can reproach myself, and I go forward on my career without apprehension, supported by an easy conscience.—Who is that?"

"It is I, my old friend, come to see you again," said Sir Hector.

"For the last time a living body!—But my boy—and that little angel, Murray, see her lift her little hands to heaven for me, when, heaven knows, *she* has more need of our prayers!—for in this dark and slippery path of life, who is to guide the innocent, to shelter the afflicted? I am easy, Murray,—easy in all but her. I leave her in your cottage a pensioner upon your bounty: you will not cast her out when she is fatherless."

Sir Hector seized his hand. "I would sooner," he said, "have died myself than have heard those words! As true as you are present, O God! at this afflicting scene, so truly will I protect them both in this life, and implore your protection for them hereafter!" He turned to look upon his friend,—but he had for ever passed away,—and with such a smile of contentment upon his countenance, that the calmness of resignation was nearly lost in the strong mark of apparent satisfaction.

"The Lord take him to himself!" said Sir Hector. As the sobs of Amelia stopped his further address, "Come, my child," he said, "this is no scene for you. Your abode is now with me: as you have well done your duty to him, so do I hope that I may be able to do towards you. Old as I am, I feel younger now; for I have a charge, and a great but a pleasant one. We must learn to bear these lessons, my child; the scene is fast closing around me, the curtain drops over my dearest friend, and day after day but makes us more familiar with that which we must all meet. It is after all but a shadow, for death has no substance: it is an imaginary evil, more feared in the distance than when nearest; and since all must encounter it, it is well to be acquainted with it. God bless you, child! your little heart will sadly mourn for this; but time will remove the first pang and impression, and kindness and attention may alleviate the affliction and console you for the bereavement."

CHAPTER XXI.

THE "SAUCY ARETHUSA," AND CAPTAIN MURRAY'S FIRST VISIT.—WEAZEL'S MISTAKE.—GAME OF "ABEL WHACKETS."

In 1806 the *Arethusa* was in Portsmouth harbour undergoing repairs. She had been, like most of his Majesty's ships in those stirring times, actively employed in annoying the enemy; the shot and shell of the French batteries had passed over and through her; the singly contested action had been fought, and there was no frigate more honoured in song than the "*Saucy Arethusa.*"

It was when she removed to Spithead, previous to her starting on another cruise, that her captain, in endeavouring to reach the shore during a heavy gale of wind, was upset in his gig and drowned; and as the body drifted on shore, the coroner and the undertaker did all that was requisite, "save the lapidary's scrawl." It was a sad accident; but sad accidents in active minds are shortly forgotten—they never remain to corrode the heart, which in seamen, during war, beats too highly and too quickly to allow of the rust of life arising from misfortunes to impede its machinery.

The *Arethusa* was all a-taunto, top-gallant yards across, her red ensign shining in the breeze; and now the pendant was masthead high, for the late captain had been buried, and the first lieutenant almost imagined himself the actual commander; but as he had received some gentle hints that a man half his age was about to take charge of the ship, he thought it best to forget his disappointment,—the decks received a higher polish from the holystone, the ropes were all taut, the yards well squared, and the *Arethusa* attracted the attention of all parties for her neatness aloft, and her clean, man-of-war-like appearance.

It was about noon, when the people were at dinner, that a smart young man, in plain clothes, came alongside.

"Keep off in that shore-boat!" said the marine on the gangway.

"Have the kindness," said the gentleman in the boat, "to give this note to the first lieutenant."

"What's all this?" said the midshipman of the watch. (The officer of the watch was playing the flute below.)

"A shore-boat, sir," said the marine; "got something for the first lieutenant."

This brought the midshipman to the gangway, who seeing a remarkably dandified young man telling the boatman to go alongside without his leave, he resolved to cool this intruder on marine discipline.

"Sentry!" said Mr. Weazel, (whose face was not a little altered since we last left him: he being now about five-and-twenty years old, and having one or two distinguishing marks in the shape of grog-blossoms on his nose; whilst his left hand was not quite so ready for mischief as formerly, he having lost two fingers in Trafalgar, and obtained, not his promotion, but the sobriquet of "Three-fingered Jack,")—"keep that long-togged gentleman off!"

"Keep off in that boat!" roared the marine, "or I'm blessed if I don't fire into you!"

"That's all right enough," said Weazel; "you see the gentleman is ready dressed for *a ball.*"

"Very likely," said the gentleman: "but I am not much inclined to *dance attendance* here."

"Dance ten dances!" said the old quarter-master. "Why, his legs arn't thick enough for scrub-broom handles! although I'm blessed if he does not stand as stiff in the boat as a midshipman on half-pay."

"None of your impudence, M'Donald, if you please," replied Weazel; "the only thing stiff such old toddles as you like is your grog."

"I'm thinking," said M'Donald, "that there are two of us in that boat, Mr. Weazel."

"Will you have the kindness to take this card to the first lieutenant?" asked the gentleman."

"Will you have the kindness, sir," said Weazel, mimicking the gentleman's manner, "to tell me if you take me for your footman? and be d—d to you!"

"I dare say beforc long," replied the gentleman, apparently a little irritated, "you will obey my orders, or I shall discharge you."

"That may be," said Weazel, "so by way of being to windward I'll just *discharge* you now; so *go off*, or this shower of rain may wet the powder in the pan, and hinder the marine's musket from being discharged, by way of *turning you off*."

"Come, sir," said the gentleman, "I cannot stand this nonsense any more: you will tell the first lieutenant that I desire to see him."

"Well," said Weazel, "that does beat cock-fighting!—But, stop a moment. I say, you sir, with the top-chain over the shoulders of your mast, are you the new captain's steward?"

"No, sir," answered the gentleman.

"Are you his footman, then?"

"No, sir, I am not."

"Are you the old captain's undertaker?—because if you are, you may heave and *Paul* where you are."

"No, sir, I am neither one nor the other; but I am——"

"Oh! never mind who you are, my fine fellow," interrupted Weazel: "if you are not the live captain's steward or the dead captain's undertaker, you must be a Whitechapel bird-catcher; so hop your twig, my boy, or you'll find we have plenty of cats to catch such birds as you are. I wonder what you would take for your watch without the wheels of it?"

"By the Lord! my finc fellow!" said the stranger, "you shall remember that word, and watch and watch shall you have time to think of it."

"It's a *repeater*," said Weazel, "and I dare say you got it on tick; it looks like a second-hand German warming-pan, and the case is large enough for the boatswain's baccy-box! Now, Moses, or Aaron, or who the devil you may be of the lost tribes and lost beards, if you take us for any of the *Men-asses*, you are mistaken! I dare say, now, you are some of John Doe's men, without your top-boots, come to nab the first lieutenant; but we know how to weather the Nab-light, however decp it may appear to be surrounded. Here's the first lieutenant coming up the hatchway; so Catchpool, look out!"

"Who are you talking to over the gangway, Mr. Weazel? I thought I told you before that I would have nothing of this kind. Have the men had their time to dinner?"

"Not quite, sir," replied Weazel, in a very different tone of voice from that in which he had been amusing himself.

The first lieutenant came to the gangway; and seeing a gentleman—for a gentleman is always known—bobbing about in a shore-boat in a drizzling rain, and hearing from the sentry, who had been giggling away on his post, that the stranger wished to see him, he ordered the boat alongside, and a smart-looking, well-made man of about one-and-twenty stood on the *Arethusa's* quarter-deck. That he was a sailor was obvious; no landsman steps up the side, touches his hat, and gives that footing of consequence which a man does from long habit during a professional life.

The first lieutenant, Mr. Jones, returned the salute: and looking at the card, took off his hat and made a low bow. Weazel saw something was wrong, and sheered over the other side.

"I am appointed to the command of this frigate," said the stranger, "and I was anxious to see her without being known. I shall come on board and read my commission to-morrow: in the mean time let me look round; and let me beg of you, Mr. Jones, not to mention who I am. I have a great desire, if possible, to repay that young gentleman for some of his civility in his own coin, and I would rather see the people I am to command without their knowing their future captain. If I stop in the midshipmen's berth, leave me there."

"Shall I send the shore-boat away?"

"Certainly. I must pay him first though.—What's your fare, my lad?"

"Three shillings, sir; and I hope your honour will give me something to drink for waiting."

"Three shillings for coming out to Spithead! There's half-a-crown, and shove off directly."

"Well," said the boatman, as he looked at the money, "you're a pretty chap to call yourself a gentleman!—why, you would skin a flea for its hide and tallow! Take care of him," said he to Weazel; "he's all outside show, like the marine's mess. I dare say he would let a poor fellow pull him to St. Helen's, and then ask for change out of a sixpence." And here the voice grew weaker in the distance; although every now and then such words as "nipcheese," "herring-bones," "hung-in-chains," and such like fag-ends of the long volleys, reached the ship, until the boatman thought he could no longer be heard, and resting upon his oars he relieved his throat.

Murray at last stood in the position he had so long pictured to himself: he was the captain of the *Arethusa*. He looked aloft from the quarter-deck, saw the neat-rigged mast, the yards square, the ropes taut—such as a man-of-war should be in appearance and efficiency; and he remembered the launch, and the little fairy who christened her; for he had been present when the *Arethusa* many years before had been launched; and Amelia, then a mere child, had gone through that ceremony; but that fairy had grown a woman, and seemed, from his father's affection for her, to be likely to cheat him of his birthright. The sister of the man who had struck him! he bit his lip as the thought occurred to him; and he fancied his revenge but half complete, since Hammerton had never been heard of from the day he had sailed. He considered himself wronged, and he felt he was unrevenged, since the object of his hate might have died uninsulted.

But Murray was himself now a captain: the *Arethusa* was under his command; the war raged fiercely; the battle of Trafalgar, for he was in it, had led to his promotion; the naval glory of Great Britain was raised upon the highest pinnacle; the ships of England swept the seas; and although in arrogance we did not equal the Dutch, who on a former occasion carried brooms at their mast-heads—a signal now that the vessel is for sale,—yet the long pendants of our ships were to be seen in every sea, in every clime. By Murray's side was his first lieutenant; and although the captain was out of uniform, he felt his own situation, and knew how to profit by it. "Mr. Jones," he began, "this Weazel played me the first frolic ever practised upon me. When I first entered on board the *Tribune*, he was then a midshipman of four years' standing; and after nine years' separation I find him in the same situation, with as little chance of advancement. What, Mr. Jones, is his general character?"

"He is, sir," replied the first lieutenant, "the life and soul of the ship, foremost in danger, ready for mischief, always excessively innocent, and every day getting into scrapes. He nearly got into one for talking to you over the gangway, for that is expressly against my orders."

"He took care to have the whole of the conversation to himself," remarked Murray, "and after calling me Moses and Aaron, a bum-bailiff come to arrest you, and so forth, he finished by calling my watch a German warming-pan, or a boatswain's tobacco-box."

"He is not very partial to the Israelites; for it was but yesterday he shaved off the beard of one in the midshipmen's berth, and stuck it on the collar of the Jew's coat, remarking that bear-skin collars were coming into fashion; he then lashed him up in a hammock, took him into the cable tier, stowed him away in the heart of it, and then told him he ought to be very happy, as he resembled his namesake whilst living and whilst dead: in the one instance, because he was always in pursuit of the promised land; and in the other, "because no man knew of his burying-place even unto this day." On the Jew being released, he threatened to bring an action against him; upon which Weazel immediately knocked him down, "by way of commencing the action," as he said. Finding the poor fellow hurt, he poured some raw rum down his throat, telling him to make the best of "the spirit of the law."

"I should like to see him at some of his tricks again," replied Murray; "and if he asks me to dinner with him after his abuse of me, I certainly will avail myself of the honour. Let us see the between-decks, Mr. Jones; and be kind enough not to give me the honour of an introduction."

Captain Murray expressed himself much pleased with the good order of the frigate; there was no useless lumber about the decks, everything was in its place, and the ship might have gone into action five minutes after she was clear of St. Helen's. The main-deck was the main-deck of a ship for service as well as for show, and the lower-deck exhibited that pride of seamen, the neatness of their messes: the men appeared stout, young, and clean seamen; and, to use a common expression, though rarely true, you might have eaten your dinner off her decks, and never felt the grate of a sand-grain.

"This, sir," said Mr. Jones, "is the midshipmen's berth," as he put his head inside the door.

The young *gentlemen* had just made preparations for dinner. In those days, the table-cloth did its duty for three or four days without being relieved; and before Monday evening the whiteness had been pretty well superseded by the lines of dirt which the expectant heroes of the navy had rubbed from between the prongs of their forks: some, indeed, preferred the easier and less laborious mode of plunging the fork through the table-cloth, leaving two large holes,—for three or four prongs were in those days considered useless, and green peas never in fashion in the midshipmen's berth. A japanned tin jug, familiarly called a "black-jack," was in the centre of the table, and contained swipes,—a liquor by no means the most intoxicating, it having been proved that a man might drown himself in such miserable beverage before he could get drunk upon it. The bread-barge contained its weight of hard flinty biscuits; and the mess, which was a republican one without a caterer, exhibited all the signs of bad government and starving populations which agitation produces. The strongest seemed to profit by this general disorganisation, and the weaker suffered in proportion. Each one daily prepared to help himself to the large half-baked piece of beef upon the "after you" principle, which may be thus explained:—When the poor wretch of a boy made his appearance with the dinner, the dish was instantly seized by one of the quickest and the strongest; another immediately called out, "After you!" whilst another, distancing a stuttering companion, had "After you!" out before the poor fellow labouring under the impediment could get out the word "After." So it proceeded; the last one getting but a very slender allowance to feed a voracious appetite, and each receiving the dish to help himself as his turn stood, on the "after you" principle. It was, however, considered a point of honour never to give the dish out of its turn; although Weazel, if he failed in capturing the beef on its passage, generally went upon the cutting-out system: he would draw the attention of his victim to some object whilst he helped himself from the plate nearest to him. Hence civil discords soon grew high, and not unfrequently blows were repeated instead of grace.

"Will you sit down, sir," said Weazel, addressing the captain, "and make yourself quite at home?"

No one had seen the first lieutenant's approach, and all hands were beating the devil's tattoo with their knives and forks on the plates, keeping an inharmonious accompaniment by singing the "Roast Beef of Old England." Mr. Jones, on hearing the invitation, retired, and Captain Murray entered the berth.

"I am very glad, sir," replied Murray, "to find that you do not consider me as either the live captain's steward or footman, or the dead captain's undertaker; and I shall have much pleasure in accepting your invitation."

"No grabbing now," said Weazel, "a strange gentleman's here; and manners, you know," in a whispering tone to his messmates. And then, addressing Murray, he said, "The dinner will be here in a minute. Here, boy, put the beef before me, and the potatoes within hail. Hold the gentleman's plate, boy. Where the devil have you been educated? don't you know common behaviour? Do you like the outside piece, sir?"

"Thank you," said Murray; "any piece will do for me."

"Hold the plate nearer, and be d—d to you, you stinking hound!" said Weazel to the boy; "you have no more manners than a kangaroo! There, don't capsize the gravy down that gentleman's collar. A potato, sir? I am sorry we have nothing better to offer you; but, unfortunately, the boy, who is the clumsiest cub in creation, fell down on the main-deck, upset the soup, and left the fish for the cat to eat. Now, gentlemen," he continued, addressing his messmates as he put about a pound in his own plate, "help yourselves, and remember *manners*."

"After you, Tom!" "After you, Harris!" "After you, Walcot!" "After you, Smith!" was instantly vociferated; and Captain Murray soon saw that, at any rate, if his ship was in good order, his midshipmen's berth was rather in a revolutionary state, and required some alterations to protect the youngster from the overbearing power of the oldster. In a minute the bone was picked as clean as if half a dozen dogs had been at it, the potatoes vanished, the black-jack was empty, and the bread-barge capsized. Murray now intimated that he would take a little piecc more; and Weazel, who was always ready, said, "Boy, run up to the galley and bring down the turkey." A smile played upon the lips of all his messmates; but Weazel, with consummate coolness, continued, as he saw the boy gaping at him, "What the devil is the matter? has the poulterer forgot to send it? or has that rascally cook let it fall in the ashes? Tell him I'll report him to the first lieutenant, and the new captain may exercise his powers of eloquence in his maiden speech to the ship's company. I'm very sorry, sir," he continued, addressing the stranger, "but we will endeavour to make amends in another way. Boy, bring the dessert, and take care not to injure the branches of the cherry-tree. Tell the captain of the fore-top to stand by as a scarecrow to frighten the blackbirds. You must see our garden aloft, sir; it's a wonderful invention—much on the plan, as the clergyman of the flag-ship said, of the hanging gardens of Babylon; it's quite extraordinary how our fruit ripens, and how we avoid blights and late frosts. Perhaps after dinner you would walk round, and I'll desire the gardeners to be in waiting."

Captain Murray kept his countenance well, although he remembered that Weazel had played him this very trick years ago, and he was perfectly aware that he now destined him to be the scarecrow, and the gardencr the captain of the top.

"I shall have much pleasure," replied Murray; "but I cannot conceive how I could have passed unnoticed the garden, for Mr. Jones——"

"Oh, Mr. Jones," intcrrupted Weazel, "is much too knowing to show thc garden: he has such a variety of South American plants which he wishes to bring to perfection before he allows them to be seen."

Here the boy entered, and, having takcn his cue from Weazel, said, "Gardener says, sir, that one of the foretopmen is in the report for having picked all the cherries, and that a flight of sparrows and blackbirds have eaten up all but a few gooseberries, which Mr. Jones has ordcred him to keep for the new captain."

"Curse the new captain!" said Weazel. "By the Lord! the service is come to a pretty pass when the gooseberries are to be kept for the new captain! But, sir," said he to Murray, "so it always is; the active and industrious starve in order that the slothful and the indolent may fatten. As sure as ever I'm first lord of the admiralty, I'll do away with all gardens on board a ship, and make the captains sow mustard and cress on the sills of the ports for the good of the ship's company"

"Clear away, boy," said a rubicund-nosed oldster, "and clap the grog on the table. The only dessert we shall get to-day is some of Bounty Bligh's bread-fruit, or midshipman's nuts, which grow better in an oven than in the foretop."

The cloth was removed, and the greasy oak table brought to view. It had divers proofs of long service; each oldster mixed a pretty strong portion of grog, taking it out of an old lime-juice bottle, most of them preferring a cup, for there were only two glasses or tumblers belonging to the mess. Weazel of course apologised; he was the very cream of civility whenever he intended mischief. It was the last roll of the ship before she rounded the Isle of Wight that smashed all their glasses; and owing to the confusion in refitting the ship, it was judged better not to receive the new glass on board until they should be ready for sea.

"You seem," said Murray, ready to lead Weazel on, "to spend a very jovial life, and to make amends for wanting the amusements of the landsmen by some constant occupation. How do you generally pass your evenings?"

"Pretty well and comfortably," replied Weazel. "When we have no theatre open, or no tight-rope dancing, we play at Able Whackets."

"Able Whackets!" replied Murray, "what can that be?"

"The most delightful game ever invented," said Weazel; "it keeps the attention alive, and warms the hands of the players more than any other. I'll teach it to you, if you like; but take a glass of grog first. When you are on board a ship, you must do as sailors do; and 'grog,' you know, or at least I know—'grog is the liquor of life.' Perhaps you would like a glass better than that cup; but

Balderson and myself think there is no use in showing how much we take, or rather how little, for fear our messmates would force us to take more. Now then, Harris, hand out the 'good books,' and let's get round the board of green cloth."

A slight explanation of this game may not be amiss, in order to show how very easy it is for a man to pay off a debt of revenge without incurring suspicion. A handkerchief is twisted up as hard as a rope, and this is called the "good money" by which you are to pay off all debts. The cards are called "good books" (they are called elsewhere the "devil's books," and as far back as memory can trace, the four of clubs has been called "the devil's bed-post"); they are dealt out exactly, and the hands count the same as at commerce. The great art of the game is never to miscall anything. For instance, if a person were to designate the hand as the hand, another would call out "Watch;" and the person having made the blunder would have to hold out his hand and receive one blow upon it from every player, just as hard as he thought proper to inflict it, the culprit being told the reason of the punishment by the man who called out "Watch," saying before he struck him, "This is for calling the good thing *flipper* out of its proper name," a hand being a flipper: thus, the table is the "board of green cloth," &c., everything having a professional name. It is obvious that the young beginner is likely to catch the most blows; and Weazel, completely blinded by Murray's manners, sought to pay him off for the "rowing" he got from Mr. Jones for talking to him over the gangway.

Murray, who knew the game well, readily agreed to the proposition; and Weazel having explained to him the game, warning him that when he had a good hand he ought to "stand Able," which gave him the privilege of inflicting three hard cuts upon the person who held the worst hand, they dealt the cards round once or twice to explain the game, and they then "served them out" properly, every one of the midshipmen being determined to pay off "the long-togged gentleman with the chain round his neck."

Perfectly aware of Weazel's character, Murray acted accordingly, and kept a guarded silence, inflicting the punishments gently, in order to show a lenient disposition, and then made a mistake purposely; upon which Weazel called out "Watch," and gave a wink to his messmates. "Hold out your flipper," said Weazel: "I demand the good money—this is for calling the 'good books' out of their names:" and smack came the hard-twisted handkerchief upon Murray's hand with all the force Weazel could bestow upon it; and it required some courage to keep it steady to meet the blows of the others, for they all served him out according to their utmost power, the last man keeping the "good money warm," as the term is. Lord Byron has since said,—

> "And if we do but wait the hour
> There never yet was human power
> Which could evade, if unforgiven,
> The patient search and vigil long
> Of him who treasures up a wrong."

Murray was like the bard's watchful man; and Weazel, equally alert, was never off his guard. At last Weazel "stood Able" upon a sequence—"king, queen, and knave;" and Murray "stood Able" upon aces. When the hands were exposed, Weazel had the worst; for each by some good luck had got better cards, and the victim was called to receive punishment. Murray having demanded the "good money," desired him to hold out his flipper, and he began, "This is for the loss of the good game called Able Whackets, this is for the same, and this is for *my* standing Able and *your* losing the game;" and at each time fell a stroke which nearly cut his hand off. At the expiration of this Weazel withdrew his hand to offer it to the next. "Avaust there!" said Murray; "hold eut your flipper again;" and he received three more most powerful cuts for Weazel's having stood Able and having lost the game. The tears started in his eyes when he found that Murray used the good money with the swing of a proficient, and amply repaid him for his former unkindness; whilst Weazel, irritated by the laugh of his messmates, who perceived the stranger to be an adept, gave vent to his wrath and got watched "three times more." Some jeered him when he offered his maimed flipper, and refused it as being so much mutilated as not to offer a fair mark; and as the blows so hardly and so constantly inflicted led to abuse, and abuse to a promise of satisfaction, Murray contrived to give the conversation a turn by inquiring when the ship was to sail, as he should be happy to meet the gentlemen again.

"Oh, sail!" said Weazel, whose tongue was not idle, for his wrath had subsided at the idea of satisfaction and the prospect of working an eyelet-holc in the coat of his enemy —Sail! why, when we get our new captain on board."

"Who is to command this fine frigate?" said Murray.

"Some booby of a lord's son, dry-nursed by a fat lieutenant, and put under the guidance of Jones to keep out of mischief."

"Why does it follow," said Murray, "that the captain must be the booby you would make him?"

"Because," said Weazel, "merit is never rewarded. Here am I, old enough to command any frigate in the service, having lost two fingers at Trafalgar, been wrecked, badgered, buffeted, swamped in a boat cutting out; cut out of my own promotion by having been knocked overboard and believed drowned, four ycars past; been mate of the deck, had charge of a watch, and being, though I say it myself, the best hand at dry-holystoning a lower deck in the navy. Now I'll bet a dish of ham and eggs for four, with grog to wash it down, that the skipper who is sent on board to be acting captain under Jones is not older than you arc to-day, and knows no more of a ship than you do!"

"That may be, and yet he may be a very proper man to command a frigate. Why, you would not like a man as old as a Spanish mule, and perhaps just as obstinate, to command you! I know you all like young slim fellows likc myself."

"Do you?" said Weazel: "then you are much mistaken! Everything is fancy: I fancy being commanded by a man older than myself—one who has been longer at sea, seen more service—one I can respect from his seniority, and in whom I can have confidenee from his services. Now you are younger than me; and although I fancy, from the way you handled that handkerchief and gave me such striking proofs of your power, that you have been at sea, yet I should just as soon sail under the orders of the bumboat woman as under yours. So now, no offence, you know; as the hands are turned up, I shall turn out of this."

"Mr. Weazel," said a quarter-master, popping his head in the berth.

"Well?" replied Weazel.

"Mr. Jones says you are to go on shore with the dockyard party in the launch."

"Curse Mr. Jones, and the launch, and the dockyard party too!"

"At any rate," said Murray, rising to depart, "you are variable enough. Poor Mr. Jones, who is to dry-nurse the captain, is old enough to suit you—is entitled to your respect from his long service, and yet you don't seem to have much confidence in his orders. However, I will not be the cause of your delay: so, good evening, young gentleman. I dare say I shall have the pleasure of seeing you again."

"D— me if ever I want to see you again!" said Weazel.

"Nor I," said Walcot.

"Nor I," said Harris; "he plays too good a knife and fork; and notwithstanding his gold chain, I don't think he has had a blow-out for the last fortnight; he's as thin as a herring, and twists about like an eel: but, by the Lord Harry, he hits hard!"

Murray overheard these unfavourable remarks; but he well knew that midshipmen's remarks were harmless enough. Mr. Jones was on deck carrying on the duty; and Murray saw by the way one or two of the officers returned the salute as he got on the quarter-deck, that Jones had given a hint that the new captain was for show. The gig was manned, and Weazel saw the shore-going gentleman take hold of the yoke-lines and steer the boat as well as any man in the navy."

"That gentleman," said Mr. Jones to Weazel, "has known you before. I suppose you shook hands with him after dinner?"

"Not exactly, sir; but he made my hands shake. We played at Able Whackets, and I fancy I got off second best."

"Had you a midshipman on board the *Tribune* of the name of Murray?"

"Yes, sir," replied Weazel; "and a gallant fellow he was, but a precious nob to be sure: he was the son of some old lord mayor, and was placed under the protection of a

Mr. Hammerton, who gave me a considerable hiding because I stowed his blankets away the first night."

"Now did he get on down below with you," continued Jones.

"Ate very well, I thank you, sir—a mighty stretching appetite. I was in hopes of showing him the garden in the foretop, or the cow in the maintop; but the dockyard party ——."

"—Will save you a little repentance. Mr. Weazel, that gentleman is Captain Murray of the *Arethusa*."

"Whew!" went Weazel, as he slipped down the side: "a pretty kettle of fish I've made of it!"

CHAPTER XXII.

THE CAPTAIN'S ELOQUENCE.—A RETROSPECT.—SIR HECTOR'S EXPLANATION WITH MURRAY.—CONFESSIONS.

The next morning Captain Murray read his commission on board the *Arethusa*. All captains make a speech—it is quite astonishing how eloquent a man becomes when no one dares criticise. Horace talks of his inspiring bumper; but the intoxication of power gives eloquence—intoxication arising from gratified ambition, knowing that all around you are subservient to you and can never be above you,—that not one of the three hundred souls to whom you deign to address yourself can ever be your superior in the service you have chosen—your stammering will be unheeded, and, like a newspaper report, the address will be printed without the blunders, on the minds of the ship's company. Thus spoke Murray after his commission had been read:—

"My men, you are aware, from the commission which the clerk has just read to you, that I am appointed by the lords of the admiralty to be your future captain; and you are instructed by that commission to behave yourselves respectfully to me and the officers placed in authority under me. I am convinced from the good order which I observed on board yesterday that I need say very little to you in regard to your several duties: I remarked with much gratification the cleanliness of the different messes, and I am well aware that your comfort below is the result of discipline on deck. My men! we are about to sail on a station where we shall have every prospect of meeting with an enemy's frigate. I shall take care that you often practise at your guns: that once effected, the bravery and courage which have distinguished British seamen in all actions, but more especially the two last general engagements, will not be forgotten by you. In conclusion, my men! I shall do my duty strictly, rigidly: you will do yours obediently. We shall not quarrel, I hope; and I sincerely trust an opportunity may occur in which you will see my readiness to lead you in danger and difficulty, when I shall have the gratification of observing and of profiting by your cordial assistance. On Saturday next we sail; it is now Tuesday: the necessary refitting of the ship will prevent my giving leave to any of you;—indeed, as we are short of complement, it would be imprudent; but this I promise you, that if your behaviour is to my satisfaction—if the duty is done as it ought to be done on board a man-of-war, when we return to harbour I will not deny you liberty to go on shore; and I hope you may have plenty of prize money to spend.—Pipe down, Mr. Calls."

As the men retired to their different avocations, Captain Murray desired all the midshipmen to remain on deck, and he addressed them: "Young gentlemen! I yesterday availed myself of your hospitality, and, I hope, gave some of you a hint that practical jokes are often repaid with interest. I admired the frankness with which you spoke your minds; but I regret to say I was very much dissatisfied with the arrangement of your berth. You are, I see, a republican mess, and, like all republics, you sacrifice the weak for the benefit of the strong; and since, where there is no one to command, there are none to obey; the regularity which distinguishes society in general is lost; the rules required by decency are laid aside; and your behaviour is not one jot better—indeed not so good—as the society of negroes who sit round a rice-pan, and dip their dirty hands in to obtain their food. Not exactly being, as you will find, the lout of a lord so flippantly denounced by Mr. Weazel, I shall show you that your conduct *shall* be altered.—Mr. Walcot! although you never wished to see me again, I am convinced you will ultimately be grateful that I am returned to you. I desire that you will be caterer of the berth, and I expect to see it much altered on my next visit; and mind, I give you all fair warning, if I ever hear of an ungentlemanly act, I shall dismiss you from my ship immediately.—Mr. Jones! I desire that you inflict some punishment upon Mr. Weazel for disobeying your orders yesterday, and for having allowed a gentleman to inquire for you, and receive an insult from the midshipman of the watch, who levelled his wit in order to obtain a smile from the quarter-master. Let the marine who was on duty be placed in the report;—I do not intend his Majesty's subjects to be shot at, or even threatened to be shot at, to please the marine or sentry; and you will disrate the quarter-master and place him in the foretop.—You will see, I begin as I intend to go on. And now, Mr. Jones, man the gig, if you please."

We left Murray, previous to his command of the *Arethusa*, a midshipman on board the *Surprise* in the West Indies. He remained under his gallant commander until he had served his time; and during that period he had learned his duty properly, and had imbibed the ideas of Sir Edward Hamilton. The service could not have wished him a better preceptor—the country could not have found him a more gallant or distinguished captain. With him Murray was taught the necessity of being occasionally a leader in any very dangerous service; with him he learnt that the bravest man is generally the most liberal and generous,—that when the flag of an enemy came down, that enemy became a friend; and the only thing he could not learn, (for that had grown with his growth and was too deeply rooted to be eradicated,) was love of money—a niggardness which led to meanness. But this had not escaped his captain, who often told him that as he grew up he would have opportunities of relieving old and shattered shipmates, and that the money spent in a good cause would yield him a million times more pleasure than in hoarding it up in trunks, or counting its increase in solitude: but all his lessons of liberality were in vain—the bad seed had been too early sown and had taken deep root; and even when grown a man, Murray would congratulate himself upon his overreaching Hammerton—for which a little more appropriate term might be found.

Before he left the West Indies, he had heard of Hammerton's resurrection: he knew that the theft must be discovered by him—that the slightest hint in conversation with his father would have led to suspicion; but in all the letters he received not one word had reached which alarmed him. He grew bolder as time slipped away; and when he heard of old Hammerton's death, and of his son's having been absent, unheard of for years, he rubbed his hands, and thanked God that he was freed from another witness of his shame.

Murray had become a good officer: under such a preceptor who could fail? His father's interest procured him a commission; he served his time in the *Phœnix*, was made commander into the *Dotterel*, and arrived at Portsmouth just in time to step into the unfortunate man's berth whose death had made the vacancy. It was nine years since he left his father: his promotion had been as rapid as the rules of the service would permit; and he had passed his examination after dinner, when the only question asked was, if he knew the Jamaica fashion of cutting up a pineapple, or preparing a shaddock. These little oversights of an important duty *did* occasionally occur; but had Sir Edward been one of Murray's passing captains, he would never have allowed an officer to be placed in any situation if he thought that officer not fit for it; he would never have given a brother-officer a chance of being lost through the incapacity of a man of fortune's son. Luckily Murray was as good a seaman as the service could show at his age—was a very promising navigator, a distinguished lad in the hour of danger, and would have passed any necessary examination.

He had now the pleasure of seeing his pendant flying on board a frigate, and had just obtained leave from the admiral to be absent for twenty-four hours. He was on his road home, and thinking of honour and glory, and stars and ribands, jolting across the country, dreaming of happiness; whilst his officers, after the grog and biscuits had superseded the supper in the gun-room, were canvassing his character in a very off-hand manner.

"Just the lad for us, my boys!" said Jones. "We shall reef topsails in forty seconds, or stand clear on the topsail-yards.—Bell, my boy!" continued the first lieutenant, addressing the marine officer; "by the Lord Harry! he will knock the pipeclay out of the Gallouts' jackets, and make them carry arms to a midshipman's coat if it's stuck on a broomstick.—Purser, my lad! your lanterns will get a kick or two of a night; for I suppose we shall sleep at quarters. And Soundings! he'll wear your old quadrant out in making you observe if we near the chase. Give me your young ones! I hate your old fogies, who potter about the deck, and are half an hour finding out a fault, and an hour thinking how to correct it. Let's have a glass to the next cruise!"

"I shall not allow him," said Bell, "to interfere with my marines."

"Certainly not," said Dangle, the second lieutenant of that gallant corps.

"Mind how you play with the bull, my lads," said Jones, "or you'll know all about his horns!"

"He cannot make me do any duty!" said the first.

"He *shall* not interfere with me!" said the second.

"You may depend upon it, my boys," said Jones, "you won't be idlers any more!"

In the midshipmen's berth all was confusion: the republicans were routed without opposition: but not one of them would pay a farthing towards repairing fractures. Weazel swore that this was the way of the world—that promotion obliterated friendship, and that he remembered the new captain a snivelling lad, who had his head combed twice a week by the corporal of marines, and his feet washed by the midshipmen's boy; two of the oldsters wrote home to get their parents to procure their discharge or removal; and all hands were talking in as much fear and trembling as if they expected the devil on board in top-boots.

The real good seamen were in high spirits: the last captain had been a trifler; and had not Jones been a smart officer, the *Arethusa* would have looked like a Spanish rather than an English frigate.

"Stand clear, you skulky!" said one.

"Ah!" said Mr. Calls, the boatswain, "I'll make some of you jump mast-high now! D—n me! but he's just the lad for our money! You Nobody—you boy who stole my grog! give us a drop here now; and hurrah for the young one! Now we shall all pull together, and the work will be light enough.—Chips!" said Calls, addressing the carpenter, "I'd recommend you to clap the prophets in your pocket, and not to kick up such a dust with your boy, singing all day; you won't be wanted now! By the Lord! you'll muster every morning with the polished pump-bolt, and stand clear the fellow who has any rust on his adze!"

"The Lord prosper us!" replied the carpenter; "my duty is aloft."

"Oh! that won't do now, Chips," said Calls; "your duty is on the main-deck; and you had better keep your eyes on your shot-plugs, and not be turning them up to the truck like a dying duck in thunder: it's no use now singing for help—you had better help yourself. Take care!—there's Weazel got a fish-hook into your beef; and knowing you have given up spirits, he has been alongside your case bottle."

"That alters the case a little," said Chips. "St. Paul recommends wine and water, and I always take the spirit separately; but I'm bless'd if I don't take the bad spirit out of Mr. Weazel if I catch him at my bottle!"

"I fancy," said Calls, "you'll brace about your yards and come round on the other tack before long!—It's no use your trying to weather the devil by singing—he's not fond of music, so give us a stave like a man."

"Mr. Calls," said Chips, with amazing gravity, "you will be weighed in the balance and found wanting."

"You be d—d!" said Calls.

Arriving at Sir Hector's gate, Murray was awakened from his dream of future greatness by the present prospect. It was dark; but the genial air of spring blew pleasantly upon him. He was expected: the gates were opened without the trouble of ringing, and the carriage stopped at the door. Old as Sir Hector was, he stood there to welcome his son: he took him in his arms, and tears of gratitude to heaven poured down his old face.

"Welcome! welcome! I see you again, Walter—I see you worthy of your name! Come in, boy, to the light: let us look at you;—altered much, of course, but still your mother's look! How long can you stay with us?"

"I must go back to-morrow evening: I sail on Saturday," replied Walter, "and have only twenty-four hours' leave;

but the admiral has promised not to inquire for me until forty-eight are expired."

"Ah, Walter!" said Amelia: and then blushing at the apparent familiarity, she drew back much confused, although she offered her hand.

Walter took it coolly.

"Why, you seem to have forgotten Amelia Hammerton!" said Sir Hector; "and yet *now*, Walter, common gratitude might make you remember the little fairy who christened your fine frigate. She is my adopted daughter: this is her house whilst I live, and if not hers after my death as an abode, I shall provide for her one as good."

Amelia took Sir Hector's hand, and looked at him as much as to implore him to think of his son and not of her. The old man caught the glance of malignant spite with which his son eyed the girl, who he fancied had pushed him from part of his inheritance, and yet Walter could not withdraw his eyes from her. There was so much mildness, so much beauty in the lovely girl before him—so much of innocence and of virtue, that in spite of the devil in his mind whenever money was concerned, he kept gazing at her until her modesty had covered her face with a blush, and she had withdrawn her hand and her eyes.

"I shall tell you more about her when we are alone, Walter; but now about yourself. Have you everything you want—everything that an officer and a gentleman should possess?"

"Everything, I thank you, sir."

"Remember, Walter, I do not put you on any allowance—you have unlimited credit at the banker's. Do not rush into extravagance, and beware of gambling. I know that young captains at Palermo frequent the conversazione. Beware of beginning to gamble; for if once it becomes an excitement—if once it becomes an object, you are lost: few men can stop in time.—But I must not lecture you now. Have you dined?"

"No; but I have told the servant to get me something."

"I ought," said Sir Hector, "to have killed the fatted calf."

"Why," interrupted Amelia, "you do not call it the prodigal's return!"

"I hate her for that," thought Murray to himself. "By heavens! it appears as if I was never to be clear of these Hammertons! One hates bankrupts and breakers, for he is in danger who is nearest to them. That girl chimes in with her remarks as if she were my father's second wife: she has a much better chancc of that than being my first."

"Tell me," said Sir Hector, "how you left your gallant captain—he who ought to be called Hermione?"

"Well, sir: as usual, actively employed, never idling his time in harbour. But I think I ought to have complimented you upon your good looks."

"A green old age, boy: I am better than I have been for years, and for a man of seventy, I think, one whom the insurance offices would prefer. Since I have adopted that dear little girl, whose affection for her poor father and attention to me warrant my warmest and most sincere gratitude, I have felt a new life. Walter, I promised her father.—There—Amelia, my child, leave us for a moment: Walter's time is short, and we must speak quickly on these matters;—I may be dead before he returns."

"The Lord of all things avert that blow for years and years!" said Amelia, as she left the room in tears.

"Walter! that girl must be your charge should I die; and if her brother should still live, you must be as a brothcr to him. Hear me, my boy!—you have risen to the highest grade—at least to that which must lead to it; you have done well, bravely, honourably, in your public service: the faults and frolics of your youth are past and forgottcn—there remains but one wish of my heart, and that is to sec you married."

"What!" ejaculated Walter, "married! I would just as soon think of giving up the navy!"

"Married!" replied Sir Hector. "Why, one would think from your scruples that marriage was a state of misery! It should be, and is to well-regulated minds, the happiest portion of life. To the libertine or the unoccupied, it is, I own, but a dreary sameness. Women hate your men who dangle in a drawing-room: but to the young, the well-disposed, thc honourable, the religious, the partner in wealth or woe enhanccs every moment of existence, and makes life a pleasant, a delightful journey. Now, Walter, the girl who would make you happy, who has proved herself a good daughter and an affectionate friend, will make the best wife; and I recommend you to rub up your old acquaintance with the *Arethusa's* sponsor."

"Never, sir, never! I will be frank with you: I hate the name, and wish she was removed from this house."

"Indeed!" said Sir Hector; "that expression I did not expect. Come, we will not talk of the matter any more, and I believe myself to be an old fool for having set to work in that manner. Had I shut her up and declared you should not even speak to her, you would have been caterwauling under the window in order to have seen her pretty face; and by a determined opposition on my part, I should have been met by a vigorous one on yours, and she would have been cut out like the *Hermione*. But mind, Walter, if this is the last time your old father should speak to you, remember that I leave that girl under your protection!"

At this moment Amelia returned, and seating herself by Walter, inquired of his doings since they parted; made him tell her over again the fearful wreck of the *Tribune*; led him on to talk of the *Hermione;* gleaned from him his first entrance into the navy, his hardships, disappointments, mortifications; and then, with a face of almost divine resignation, she asked him his opinion as to the probability of her brother's existence.

Walter, who had now become more charmed with the affectionate manner of Amelia, and who felt his consequence from the manner his opinion had been asked, replied that he hardly knew the circumstances under which Frederick sailed sufficiently to form an accurate opinion.

"He sailed in the *Rover* packet five years since to join his ship, supposed to be at Malta; he arrived at Gibraltar twelve days after he left Falmouth, and was to sail the following day. From that moment to this we have never heard of him, neither have we received any tidings of the vessel: some imagine she must have been wrecked on a hidden rock, others that a white squall might have overset her; and many have mentioned that the Algerine pirates may have captured her; but all is conjecture, and hard it is, Walter, to mourn for a dear brother of whose death we are not certain. Even in my prayers for his eternal happiness, hope appears and cheats me of earnestness. We have not heard that he *is* dead; hope, therefore, and hope alone, can inspire me with fortitude to think and to talk of it. If we did know it, I should pray for resignation to bear what I cannot or could not avert.—Now tell me, Walter, your opinion."

"I have never, Amelia," he began, while he managed to take her hand,—"I have never been in the Mediterranean; but from all I have heard I should say the chances are ten to one that he was taken by a Tunisian or Algerine pirate: if so, and he did not fall in the action, they still preserve him as a slave;—Frederick Hammerton, who risked his life so generously for others, ought not to let a chance escape of saving his own. I would encourage hope, whilst I would be prepared for the worst." Amelia paused a moment after he had ceased speaking, appeared hesitating which colour of the prospect she should adopt, and proceeded thus:—

"He always wrote to us affectionately and fondly of you, Walter. In all his letters from America your welfare was ever uppermost, and his last words to me were, "Remember me to Murray; he will forget the only difference we ever had as a Christian ought to do, and we may again sail together."

Sir Hector watched the countenance of his son, which seemed to give way to a pleasurable sensation, as if revenge had been gratified. Amelia continued:—

"It was in endeavouring to save you—nay, I believe he fastened the rope round you—that all his misfortunes commenced. He might have escaped the wreck as you and others did—he might now be here to thank your father for his more than fatherly care of me; he might have thanked him for his generosity at Halifax, which, however it miscarried, was intended at a moment of need to have been useful."

"What's that you refer to, my little Mimic?" said Sir Hector, affectionately, whilst a deep blush covered Walter's face, but was instantly chased away by a paleness that would have defied the art of those most accustomed to conceal the defects of nature.

"Frederick told me that after his return to Halifax from

Virginia he applied at the post-office for letters. He found one from you which mentioned an inclosure; but the generous gift you had omitted to send in the hurry of business."

"Impossible, my child," interrupted Sir Hector. "I have been a man of business all my life, and never made such a mistake: besides, I have a clear recollection of the payment of that bill. The letter was sent by the same packet—nay, under the same cover, as your father's letter. I remember my bungling manner of folding it; but my diary will tell—I will look at it directly."

"Stay, sir," said Amelia. "What can it signify now?"

"Signify! child. Why, if I omitted to send that nearly ten years ago, I must have been unfit to manage my own affairs. We old merchants don't make mistakes in that manner!"

"At any rate, sir," said Walter, "let us leave it until to-morrow, for I am very tired with my day's work, and shall be glad to get to bed: so I will wish you good night."

"Good night, boy!" said Sir Hector, as he lighted a candle, resolved to look up his ledger, his diary, and every other evidence to convince himself that he had made no such careless omission.

"Good night, Walter!" it was Amelia spoke. "You really do look so fatigued and jaded, that bed is the best place for you now. I hope, though, I am not the cause, nor my tedious conversation, of your sudden departure."

"Not the least, child," said Murray, hurrying by her, and seeking the solitude of his own chamber to conceal his feelings. "Dolts, asses, fools, idiots, that we are," said Murray to himself, as he closed the door, "to allow the inclination of a moment to be the cause of everlasting shame! I, who could have had any money, to have taken this infernal cheque, and even to have since derived pleasure from the thought! Now would I give all the wealth of the world to avoid to-morrow!—I would go back in life to be the shipwrecked boy that I was, and begin the world anew, to rub out that d—d spot which will remain a stain for ever! What miserable, weak creatures we are! I could withstand the temptations of the West Indies—I could give up the wine which I once loved—I could correct my language, control my passions; but this devilish itch for money, even though I have an unlimited amount of it now, governs me still. By heavens! the very words of that girl shall make me overcome this meanness! The discovery now, and by her too—by a Hammerton! I would rather cut my throat!—Who the devil is this?"

Whilst he thought thus, he saw the door open and his father come in, holding in his hands a diary, a ledger, a banker's book, and a slip of paper.

"Now, look here, Walter, and see if I can be mistaken," he began. "Here is the very entry, the date—nay, here is the memorandum of my having enclosed it.—This must be looked to; it would become a practice to defraud others, if we negligently closed our eyes over the committal of a crime. The long time elapsed since it happened will be no bar to the discovery. The hounds of justice, though slow, are mostly sure; and no man would have greater pleasure in bringing such a villain to his proper punishment than I should have. The robbery, if committed at Halifax, is doubly bad; for the ship must have been lost before the arrival of the packet; and he who could have robbed a poor shipwrecked boy must be a villain so black, so——"

"Hold! I implore you."

"What! would you not have me curse the thief who ——"

"No! no! *I* am that thief."

"Merciful God!" said Sir Hector, "strike me deaf as him who blessed you when he heard a daughter's voice! You, Walter!—you descend to such meanness! Surely you said it to try my patience—to see the burst of despair which a father might give vent to, and then watch the working of nature as all the parent returned. Come, come, Walter, unsay it—nay, nay, you did but jest."

"I scorn to add a lie to the crime. I am sensible of my error; I did it—I opened the letter, took the money, spent it; but I thought he was drowned, and could never rise to brand me with the felony."

"This is but a sorry extenuation of the fault,—nay, it is a repetition of the former crime. Strange that a man who could face any danger, who could risk his life to save another's, who but a week before had seen 'how in the midst of life we are in death,' should thus run the perilous chance of being swept from the living with a sin so great upon his memory! Still I am your father—still I know it is my duty to forgive as I would be forgiven: nor am I Roman enough to pronounce a sentence on my own child. But, Walter, think,—ay, think,—if you, standing in the command of the *Arethusa*, ordering a punishment on one of your men for theft, were cursed at that moment with the recollection of the past, how could you uphold the required discipline, when every lash that fell would be to you the most appalling conviction of your own deserts?—and should some malicious person have treasured up Hammerton's disappointment,—nay, more, engendered a suspicion, how could you look on a captain, yourself a culprit self-condemned? Here, see me tear every remembrance, every record of the foul act: to your bed, to your prayers, and bury the secret with you! Let not Amelia hear it; *she would* hate you—she who alone can reform you. God protect you this night, and so bring to your mind the fearful remembrance of your crime, that it may be now and for ever a rock to be avoided, a mountain to be levelled! I go to bed, but not to sleep. Walter! Walter! you have blighted my old age—you have withered my hope! Well may I say,

> "'How oft a day which fair and mild appears,
> Grows dark with fate and mars the toil of years!'"

The son's return has caused his father's curse.

CHAPTER XXIII.

MURRAY'S REPENTANCE AND SIR HECTOR'S FORGIVENESS.—LOVE SCENES.

THE night passed differently with our three principal characters. All virtue, all modesty, all gratitude, the beautiful Amelia knelt and returned thanks that Walter had come as a bright sun to give life to the old age of Sir Hector. She laid her head upon her pillow without a crime to upbraid her; her eyes closed in refreshing sleep; and if she startled during her slumbers, it was when she dreamt her brother stood beside her, thanking Sir Hector for his kindness, praying for his health and happiness.

The bed of scorpions on which Walter reclined gave him but a short repose: his eyes closed, for he was tired; but all the misdemeanours of his boyhood rushed before him. It is true he saw in them faults not trivial, but such as might be forgiven: his age at the time, the manner of his education, the belief of his friend's death, all came more or less consolatory. But when he viewed the faults as fixed upon a man—upon a captain in his Majesty's navy—his whole soul revolted against himself, and he saw his errors in a stronger light; his mother's locket he more than once clasped in his startling slumbers, and in his dreams he vowed reformation.

Now, taking human nature as we find it, there are few who have not been guilty of crimes as aggravated as Walter's. A sailor—one who roams the world, dissipates dullness in foreign climes, and drives out by the activity of his life the poignancy of grief, forgets the trivial faults which cloud the remembrance of those who drivel through days in monotonous melancholy: to these the slightest fault clings with fearful tenacity, and, accustomed to view their own trivial sins as great, they shrink from men whom they believe to have wallowed in the enormity of guilt. The fault was a great one, but it was committed by a heedless boy: no one felt the error more than Walter; he disregarded it in youth, but felt it in manhood; he slept as those sleep whose minds forbid repose, he dreamt as those dream whose waking thoughts survive the mimic death.

With all the poignancy of regret which such a discovery was likely to make, Sir Hector threw himself on his bed. No man had more real religion than the baronet—no man could cling to an only son with greater fondness. The first ebullition of rage having subsided, the calmness which succeeds the night's devotions recalled to him the language he had lately expressed; he had forgotten the early disposition of his son, and surveyed him only through the medium of his hopes; he had heard him spoken of as brave and as generous in offering his own life, but he forgot that the seed sown in youth is not easily eradicated,—it is a nettle which always stings and fructifies immensely. One thought now occupied the old man's mind—it was forgiveness. His son, his only son, once more claimed his forgiveness, and could he withhold it? With this blessed resolution, his mind became more composed, and he sank into sleep.

It was early, and Walter had not risen, when his father stood before him. "I have considered, Walter, of last night's conversation," he began.—"I see in *that* fault your former follies breaking loose—I see you now as a man ashamed of the act: it is sufficient. I wonder if you have retained your mother's locket?"

"It is here," interrupted Walter, as he took it from his neck.

"And did it not guard you in the hour when your honour was forsaking you?"

"It did, father, and it saved my life when the *Tribune* was lost."

"Keep it as your best guardian, and remember these last words on a painful subject: The follies of youth are disreputable actions in the man; the schoolboy's thefts, which the lenient master punishes so lightly that they are forgotten when over, become transportable offences in after life: but the shame of discovery is ten thousand fold more when the crime is brought forward in later years, and when the blot upon the escutcheon is pointed out. Consider your station—consider the responsibility of your rank; and as you value your future repose in this world, become more liberal to yourself and others. I know your faults and your failings—you know them, and that knowledge will best guard you against them. Remember, you have wealth at your command—use it with a generous disposition: the hoards of the miser are merely a temporary pleasure; his successor generally bestows them in a worse channel than even avaricious niggardness could dictate. Be for the future, my dear Walter, the generous, straightforward sailor. No men have characters with so few tarnishes as seamen: they have occasional wildness, occasional levity; but for liberal notions and feelings, generous dispositions, straightforward honesty and honour, no men surpass them. I ask you only to act up to the character of your profession, and be the worthy type of your old captain in the *Surprise*. Now, boy, get up! your time is short, and I have much to say—much to propose to you. I want you to suggest any alterations or improvements you would like done. My days are numbered, and already I have outlived my most sanguine expectations. I want this place to become such a residence as you yourself will be happy in; and as this may be our last meeting, I should like you to be convinced how much I have your happiness at heart. All the past is forgotten; all the future will, I trust, be brilliant."

Sir Hector, having delivered himself of this oration without stammer or blunder, retired from his son's bedside; and before half an hour had expired Captain Murray was suggesting one or two slight alterations, to which his father listened with much attention: suddenly he turned round and said, "Walter, when will you marry?"

"I am," replied the gallant officer, "much too young to think of that, sir. I stand alone nearly in our profession: every midshipman at Halifax has tumbled into love, and every messmate I had as lieutenant unburthened his overloaded heart to me, and told me of dear little budding creatures left to pine away in solitude, weeping for their lost and truant lovers. Now, sir, you will think it odd, but I never was in love in my life—I do not know that I ever saw the woman who made my heart ache for a second. I have always thought of my profession, and faith, Captain Hamilton gave us no time to think of pining and whining at a woman's tail."

"Have you never written a poem yet, Walter?" said Sir Hector, with a smile.

"Never wrote a line with a rhyme to it in my life. I have seen midshipmen spoiling paper, getting rhymes ready-made and writing up to them, lugging out a fathom of hair which they had coiled round their necks, and ultimately washing their love's image out in strong grog; but I never knew more than four midshipmen married in my life, and they were proverbially the greatest fools in the navy. If I live, and the *Arethusa* sails well, we may yet do something more worthy of being remembered than running after a petticoat."

"But, Walter, remember you are an only child, and the title must die with you unless you marry. It is my fondest wish to see the child who is to inherit it, and you deny me the only object I wish to see before I die.'

"Children! my dear father. Why you add up all the

miseries of matrimony in a breath, and ask me to take them in my arms and fondle them. Never was man in better health than yourself. By your days being numbered, I presume you are seventy: now I see no reason why you should not live until ninety, and during those twenty years I will promise you at least four grandchildren. But even supposing I was inclined to get spliced and have a few little rope-yarns, who the devil am I to marry?"

"Amelia."

"Amelia! Why, would you have me marry the daughter of a bankrupt merchant, who could bring neither family, connection, nor wealth?"

"As for the family, Walter, I never knew a girl more likely to have one. Connection you will have, and wealth you have abundant. Are your scruples overruled?"

"Not a grain of them, father. Would you have me leave a service to which I am passionately devoted, at a moment when the English navy is at its highest honour, and when every man is anxious to imitate him who fell at Trafalgar? I tell you I should be miserable: I would rather command the *Arethusa* than all the harems at Constantinople."

"At any rate, you do not dislike Amelia?"

"No, certainly not. She is a very pretty girl, affectionate, grateful, lively, even-tempered, well-proportioned in all but pocket. I would as soon marry her as any one else; and if all the world were obliged to pair, like the animals in Noah's Ark, I should have no objection to her."

"I see, Walter, you are too light-hearted at present to think of any such serious matters. Remember, however, what I have told you: I have adopted her, and I will never forsake her. If I find you are not disposed to share her fortune with her, I must leave her independent of you. The cottage where her father and mother both died, I have left to her and those after her, and I have made an ample provision for her from the money I have saved. We cautious old merchants never live up to the full stretch of our incomes; as you sailors say, we always keep enough to veer and haul upon. You will find your fortune greatly diminished by this arrangement, although I have left a clause which will make you master of the whole under certain conditions. Come to breakfast. I have told you the wish nearest my heart, and my reasons for having selected her. I tell you again, the girl who is an affectionate, dutiful daughter—a kind, benevolent, active, feeling sister—will never make a bad mother, an indifferent wife, or an insincere friend. Believe me, Walter, the best guide in the choice of a wife is the character the girl has maintained as a daughter. The devotedness of that girl to her parents was never surpassed; and her undeviating friendship for me and her affectionate fondness for her brother place her very far above her sex in general."

They found Amelia at her post, and where a female reigns supreme. She rose to receive Walter, and as he gently pressed her hand a blush glowed in her face. The conversation soon relieved her from the betrayal of her feelings, and her usual animation was a sufficient excuse for the glow.

"I hope, Walter," she began, "that my godchild, the *Arethusa*, meets special favour in your eyes."

"She does, indeed, Amelia! Of all ships in the navy, she was the one I most wished to command. I suppose you remember all the circumstances of that day?"

Amelia crimsoned; she thought of the gipsy.

"Why, how now!" said Sir Hector. "You show as many colours, my little girl, as a pirate. What is there connected with that launch which seems to influence you now?"

"Nothing, sir," replied Amelia, "that is, nothing of any consequence. The remembrance of some words made use of by some sailors of one of the ships, and the effect they had upon my poor father, who was then in affluence, caused me perhaps to betray my feelings: but I must learn to forget that I was once the rich merchant's daughter."

Now this was Amelia's first falsehood, deliberately uttered and backed up by a circumstance. She was—and who would deny it?—perfectly justified in telling the white untruth rather than answer the question directly, which would have led to a confession every maiden may conceal within her own heart. If Amelia loved Walter for his father's sake, or if it were the general recollection of youth which no other object had eradicated, or if it were the appearance of a handsome young man, his eye proud of his situation, his figure perfect, which it was, (a kind of Sir Peter Parker, such a man as the navy had rarely shown,) may be open to doubt; but that she had admitted some few hopes and fears into her heart was evident: she seemed to forestall his every wish—she seemed to listen to the voice of Walter as if there were a fascination in each word; and the eye which formerly seemed to deaden as imagination pictured to her mind scenes long since passed, was now restless and impatient. It was scarce a second without being fixed upon Walter, and he never once darted a sudden glance at her without finding hers reciprocate. This is the first general demonstration of love: each look generally makes the matter worse; for as detection takes place the face becomes a pretty sure index of the mind, and hence to careful observers the secret of a young heart is easily betrayed. It is an amiable weakness of which the experienced take advantage: the cool deliberate villain sees his path clear before he attempts to walk forward, and danger and misery attend his detestable steps.

After breakfast, Sir Hector, who was now as active to forward his matrimonial projects as the most acute of scheming mothers, left the young people alone. The conversation was well sustained by Walter, who made a greater impression than he was aware, and used the most dangerous weapon in relating several anecdotes. The light heart of Amelia was easily moved to laughter when Walter told all the vagaries of Weazel after the shipwreck: she was pleased; and when we are pleased we easily fall into that pleasant disposition which becomes an inclined plane towards love. But when he stood before her as a hero,—when in animated language he drew the picture, which no one could colour too highly, of his desperate enterprise at Puerto Caballo, the girl's eyes, like a second Desdemona's, were riveted on him who had shared the dangers of that night. This was followed by a vivid description of the midshipmen's berth of the *Shark;* and as he described the last moments of that victim to a friend's invitation,—when he pictured the last horrors of madness—and when he told her of that young man's love, his remembrance of the girl at the last hour of existence, when the fatal lull restored him both reason and memory before he sank for ever,—the colour of Amelia's cheeks was alternately suffused or blanched, and catching the enthusiasm from Walter, she said, "Oh that I could find in the man I love equal attachment and sincerity!"

Walter had been pretty considerably initiated in the mysteries of the female heart. His life had not been one dead prosing over Hamilton Moore or Norrie's Navigation: Robertson's Elements and Mendosa Riou's Tables are but dry study, whilst the warmth of the West Indies produces from its hotbed the precocious buddings of the human creature. He never loved, but he had often flirted. Catching, therefore, at the exclamation of Amelia, which was partially softened by the words, "What devotion! what sincere attachment!" he replied, "So, Amelia, you love, do you? Pray, who is the envied object of your love?"

"That," replied Amelia, recovering herself, "Mr. Father Confessor, I shall not tell you."

"I think," said Walter, without intending any kind of romance, "that you ought to give me a little of your love, for the affectionate charge I have taken of your sea-nymph, the *Arethusa;* she is dressed out in her proper ornaments, and looks as pretty in her element as her sponsor does in hers."

It was the first civil remark, or one approaching to a compliment, he had ever made the poor girl, and she blushed. Everything was natural with Amelia: she had never had all those fine and tender feelings which nature engrafts on the female mind rubbed off or deadened by the cold, unfeeling world by which we are surrounded. From her infancy to the ripe age she had gained, she had scarcely ever left the neighbourhood; from the moment of her mother's death she had become necessary to her father's existence; at his death she had but one friend left in the world, and he had now relinquished public life and settled in the country. Amelia's mind was a natural, yet an artificial one; it was stored with history, poetry, religion: but she had never seen any of the world's ways, and in that respect was a perfect infant.

"Rather a pretty plaything this," said Walter to himself. "By Jove! it is astonishing how people can fall in love, and make tom-fools of themselves, when, if they only cast about, they may find girls who will make eyes at them, and yet hardly know that their heart is getting under weigh for another harbour."

"Do you sing, Amelia?" said Walter. "I remember, when I last saw you, you used to open that little mouth of yours like a young thrush in a nest, and scream out a psalm."

"I have never been taught, Walter; but I will do my best;" and she sat down and sang, in a plaintive, sweet, and harmonious voice—every note strictly in tune, but without flourish or ornament—"How sweetly along the gay mead." Walter looked at her as her swelling voice gave out, "Shall man, the great master of all;" and after having watched every tremulous motion of her lips, and gazed upon the calm face of the girl, he turned round, saying to himself, "I had better be off, for I feel my heart bumping against my waistcoat buttons. I shall make an infernal fool of myself! I'll be hanged if I shan't be captured!—I really do think she is perfect!—What a fool I am to go bobbing about in the Bay of Biscay!—I never felt so curious before, since I was sea-sick.—D—n me, if I'm not in love!"

By the time Walter had got to that pitch of admiration, Amelia had ended her song, and was about to make some apologies for her want of talent, when Murray, very like a young, ardent sailor, caught her hand, and giving her a gentle turn towards him, allowed his feelings to overcome his determination, and imprinted a kiss upon her moist, rosy lips, saying, "You are perfection's self."

Amelia did not take this as a liberty, for she had often when a little girl kissed him; and although she felt perhaps somewhat more curiously, with palpitations more rapid, while the blood mounted to her cheek and she trembled at every limb, yet she regarded it merely as a repetition of former friendship; nay, she had wondered that Walter had not been gallant enough to salute her according to his former custom. Rare innocence! and perhaps not the more valuable for being rare; for girls like Amelia love but once, and every instant is embittered after the object is removed from their sight; the man who engrosses such affections has all the odium of the other sex attached to him, if, by any unaccountable folly, the young lady goes into a consumption, swallows poison, jumps into a river, swings from a tree, or commits any of the fifty-six different methods of suicide so admirably related by a Frenchman for the benefit of the human race. Now, in fashionable life such an event never occurs : another lover usurps the place of the former, as generation succeeds generation, or wave follows wave; the young creature's heart is relieved by a ball or an opera, and in six months it is by no means uncommon to hear that both parties are married, though not exactly to each other.

Sir Hector had left them together for a long time. The yarns Captain Murray had spun were not run off the reel in too hasty a manner—the song, the kiss, &c., altogether occupied more than two hours ; and yet so unaccountably stupid were the principal actors, that they could not believe their ears when the clock struck twelve as the baronet came in.

"Walter, my boy," said he, "at what time must you leave us?"

"At four o'clock, sir."

"Not so soon as that, Walter," replied Amelia, her large dark eyes exhibiting a brightness such as moisture might occasion. "Surely you can stay another hour; you can always make up the distance by a little silvery persuasion to the postboy."

"Indeed, little darling," he said, (old Sir Hector rubbed his hand and gave one foot a kick with the other, an apology for a caper in the air,) "my time is limited: I shall run it very close indeed, even at four o'clock. I must be at the admiral's office by ten to-morrow; and dark nights, muddy roads, windy, rainy weather, may make the pedantic remark of an Irish lady true: 'The humidity of the atmosphere prevents the velocity of the quadrupeds.' But if anything could persuade me to run the risk, it would be your sweet self: but duty, you know—at least my father knows—duty is uppermost in a sailor's mind."

"And love," interrupted Sir Hector, "in a woman's."

"Still, Walter, I am not satisfied; you must stay half an hour longer: so I will ring the bell and tell the servant the carriage will not be wanted until that time;" which she did without receiving any interruption from

Walter, who merely remarked to his father: "That girl would have made even Nelson forget his duty."

"Thank you, Walter, for the compliment," replied Amelia; and adding as she flew past him, "You see you can obey orders from the ladies," she left the room.

Sir Hector watched his son as he kept his eyes upon the door as if to welcome her return, and then touching him upon the shoulder, said, "I see, Walter, I shall have no reason to leave that clause in my will, of which I spoke to you this morning."

"Why, what do you mean, sir?" asked Walter.

"Merely, boy, that you have found Amelia a very charming girl, and that you are half in love with her already. Now tell me this: don't you feel very much annoyed at going away so early?"

Walter smiled, and taking his father's hand, said, "I hope I shall never disappoint your wishes: she is a very charming girl, and I have openness enough about me to say, that I should like to see more of her. I never thought I could have entertained such a wish for any Hammerton under the sun."

Between twelve o'clock and half-past four a very considerable advance was made in their love affair: they had walked out together, they had found a similarity in each other's wishes; they had become, as it were, dependent upon each other. Walter had got so far as to say, "You will not forget me, Amelia, during my absence;" and she—for she scorned to sail under false colours—had replied, "Walter, you are much more likely to forget me." Then came a most magnificent oath from the son of the sea, swearing, that although sailors had been called the emblems of inconstancy, cradled in inconstancy, rocked by the inconstant wind upon the still more inconstant ocean, yet he would be the exception to the rule, and that Amelia alone occupied his heart: he talked about the anchor of his hope; and if he had been provided with utensils, he would have proved his father a good judge of lovers' affairs, and have written a verse such as—

"Oh, I have found that haven heart;
  Life's roughest gale may blow in vain—
Nor canvas shake, nor cable part,
  To force me o'er the sea again;

For now affection proves its sway,
And love that cannot, shall not fly,
May blaze his torch at life's decay,
And light us to eternity."

By five o'clock Walter was in his carriage, and arrived at Portsmouth without accident.

CHAPTER XXIV

IMPRESSMENT; FOR AND AGAINST.—CAPTURE OF JONATHAN CORNCOB.

WALTER, as he jumbled over the roads, slept but little. He had partially committed himself in regard to Amelia; and although he imagined he loved her whilst she was present, yet he certainly thought more of his frigate and her officers than of his lady, as he grew nearer to the one and more distant from the other. He was too young, too volatile, too vain, to be much in love; and there was always considerable danger that his hatred of the Hammertons would greatly tend to reduce the trifling affection he had formed for Amelia.

Notwithstanding all his vows of reformation, all his glorious disregard for money whilst no one assailed his pocket, still there came over his mind not the most genial reminiscence of what his father had said relative to a certain sum being very likely to belong to the lady which ought in common fairness to have belonged to him. There is not in the whole range of classical quotations one truer than that "*Amor nummi crescit quantum ipse pecuniæ crescit.*" A man may have enough of love, friendship, wine, children, weekly bills, and other domestic nuisances; but he never can have enough of money: it grows with its growth, and increases with its increase. If a man had the large pyramid of Egypt in solid gold, he would wish for a weathercock of the same, merely to see the sun's rays dazzling over his massy hoard. It is human nature: wealth is power, and every man is desirous of power.

"Some letters from the admiral's office for you, sir," said Mr. Harris. "Mr. Jones desired me to give them to you on your arrival, as he believes they are of consequence."

"Have you breakfasted, Mr. Harris?" A midshipman

has never breakfasted *sufficiently;* so Mr. Harris responded that he had not.

"Where is the boat?"

"At Sally-Port, sir."

"Tell the coxswain to take care of the crew, and bring one of the men up here: I've some things to send on board."

Whilst Harris scudded down to the boat, Murray changed his dress for his uniform, and more than once looked at his right shoulder, and regretted he was not three years older, in order that his left also might have an epaulet. His servant had provided breakfast, and Mr. Harris and the captain sat down to a very disagreeable *tête-à-tête;* the midshipman by no means liking the look—the *mild* look—of his commander, and Murray being very anxious to read and answer his letters. The first was from the admiral, desiring Murray to complete the complement of the *Arethusa* by pressing men; a circumstance which was by no means congenial to his notions, for he had imbibed many of the ideas of his former captain, and amongst others this,—that in pressing men you invariably get the worst kind, for it is only the idle and the worthless who are to be taken. You have then to run the risk of contaminating the better men, by mixing them up with a set of low, worthless vagabonds, who are addicted to every vice, and who would commit any crime rather than labour for their daily bread. There is always danger in such heterogeneous mixtures; and although many of the pressed men have turned out the best seamen, yet, generally speaking, they do not come to their duty with that alacrity which the man does who has chosen the sea for his profession, and is anxious to excel in the path of life his own intentions dictated.

"Well, Mr. Harris," said Captain Murray, "I suppose you are a little more comfortable in your berth since you gave up the republican mess for one more consonant with the feelings of gentlemen?"

"Yes, sir," replied Harris, thinking at the same time just the contrary; for he was a stout young lad, and made more by force than he could get by equal distribution.

"I am astonished," continued the captain, "that you should have chosen a manner of life which can be beneficial only to the strong, and which must often leave the weak and the sickly to have recourse to very improper methods to get a dinner."

"It is a common saying, sir, 'Every man for himself, and God for us all.'"

"If every man in this world, Mr. Harris, only thought of himself, one half of the living would die of want, of cold, of sickness, and there would be an end to all friendship, all affection, all love."

Here Captain Murray saw a most unofficerlike smile upon his guest's countenance; however, he discovered that the disrespect in the midshipman did not arise from any levity of conduct during the "wise saws" of his captain, whose fancy was straying in Somersetshire, and who had jammed the admiral's order into the teapot, making tea of the letters instead of the leaf. He smiled himself when he discovered his own absence of mind, for which he could give no very satisfactory reason even to himself, and which became doubly annoying when he afterwards found himself filling the cream-ewer with boiling water, instead of the teapot. His mind was wandering between his affection for himself and the discipline which he intended to enforce, with an occasional ramble through his father's shrubbery, which caused him, instead of asking his midshipman if he would take some more toast, to sing,

"Forbid it, devotion and law;
Forbid it, affection and love."

The fact was, that Mr. Harris returned on board perfectly satisfied that his captain was only fit for a berth in Bedlam; whilst Walter Murray was quite annoyed to think he should have such a very inattentive midshipman as Mr. William Harris.

Captain Murray waited upon the admiral, received his orders, and then went on board to make preparations for the evening, with the intention of dining there in order to see what he did want. Mr. Jones was invited, and at four o'clock, the feeding-hour, the surgeon and Mr. Harris walked into the cabin: Captain Murray then eating his first dinner on board his new ship.

With regard to the decorations of the table, it has been admitted that no man in his Majesty's navy could surpass

Walter Murray's; and there no man could be more thoroughly a gentleman in his manner. But there was always a little of the old failing: under the covers of the silver dishes there was a great deficiency of come-at-ables; the saving propensity was marked even in the number of potatoes; and more than one officer had observed, that, like the marines' mess, Captain Murray's table was all outside show. It was, as another said, "great cry and little wool;" and every one who had dined with him during his former command, remarked, "that he was prodigal of show, but very niggardly in substance."

The dinner passed off as all dinners do in a captain's cabin. If he is familiar, easy, and cheerful in his manner, his officers are the same; if distant, sullen, morose, there is little said and the time is curtailed. On this occasion the company were remarkably cheerful—a sure sign that the barometer of Walter's good-nature was rather high.

The feast over, Captain Murray began the conversation nearest his heart—his abhorrence of impressment.

"I cannot," he began, "Mr. Jones, sufficiently express to you how grieved I feel about this order to complete the ship's company by these means, for I have long entertained the same opinion as my former captain,—that forcing men to become sailors, taking them from their own firesides, leaving their wives and children to the chances of life, cannot be upheld as a laudable principle by any one; and I regret that my duty as an officer must overcome my feelings as a man."

"I do not, I confess, sir," answered Mr. Jones, "look on this question in the serious manner you do. It is evident somebody must do the work; some men must be made seamen, or we should never be able to meet our foes; and, as in days gone by, we might see an enemy's fleet off Fort Tilbury. Besides, on board a ship, they are clothed, fed, weaned from their light-fingered propensities, and made respectable servants of the state."

"I rather fancy, Mr. Jones, that is more in imagination than reality. During their early lives, it is true that the constant employment, the continued exertion, the hope of prize-money, the delight with which they welcome the land after a long cruise, their frequent visits to foreign harbours and strange countries, may make them forget the cruelty of the force which compelled them to become sailors, and which compulsion is only acted on in the cases of the wretched and the miserable. The rich talk of liberty, while they enslave their fellow-men! Tell me, upon what grounds can you justify the proceeding which takes from an Englishman his natural liberty, and makes him as subservient to the caprice of the articles of war as a Russian serf in regard to his master?"

"Upon the principle, sir," replied Mr. Jones, with much eagerness, "of necessity. Necessity, they say, is the mother of invention; and it has invented this, the only way of manning the navy; and certainly it is the only efficacious mode I have ever heard of. In reality you do the man a great favour,—exactly as much as in the slave trade. You take a poor wretch who is dying of want; you feed him, clothe him, attend him in sickness, contribute to all his comforts; and, in return, require of him merely his manual labour."

"You tear him from his friends," interrupted the captain; "you forcibly dissolve all the ties by which he has bound himself to his family; you deny him his choice in what manner he may benefit the state; by force you take on board a man habituated to the land, and with one cut of the sailmaker's shears, you make outwardly a sailor, and inwardly a discontented being. Having exhausted his strength, ruined his health, brought on premature old age—for sailors are always older than their fellow-creatures—you turn him adrift, to die in some ditch, to be taken as a subject for anatomy; and in this case bring him in comparison with another ill-used animal; for very few have ever seen a dead donkey or a very old sailor."

"Surely, sir, you overlook the reward of faithful service in Greenwich Hospital. There a man injured by the wear and tear of the service comes safely to anchor, until declining life hauls down his pendant and puts him out of commission; his hull, when broken up, is safely deposited. Having enjoyed 'a youth of labour with an age of ease,' he is followed to the grave by his former messmates, and his name is left on the records of the Hospital as one who had done his country good service."

"Mighty poetical, Mr. Jones!' interrupted the surgeon; "but how many ever get into Greenwich? and how many ever have the curiosity to read over the long list of Smiths, Browns, or Joneses, which fill up the soiled leaves of the Hospital books?"

"Why, twenty thousand men are provided for by Greenwich. And I have ever been taught," said Mr. Jones, "from the first day I sailed in the *Agamemnon* with Nelson, up to this date, to consider impressment as a necessary evil, and for which the wisdom of man had never been able to find a substitute."

"I do not consider the case," said Walter, "so desperate. I know it was and is the opinion of as gallant an officer, and a man who has the interest of the navy as much at heart as any one alive, that the navy might be manned at all times in the following manner.—Never mind the coffee just yet, steward; bring another bottle of wine."—(the steward had given the guests their allowance, which was a pint a man, and according to Murray's instructions, in order to save the expense of another bottle, had brought in the coffee; a gentle hint that the allowance was finished, and that the last turn of the white wine would finish the repast.)—"Each county in England," continued the captain, "provides a certain number of men drawn for the militia, and these men take to the line of life thus selected for them with apparent, and mostly sincere, contentment. Remember, if they have been industrious, they can buy a substitute; and the substitute receives his reward much in the same manner as a volunteer receives the bounty money. Now, why is it impossible to draw men for the navy in the same manner, charging the county, which has to provide a certain number, with all the expenses of their removal from place to place? Let the government make it worth a man's trouble to become a good seaman, by giving an increase of bounty at a certain period after the man is first received on board. As the inland counties would not be able perhaps to find volunteers for the sea-service, let those counties find a double proportion of militiamen, and the maritime counties be released in proportion of the militia, doubling the number of seamen. Here there would be no force, no compulsion, no landing after dark to pounce upon an unfortunate wretch in bed, to drag him on board a ship, to place him shivering under the half-deck, and, in fact, to make a man a prisoner until he can be tamed into being trusted at large."

"The plan, no doubt, is a good one, sir," replied Mr. Jones: "but it is not, in my mind—and I hint the difficulty with great deference—quite satisfactory. Suppose, sir, you require to man a fleet suddenly: how are you to get these men? For instance, here we are forty men short of complement; and although, thank heaven! these forty men would not make us inferior to a French frigate which had twice our number, yet we should feel a little more at ease with our enemy if we had them. We are to sail the day after to-morrow. A circular written to the different authorities would not reach them before we ought to be at sea; and if this is the case in a frigate, what would it be with a fleet?"

"There again, Mr. Jones, I shall meet the difficulty: the object of my plan is only half-developed to you. I should have a regular depot of seamen on board the guard-ships in the different harbours. These men, by being in the first instance removed to the guard-ships, would gradually get reconciled to their situation; the songs of the older seamen would give them a little enthusiasm in the cause; and our forty men, whom we require at so short a notice, would be drafted on board this very evening. The emptying of the prisons, and the impressment of seamen, are both calculated to disgust the real straightforward, honest sailor. He finds himself obliged to associate with a man who has escaped the gallows merely because he is required as a seaman; and you know, Mr. Jones, it is a custom to place these wretched men in messes with the best and most steady seamen; so that the honest man and the convicted rogue are forced together, to the great injury of the first, and perhaps to the dislike of the latter;—oil and water never mix."

"If such a plan could succeed, sir," replied Mr. Jones, "I have no hesitation in saying it would be preferable; nothing can be worse than the present system; and, at any rate, it might be worth while trying. But I fear, sir, to-night we must go on the old beaten track, and try our luck as others have done before us."

"Have you made all arrangements, Mr. Jones, for this night's marauding?"

"Yes, sir; in all but one instance. Mr. Weazel is on shore on leave, and he is the best hand at a press-gang in the navy: no difficulty daunts him, and he keeps his temper under every circumstance; he begins by a joke, and uses force only when it is absolutely necessary. He has a wonderful talent for addressing a mob; and all the taunts and jibes of the ruffians by whom he may be surrounded only keep him in better humour. I am very sorry he is not here; and as to finding him, he is much too knowing for that: directly he goes on shore, he gets into the most out-of-the-way places, but he comes back to his time as regular as a chronometer."

"I fear," remarked the captain, "that his morals are none of the best."

"Morality in a midshipman, sir," interrupted Mr. Jones, "is as unlikely as generosity in a miser!"

"Steward, bring coffee! Will you take some white wine, Mr. Jones?" Thus the hint was given that the dinner was over, and that every man should retire.

About nine o'clock the boats of the *Arethusa* left the ship, in order to make out her complement by impressment. Mr. Jones himself took charge of the expedition: he landed on the Gosport side of the harbour, where he was met by a magistrate, without whose presence Mr. Jones could not have forced an entrance into any but a public-house. As plenty of ships had latterly been obliged to recruit their numbers by the same means now employed by the frigate, the idle and dissolute took care to remove a short distance from their usual haunts about dusk; and although house after house was ransacked, not one was caught. At last there was a cry of "Lug him out! never mind his kicking; he is just the build for us!" and a round, thick-set young man was pulled out of a house, with a silk handkerchief round his head, which had served as a nightcap. He was sufficiently dressed to be decent; and endeavoured to make good his escape by using his fists pretty freely. "Down with him!" said one; "Give him a crack over the figure-head!" said another; "Hold him fast!" said a third; "Trip him up!" said a fourth; whilst he manfully defended himself, doubling about like a hare, and facing his enemies at every turn. At last he was seized, and tumbled into the boat. The night was excessively dark, and no one had troubled himself to look at the features of the victim; it was sufficient that he was young, stout, and active; and as he lay particularly quiet, no one disturbed him with questions. Two hours had been lost, and only one man taken, when it was resolved once more to beat up the rounds: this was done without success, the whole press-gang returning towards the boat by the broad street of the town. They had not proceeded far before they fell in with a man dressed as a seaman, with a Panama hat, large enough for an umbrella: he was steering a little wildly, and was brought up all standing by Jones.

"Holloa, my lad!" began the first lieutenant, "who are you?"

"I expect that's a tarnation piece of impertinence of yours, which I calculate is not likely to be gratified by an answer."

"Who are you, I say?" repeated Mr. Jones.

"Why, I'm a real Virginia man, born and bred; and I guess I've grown more tobacco than either you or your gang here ever smoked."

"How came you here, sir?" said Jones.

"That's what I call a pretty particular piece of impertinence," responded the stranger; "but as I'm a civil kind of a person in a foreign country, I'll tell you."

"Come, sir," said Jones, "cut short that long yarn, if you please; we are not going to swallow your nonsense. What are you—where do you live—where do you come from, and where are you going?"

"I expect," remarked the stranger, "that no man in the States ever asked so many questions at once without any probability of getting an answer."

"Are you an American?"

"Yes, I calculate."

"Are you a sailor?"

"I expect I am, too."

"Have you got your protection?"

"Yes, in this stick, I reckon."

"Then you reckon very wrong!—Hand him down to the

boat; if that's all the protection he has got, break it over his own head if he does not walk quietly along."

The men instantly seized the American, who, finding all opposition vain, kept saying, in the usual nasal intonation of that country, "This, I calculate, is too bad! I reckon our President will go to war about it; and if we don't pull down the pride a bit of you Englishers, there's no snakes in Virginia."

Mr. Jones cared very little about such a threat and such consequences. Grumbling at his ill-success, he returned to his boat; the men took their respective stations, and were soon alongside the frigate; the pressed men were safely lodged on board without being bound or shackled; the boat was hoisted up, the men sent down below to their hammocks; but when the midshipman of the watch turned round in order to place the two pressed men under the half-deck, where a sail had been spread for their slumbers, only one could be found, and he was the American.

The boat was lowered directly, the ship was searched, and although an hour was wasted in pulling backwards and forwards, the man who fought so well for his freedom could not be found; it was quite evident he had escaped, and this too whilst numbers of men were on deck. It was a strong ebb tide; and had the poor fellow taken to the water he must have been swept out to St. Helen's.

"This is bad work, indeed," said Mr. Jones, "if a man to avoid serving his king prefers losing his life! If that man went overboard, he is drowned to a certainty. Faith! this would make me of the captain's opinion." And, not a little vexed at the loss, Mr. Jones turned in.

At daylight he was roused up by Mr. Weazel, who gave him a letter from the captain, desiring him to have the *Arethusa* in readiness to weigh at nine o'clock; that orders had come down for her to sail directly, and that the hour above-mentioned would certainly be the latest allowed.

"Why, Mr. Weazel," said the first lieutenant, "this is the first time I ever recollect your coming off before your leave was expired. Did you meet the captain last night?"

"No, sir," said Weazel; "I was *obliged* to come off much against my will."

"Turn the hands up, unmoor ship," said Mr. Jones.

"And here, Mr. Weazel," he continued: "pray, has the other pressed man escaped?"

"No, sir," replied Weazel: "I saw him in the spare topsail under the half-deck as I came down the hatchway"

"Ah!" ejaculated Mr. Jones, "I would give ten pounds to hear that poor fellow was safe who went overboard last night. I never shall be a happy man again! for I consider myself the cause of his death."

"Which anchor shall we weigh first, sir?" said Weazel.

"Tell the master we are going to unmoor," was the reply. The master was called, the messenger passed, the small bower weighed, the ship hove short upon the other anchor, and before eight o'clock the *Arethusa* was ready for a start —the decks clean, the ropes coiled down, and all those preparations made which mark a well-disciplined ship. It was quite astonishing with what readiness Jonathan Corncob, the impressed man, fell into the necessity of turning all occurrences to the best advantage. Before the first anchor was weighed, and whilst Mr. Chips was seeing his crew at work shipping and swifting the capstan-bars, Mr. Jones desired the new man to be sent on deck, and shortly afterwards Jonathan appeared. His Panama hat was crushed upon his head, his dress was soiled with mud, his face begrimed with dirt, and his whole appearance that of a sailor in a long coat, fatigued by a debauch overnight.

"Last night," commenced Mr. Jones, "you told me that you were a seafaring man. What part of the ship have you done your duty in?"

"In the cabin, I expect," said Jonathan.

"None of your nonsense, sir!" said Mr. Jones. "Mr. Chips, knock off that fellow's skull-thatcher—that roof of straw he has jammed over his head!"—(The carpenter did as he was ordered in a quiet manner, whispering into Jonathan's ear, "A mild answer turneth away wrath.") —"I'll teach you manners with a rope's end for a master in a minute!" said Mr. Jones. "Where did you do your duty, sir?"

Jonathan saw it was no use warring against such elements; so, moderating his independence, he said with a look of submission, "I expect, sir, it's no use my telling you, for you won't believe me; I am a gentleman in the

States, and came over in my own vessel, now lying in the harbour."

"Stuff and nonsense!" interrupted Mr. Jones, who in reality did not wish to hear anything that was likely to leave him minus a man. "Sailmaker, cut off this chap's tails!" (it was done in a moment;) "there, lay into the bars." Jonathan was placed the outside man by those who preferred doing the least, and felt no inclination to jump over carronade slides, the inside man being invariably a skulker, and having one-half less to do than the outside man. "Hold on below—heave round!" and Jonathan Corncob found himself performing much the same occupation as a horse in a mill. Finding himself obliged to work, he did it freely; but whenever he passed the first lieutenant, he got out as much of himself as he could,—"Daughter ashore, I expect." By the time he had delivered himself of that, he was on the other side of the deck. As he successively came round, "Protection" and "President"—"Poor child all alone!"—"I expect I am done clean slick"—"All over before dark"—"Captain shall give satisfaction"—"I reckon those who take a scorpion by the tail get a sting in their paws."

The men, as Jonathan worked away, could not help laughing, and they ran round the quicker in order to work him the more. The anchor aweigh, the capstan pauled, Jonathan took out his pocket-handkerchief, and, wiping his face, turned round to Mr. Chips, and said, "I calculate this is hot work; it beats Shadrach, Meshech, and Abednego to immortal smash!" Chips was perfectly horrified, and, looking at the American with an eye of commiseration, said, "A wise man keepeth a silent tongue."

No sooner was the duty done, than Jonathan found a good-natured seaman to lend him some paper; and he forthwith wrote a letter to his daughter, detailing his situation, and desiring her to go immediately to the agent, mention the circumstance, and get him released. For a long time he endeavoured in vain to give his letter to the bumboat-woman; the sentries on the gangways having particular orders to keep a good look-out that he did not escape. He gave the old woman a dollar to carry it on shore directly; but the old lady, finding that her bread and butter sold well as the ship was going to sea, did not shove off until the hands were again turned up—the captain close alongside.

No sooner was the captain on board, than the boatswain's whistle was heard, and "Hands, up boats!" followed. This required but a minute; "Up anchor!" followed; and before Jonathan could get near the captain, the anchor was aweigh, the sails set, and the *Arethusa*, under a crowd of canvas, standing out of St. Helen's. Captain Murray had gone below to look over his orders; and before he returned on deck, Jonathan was stationed, quartered, messed—had a hammock and some purser's slops served out to him, and was as regularly in for the cruise as any seaman on board the ship.

CHAPTER XXV

UNEXPECTED MEETING.—FREDERICK HAMMERTON.—CAPTURE BY AN ALGERINE PIRATE.

WHILST the *Arethusa* is standing out to sea, we must look back to Sir Hector Murray Desirous of keeping up the affection which he thought had been kindled on both sides, he proposed to his adopted child Amelia to start for Portsmouth, in order to see his son in his proud situation. He knew enough of the female mind to be aware that the deference and respect paid to Walter would greatly tend to forward his views in the heart of Amelia;—that ladies, however modest in themselves, are partial to men who are placed in authority; and that nothing tends more to smooth the difficulties of love than public notoriety.

Amelia, who had seen and been a principal performer at the launch of the *Arethusa*, wished to see her in trim order, with the only man she ever cared the least about as her captain. Walter had given a rather flourishing account of the power he possessed; and there is something in power mighty fascinating even to a woman. Amelia, therefore, coincided with Sir Hector on this point, as she invariably did upon every wish he expressed; and early in the morning following Walter's departure, Sir Hector and Amelia were on their road to Portsmouth.

They arrived, having slept on the road, just in time to see the ship standing out under a crowd of sail from Spithead; and Sir Hector thought he remarked a tear start from Amelia's eyes, when she saw the gallant frigate, with him she sincerely loved on board, every moment growing less in the offing, whilst sail after sail was crowded, as if he who commanded her was anxious to increase his distance. Sir Hector watched the frigate; his pride to a certain degree was satisfied, for there is no situation more enviable than that of captain of a frigate to a young aspiring man at the commencement of or during an active war. He overheard with delight the remarks of the old seamen and boatmen who were standing on the Parade Battery, making their observations upon the manner with which the sails were set: she really "walked the waters like a thing of life," and well merited the name of the "dashing *Arethusa.*"

Whilst Sir Hector and Amelia were watching the frigate, she gradually drew from the shore, and lessened on the view. Neither spoke; but their attention was soon aroused by the sudden appearance of a girl, dragging, rather than accompanying, an elderly man.

"He is there, I tell you," pointing to the *Arethusa*; "that is the ship he was taken on board of last night. Do, sir,—do run to the admiral!—a signal might yet be seen!—Oh, sir, for mercy's sake—for the sake of a poor child left fatherless, to starve in a foreign land!"

The tone, the manner, the words of this application awakened all the generous feelings of Amelia, and she instantly turned to the object in such poignant distress. She saw a fine young woman on her knees before the old man, whose feelings evidently were not so much excited as the applicant's.

"Gently, gently, young lady; don't be in such a hurry—have patience."

"Patience, indeed!" replied the poor creature; "you ask me to have patience when every moment renders it less likely to recover my father. Sir, sir," said she, addressing herself to Sir Hector, "you will have some mercy—you will assist a poor forlorn stranger, whose father was last night pressed by mistake, and sent on board that frigate now sailing away."

"The *Arethusa?*" interrupted Amelia.

"Yes, miss, yes; that old man is my father's agent. Oh, sir, quiek, quiek—every moment renders me more and more miserable!"

"I fear," said Sir Heetor, mueh moved by the girl's eager manner, "that it is now too late; but I will go instantly to the admiral. The ship is eommanded by my son, and perhaps I may have interest enough to serve you."

"I ean show you the way, sir," said the girl. "Turn to the right after we leave the parade;—quieker, sir, quieker!"

"Quieker, ehild, quieker! Why, you think that my old limbs ean run a raee with youth! My intentions might rival your own—my wishes to serve you might be equal to your wishes to be served; but my legs will not be a bit the less stiff, or my joints a jot the more supple. There—walk over to the inn with Miss Hammerton, and she will take eare of you until my return."

"Miss Hammerton!" eried the stranger; "then I may yet find a friend. Have you a brother, miss, in the navy?"

"I have, or had," said Amelia, with a sigh.

"Was he ever left to wander on the world a stranger, without a penny, without friends, without assistanee?"

"All, all, and ten times worse," replied Amelia; "but he found a friend on the shores of the Chesapeake, and was grateful for the kindness he reeeived."

"Oh, heaven, I thank you for this unlooked-for kindness! Then you know the name of the man who was a friend to him—of the girl who ——?"

"I do," replied Amelia.

"Then, to the sister of the man she onee sheltered, Maria Corneob now asks the only kindness she ever asked in her life from friend or stranger. My father is torn from me—he is made to serve a foreign nation—he is a eommon pressed sailor on board the *Arethusa.*" Here the poor girl fell down upon a sofa, (for they had reaehed the apartments oeeupied by Sir Hector,) hid her faee in her handkerehief, and sobbed bitterly. She heeded not the kind words of Amelia, but, suddenly raising her head, eontinued, "I must not be idle here; I must go and throw myself at the admiral's feet—I must."

"Stay, stay," said Amelia; "you have awakened feelings not easily lulled: you have sheltered my own, my only brother, and he has told me still more than has escaped your lips. Remain quiet; leave it to me and Sir Hector Murray: the girl who was engaged to be my sister-in-law will not find a cold friend in her probable relative. It is useless, however, blinding oneself with hope; this breeze, which has so unfortunately freshened, has long since driven the *Arethusa* from all signal-distance: but be assured that your father will not be hurt on board, that a few days will see him returned, and that during his absence his interests will not suffer. In these times ships sail and return every month: the admiral will tell Sir Hector to what station the ship is sent, and you have only to keep quiet, and endeavour to reconcile yourself to what for the present is unavoidable."

"Your brother Frederick," said Maria, with a faltering voice,—"is he on board that frigate also?"

The blood forsook Amelia's face. Her brother! who could tell that she had a brother? and who could be so void of feeling as at that moment to have crushed the hope which evidently had taken root in Maria's heart? A little dissimulation, a slight variation from the actual truth, could not be culpable: "He is not on board the *Arethusa*," she said; "but I hope and trust he is well, and soon likely to return."

"One question more, Miss Hammerton, and I *will* be satisfied. Has he ever thought of—?"

"—You," interrupted Amelia. "Often, often has he told me of all your father's kindness when he was a beggar upon his bounty. Your father was repaid, I believe, by Sir Hector Murray, who will now be glad that an opportunity has occurred to return the attention you and your family bestowed upon Frederick. That is Sir Hector's step; one moment's more anxiety, and you will be, I trust, satisfied."

"Sir, sir," said Maria, as the baronet entered; "is the ship stopped and poor father released?"

"My good young woman," said Sir Hector, "sit down; don't agitate yourself, you really confuse me—old men must have their own way. Now listen, and don't do as most women do—cry about nothing. I have been to the admiral: the signal was made for the flag-ship at Spithead to recall the *Arethusa*, and the answer was, "Out of signal-distance." It was unfortunate, but could not be remedied. I asked the frigate's destination: she has sailed under sealed orders, and on that account I can give you very little information as to your father's destiny. There, now, don't cry—it is nothing at all: my son is as mild as milk—he would not hurt the most insignificant thing alive; and when he finds out the mistake, he will of course send back your father by the pilot-boat. Pray, what is your name?"

"Maria Corncob."

"Maria Corncob! Why, Amelia, I have some recollection of that name; but I'm sure it was not fifty years ago, or I should remember more about it. Events do not fix themselves now so strongly as in youth; and old Time rubs out the picture as quickly as it is painted on the brain."

Here Amelia interposed, and mentioned the preceding conversation, with some trifling additions which may be easily imagined. Sir Hector immediately rang his bell, and having learned the address of the agent to whom the *Matchless* had been consigned, took every precaution to insure the amount of the cargo. He left particular directions for all accounts to be forwarded to the daughter at his house in Somersetshire; and having given directions that Maria's wardrobe might be removed from the schooner, which vessel was to be kept in good order at Sir Hector's expense, two hours after he had left the admiral's office, Maria Corncob was safely placed in the baronet's carriage, and was rolling away into the country, whilst her father was *rolling* away from it; one in a very comfortable conveyance, going to a remarkably comfortable house—the other having before him the constant dread of a captain in his Majesty's navy, liable to all calls, and with every prospect of having his way freshened by a boatswain's mate, being a seaman under one of the smartest men in his Majesty's navy.

Maria Corncob was duly housed in Sir Hector's habitation, and the friendship of the ladies increased with the length of their acquaintance. Sir Hector found his evenings pass more cheerfully, Amelia had a virtuous companion, and Maria was soon benefited by the society in which she was so fortunately placed: the American idiom and nasal intonation were soon changed for the English pronunciation; Amelia found a cheerful friend, Maria an instructive companion.

In the mean time we may give some account of another of the principal actors in life's drama as belonging to our story. It has been mentioned that Frederick Hammerton had embarked on board the *Rover* packet, in order to join his ship in the Mediterranean. Malta was at this time become a harbour of much importance to England: the surrender of that important island had been followed by its conversion into an English arsenal. The islanders, soon convinced that a greater protection would be afforded them by belonging to a powerful nation than being under the influence either of their own body or of the beaten French, wisely became good and quiet subjects. They were allowed to retain all their religious prejudices; the governor, Sir Alexander Ball, being a man well suited both from his courage and his kindness to enforce and to maintain obedience.

At Gibraltar Hammerton heard that the *Leonidas* was at Malta, or likely to be near that island; and again the packet was under a crowd of sail for her ultimate destination. The wind was fair, and she soon came into the tideless sea under a crowd of canvas. She had passed Oran without seeing a stranger; but at daylight, when nearly abreast of Algiers, a very suspicious sail was seen to windward: she was lateen-rigged, low, and being plainly visible, was discovered to be full of men.

The wind, which had blown a moderate breeze, now died away into a calm, and both vessels lay about four miles apart, apparently without noticing each other, for no colours were shown; but very different was the case in reality. On board the packet every glass was in requisition: the vessel—the low, lurking vessel, was seen to have altered her position, and two sweeps were discovered at work keeping her head towards the packet. The useless sails, as they swung from the long unwieldy yards, showed in their flapping a long gun mounted forward in the vessel, and it was evident that the men were busily engaged in getting it ready for service, which accounted for only two sweeps being in use.

No time was lost on board the packet in making preparations for the coming fight. The captain, a bold, straightforward seaman, was by no means inclined to despond; he saw in his adversary but (comparatively speaking) a boat, with, as he termed them, a ragamuffin crew of dirty Turks—a kind of boat with only one gun; whilst on board of his brig he could show six, and could muster thirty men, all good seamen, with their hands ready to obey their hearts. No precaution, however, was neglected: the men were mustered with their arms; the guns—if such pop-guns as six-pounders can be dignified into great guns—were examined, loaded, primed; precautions were taken to secure the yards, and, in fact, all the little circumstances of war rigidly attended to.

On board the Algerine pirate, for such she was, great exertions had been made. The long gun which now peeped over the bows had during the breeze which commenced the night before been lowered into the bottom of the boat: the sight of the packet at daylight, their vicinity to a friendly port, decided the Algerines to make an attack as soon as possible, and, as is mostly the case with the strongest, every circumstance tended to favour them. The calm was much in their favour,—the enemy could be approached on her weakest point; by the aid of her oars the Algerine possessed the power of flight if it were requisite, and in commencing the action, of a guarded and optional approach.

These marauders of the seas knew well that the vessel in sight was not a man-of-war. She might have hoisted a pendant as long as herself; but her build, her sails, would be the strongest evidence against the fact. The Algerines, long used to attack the unwary, were seldom caught by any disguise: they knew their victims, and when and where to pounce upon them.

It was about seven o'clock in the morning that the captain of the packet observed the Algerine brail up her sails, hoist her colours, and put in use about thirty oars. The brig was at this time in a dead calm; not the slightest flaw of wind disturbed the smooth mirror of the ocean, and not the least hope could be entertained by reference to the clear unclouded sky that any breeze would come down to give her steerage-way. It was useless fearing the danger—the best plan was manfully to oppose it; and Hammerton, who had been in many an action, cheered up the crew by his resolute behaviour.

There were some females on board, one a girl of much pretension to beauty. These, fortunately, were not aware of the danger: they saw the felucca coming towards them, but she looked so insignificantly small, that not one of the sex considered herself as in the slightest jeopardy. But when they saw the anxious look of their captain, and the energetic manner of Hammerton, who had conquered the whole of them by imitating Othello, and talking of his hair-breadth escapes, they began to think that something a little more than they expected was likely to be the result.

When the captain persuaded them to go below, they manifested not a little surprise; but the whiz of the long gun, as the shot of the pirate passed over their heads, freshened their way down the hatchway, and in two minutes they were all at prayers in right earnest, fully persuaded that they were already victims to the pirate's fancies.

On the receipt of this iron messenger, the captain was for returning the compliment; but Hammerton, who knew their only chance was in close action, persuaded his commander not to fire until he was quite certain the shot would go over her: "for," said he, "if they find our pop-guns will not reach, they will remain out of our gun-shot, and riddle us with that long Tom, which seems to be well managed, for that last shot struck us. If we can get her alongside, we may clear her open deck with some grape and canister; and if it comes to boarding, we shall have all the advantage of British seamen used to such service, and ready and willing to maintain aloft our glorious flag."

Another shot, which passed through the main rigging and grazed the mainmast, convinced the captain that practical gunnery had been a favourite pastime with his enemy; and he suggested that by firing in the calm, the smoke might prevent the Algerine from being so sure of his mark.

Hammerton opposed it. "Take it coolly," he said, "for that is our best chance. Let the men lie down; and don't attempt to show our weakness by firing those twopenny-halfpenny things, which if they were blazed in a salute during a squall, the man to windward would never know that the lee gun had been fired. We must get them close before we fire: but we may as well let them see the ensign, which just now is all up and down like a donkey's fore leg."

The Algerine was not slow in returning the civility. She hoisted her flag upon a little ensign staff which was shipped on her taffrail, not being ashamed to show the Algerine colours; then, by way of drawing attention, she fired another shot, and altered her course, so as to render it plainly perceptible. Again she steered for the packet, being about a mile and a half distant.

The women, whose ears were quick, when the real danger was known, proposed an instant surrender; but Hammerton soon gave them to understand that Turks and pirates never listened much to terms of surrender, and that the worst part would come after they had possession of the packet.

In the mean time, the Algerine advanced, firing well-directed shots at her opponent—hardly one missed: Hammerton, who perceived the courage of the men around him gradually growing less as every shot told, began to alter his opinion about reserving the fire; and as the pirate was now well within reach, he hinted that if all the guns were brought over on the larboard side, and fired steadily one after the other, the six guns might be doubled in the apprehension of the cautious Algerine, and prompt him to relinquish the contest. This was accordingly done; the captain firing the first gun, and Hammerton the next. Great care was taken to point them well; and thus the action commenced on the part of the packet. Although every shot went in a good direction, not one struck the felucca: some fell close alongside, the others went over her. No sooner was the smoke cleared away, than the pirate was seen to have altered her course, and to have put her head the other way, pulling hard. It immediately struck the captain that Hammerton was right in his calculation; and they continued firing at their retreating enemy until it was evident that the short sixes would not reach their destination.

The Algerine now faced about, and again had recourse to the long gun; and it was evidently not his intention to come within reach of the sixes until he had completely vanquished his enemy. There was no sign of a breeze—not a ripple visible upon the water; and all hope from flight, or being enabled to close with the enemy, was soon relinquished. The only chance was creating a smoke, which might serve as a cloud to conceal the packet, and thus avoid offering so fair a mark:—a breeze might spring up; and, if so, a little retaliation might be played off upon the Turks. But Hammerton was aboard: he was a Jonas—every step of his life had been unfortunate; he had met with more reverses than half the profession put together, and he foresaw in his present situation a climax to his woes.

Every shot of the Algerine took effect. The smoke from the packet's guns shrouded the unfortunate vessel; but there was not an air of wind to spread it—it hung over her, making her, if possible, an easier mark. Considerable damage had been done to her mast and yards; her hull was cut in all directions; five men were killed, and about twelve wounded, when the rest came aft, and requested the captain to strike, as prolonging the contest was a wanton waste of life.

Hammerton here interposed; and after stating that in fair and upright warfare he would be the last to suggest a treachery, yet on this occasion, when their lives would be sacrificed by the cruel disposition of the pirates, he thought all deceit was fair to practise in order to escape. He seconded the idea of striking the colours and of ceasing to fire: "but," said he, "we will keep armed and ready; and if she runs us on board, we will die like men, with swords in our hands, and not be slaughtered like sheep by such butchers as these pirates."

When a brave man stands forward to address sailors in any emergency, it is quite astonishing how readily they follow his advice. An instant murmur of applause followed the development of the plan; the firing ceased, and the colours were struck. Instantly another thought occurred to Hammerton, and he called out to the men again to hoist the colours, and renew the fire; and they obeyed him without asking why or wherefore.

"Now, sir," he said to the captain,—"now is our time, I think, to try to effect an escape, or to drive the enemy away from us. We have three boats; let us get them out, and keep them on the starboard side ready for use. One of two plans may be adopted: either to place the passengers and the crews in the boats, and leaving some oakum to smoke in different parts of the decks, shove off, keep the pirate and the packet in a line, and pull right away; or to put the best and bravest of the men in the boats, give three cheers, and make an attempt to board the pirate. In the first case, we must not forget the provisions; I have had one turn at starvation, and don't like it at all; and the boats must take each other in tow, placing the women in the centre boat. Or, if you are for a desperate rally and a little revenge at our turban-headed antagonist, I will either lead the boats, or obey your orders should you propose to command."

"They are both good plans, Mr. Hammerton," said the captain, "and show how cool must be the projector. I think in this affair we had better consult the ship's company."

"On no account," said Hammerton. "Call them aft, and tell them which you are resolved to do: they will follow you anywhere. If you leave it to choice, there are always one or two not so brave as the rest; and if they happen to speak out, you will have a run-away proposed: fear soon spreads itself—it is quicker than an electric shock, and every one feels afraid before the shock is actually communicated. You may read a proposition for flight half an hour before it is spoken; and if once you get a retreat into a sailor's head, the devil himself, horns, tail, and all, will never rally them. For my part, if you ask me which I vote for, I tell you at once I would rather face fifty Algerines than have one long pull in a boat with a scarcity of water and short of provisions:—a burnt child dreads the fire, captain."

The captain smiled at the cool manner of Hammerton, and, being himself a brave seaman, he readily agreed to the more desperate undertaking. The men were called; they were told what was proposed and determined upon, and, giving three cheers, they jumped into the boats and got the oars ready to pass.

The captain was in the quickest, Hammerton in the slowest boat; the plan being to tow each other, steering a direct course for the pirate, and, when perceived, to separate: the captain's and the other boat to board on the starboard quarter; the launch, as she was called, to board on the bow. Three or four boys were left on board the packet to fire the guns occasionally without shot, and to keep some oakum and shavings burning, so as to disguise the attack The seamen, now sure of a hand-to-hand contest, exhibited symptoms of that daring, unconquerable spirit which was so conspicuous during the whole of the long war. For some time they were unperceived; indeed they had neared the Algerine to half a mile before a discharge of grape, canister, broken nails, and all manner of deadly ministers came rattling into the boats. "Cast off! cast off!" was the cry; one boat cheered the other; the seamen bent their backs with a good will, each steering for the station already agreed upon. They forced their boats through the water, and never looked behind them to see the position of the enemy, but left the steerage to their commanders, well convinced that the shortest route would be preferred.

No sooner did the Algerine perceive the force likely to be opposed to her, than she ceased firing until the smoke was quite clear: indeed, so coolly did they take the whole concern, that after they fired, they pulled a stroke or two in order to get clear of the cloud they had created. It was evident that the two boats would reach the pirate before Hammerton's could get to his station; and the plan they entered on was to devote their gun entirely to keep Hammerton in check, and allow the other two, which they saw were smaller boats, not containing altogether more than twelve men, to approach; then to pull the felucca as if in flight, so as to keep up a steady long fire upon the captain's division, and to take their enemies, or allow them to attack, in detail.

The good effect of this plan was soon obvious: the third shower of grape directed at Hammerton's boat disabled four of the oars and wounded two of the men. In the mean time, the muskets were not idle; and to the inexpressible grief of the gallant young Hammerton, he found after a short time that he had only four oars with which to pull the boat.

Now it was that the felucca pretended to escape. The

captain, convinced that a panic had seized them, pushed gallantly alongside, leaving his companion far behind: the sweeps were dropped over his boat, a grapnel with a chain was instantly lowered into her bows, and the six men were handed out without a chance of resistance; they were disarmed, ironed, and sent below.

The chief mate, seeing his captain effect a boarding, and observing that the Algerine no longer attempted an escape, believed that she had surrendered. They came up upon the quarter without expecting to find resistance, were seized by the concealed Algerines, and soon found themselves prisoners.

Hammerton came up slowly, and finding that no hostile gun was fired at him, and seeing the captain of the packet on deck—for the Algerines had brought him up in order to follow up their plan—came alongside and was seized in the same manner. His fertile mind instantly pictured to him the horrors for which he was destined: the cautious manner that the Turks had avoided firing into the boats—their care not to wound or maim their adversaries, at once convinced him that his comrades and himself in adversity were destined for slaves. They were lashed back to back, placed in the hold, the gratings clapped on; death was now more likely to ensue from suffocation than from a sword. It was useless to repine; they were caught in their own net, and had nothing left for it but patience and strong legs.

The men who had been wounded were taken to a more airy part of the felucca, which was forward. A man who enacted leech applied some simple remedies to those whose hurts were trivial; whilst, as an especial act of favour to those whose loss of limb rendered their room more desirable than their company, they were first of all stripped, the limb carefully examined, hauled about to satisfy the most sceptical as to the compound fracture, and afterwards thrown overboard,—not one of the Algerines being kind-hearted enough either to tie their hands together, or to forestall the cruel and protracted death which might ensue from drowning, by planting a dagger in their hearts.

The packet was now the object. Having gleaned from one of the poor wretches, who thought that by giving the information his life might be saved, that no further resistance could be made, the felucca's head was directed towards the vessel, the sweeps were again in use, and by eleven o'clock she was alongside. The shrick of the women was beautiful music to their ears : they dashed on board, dragged the screaming wretches from their cabins ; heeded not the cries, the groans, the tears, the prayers of the captives ; but, giving a cheer of "Allâh il Allâh !" they hurried them to the felucca, and using only violence sufficient to restrain any suicidal attempt, left them abaft on the small raised deck to witness the conclusion of the tragedy.

The wounded men found on board the brig were very unceremoniously tossed overboard : their shriek, as the water bubbled from their mouths when they rose to the surface, was answered by onc louder and less impeded from the women. Some of the sufferers whose arms were unhurt struck out and maintained themselves above water, calling loudly and vainly for assistance. Thc ruffians, accustomed to such deeds, smiled at them with horrid delight, imitating the action of swimming and panting, and then, with savage calmness drawing their pistols, took delight in wounding, not killing, their victims. It was the captain of the pirate who found the groans too loud even for his accustomed ear,—who, after laughing with one of his crew as if wagering the part he would hit, sent the sufferers to that grave which under such circumstances may truly be termed the place "where the wicked ceasc from troubling, and the weary are at rest."

The savage pastime ended, and the women quiet from exhaustion, it was resolved to burn the packet, after they had cleared her of all that was easily removed, and of that which was most valuable. The powder and shot were considered objects of the first value ; the cutlasses they cared little about, being more accustomed to their light, sharp weapons, and rather despising the hcavy, hacking sword, which fatigues the wearer and requ res a Hercules to wield.

Although Turks have a religious fear of rum, they have a very Christian-like appetite for the spirit ; and those who had got so far into the bowels of the vessel soon exhibited proofs of their having transferred some of the liquid into their own. There seemed to bc a very summary punishment for drunkenness, and one which when seen might deter any offender from the repetition—much more than all the cat-o'-nine-tails ever flourished over a seaman's back: it was merely the cutting off one ear. But this was never inflicted whilst the culprit was intoxicated: the operation was reserved until the following morning, when the ear would convey to the owner the sad tidings of its own departure. But now that the rum was at hand, ears or heads were not valued in comparison with the liquor, and the fury of appetite soon prompted every vicious thought.

The captain well knew what would be the attempt. He placed his best men to guard his plunder, his women, and his prisoners; and with the rest of his crew soon rid the packet of the noisy Turks who had thus broken through the laws of discipline and of religion. With his own hand he fired the brig: the flames flew up the ropes—the victims returned to their vessel, and pulling some short distance from their prize, watched her with curious eye, as flame after flame rushed like a rocket to the mast-head, ascending the tarred rigging. A light sail aloft would suddenly burst into fire, and from its pendant position blaze and die, like woman's beauty; some fantastic flame would wind itself round a particular strand of the rope which it consumed, in its tortuous track wreathing itself slowly and slowly to the mast-head—not a bad emblem of the subtle lawyer, who insures the exhaustion of his client the more nearly he embraces his cause, and who cares not for the ruin he engenders, so that his aspiring ambition is gratified. But now the hull broke into a blaze—all was ruin and desolation: the smoke burst through the scuttles, whilst the flame followed it, lighting the tarred sides of the devoted vessel, and devouring her in its course.

There was no breeze to fan this fire; it was a beautiful, calm, unclouded day, as if God smiled upon his creatures. The artificial cloud, the groans, the shrieks, the screams, seemed sadly contrasted with all the splendour of the morning; and when at last every part of the packet lighted up in a stronger and more brilliant flame, it was but the mockery of the glorious splendour of the setting sun, to be superseded by the darkness of night. The hull sank before dusk, and the refreshed pirates, taking advantage of a light breeze, steered their course to Algiers.

CHAPTER XXVI.

SLAVERY IN ALGIERS.—PUBLIC AUCTION.

It is not every man who has philosophy enough to lie down quietly in captivity and dream of happier hours in store for him;—but the chances of eluding the vigilance of an Algerine were at all times slight, and the idea of gaining liberty by any but a desperate act never could come within the scope of any philosophy excepting that which occasionally falls to the lot of a midshipman. We hold the summit of philosophy to be, receiving a bastinado without a murmur, or to be confined, lashed down as a prisoner, without venturing a good substantial curse. Nothing eases the mind of a rough sailor like a good round oath: it means nothing, and it can scarcely be marked down in the grand catalogue of his iniquities; it is as often vented on a marlingspike as on a human creature, and is with honest Jack nothing more than lightening his heart of a load with which even conscience interferes; and as soon as uttered it is forgotten. Such was the loud, deep damnation which fell from the *ci-devant* captain of the packet, as he was bundled neck and crop into the hold, after having been the means of decoying Hammerton into captivity.

Hammerton had been well nurtured in adversity, for he was born rich and made poor: he had faced all dangers, and had outlived nearly all his companions; he had returned to give his father the shock which ultimately killed him; and had found himself robbed by the very lad whose life he had risked his own to save. His last adversity, his capture, as yet gave him no uneasiness, except what he felt for the women,—even bondage was a luxury to his cruise in the *Tribune's* boat; and as he calculated all evils by comparison, he very quietly betook himself to sleep, not even once dreaming that he was a prisoner.

At daylight, however, the next morning, he was perfectly convinced that he was reserved for hardships which as yet he had evaded. The prisoners were brought on deck, lashed together, they were examined, their pockets lightened of any superfluous load, and they were paired off; it being a principle with the Algerines to do just as some of our reputable class of horsedealers are apt to do—put a quick nag with one rather slower; the power, capacity, and sprightliness of the one is pulled down by the slow, lagging pace of the other, and the owner soon finds it requisite to match the quick one; the lazy animal is bought in at a very reduced price, and the quick one matched at an exorbitant sum. Now, slaves are often turned to the same account;—the lazy one would rather receive the stick than work, the active would rather work than be beaten: so that the pair thus matched do between them a fair proportion of labour; the one getting stout upon his sluggishness, the other dwindling in flesh in an equal ratio.

Hammerton was paired off with the chief mate, who was an obstinate, stubborn, lazy fellow, and who hauled and yawed about like a pig in a high wind. He was, however, a little tamed by being an eye-witness to the punishment inflicted on the Algerines, who had forgotten their duty to Allah and the captain by getting drunk during the plunder of the packet.

Whilst the prisoners were undergoing inspection and assortment, the two Algerine culprits were receiving without a murmur a most satisfactory beating on the soles of their feet. No one paid the least attention to them, and the executioner continued to do his duty most ably, until one of the unfortunate wretches thought proper to ask if he was to receive any more. The captain, as if quite unconscious that such a punishment was going on, coolly took his pipe from his mouth as the stripes continued, and after leisurely puffing out a long column of smoke, answered "Yok" (no): whereupon the poor devils, whose feet were beaten to jelly, crawled up to their chief, thanked him for the punishment, and expatiated upon his moderation. The executioner, however, seemed to know that a little more was yet to be administered, and coming before the chief with the culprits, made a kind of Oriental salaam. The captain's head nodded an assent, and in a moment both prisoners were released with the loss of the left ear. Not a groan escaped them—not a murmur of complaint was heard: it was fate which ordained that they should get drunk, and the punishment was *takdeer* (destiny). Happy people, who can thus meet all adversities, and find consolation in misfortune!

Hammerton, who saw this deed, said to his companion,

the chief mate, "I think, if we are prudent, we shall do as we are bid; for if for getting drunk a Turk loses an ear, we shall in all probability, if we neglect our work, lose a head."

"I shan't work," replied the sulky cur: "I would rather they killed me outright."

"Have you no brother, no sister, no parent," asked Hammerton, "for whom you might wish to live? and cannot you muster up energy enough to let your heels save your back?"

"If you are so fond of work, my lad," replied the mate, "you can do a little for me."

Here, as a little bad feeling was already engendered, the blackguard hauled one way and the gentleman coaxed the other. This was soon put a stop to by an elderly Turk, who seemed to have much authority, thrashing both of them, and making them lie down and keep quiet. It, however, appeared that the mate was not quite so silent under his punishment as the Turks, for he bellowed lustily, upon which the Turk redoubled his blows, thrashing him until he was silent; much in the same manner as one often sees a brute of a coachman whipping his horses to make them stand still. During the shower of blows Hammerton never moved or said a word; and if by accident the old Algerine let the stick fall upon him, he stood as still and resolute as a donkey. The rest being paired, and the women duly kept apart, they were again placed in the hold, and that evening the felucca cast anchor in the mole of Algiers.

The next day, preparations were made to get the prisoners in condition for sale. They were rubbed down like horses, fed better, and had some wine, kept for the purpose, given them: and although the head master of the prisoners called them giaours and infidels for drinking the wine, yet he took especial care, when left alone, to taste this fire-water of the Christians; and not being able to make up his mind as to the taste, he tried it again and again.

"Now," said the mate, "if that turban-headed vagabond would but get drunk, I would pardon him the thrashing he has given me, and now's my time to pay him off;" here he edged towards the old man and gave him such a tremendous kick on the shins, that down fell Turk, bottle and all. The infuriated Mussulman, after rubbing his legs until the pain had partially subsided, coolly walked off for his stick; but the mate, as he approached, made him understand that his ears were in danger, and nodded at the broken bottle.

The Turk understood the hint, and likewise the remedy. In order to prove he was not drunk, he administered such a drubbing on the legs of the mate that he was obliged to lie down, and cried like a child. This only inflamed the Turk the more; and calling him a woman, a dog's son, and swearing he would defile the grave of the fathers of all the giaours, he thrashed him until his old arms were fatigued and he was obliged to sit down to take breath.

"I hope to God," said Hammerton, "I shall not be sold with you! for you have already broken my spirit; the sound of that stick is dreadful to my ears."

"It is devilish painful to my legs and arms," said the mate; "but I will kill that old fellow yet: if he does not lose his ears, I shall regret my thrashing the more."

"Take my advice—grow wiser by the experience you have gained. You see he can do as he likes with us: therefore smother your wrath, and strive to avoid the stick."

"I would not be such a cursed craven cur as you are, to be beaten and not to dare to howl, for all the Turks in the world."

"And I," said Hammerton, "would not be such a fool as you are, not to bow to circumstances which you cannot control, for all the world put together!"

"See if you can bow to that!" replied the irascible mate, as he trod with all his force upon Hammerton's feet.

"I forgive you, mate," was the meek reply; "for you have misery enough in store for you:—that old Turk will not forgive the insult, and you will have eight times the thrashing to bear; learn then to bear them, as I have borne your insult to me. Here we are tied together; let us work with as much cheerfulness as we can command, and use our utmost exertions to please our new masters."

It was in vain that Hammerton, who had been schooled in adversity, recommended patience and obedience; his companion was resolved rather to die than work.

Near the gate which leads from the mole to the interior of the town there is an opening of some extent; and here it was customary some years since to expose the slaves for sale, and to show off their several capacities. The human cargo thus to be disposed of was, previous to any bidding, shown in a state of nudity, and the buyers of these animals overhauled them with all the caution of men used to mark the maladies of our nature. On this spot by daybreak the following day some mats were spread, and many grave-looking personages assembled. The government had deputed men to purchase some of the stoutest, in order to complete the fortifications round the mole-head, and likewise to carry the large stones which were destined to finish the mole itself; it being beyond the wisdom of these barbarians to carry the stones on trucks, they preferred the method handed down to them with their turbans, which was to sling the stones between two poles, and make the slaves carry them by placing the poles on their shoulders. The whole cargo was landed together; and no sooner were the prisoners brought into the open space, than the wife and daughter before mentioned rushed into the arms of the husband and father, and, hiding their heads, gave vent to a flood of tears. The unmannerly Turks instantly advanced to separate them, while Hammerton, forcing along with him the lazy hound to whom he had been tied, endeavoured to clear the Turks from their prey. With almost supernatural strength he succeeded, having his right arm free, in tearing the old man away; and giving the tottering Turk who had held him a sudden twirl, he dismissed him with such headway that he fell into the water. There was a laugh even amongst the Turks; but the rest, in spite of cries and entreaties, the stronghold of affection and love, succeeded in separating the parties. In vain the poor creatures knelt to their captors—in vain they implored heaven for its interposition in their favour; the strained attitudes of the females only heightened the biddings for their charms; and as one was young and lovely, the other gradually waning into years, they fell to the lot of different bidders.

A veil was thrown over the faces of mother and daughter, and they were borne away to different houses,—one to be sacrificed to the lust of the buyer, the other to be condemned to all the drudgery—the slavish drudgery—which religious rancour could inspire and brute beast could perform. The husband saw the money paid down for his wife and child;

he saw the lewd jest which heralded his daughter's infamy; and although he again and again made an effort at a rescue, he was condemned to see the buyers of all he held dear in the world order them to different harems, themselves following their purchasers.

Now began the auction for the men. They had been inspected by the intending purchasers; many a hand had been passed down the back sinews of their legs, the muscles of the shoulders had been pinched, the size of the arm-bone had been measured, the head had been examined for gray hairs—in short, every part had been duly scrutinised, and the price to which each bidder would go was settled in his mind.

The first couple disposed of was the captain and one of his crew. In order to show the strength of the animals, they were placed under the pole, to which was attached a stone of considerable weight, and they were told to lift it. The slings were of such a length as to require both the prisoners to bend down a little, before they could get the poles placed upon each shoulder, and this position showed the muscles of the legs and back to the greatest advantage. In vain they tried—evidently tried; the weight was more than their united power could apparently move. The price fell,—the enraged pirate asked what would be the highest bidding if they lifted the stone, and a considerable advance was immediately offered by the government if such should occur; whereas, in the event of a failure, the price was so much depreciated as to very materially discomfort the pirate.

He called four of his men, who were armed with long sticks about the circumference of a man's finger, and he placed them so as to command a good position for inflicting the blows which were to follow. Having again agreed with the bidder as to the price should the stone be weighed, he gave the order for the unfortunate men to try again.

With a fearful knowledge of the punishment which awaited them, they both tried. The muscles of the leg seemed bursting through the skin—the perspiration started like a fountain from their bodies—their backs groaned to achieve the task; when the pirate, fearful that they might not succeed, beckoned to his men, and they began to strike the prisoners with all their force over their legs, urging them as if they were horses, and goading them to the fearful trial. Escape was impossible, and to turn impracticable; they again tried, and succeeded in weighing the enormous weight, both falling down over the stone almost dead with exhaustion. The brutes now plied their sticks again until the poor fellows were sufficiently recovered to stand erect; when the marks of the blows, and the tender manner in which they walked, evidently showed how severe had been the punishment—how exhausted were the sufferers.

An objection was taken on the part of the purchasers as to the fair lifting of the stone, and the pirate offered to make them do it again; and when taunted with the impossibility of making such exhausted creatures raise so heavy a weight, he crossed his fingers, emblematic of the creed of his victims; and after spitting in their faces, and kicking them for cowards who were afraid to work, he made a trifling reduction of the price, and the unfortunate captain and his man became government slaves to the Dey of Algiers.

They were kept on the spot, in order that if a larger purchase was made, all the slaves might be driven away together, to carry sand like donkeys, to weigh stones for the fortifications, and to have black bread and bastinadoes for their pay.

It was now the turn of Hammerton and his sulky companion to be brought before these devils in Turkish garb; and no slight burst of pleasure was manifested as the two were brought forward. One was a miniature Hercules—short, compact, sturdy, and stubborn; the other slim, well-proportioned, handsome, and active. Such a contrast could never assimilate. The man who bade for the government fixed his eyes upon the mate, and made a liberal offer for him without a trial. The pirate raised his price, of course—(Turks are as subtle as Indians at a bargain)—a controversy arose, and the pirate, swearing a good Mahomedan oath, bet his value, as named by the government purchaser, that the slave should lift the stone by himself, which the two others, both stout men, had nearly failed to accomplish. It was a bargain, because it was safe betting on the one side; the Turk, of course, had he gained the bet, would have got his slave for nothing, and charged his master a wholesome price: on the other hand, it was one of those angry offers which losing gamesters are apt to make when they run a tilt against fortune, and are sure of being worsted.

Two of the pirate crew now stepped forward and unbound the captives. One was sullen and reserved, as if winding himself up for an act of desperation; the other quietly and modestly succumbed to his fate, with a countenance truly resigned, yet resolved to do his utmost in any trial. They were now both unbound, and standing beside each other: the mate remarked, with a sullen curse, that those turban-headed fellows should feel his wrath if they attempted to harness him as they had done his captain.

Hammerton sighed, as he said, "We had better do our utmost at first; and then we may avoid those cruel sticks."

"If I lift it may I be ——!"

Hammerton merely replied, "Your determination will ruin us both."

Two of the pirates, who carried sticks, one the old Turk who had been insulted by the mate, now advanced, and giving the mate a sharp blow on the bare shoulders, pointed to the stone. The unexpected salute sent him into a boiling rage; he turned round—grasped the offending pirate, shook him like a child—seized the fellow's stick, and with one blow broke it over his turban.

A furious row instantly ensued. The sturdy Englishman, seeing the coming storm, grasped hold of an idler, who had been attracted to the scene by the crowd, and seizing his scimitar, dismissed him to his companions, going at a quicker rate than was customary, owing to an impetus behind which propelled the Turk beyond his usual grave and lazy pace. The lion was now fairly roused;—he stood like Spartacus after he had broken his chains; he merely made a few backward steps, so as to get the water in his rear, and then offering himself as a fair mark, called out in English, "Now, come on, you ruffians, and see who will make me lift the stone!"

To kill such a valuable slave was no part of the pirate's plan, and now was the time to strike a good bargain. His price rose; but the wary old Turk said, "If he does not lift the stone, he is mine."

"There was no *time* mentioned," said the vendor; "and we shall see if we cannot wear him out."

He now directed his crew to get some long stout sticks, and make a regular advance to push the mate over the quay; whilst others were sent in a boat to seize him in that helpless state, and bind his arms. The Turks advanced in a semicircle, and making one determined rush, they succeeded in effecting the plan; the poor fellow, tottering back, fell overboard, the scimitar dropping from his hand as he attempted to recover himself. He was instantly seized by the hair of the head, and kept from entering the boat until his arms were secured; he was then landed, brought to the fatal stone, and harnessed.

And now the Turks found that it was impossible for the man to lift the stone, in consequence of its size hindering him from standing right over the weight. A platform was soon erected, through the centre of which the slings were led; they were then fastened over the mate's shoulders in such a manner that he could not extricate himself, at the same time bending him down; and the Turk whom he had so signally disgraced appeared by his side, with a brighter eye, a more resolute arm, a thicker stick, and a more willing heart.

The victim being secured, the pirate captain gave the nod to the administrators of his law, and heavy and thick fell the blows. The insulted Turk did not confine his operations to the calves of the legs alone, but every part of the naked body was shortly in large weals. Still the mate would not make the slightest effort to lift the stone: sullenly, and without moving or flinching, he bore the repeated strokes, until he sank down unable to move, even had his inclination been to have done so. The beating was continued, and fresh sticks supplied the place of those which were broken; but the insulted man,—he who had been beaten by an Isauri—a dog of a Christian, a cursed giaour! —although almost fainting with fatigue, continued to ply his strokes. Still more enraged than the rest, the pirate captain raised his sword to despatch him; but the government purchaser claimed him as his own—all further persecution ceased; the wretch was unbound, and the captain and the man already bought were ordered to carry their fainting shipmate to the prison destined for their reception.

The rest of the crew saw the mate carried on the

shoulders of their purchased shipmates, another set of them freshening their way as they were hustled through the gate leading into the town: a good lesson had been inculcated—never to strike a man in authority when there is no chance of reversing the tables. They were now all brought forward and disposed of but Hammerton: every one fell to the lot of the government but he—they would have nothing to do with such a slim, woman-looking youth; he was reserved for the captain, who, making an allowance to his crew, retained him as his own slave.

Hitherto the captain of the pirate ship had not shown himself a very bloodthirsty fellow; throwing the wounded part of the crew overboard was nothing more than a benevolent spirit to ease them of pain and broken limbs, of which they could not have been cured; but his wish to have killed the mate was the hasty ebullition of the moment, which prudence and the love of money would have stifled. Hammerton turned all this over in his mind, resolved to do his utmost in his new situation, inwardly hoping that he might be retained on board the felucca; for the hope always glimmered that she might be taken and he recaptured. He soon found that he was reserved for another service, and that his master was a very knowing performer in the art of traffic.

Hammerton was removed in the first instance into a kind of coffee-house which stands down by the quay, and placed in a corner. Here he snuffed the savoury kabobs which were handed about to the different people; he saw the fragrant coffee and the still more aromatic pipe offered: and never did sweet odours come more inopportunely upon his nostrils; for the recovery from his fright, and his finding himself with a mantle to cover his nakedness, had brought back the common feelings of our nature, hunger uppermost.

His master was busily employed in playing a game of trictrac (a species of draughts), and was evidently much interested in the result. An old Turk who had been bargaining for some of the slaves was his opponent, and a large bag of sequins and dollars rattled upon the table. Although the room was filled, each Turk smoked his pipe in sullen silence, with the exception of those who had a little of the mania for gambling: these fellows played either chess or trictrac, moved the men without breaking silence, and lost or won without excitement or despondency.

Hammerton watched them narrowly, and was thankful that he had before him these living specimens of predestination. He himself had imbibed his father's knowledge on this subject; and it certainly was this which taught him to bear up manfully against the storm he could neither allay nor control.

As he had been placed in a corner there he remained. He saw some poor miserable beggars wander from table to table, picking up the crumbs in reality which fell from the board of the wealthy; and once or twice he thought of following the example: but the sticks were ever before his eyes—the swollen bodies of his late shipmates checked even hunger when he thought of them, and once, when advanced about a foot from his corner, a kind-hearted waiter kicked him back again. Both mind and body grow callous by custom: Hammerton hardly felt the kick, and certainly evinced no inclination to return it.

Notwithstanding the general sullen indifference of the Turks, Hammerton thought he saw his master under rather unusual excitement, and he knew enough of life to be aware that his spite would be vented upon himself. He saw the pirate leap from the table, and resuming as much gravity as possible, walk, without noticing his slave, out of the door.

The old Turk with whom he had been playing now pouched all the money—called for a dish of kabobs, another pipe, some coffee, and, folding his arms with most Oriental elegance, awaited the arrival of his food.

"Now," thought Hammerton to himself, "if I were in any other place than this, I would most assuredly make an attempt for my liberty. But how can I manage it here? There is no friendly ship which could receive me; and if I merely put one foot before the other, I shall be kicked back into my corner. It will be better to wait until I am kicked out, and then it will be my fault if I don't make the best use of my legs."

The idea soon occurred to him that he had been the object of the gambling, and that the bags of money which he had seen, about twice his esteemed value, had been staked. If the old Turk won, he was to have the slave without payment; if he lost, he was to lose double the value of the slave, but to retain him. He had now got him for nothing, and was in a very excellent humour. The old boy seemed right well to know that his new purchase could not escape; and in the plenitude of his joy in having over-reached a pirate, he ordered a dish of kabobs to be given to Hammerton, who stood in the corner like Patience on the lee cathead grinning at wet swabs. When the man who enacted waiter gave him the food of which he stood so much in need, he gave him a long stick on which were stuck pieces of fried mutton, about the size of a very small veal cutlet, which, being served quite hot, is one of the most esteemed dishes the culinary wisdom of Turkey has yet discovered. Hammerton's hunger would have made him believe that a piece of shoe-leather fried in train oil was delicious, but the kabobs (who has ever eaten a kabob and not relished it?) were truly good.

A little refreshed with his dinner, and quietly chuckling over his having escaped the blows so plentifully showered upon his old shipmates, and which were likely to bring the mate to his senses, he turned his inquisitive mind to inspect the scene around him. Although the room was crowded, there was scarcely a word spoken. The slaves who attended on the company slipped silently along in their papooshes; some were barefooted; and the only sounds audible were occasionally the chink of money, or an Oriental sigh, which, after having puffed out a column of smoke as long as a frigate's pendant, seemed to lighten the lungs of the lounger. The coffee, in a small neat coffee-cup, placed in a gold filigree saucer, was almost the only beverage drunk, saving now and then some of that truly delightful liquid, sherbet. As each man finished his scanty repast, the money was placed upon the table, and the grave Mussulman retired.

Hammerton observed the company one after the other, each with that never-failing attendant a pipe, retire. His master, or the man believed to be his master, was seen busily employed in devouring a pillau. His greedy fingers were now dived into the dish, and now they threw up the rice, and as it oozed through his claws, he appeared more like a bear than a man.

"Egad!" thought Hammerton, "I must indeed be a fool to wait here whilst that old fellow is feasting! I will try if I cannot give my master the slip: perhaps there may be a Portuguese or a Spanish craft in the bay; and if a swim will accomplish it, I may yet have a chance."

Watching, therefore, until the eyes of some casual spectator were withdrawn, he slipped out, and once more thought himself free. The sun was now near the horizon, and only a few Turks were lounging about the pier. The loose shawl which had been thrown over his shoulders concealed his otherwise naked limbs; and he found that few remarked or paid the least attention to the forlorn wanderer. To his great joy, he saw a neat, trim vessel in the bay, and from her peak floated a long Sardinian ensign: she seemed to have some pretensions to a man-of-war.

"Now," thought the poor fellow, "if I can but get to the point round the mole-head, I may make a start." He looked round the little bay which formed the harbour in hopes of seeing a boat; but although there were many large ones, there was not one of a size to allow of a pair of oars propelling it fast enough to effect an escape. He therefore walked boldly forward, and made up his mind to have a swim for it.

He had arrived at the extreme point without the least interruption, and was preparing to disrobe himself, when a very stately man, armed with a long silver-mounted pair of pistols in his girdle, stopped him, and asked him in good Turkish, what might be his pleasure in wandering so near the water? To this question Hammerton, who had made up his mind to have a fight for his liberty, answered in English that he did not understand a word he said, and pursued his walk: upon which the Turk immediately seized him. Off went the only covering, and the slave who had been sold in the morning stood before the very man who had attended in his official capacity at the mart of human flesh. A pistol was instantly drawn and cocked and pointed at him, with an intelligible hint that if he moved he was a dead man.

Hammerton's master had by this time finished his repast, paid for it, and walked to the corner. Finding his slave gone, he obtained the assistance of some ferashes, in order to pursue the runaway. On inquiries at the gate, it was evident he had not passed through it. They then ran to the mole-head, and there found him, facing the Turk, but quite unable either to attack or escape. They directly began with their long sticks to belabour him, and continued unmercifully to beat him until he arrived at his master's house, where, being kicked into a hole which would have been purgatory to a turnspit dog, he was left alone and in the dark, to ponder over his folly, and to make resolutions of greater caution for the future.

In the mean time the sun had set. The last prayers of the devout had been offered up; and as the curtain of night began to descend over the landscape, the weary and the wretched lay down to sleep, and endeavoured to forget in deep slumber their toil and misery.

Hammerton now employed his leisure in rubbing his sadly swollen limbs, and in vain regrets that he had been guilty of such egregious folly as to risk the displeasure of a master who had ordered him some kabobs. We are told "Repentance ever comes too late," and our prisoner had full time to ponder on the truth of this wise saw. By degrees, he became more reconciled to his situation, since it seemed predestined he was not to escape; and believing that his repose would be most unceremoniously disturbed in the morning, he endeavoured to compose himself to sleep.

His rest, however, was soon interrupted by the loud piercing shriek of a female. The sound chilled him to the heart; for on listening to the words which followed—imploring God to protect her—he recognized the voice of the poor girl who had been that day sold. He instantly rose, and tried every means to effect his escape in order to run to her rescue. Vain, however, were all his endeavours. He knocked his head against stone walls and wooden rafters, but he could not find any exit; and was at length obliged to desist, although he was not a person to be disheartened easily. At last the screams grew fainter and more faint, and at length entirely died away. Still he listened with painful anxiety; but not a footstep, not a sigh could be heard; there was a fearful silence all around. The victim had evidently been dragged to some remote corner, and he shuddered as he reflected on the melancholy fate of that poor and beautiful girl.

When morning dawned, whieh was at a very early hour, a man brought him a kind of Greek dress : it consisted of enough to eover him, with a red skull-eap, to ward off the rays of the sun. He was desired to follow his guide.

At the doorway he was pinioned; and as he had previously manifested some inclination to escape, a large piece of wood was fastened to his right leg; and after a piece of blaek coarse bread and some water had been given him, he was marched off. By way of a gentle hint, he was in the first instanee eonducted to the mole, where he saw his shipmates at work. The captain and his companion had done their duty without the aid of the stiek; but the mate, who resolutely determined to refuse to labour, was tied to a stone, with two• or three people employed in giving him a severe bastinado.

His guide, after pointing out the mate to Hammerton, shook a stiek he carried in a very ominous manner, and leading him by the captain, who had a very heavy load of sand on his back, he was conducted through that wretched town, and passing out of a gate to the westward, was released from his log, and commanded to quicken his pace into the interior.

Hammerton, finding all chance of escape now impossible, wisely made the best of his situation. His guide spoke a little of the lingua Franea, and the eaptive began to turn the moments to some aceount by learning the Arabie names of different things as they proceeded. By his eheerful manner he soon gained upon the Turk; and in short, a doubtful friendship was soon established between them.

They had walked some miles into the interior, when they arrived at a large earavansary, into whieh they entered and reposed for some time. Loitering about the house were some of those strolling story-tellers so often met with in the East; but as Hammerton did not understand a word they said, and as his guide fell asleep, the wandering romancers soon gave up their avocation. Hammerton followed the example of his friend, and quiekly sunk in a deep sleep. In this caravansary they remained during the heat of the day.

Towards evening they again set forth, steering a little to

the southward, until they came to an old rambling kind of building. Here they were saluted by about fifty dogs, which came rushing forth, howling and barking at the intruders. The old guide called them by different names;—one wagged his tail, another growled into his corner, and the rest slunk off upon the reception of a heavy and well-directed salute of the stick.

Hammerton was led into a miserable room, which had no furniture but one or two planks supported upon a rough unbarked stump of a tree, to which the Turk pointed, and closing his eyes and giving an initiative snore, plainly gave his companion to understand that that would be his bed. Hammerton was then left alone, but shortly afterwards the savoury smell of kabobs met his nose. Some black bread was soon brought, with which, and a few pieces of mutton taken from the Turk's stick, both Christian and Mahomedan made a somewhat satisfactory meal.

Here the Turk gave him to understand that his comrades would have to drag on a life of eternal slavery and hard labour, unless they could purchase their freedom; and that long before he returned to Algiers the stubborn mate would have become a good servant or be starved. He made Hammerton clearly understand, however, by means of his lingua Franca, that he was reserved for a life far more pleasurable, and that his old master was sorry when he found the evening before that he had attempted to escape. He told him that their present abode was only for the night, as his master's house was further in the interior, and that, at the expiration of a fortnight, the whole establishment would arrive.

A kind of friendship having sprung up between Mustapha and Hammerton, the latter became more cheerful, being only a little saddened whenever the former, with much gravity, endeavoured to persuade him to become a Turk, indicating that he himself could assist him in the first necessary operation, and that afterwards he would become much higher in the estimation of the inmates of the house.

The next day they again moved forward, and, after a tedious journey of fourteen days, during which they sometimes got a ride on a passing camel, they arrived and were fairly established in the country house of Mohammed Benzali Berzroom.

CHAPTER XXVII.

CORNCOB'S NOTIONS OF EQUALITY.—CAPTAIN MURRAY'S DISCIPLINE.

THE *Arethusa* having cleared the land, shaped her course down Channel, and ultimately arrived at the latitude of Cape St. Vincent, off which about a hundred miles Captain Murray was directed to open his secret orders. He then found that he was directed to cruise in the vicinity of Madeira for four months: after which he was to proceed to the coast of Africa, to visit Goree, Sierra Leone, and sweep that inhospitable shore down to the Bight of Benin. He was then to return to Gibraltar, where further orders would await his arrival; if, however, these should not have arrived, he was to place his ship under the directions of the commodore there. The accident which occurred to her in the Bay of Biscay, however, frustrated the completion of these orders.

The morning after her departure from Spithead, Captain Murray learned from his first lieutenant during breakfast the whole failure of the press-gang; at which he rejoiced, although he did not allow his pleasure to escape his lips.

"One, do you say," he began, "rather than serve risked his life, perhaps lost it in attempting to desert?"

"That was the first impression, sir," answered the lieutenant; "but I have been informed this morning that he is safe on board."

"Poor fellow!" said Murray, "I cannot find it in my heart to censure that which I cannot but applaud. Was he stowed away below, or concealed in the mizen-chains?"

"No, sir, he was discovered fast asleep in Mr. Weazel's hammock. The fact is, that the American, who is as extraordinary a piece of machinery as ever worked, came aft to know why he had not the same advantages as the other pressed man; saying, "he thought it was tarnation hard that he should be jammed up between two of the starboard watch, and have to wash out the mess-kids, whilst the man who was taken with him was amusing himself with his three fingers playing the flute, with a servant to wait upon him, and swinging-room for his hammock." This led to a little inquiry, and we found out that it was Mr. Weazel we had pressed sorely against his will, and who, during the time he was lying in the stern-sheets of the cutter with Corncob, was amusing himself in rubbing the American's face with some of the dirt into which he himself had been rolled; and as far as three fingers could do the deed his did it effectually, for never was a dirtier American handed up the side of any of his Majesty's ships of war."

"Pray, Mr. Jones, where did you find Mr. Weazel?"

"In rather a questionable place, sir—where he left some of his clothes behind him. No sooner was he sent aft on the quarter-deck than he walked over the mizen-chains, got into the main-deck port, and turned quietly into his hammock."

"That fellow," remarked the captain, "is always in some mischief; but on this occasion I must say that I cannot help being pleased with the result. We must now, Mr. Jones, turn our whole attention to practising the guns: they are smart enough aloft in reefing and furling, and they certainly work the ship in good style; but I must also have them expert and active at their quarters. You must desire the gunner to look after the magazine; to-night we must fill the powder: and even if we fall in with two frigates, I shall, I trust, have confidence enough in my crew to face them without hesitation."

"I hope, sir," said Mr. Jones, "that such an opportunity may occur. I am perfectly satisfied that the *Arethusa* will always maintain the high opinion she has hitherto deserved. But I really think we shall have some trouble in making the gunner attend to the magazine to-night, for it is Saturday night."

"I hope, Mr. Jones, he is not addicted to drunkenness? If he is, as sure as he is now the gunner, he shall shortly be before the mast."

"On the contrary, sir," replied the first lieutenant, "he is the most sober, steady person in the world: but he is very religious, and directly Sunday morning comes he will walk off to his cabin, let the consequences be what they may."

"I respect him for his feeling, for it gives proof of his sincerity. Let the lights be put out at ten o'clock, and his duty will be done by midnight. This new man—this Corncob, what is he like?"

"Really, sir, he talks and acts like a true American: he declares that we shall have a war on account of impressing him, and speaks, I understand, largely of his vast possessions on the shores of the Chesapeake."

"Had he a protection when you pressed him?"

"None, sir, but a stick, which he called such, and used with a strong arm."

"We shall make a sailor of him, and go to war too, if it is necessary."

The first lieutenant now walked on deck; and shortly afterwards Captain Murray made his appearance there also. His quick eye was aloft in a moment; but every sail was properly set—not a yarn hung like an Irish pendant from any of the ropes—everything was neat aloft, whilst the quarter-deck was clean, the ropes nicely flemished down, and everything bore witness to the order of the frigate and the care of her first lieutenant. The frigate was then standing down the Channel with a favourable breeze, and Captain Murray was looking over the gangway in order to estimate the sailing of the ship, when he felt some one smack him on the back: he turned round, for he had his epaulet on his right shoulder, to punish such want of respect, amounting to a violation of discipline.

"I just expect," said Jonathan Corncob, "that you call yourself the captain of this ship, and I'm pretty considerably mistaken if I don't get satisfaction for my ill-treatment. Here am I, Jonathan Corncob, citizen of the United States, lugged like a beaver out of a trap, jammed down into a swinging bed, crammed into a mess with very little to eat, my coat-tails cut off, my Havannah hat chucked overboard, my hair snipped by a rascally ruffian,—and all because I was walking home to go to bed at the inn at Gosport! This is pretty considerable tyranny, I calculate; and I'm not the man to put up with it for all the English frigates or brass-bottom serpents that ever crossed our seas. You speak American language, I expect: so now out with your answer, and no flustification."

If anything could have taken a young captain aback, it was such an attack as this when the eyes of half the ship's company were upon him, and where he knew every word was weighed—every action noticed.

"Mr. Jones," said Captain Murray, with the greatest coolness, "is this the man who was pressed? or is he one of the ship's company gone mad? Take your hat off, sir, when you stand before your captain."

"Take my hat off!" replied Jonathan; "I expect I shall do no such thing, or I calculate I may get a breeze of wind in my hair; and I have not yet got over my giddiness when they put me to the bars and made me run round and round like a squirrel in a cage."

"Is he mad, Mr. Jones?"

"No, sir; I have not seen anything like it before now; but, on the contrary, I thought he went to his duty with cheerfulness."

"Send the clerk here," said Captain Murray.

The clerk came. "Get the articles of war and read them to this fellow; let him understand what is the penalty of insubordination, disrespect, disobedience of orders; and report to me when they have been read to him."

"I tell you what it is, captain: you think you have brought me to a tarnation uncomfortable fix; but I calculate I shall get along yet."

"Here, sir," said Captain Murray; "listen to me. You seem to be what you say, an American, for no Englishman would be half so impertinent; but you have not any protection, which, as an American subject, you were bound to have produced. Failing that, I have a right to consider you an Englishman, who, not having any calling or trade, is liable to impressment. You are pressed into his Majesty's service: you have a duty to perform; it is mine to see that it is done: and be assured, do it you shall, whether you like it or not. Had it been light when you were taken, in all probability you would have been released on account of your age: but, being here, we are obliged to keep you; and as this is the last time I shall speak to you on the subject, let me advise you to do your duty with alacrity, and spare me the trouble and the pain I shall experience in enforcing obedience to my orders."

"I'm no Englishman, and I'll not do anything. I am a man of land and dollars in the State: and I tell you, captain, that I have, in my house on the borders of James River, sheltered your countryman in distress; and (though to be sure I was repaid—ay, and by a man of your own name, only he called himself Hector) I gave money to take the poor fellow back to his own country: and this is the return! But I expect I'm a free man, and no power on earth or on the sea shall make me do one moment's duty, or consent to have the yoke placed round my neck to be driven to work like an ox. You may flog me, if you dare; but I calculate vengeance shall fall upon you, or else I have mistaken the courage of the man I assisted—and that man's name is Hammerton."

It immediately occurred to Murray that this was the American of whom he had heard his father speak. This became evident by the conversation which ensued; and as our hero was in all but in money more inclined to generosity than to its opposite extreme, he desired that Corncob might be released from the thraldom of the first lieutenant, be placed to mess with the gunner; and having been fitted out in a coat with long tails to it, he was invited to dine with the captain, instead of being seized up to the gratings.

Corncob was a man of highly independent mind—one of your upright and downright liberty and equality men, who believed in anything rather than the divine right of kings, or the legal dominion of smaller sovereigns in command of ships; and to Corncob it was the same if he shook hands with the sweeper in the waist, or with the captain in all his glory. His messmate was, on the contrary, one who had all his life listened to nothing but martial law, and the law which he in his ignorance had construed from his religion; and thus with such an acid and alkali it was not likely that a very friendly effervescence would be produced.

Whilst the gallant frigate is shaping her course southward, we may as well record a conversation illustrative of the gunner and Corncob. It began at noon, on the day that the discovery was made relative to his being an American gentleman, as a piece of salt beef was placed on the gunner's table, which was not quite alone on the festive board, there being two potatoes and some biscuits, whilst a considerable fid of duff, as hard as a tennis-ball and as heavy as a shot, made up the meal of the happy and contented gunner.

"I'm expecting, Mr. Gunner," began Corncob, "that

this cursed fix into which I am brought by your slave-catcher Jones on deck is not the most likely to make me a happier father, or my child a better daughter! I guess the whole batch of you are no better than Coast of Guinea niggers, who forget you are men, and let yourselves be whipped like boys. I expect, if that young chap of a skipper had touched me, it's not Jonathan Corncob who would have failed to level him on that quarter-deck of his just as flat as any flapper's tail in the high seas."

"Then," replied the gunner, without altering his sanctified face, "you'd have been hung to the fore yard-arm just as sure as your name is Jonathan Corncob! And what would have become of your precious soul," said he, as his eyes went up to the carline of the deck above,—"your precious soul, Mr. Corncob?"

"I guess, if he had strung me up to the fore yard-arm, as you call it, that there would have been more souls to have been looked after between that day and Easter. What right has any set of men to hang a fellow-creature? We are all men; and I calculate that if a man strikes me, it's the law of Nature that I should knock him down."

"Very likely, Mr. Corncob. Then come the articles of war, which, next to the Bible, I hold to be our best sailing directions. If you disobey the articles of war, you are convicted in this world; and if you disobey the Bible, you will be convicted in the next."

"That's long credit, Mr. Gunner; and if a person can 'weather the storm' here, he may trust to luck for the rest."

"To luck!" said the astonished gunner; "by the blessing of Him above, I will make you a sensible man before we part. This it is, Mr. Corncob: in your country you believe all men equal, whereas we have here just the contrary idea. Now, if all men were equal, how would you get your dinner dressed? how would you get your land cultivated? how, in short, would you get any one thing done which you could not do yourself."

"Why, I calculate, by paying for it; for money, I guess, is the grand leveller."

"It is just the contrary, I calculate," said the gunner; "for if you pay a man for his work, it argufies two things: firstly, that you can command his services, which his poverty obliges him to give; and secondly, that he is above you in knowledge—at least, in the knowledge of that particular business for which you have engaged him. Now you see that there is a difference, and consequently no equality."

"Just the contrary, I expect, Mr. Gunner; because if I'm above him in money, and he's above me in knowledge, why two and two, I guess, make four; and that's equal all over the world."

"But, Mr. Corncob, if all the world was equal, we should all go barefooted: and in a ship there would be no master to navigate, no captain to command, no seaman to go aloft, no carpenter to swift the bars—"

"And," interrupted Corncob, "no pressed men to run round like a horse in a mill. I expect, Mr. Gunner, you know more about your powder-boxes than you do about liberty and equality; and I say it is a right-down tarnation shame that your boy should stand here to help you to swallow your dinner whilst he's as hungry as a shark."

"There's one bell, boy," said the gunner; "go up for the liquor:—it's not, Mr. Corncob, that I ever drink it myself, but I don't want others to forget their duty and become liberty-men. I tell you, Mr. Corncob, that if I can guess the character of our young captain, he won't let any man in this ship be his equal. Now, here's Mr. Weazel, a man who's been in Trafalgar, who sailed under Nelson,—we'll just put the question to him, and you will see what he says about the business.—Mr. Weazel," continued the gunner, "will you sit down on the corner of my chest there, and settle this question? Mr. Corncob says the world are all equal, but I say they are not: now just you give us your opinion upon it."

It was the custom of Weazel to pay the gunner a regular visit about this hour, during which he allowed him to believe he was working his conversion whilst he drank his grog; for Weazel used to remark, that if the gunner possessed an inward spirit, he had no occasion for grog.

"Why," said Weazel, as he helped himself, "I think Mr. Corncob is right."

"No doubt of it, Mr. Weazel: and by way of being upon an equality with you, I'll just trouble you for that case-bottle, because at present, I own, we are not."

"I wonder, Mr. Corncob, why you allowed the ship to sail and take you away from your family. Had I been you, I should have said, 'Captain Murray, if you think you are going to sell me for a nigger on the coast of Africa, you are mistaken!' Now, as he has asked you to dinner, you ought to ask him in return."

"And I just calculate that I shall, Mr. Weazel."

"And as he has courted your acquaintance, I would be civil—it's Christian-like to forgive injuries. When you see him on deck, walk with him and be kind to him. He is rather reserved in his manner, and may appear shy; but you will soon get over that for which all sailors are rebuked. You can talk to him about America, and let him see you are not proud by your shaking hands with the quarter-master. I never saw a person so shocked as the captain was when he discovered that you were likely to be President of the United States: for as all are equal, you are as likely to be president as any one else. By-the-bye, Corncob, I think you have not been quite so civil as you might have been in offering the captain some of your tobacco to chew."

"That's as true, I calculate, as that alligator's skin makes everlasting particular shoes; but I'll not forget it. Now, I should be most particularly curious to know why I, Jonathan Corncob, with a whole pack of niggers, a schooner, and a store at Norfolk, aint every bit as good as Captain Murray?"

"And I should like to know why the niggers," said the gunner, "are not as good as you?"

"Why, because I bought them, to be sure: they're the same to me as my cattle; and I should as soon think of putting a cow in corduroy breeches as clapping a pair of shoes on a nigger's hoof. I tell you, Mr. Gunner, you don't understand argufying a difficult question."

"Oh, then, I am not equal to you in sense?"

"No, I calculate you are not; your 'cuteness will never blind even a buskin. May I be most particularly kicked to death by mosquitoes if I don't think you would swim all day amongst alligators without finding out they had scales on their backs!—ay, Mr. Weazel?"

"Ah!" said Weazel, as he finished the gunner's allowance, "it's quite astonishing how blind some men are!

It's as plain as a pikestaff that we are all equal, excepting niggers, and that you and I are just as good as either captain or first lieutenant."

"Mr. Weazel," said a quarter-master, popping his head inside the gunner's cabin, "Mr. Jones desires you'll go on deck this instant, and hopes he shall not have to send for you twice."

Up jumped Weazel in a trice; whilst the gunner smiling, said, "There's a proof of liberty and equality, Mr. Corncob! Don't you mind what he says: he is as full of mischief as the devil himself. Take my advice—read this book: in it you will learn obedience to those placed in authority over you; and you will see that if every one was equal, you would not be able to grow tobacco."

As the gunner at two bells went on deck to do his duty, Corncob stretched himself on the chest and fell fast asleep; whilst Weazel, his imagination being excited by the grog, endeavoured to find out some trick which would create a good laugh.

Corncob slept soundly, forgetting half his miseries since he was allowed a life of idleness; and being naturally a very easy fellow, he began to think his fate not quite so bad, and that he might see a new part of the world before he returned to Portsmouth.

In days past, marines wore tails. They did not grow from their heads, but they had regulation tails, made of whalebone covered with a tuft of hair at the end. They had fair and foul weather tails; and as the breeze blew, so they took a reef in their tails, or shifted them altogether, like a storm main-topsail. Corncob soon had one of the small tails appended to his collar; but the tie was of similar magnificence to the fastenings of the tail in a Spanish colonel's horse: Corncob's tie was an exuberance of bunting most fantastically arranged.

The weather being very fine, the trifling motion of the frigate nursed him to sleep: the gunner's grog, with a plentiful allowance from some reserved case-bottles, had bewildered Corncob, who slept soundly until one bell after four o'clock. Then Weazel appeared with his side-arms and cocked-hat; and having restored the senses of the American by a somewhat rough shake, he began, "Mr.

Corncob, Mr. Jones has desired me to speak to you on a subject of some importance, with which I beg to engage your undivided attention."

Corncob gave an American sigh, which was strong enough to upset a jolly-boat.

"Captain Murray is well aware," continued Weazel, "that you possess the spirit and the integrity of your countrymen, and being a free man, would not like to go to prison."

"Ay, but I calculate that I'm a prisoner slick enough just now."

"If you call being amongst friends being in a prison, perhaps your remark might be admitted to be true. But Captain Murray looks at the subject in a different light: he wishes to know if, in the event of our falling in with a French frigate, you would prefer a post of honour and command, to skulking below with the doctor in the cockpit, holding the fag end of a broken arm whilst the surgeons cut it off from the stem. As he wishes you to make your own choice, he has deputed me to mention the subject, being well aware that an American—one belonging to that great nation—would only be insulted if he were *desired* to go below in security when his comrades were in danger upon deck."

"Your captain's a man, I expect," said Corncob; "upright and downright, like a donkey's fore-leg; no skulking about like a strayed nigger in a bush, all blazing and fire like a pine lath, and as straightforward as a fox's tail. I guess he's made no mistake in his man; for although I'm not half horse, half alligator, like a Backwoodsman, wherever the danger is, I calculate there you'll find Jonathan Corncob. I don't know much about a ship, but I can gallop along the decks like an Indian in a forest; and therefore, with all due thanks for your captain's kindness, you may tell him that I shall be by his side,—for he will be in the thick of them, I calculate."

"You have justly estimated the captain's character, Mr. Corncob: he is under some obligations to you for your hospitable treatment of one of his and my old messmates, and therefore he has desired me to offer you the command of the horse-marines. Although at present, of course, a dismounted corps, yet they are so called because in the event of landing they become the cavalry, if horses can be found for them. I am desired to offer you a uniform, which your servant, one of your own corps, will bring you directly: we shall beat to quarters in about twenty minutes, and your station will be on the quarter-deck near the captain. You need not change your coat; but it would be better if you put on your boots and spurs, which your servant has prepared, in order to show the men what command you hold. I will lend you a cocked-hat with the proper cockade, and you will do famously."

From the time Corncob had mentioned to Murray the circumstance of his having befriended Hammerton, he had perceived the very marked difference of manner in both officers and men: he had been released from his slavery, had dined with the captain, had drunk grog in the gun-room, and had expressed a wish that he might be stationed in some post of danger in the event of a fight. Weazel had taken the hint from this, and followed it up well. The marine who brought the well-cleaned boots wore also himself a pair of boots and spurs; and Corncob, from the subservient manner of his *valet de place*, believed he was acting rightly and respectfully to the men with whom he had to serve. His toilette was completed just as the drum beat to quarters, and a minute or two was allowed to elapse before he was told that the tune just played, "Come, cheer up, my lads, 'tis to glory we steer," was the air which summoned him to take his station on the quarter-deck: and accordingly Jonathan Corncob, in a pair of old top-boots, spurs, striped jean trousers, a yellow waistcoat, with a blue coat, cocked-hat, and regulation tail, having swung round him a ship's cutlass, walked on deck, and crossing over to windward, thus announced himself to Captain Murray:—

"Well, captain, here I am, I expect, booted and spurred, and ready to stand by you if the Frenchmen come even as thick as mosquitoes on a damp evening in Maryland. I'm told this is my station by your side, and here, by God, I'll stick as close as cobbler's wax to cobbler's twine!"

"Mr. Jones had been attending to his quarters, seeing that the men were sober and all present, and consequently did not see Corncob, who cut a more ridiculous figure behind than he did before; for the tie of his tail hung down to his stern-post, and was done up of all the colours of the flags allowed in his Majesty's ships. There was a titter fore and aft, but not a man dared laugh—the *Arethusa* was in much too high a state of discipline for that.

Captain Murray looked at him, eyed him from head to foot, and then said, "Pray, Mr. Corncob, what situation do you intend to hold, by wearing that dress?"

"Captain, I calculate, of the horse-marines. I can ride, I expect, anything between a donkey and an elephant; and as for shooting, I guess I could knock a man's eyebrow off without touching the skin at seventy yards."

"Go below, Mr. Corncob," said Murray, scarcely able to refrain from laughing: "we shall not want your corps to-day."

"Go below, captain! not I; I'm not a man to hold the fag end of a sailor's arm whilst the surgeon cuts it off at the stem. Jonathan Corncob has been shot at often enough on shore, and cares no more for the whiz of a ball than he does for the buzz of a humming-bird."

"Then, Mr. Corncob, I must desire you to go below: some one has made a fool of you, and dressed you up in a manner more likely to be serviceable in one of Richardson's booths at Portsdown fair than on the quarter-deck of the *Arethusa*."

"I heard you were shy, captain; but never mind, I expect before long you will have rubbed off your modesty. Why, dang it, man! we are all equal: why should you feel so overcome-like by seeing one near you who will protect you? I'll stick by you, I tell you, foul wind or fair wind—blow high, blow low; and when you dine with me to-morrow, I'll show you what a friend I am when I set about it."

Captain Murray, seeing that the American had got this crotchet into his head, called Mr. Jones, told him to send Mr. Corncob below; and by the help of a party of marines he was placed in the gunner's cabin and divested of his tomfoolery.

At quarters Murray manifested his intention of doing away as far as possible with a part of the idlers. The marine officers were desired to keep watch, to take the first and middle watches by turns: this did not suit their notions, and they remonstrated. Murray was quite prepared for the objection, and insisted upon one of the marine officers going round the decks every half-hour to report that all was safe below, and that when the watch were required to effect any manœuvre, they were to see the marines worked at the rope.

This order, unusual, it is true, was not likely to make the young captain much beloved by the marine officers; still the order was sullenly and silently obeyed.

"Reef topsails, Mr. Jones," said the captain. The hands were turned up, and Murray with his watch in his hand stood close to the binnacle. The weather was calm, and the reef taken in and topsails at the mast-head within the minute. "Reef topsails again, Mr. Jones: I must have it done in less than forty-five seconds this evening, or I shall go on all night until it is done. Forty-six seconds," he said, as the topsail-halyards were belayed. "Shake both reefs out, Mr. Jones, and try it again. Forty-four seconds," said Captain Murray: "I thought we should manage it within the time. Before we have been a week at sea, it will be done in thirty seconds."

"Well, I calculate," said Corncob, who had broken adrift from his confinement and got on deck, as he stood by the side of the captain, "that is tarnation smart work, and beats monkeys in cocoa-nut trees to eternal shivers."

Captain Murray did not dislike the compliment, although he wished Mr. Corncob elsewhere.

"Here, captain," said Corncob, "take a quid; it's real Virginia cut—it will do you good, and help to get over the shyness. Why, you're as coy of a man as a black-foot Indian is of a mosquito!"

Captain Murray walked below, and sending for Mr. Jones, desired Corncob might be taught naval manners, and made acquainted that any indiscretian in the way of drunkenness would be, in spite of his situation, most severely punished. Jones took the affair in hand kindly, and Corncob was soon convinced that he had been hoaxed, that the gunner was his best friend, and that Weazel was nothing more or less than the devil in uniform.

In spite of all Corncob's growing respect for the captain—for he easily perceived that all on board bowed to him, young as he was—the American, although gradually becoming more and more a convert to discipline, could not entirely eradicate his early notions of liberty and equality. Although it was evident, even to his not unprejudiced mind, that where one commanded and the rest obeycd, there was more order and regularity, more concentration of power, more effective force, than in the disjointed efforts of an undisciplined band; and although Jonathan Corncob often administered the lash on the backs of his niggers, yet he shrunk at the very notion of there being any inequality between white men. The gunner gradually enlightened his mind, and kept him from sporting those republican notions which tend to disorganise society on shore, and are sure to ruin discipline on board.

CHAPTER XXVIII.

A CHASE.

THE *Arethusa* had cleared the Channel, and was in the Bay of Biscay, when she encountered one of those furious gales of wind, creating enormous seas, which poets have dignified as "rolling mountains." A frigate well managed, with good sea-room, is, however, as safe to its inhabitants as a cradle rocked by a careful nurse to the babe within. The ship mounts the wave, tops it, falls gradually down into the vale beneath, and so continues until the wind and sea subside.

On shore, woe betide the poor fellow who passes along a narrow street in a storm! Tiles, chimney-pots, leads, come sweeping along the narrow pathway, dealing wounds and destruction. In the fields the trees are torn up; upon the road the passing vehicle is upset. And so said Tom Turner, the captain of the forecastle, to a knot of seamen who crowded round him as the *Arethusa* was rolling over the high seas of the Bay of Biscay.

"I tell you, boys," said he, "that them poor devils on shore are always in danger; they can't go from home to buy a pound of pigtail without being fired at from the roofs of the houses, or being jammed to death by a capsized cart, and the cargo falling upon them. No, no, my lads! here we are in a fine stiff breeze, with only a close-reefed main-top-sail and forestay-sail set; the higher it blows the steadier we remain; and as we have nothing to do in the shape of work, we can pass our lives merrily, and sing a song or two to the honour of our frigate, which, if I don't mistake, has got just as noble a captain as ever swam."

"He does not send out much of his fresh meat to the sick, though; and when, the other day, Bill Halliday was near giving us the slip, and getting discharged dead on the books, the steward would not give a drop of wine out of a nearly emptied decanter, because he said he had seen the captain, when the officers were gone, pouring it out into a tumbler to measure it, and then clapping it back into the bottle. He may be a devil to fight, but he'll never pay much to paint the ship; and if we get a little black outside with a Frenchman, and knocked about on board, I'm blessed if we shan't come out in a new suit of dockyard yellow!"

"Why, he got the purser to give the Yankee a coat, although he might have rigged him out from clew to earring himself."

"All the better, boys, for us!" said the first speaker. "If he's so precious fond of money, he won't let a strange sail pass without overhauling her; and when he gets paid himself, he'll take care we get our share also. Let's see," continued the old tar; "sailed on a Wednesday; that's a lucky day, although I don't think the officers of the jollies like it: there they walk the deck as stiff as a midshipman on half-pay. I thought he would make them do something for their money!"

"Well," said another, "it's all right enough; every man to his station, and the cook to the fore-sheet. I fancy, from the 'reef topsails' the other night, we shall all be known according to our qualifications, as the purser's steward says. That fellow launches more long-winded names than can be found in the open list of a three-decker! Well, it's an ill wind which blows nobody good; and the smarter the officer the more justice is done to the active man. Come, Tom, give us a song: if the wind does not get in your throat and blow the words about, you're just the man that can turn a stave. Let's have that one about the *Arethusa* and the frigates, you know, when the jolly craft tackled three of them."

Tom Turner here cleared his voice, which was as rough as the links of a chain-pump; and after clapping his quid in his pocket to keep it warm until he wanted it again, he sang the old song:

"Come, all ye jolly sailors bold,
Whose hearts are cast in honour's mould,
Whilst English glory I unfold—
Hurrah for the *Arethusa!*

"She is a frigate stout and brave
As ever stemmed the dashing wave;
Her men are staunch to the favourite launch;
And when the foe shall meet her fire,
Sooner than strike we'll all expire,
On board of the *Arethusa.*

"'Twas with the spring fleet she went out,
The English channel to cruise about,
When three French ships in sight so stout
Bore down on the *Arethusa.*

"The captain hailed them, Hoh! ahoy!—"

"A light on the weather-bow!" said the look-out-man forward. The song was instantly stopped, and one of the ring jumped aft. The wind blew so strong that the voice was with difficulty heard; but the officer of the watch was apprised of the stranger being in sight.

"Jump down, youngster, into the captain's cabin, and bring up the night-glass. And if the captain asks you, tell him that there is a light seen on the weather-bow; but that as yet I have not made it out."

The officer of the watch now stood upon the foremast quarter-deck carronade slide; and when the *Arethusa* rose to the sea, he caught a glimpse of the light. The bearings were instantly taken, and the watch turned up to make sail. As the *Arethusa* was hove-to in the gale, coming up and falling off, the stranger appeared one moment broad on the weather-bow, and the next nearly ahead. It was with great difficulty she was caught in the field of the night-glass; and it was more of a guess than a certainty that the stranger was a large ship running before the wind under her topsails and foresail.

No sooner was Captain Murray apprised of this than he was on deck. Naturally sanguine, and eager to show the

Admiralty that they had not confided the *Arethusa* to one likely to be a discredit to the service, he was resolved, even if the stranger had been an eighty-gun ship, to try his men and his metal against the superior force. At first the wind and the spray prevented his seeing the stranger; and it was not until the *Arethusa* came up to the wind, and the light was seen on the *lee*-bow, that it became evident the lieutenant was right in his guess, and that the vessel, whether friend or foe, was running before the wind. There was, however, a doubt if the light seen was the same as had been previously discovered, and no orders were given to make sail until after a lapse of some minutes; when, in a hurried glimpse of moonlight, the vessel herself was seen on the lee-bow.

"Turn the hands up—make sail," said Captain Murray: "set the foresail, and keep her away four or five points. Tell the carpenter to see the fire-screens all ready: and, youngster, tell the master I want him immediately."

Mr. Jones, a smart, active officer, was soon on deck and took command. The captain desired him to set the fore and mizen topsails, and to get everything ready for action, but on no account to cast loose any of the guns. "Stow the hammocks, Mr. Jones," he continued, as he went below to his cabin, followed by the master.

The chart was soon on the table; the compasses and the parallel rulers were in requisition; the distance of the frigate from the lighthouse of Cordovan was measured; and the swinging compass overhead pointed out that the *Arethusa*, if she kept two more points away, would be running directly for that place, being distant from it two hundred miles.

"What do you think she can be?" asked the captain.

"She must be either a French frigate steering for the lighthouse, or an American ship making a run to Bordeaux."

"Either would do for us," said the captain, rubbing his hands; "but if she gives us a hard run, we shall get on a lee-shore: we must therefore carry all sail we can bear, and endeavour to bring her to, or to action, before daylight. At the rate we are going now, which, I should fancy, cannot be less than ten knots, we shall by eight o'clock to-morrow morning have neared the land to one hundred miles: and if the gale blows home to the shore, we should find ourselves quite near enough at that distance."

Mr. Stowage, who was a rough seaman, merely remarked, as he rolled the chart up, that the stranger must be a good sailer to outspeed the *Arethusa;* but that under any circumstance, with the gale so heavy as it then was, it would be imprudent to venture nearer the land than eighty miles.

The first pipe of the boatswain's mate was heard, in spite of the creak of the ship as she surged over to leeward in the gale; and every man fore and aft was instantly on the alert. Sailors, from long custom, awake to the minute when their watch begins, and their ears are always susceptible enough to catch any unusual sound between the eight bells of one watch and the eight bells of the next.

"Tumble up, every mother's son of you, fore and aft!" said the boatswain, as he ran under the hammocks, lifting some out as he raised his back, and shaking every lazy fellow as he trotted along: "Tumble up, there—make sail!" The first order was followed by the pipe of the boatswain's mate at the main hatchway, which was answered by the boatswain on the lower deck. "Up all hammocks—heave out and lash up, my lads—look alive!"

"Call the drummer, there, below!"

Every man knew at once that he was wanted to beat to quarters; and it required no words of the boatswain to hasten the men: regular good seamen, ripe and ready for any action, they were quick enough, and in an incredibly short time the lower deck was clear, the *Arethusa* under her treble-reefed topsails and reefed courses, with the wind abaft the beam, going at the rate of twelve knots an hour in chase of the stranger.

Although hope is ever alive in the hearts of seamen, and, like the rest of the world, they are willing to believe that which they most wish; yet, sanguine as every man fore and aft the ship was, it was but too evident they did not near the chase. She was right ahead; and as now and then the thick clouds blew clear of the moon, she was seen staggering under the same sail as her pursuer, and steering a steady course for Cordovan lighthouse. Every eye was directed towards the stranger; and to the constant, almost momentary, question of "Do we near her?" the same answer was given: "Yes, sir—yes; coming up fast!" Stowage, the master, and the gunner, were the only two who put a decided negative on the question; the first saying that a dollar split into bits would occupy all the space the *Arethusa* had neared the chase, and the gunner murmuring, "Truth is truth!—we rather drop astern than forge ahead."

"I calculate," said Corncob,—who, although Weazel had endeavoured to persuade him that he might when the hammocks were stowed, being a passenger, lie down on the captain's sofa, had been one of the most vigilant,—"that trying to catch that frigate is like trying to hold on a nigger on a hot day: he's sure to slip through your fingers."

These discouraging intimations agreed but indifferently with the sanguine mind of Murray. To have fought an action in his new command was the object nearest to his heart. But now came all the horrors of a leeward shore: the gale, far from diminishing, seemed to increase as they neared the land, and it was hopeless endeavouring to creep off the shore; for the ship, had she been rounded to must have been placed under her storm staysails.

"I'm blessed," said Tom Turner, "if ever I have seen the light yet! and I think we are chasing the fore-topmast staysail sheet-block, which is dangling about there like a purser's shirt on the clothes-lines."

"How many bells is it?" asked Captain Murray.

"Past six, sir," was the reply.

"How many knots are we going?"

"Twelve and a half, sir."

"Mr. Stowage," see how many miles we have run since we bore up."

The master went under the half-deck, and there added up from the logboard the distance run, and reported that the ship had already run sixty-six miles, and that four more might be allowed for the heave of the sea.

Murray was a young captain, and he began to be slightly fearful of the heavy responsibility he incurred. Walking aft with Mr. Stowage, he asked his opinion in an open manner, for he was not ashamed of confessing that he had some fearful apprehensions of a lee-shore.

"It is beyond a doubt, Mr. Stowage," he said, "that we do not near the chase; and if I had not seen her myself, and made out during a glimpse of moonlight the very sail she was under, I should be inclined to yield to Turner's opinion, that we were chasing the fore-topmast staysail sheet-block, instead of a French frigate, so exactly does she appear to me to keep her distance. We have yet three hours to daylight; by that time we shall be within ninety miles of the land. The gale increases, and I see no chance of its diminishing."

"I can give my opinion," said Mr. Stowage, "without being afraid of any man's saying I did it from fear; and I do so now fearlessly. As master of the ship, I consider it my duty to point out the danger in nearly the same words you have used; but if I could shut my eyes a little, I should like to go on until daylight, and have one shot at that long-legged frigate; for she is the first that ever held way with the *Arethusa*.

"Then you consider it imprudent to continue the chase, Mr. Stowage?"

"I think, sir, we might try it an hour longer."

"Very well," said the captain; "we will stand on. But I should like to prick her off on the chart. Come below, Mr. Stowage."

The point of the compasses was soon placed on the spot; the ship would be embayed by daylight, and no power could have crept her off. Murray had some fearful remembrances of the *Tribune:* the awful roll of the surge came upon his ear with a kind of death-howl; the desperate struggles of the drowning crew were plainly before his eyes, the men fighting against a certain death; and all the horrors of that dreadful event came as a warning to him to forego the fame which might be acquired, and the money which might be his. This last was the bitterest of all: he saw that his men—nay, himself, might be sacrificed to the love of money and ambition. Again he walked forward on the forecastle; he took the night-glass from the midshipman whose duty it was to keep his eyes upon the chase: he felt the fresh gale which blew from the foresail; he saw his ship flying before the wind like a scared bird; and at every surge of the *Arethusa*, as the foam was driven on before her, he felt a sickness of heart, which he knew did not arise from fear of anything but a shipwreck. It was impossible for him ever to forget what was so indelibly stamped upon his memory.

Murray argued with himself, "If I round to now, and

give up the pursuit, my men, who hardly know me by sight, will attribute it perhaps to cowardice." The very thought nearly suffocated him. "I will act for the best, according to my opinion," thought he; "and will not allow any apprehensions of expressions, however disagreeable to my feelings, to sway me in my duty."

"We do not near her an inch," he said, addressing the midshipman. "Do *you* see her plainer than you did?"

"No, sir: on the contrary, I begin to think she draws away from us."

"I expect it's the sea-serpent," said Corncob; "and if you make the tail by daylight, you'll have to go a hundred miles before you get upon its broadside! I calculate it's either the *Flying Dutchman*, or the devil on an alligator cutting off his scales to make fire-proof shoes!"

"Do you think, Turner," said Captain Murray, "that we near her?"

Turner took off his hat, and replied, "Not a fathom, sir, since we bore up."

Mr. Jones came forward: he was of the same opinion.

"It's confoundedly against my inclination; but it must be done! Shorten sail, Mr. Jones; furl everything; round to on the starboard tack, and put her under the fore and main staysail and trysails: mind what you are about in rounding her to."

"Hands, shorten sail!" cried Mr. Jones.

Every sail was reduced in a seamanlike manner; and watching a time when the sea was more moderate in its height, Mr. Jones ordered the master to round her gently to. The man at the helm hardly put the wheel two spokes a-lee; the frigate flew up to the wind; and in spite of the master's warning voice, who, standing on the gangway, saw that a sea would strike her before she had her bow to it, and had cried out, "Right the helm!" a tremendous sea came foaming and towering along, burst right on her beam, and spent its whole force on the broadside of the *Arethusa*. The ship shook fore and aft as if she had struck the bottom; the bulwark by the main-channels was washed away so far as to endanger the mainmast, and the mainmast itself was supposed to be sprung; the foremost quarter-deck carronade broke adrift; four men were washed overboard. It was a moment of considerable anxiety. Mr. Stowage called out that the ship must be wore instantly, to save the mainmast; whilst some anxiety was expressed by the carpenter in regard to the injury.

In the confusion which occurred, the captain was missing: but he was heard in the larboard-quarter boat, where he had jumped, and was urging the men to their utmost. He seemed suddenly to recollect that he was the captain, and required to give the orders; he left the boat, resolved at all hazards to make an attempt to save the poor fellows. The first lieutenant strongly urged him to relinquish the rash desire; the sea ran high, and if the mainmast fell, more men must be sacrificed.

In the mean time the confusion increased. The gunner had secured his lost gun to leeward, which, fortunately, had brought itself up by running against its opposite neighbour; and when Corncob tumbled in amongst the men, saying, "Where can I be of service?" he received the consolatory answer, "At your prayers!"

The men who had gathered abaft held the boat's tackle clear for running, whilst some strained their eyes on the weather quarter to look for their lost shipmates.

"Hold on—hold on the boat!" roared Mr. Jones; "no boat can live in this sea."

"All ready for lowering!" screamed Weazel, whose voice hardly reached the deck, so high was the wind.

Not a trace could be seen of the poor fellows; the loud-bellowing sea breaking into foam lighted up the ocean, but not a mark was visible—no hat floated to give a hope, and the wide and wild surge sung the death-song of these seamen so suddenly snatched away.

Murray turned his eyes away, for he could no longer see, and reproached his men: "Had I not been captain, and my presence was required here, I had been there!" and he pointed to the boat.

There were volunteers even then. "I'll go, sir!" said Turner.—"I'm ready!" said Smith.—"And I! and I!" said others.

"Let's have one good try," said Weazel: "we can but be drowned; and my promotion is running to leeward!"

It was useless now. The boiling surf had long since overpowered the strongest, or the spray blown from the top of the sea would have drowned them. They were gone—lost for ever, without an effort to save them—snatched from their companions, and in the pride and prime of life hurried into eternity.

"Hands, wear ship!" was now heard. The fore and mizen topsails had been furled: but the men had been called down from the main rigging, and the topsail flapped in spite of the buntlines and clewlines, until it split to ribbons, and was blown in fragments to leeward. The fore-staysail was run up, and the *Arethusa's* head paid off to the breeze.

"Keep every man clear of the mainmast," said Murray; "and let the carpenter and his crew come aft with their axes. If it goes at all, Mr. Stowage, it will be when we are before the wind."

The old sailor nodded his head, but did not return an answer. Again the frigate forged ahead, and the remnant of the maintop-sail, with the courses, caught the wind. She was now before it; and Mr. Stowage might have been seen with his eyes fixed aloft, and grasping more firmly the stanchions of the hammock-netting as he watched with impatient glance for the ship to roll back and regain her equilibrium.

Murray stood by the capstan. There was a cool disregard of danger in his manner as he walked to the main-bits, and giving the starboard fore-brace into the hands of his men, he stood on the larboard side to ease off the lee-brace as the head-yards were rounded in.

"By your leave, sir," said the captain of the after-guard—"this is my station; and Mr. Jones did not place me here to hold on the slack of a rope in fine weather!"

The ship at this time rolled heavily over, and some one called out, "Stand clear of the mainmast!" The captain felt himself rudely pushed away from the bits, and the old sailor held the brace, which he slackened as coolly as if he were working into Spithead in a moderate breeze. Carefully was she rounded to on the larboard tack; she rose beautifully to the sea, and by five o'clock the mainmast had been secured by the runners and tackles. Hawsers were passed round the mast-head and hove taut; the hammocks were down, and half the crew asleep.

The gunner was the only man who denied himself the blessings of repose. His swinging light might be seen surging over from side to side as the ship rolled; and he might be perceived in earnest prayers, and heard returning thanks for his own safety, and praying that those who had been swept from the living might not die the death eternal.

Heavily passed the rest of the night with Murray. Some of his shipmates had perished; whilst the remainder, who looked to their captain and stood prepared to obey every order, might be brought, if the gale continued, to the same untimely end, or walked as prisoners to a French garrison.

CHAPTER XXIX.

A FIGHT.

The lowering morning at last dawned; and daylight was no sooner established, than the carpenter was seen mounting the main rigging to examine the mast. On his arrival at the catharping-legs, he saw the gunner, who was ever at his post, overhauling the main-yard. It was soon ascertained that the mainmast was sprung, and it became requisite to secure it more effectually. For this purpose the top-gallant mast and maintop-sail yard were got on deck—the maintop-mast was struck, and rendered into a powerful fish by being lashed to the mainmast.

The wind increased as the sun rose, the fiery appearance of the clouds augured no favourable change, and the *Arethusa* was rolling heavily on the sea as she drifted every hour nearer the land.

Various were the opinions on board the ship as to the conduct of Captain Murray. The marine officers curled their lips as they spoke of the smart captain: one, indeed, said, "Had he commanded, the *Arethusa* would have run the stranger on shore, if it had ended in the loss of his own ship."

"I am not sorry, Mr. Stowage, that I gave up the chase when I did," said Captain Murray. "Had there been no harbour open for her, I should have deemed it my duty to have insured her loss at any risk: but to run after a vessel which can enter a friendly port, whilst the only chance left to the pursuer would be the choice of evils, either a shipwreck or a prison, would be the height of rashness, and savour of madness."

"If this gale continues, sir, we shall have enough to do to save the frigate. Supposing we only drift two knots to leeward in the hour, by this time to-morrow we shall be on shore: at present, carrying sail is impossible; if the worst comes to the worst, we must run into the Garonne."

Captain Murray turned away from the plain-spoken Mr. Stowage, and taking Mr. Jones abaft, he asked the names of the men washed overboard, and if they were married.

"Poor fellows! poor fellows!" he murmured.—"Oh! I thought I had forgotten something. Send the captain of the after-guard aft—the man who was stationed to attend the fore-braces."

The sailor came aft, and Captain Murray addressed him, "I allowed your conduct last night to go unobserved, and I have forgotten your insolence in your courage. You were one of the men in the boat also. I shall give you a better rating on the first opportunity: and mind, sir, the next time you wish your captain to move, even if the mainmast is falling, touch your hat when you speak to him. That will do."

During the whole day the gale continued; but at sunset the squalls came less frequently, and the scud aloft flew in a more southerly direction. The reefed foresail, close-reefed fore and mizen-top sails were set, and Mr. Stowage began to rub his hands and look more pleased. The *Arethusa* ultimately weathered the danger; and the wind having become fair for Gibraltar, Captain Murray steered for that port, and anchored therein.

No sooner was the ship at anchor than Mr. Corncob was sent for. He was told that he had better take a passage in the packet, which was to sail the next day. "Take care," added Murray, "how you walk about Gosport again with nothing but a stick for a protection!"

"That's all particularly pleasant, I calculate," said Jonathan; "and I guess I shan't be unhappy to get along again out of this infernal fix, where one day a man's made captain of the horse-marines, and the next told that there is as much difference between a captain of a ship and Jonathan Corncob as there is between the President of the United States and a nigger. Ah! Weazel, I reckon, is a sensible chap; he is the only man who could make that straight-haired gunner understand that a man who has two legs and arms is no better than his neighbour.—But, captain, I calculate it's all well enough to talk about packets; but packets don't take passengers without being paid: so, if you are the man I take you for, shell out the dollars, and trust Jonathan Corncob: he won't sleep in Portsmouth one night before he's cleared the score, with five per cent. interest."

"I'll endeavour to get you a passage in a man-of-war," said Murray, the old complaint still sticking to him.

"But I reckon I don't like your men-of-war," said Corncob; "for if I had not just by accident mentioned Mr. Hammerton's name, I calculate—ay, captain?" and here he made an intelligible sign in reference to gratings and cat-o'-nine tails."

"Well, well," said Murray, "we will see about it: but I suggested the man-of-war because there you would have gone free of all expense."

"Tarnation particularly take expense! I guess I'm a man who can count dollars in bags; and if I dip my hand in, I calculate my head will find means to fill it again. I won't go in a man-of-war; and if you don't like to lend me the money, I dare say your steward—we are all equal, you know—will not be quite so nice."

This was a regular hard hit, and Murray felt it. He himself, however, was determined not to pay; so he drew a bill upon his father for thirty pounds, and told Jonathan any one would cash it on shore.

Although Murray had conquered his bitterness of feeling to a great extent against Hammerton ever since he had fallen in love with his sister, yet he could not overcome his love of money, or his fear of parting with it by any act of his own. He was aware of the meanness; but it had grown with his growth, and had become perfectly rooted.

Corncob took a kind leave of all—he shook hands with every man fore and aft, from the captain to the sweeper, and gave them all invitations to his house in Virginia; before he sailed, he had paid his passage-money, and given all but a couple of pounds amongst his old shipmates. "I calculate," said he, "that you are all a proper set of men, with no more fear about you than a monkey in a cocoa-nut tree. There's something to remember the man you pressed; and although we have not had a smooth passage, or turkeys and ham to eat, yet I've seen enough to know an English seaman, and to love him as much as my own brother." And as he went over the side, a tear filled the generous fellow's eyes. Murray wrote home to his father by the packet, and desired a fonder remembrance than usual to Amelia.

At Gibraltar the *Arethusa* was repaired, all deficiencies made good, and she was once more in a state of efficiency. The packet sailed—Corncob had got upon the wide Atlantic; and the senior officer, having some need of a frigate elsewhere, despatched the *Arethusa* to Malta.

Previous to Murray's sailing, he made many inquiries concerning the loss of the *Rover*. Nothing certain was known about it at Gibraltar; but the conjecture was, that she had been captured by an Algerine—that she was much too fine a vessel to have been capsized in a white squall; and had she been wrecked, some tidings of the melancholy event must have reached Gibraltar. But one circumstance was communicated which gave Murray much pleasure: it was the remark of a trading captain to his employer, who mentioned having met at Smyrna a smart-looking craft engaged in the same trade as his own; and after giving some opinion as to the success of her voyage, he added, "If we had not heard the *Rover* had been burnt, I could have sworn to her build, although the figure-head has been altered."

This conversation, which had been related by the merchant to him, afforded Murray an excellent opportunity of writing to Amelia. He did so; and by way of filling up his letter and making it more palatable, he dressed up the story of the horse-marines, with a few additions, to cheer the dinner-party of Sir Hector.

The *Arethusa* arrived at Malta. The commander-in-chief was at the time off Toulon, and she was despatched off Cape Secie in order to meet him. As the admiral himself intended cruising off the port for some time, Captain Murray received orders to cruise off Naples for three months, and then return, after having provisioned at Malta, to Port Mahon.

She arrived off her station. Captain Murray, a young officer, eoger to distinguish himself, and knowing the power of boats when night conceals the force and renders it difficult for the attacked party to make a sure resistance, was constantly on the alert to annoy the enemy. No vessel coasted in security along the shore, and the fort of Terracina more than once had fired into the frigate. Every prize captured only made the captain more anxious for another: in secret he counted his money; and as his avaricious disposition increased, while he calculated his increase of wealth, he grew the more niggardly to himself, although to his officers his table was ever open.

On the 17th of April, 1806, the *Arethusa* was six or seven leagues to the westward of Civita Vecchia, when a small boat was discovered to leeward. As the wind was fresh, the frigate soon came up with her, indeed she never attempted to escape, but pulled towards the *Arethusa.* There were only three men in her: two pulled, the third steered; and this last ascended the side, and walking over to Captain Murray, produced a paper, which after he had read, he desired the stranger to walk below to his cabin.

This man was a spy—one who had often escaped the death he merited as a traitor. Paid well by the British Government, through some of the officers on the station, he risked his life to give information tending to ruin those with whom he resided in amity and good-fellowship. In the present instance, he gave information that a French flotilla were to sail that morning from Civita Vecchia bound to Naples; and that if the *Arethusa* stood at once for Naples, she would cut them off. The spy further added, that he would rather be left in his boat than towed by the frigate; as, when night fell, he knew of a sheltered cove where he could land in security. A certificate was given as to the intelligence, and the boat of the traitor shoved off; whilst the *Arethusa*, under a crowd of sail, stood in-shore towards Naples.

At a quarter past four P.M. the man at the mast-head reported several vessels under the land. They soon proved to be the objects of pursuit: one vessel, ship-rigged, appeared a formidable vessel; there were three brig-corvettes, a bombard, a cutter, and three gun-ketches. As the frigate neared the flotilla, the immense disparity of force became evident; the larger vessel was made out to be a large corvette; and when one of the marine officers hinted that there were a good number of them, Murray remarked, "the more the better: they are but small craft."

"Ah!" answered the first speaker, "the Lilliputians overcame Gulliver."

"Nonsense!" said Murray.—"Mr. Jones, send every man aft." When they were assembled,. Murray thus addressed them:

"My lads, I was in hopes to have run you alongside the French frigate in the Bay of Biscay; and most fortunate it was for us that I relinquished that which was my greatest ambition. The wind this time appears to favour us. We have some work before us; but I know that in this ship every man will do his duty as becomes an English seaman. I shall do mine by placing you in the midst of the enemy, and leave it to your gallantry and good conduct to get me out again with some prizes fast to the tow-rope.—Beat to quarters, drummer.—Mr. Jones, pay attention that everything is in its place."

"The flotilla, sir," said the officer of the watch, has formed a line and hove-to."

"Give me the glass.—Mr. Stowage," said Murray.

"Sir," answered the master.

"Take good bearings of the mouth of the Tiber; those vessels are at least two leagues from the shore, and, I think, hovering about that shoal we noticed last evening: let me know if I am right. Egad!" he continued, talking aloud, "they offer battle nobly: what a set of little dirty boats to fire on a frigate! Let me see—I must go in ahead of the ship-corvette, and astern of her second ahead. We will take these two first; and if the rest only wait and amuse themselves by firing at us until we have succeeded in the first attempt, I will answer for it none of those lads dance at the Carnival this year!"

The flotilla at a quarter before seven o'clock opened their

fire. The water was as smooth as a mirror; and the steady aim taken, with the determined appearance of the flotilla, made one or two who calculated chances more than prize-money look a little doubtful as to the result. "If the wind falls," says one, we shall be in a nice predicament!—close to the shore, surrounded by a flotilla, night coming on, the calm almost certain."

Murray walked up and down the deck a little quicker than usual; and as the grape and canister rattled aloft, and the round-shot whizzed over his head, he appeared to be more gratified than at his own table when ordering another bottle of wine. "Take it coolly, my lads," he said; "it will be our turn in a moment: both broadsides, at once—take good aim. I'll place you close enough.—Starboard, Mr. Stowage, a little; go right between the ship and the brig, but closest to the ship. Stand by, my lads, on the main-deck; now then,—fire!" At the word, the roar of the two broadsides followed, the thick smoke enveloped the frigate, and cries from the brig gave ample notice of the destruction which had followed.

"Round to, Mr. Stowage;—sail-trimmers, to the larboard-braces. Take care, Mr. Stowage, not to shake her in the wind, but to keep good steerage-way: over to the starboard side, every man."

The *Arethusa* now ranged up alongside the brig. The ship-corvette filled instantly to support her companion; and the brig, not relishing so powerful an adversary, took advantage of the smoke and shot to pass the frigate. The corvette now came gallantly alongside, and commenced a very spirited attack; whilst the brigs took up raking positions, and poured in their unreturned fire.

It was past seven P.M. when the action commenced on the part of the *Arethusa*; and although she was close alongside of a vessel of far inferior force, yet so determined was the resistance and so well maintained was the contest, that it was nine o'clock before the corvette surrendered. This seemed a general signal for flight: the conquered vessel was taken possession of, and sails trimmed in pursuit; and although the desperate resistance of the one vessel proved how gallantly the French were disposed to meet their enemics, yet Murray viewed the whole force through a diminishing medium—they were never in appearance too ample for his grasp, or too powerful to be subdued by his skill and intrepidity. In spite of all his endeavours, however, he was doomed to be again balked: the small vessels soon began to sweep out of gunshot, and by ten o'clock every one of the vessels but the *Bergère* was under shelter of the forts, and escaped from all further attacks of the *Arethusa.**

The very determined resistance of the *Bergère* reflected the highest honour on Commodore Duclos, who commanded her; and the other captains of the flotilla were solely indebted to the disabled state of their opponent, and the danger of approaching the shore, for their fortunate escape.

The prize was soon manned, and despatched that same evening to Malta. The killed were buried with all the honours of war, Captain Murray being well aware that seamen are particularly alive to any attention paid to their messmates under such circumstances: a volley or two of musketry, the band playing sacred music, and the service read in a properly impressive style, make upon the survivors a deep sensation of gratitude. In this action the *Arethusa* lost eight men killed and twenty wounded; and she was further weakened by her spars being damaged, her hull struck, and twenty more men absent in the prize.

The next morning was devoted to shifting topmast, repairing sails, reefing new running-rigging, and making the frigate look as if she had not been in action.

Murray now felt the conscious glow of self-approbation as he penned his first despatch: the immense disparity of force was evident. After giving an account of the number of vessels and guns, he never for a second dwelt upon the superior force to which he was opposed; he spoke in high terms of admiration of the conduct of the French Commodore, and thus enhanced his own valour by affording deserved praise to his antagonist.

We have had two or three occurrences worthy of being remembered in the service, which have been thus described in the despatch:—"I have the honour to inform, &c., &c., that his Majesty's ship under my command captured, on

* The nautical reader will remark, that the action above recorded is taken from the gallant exploit of the *Sirius*, Captain William Prowse.

the 20th of June, the enemy's ships named in the margin; and I have the honour to be, &c., &c." The enemy's ships "in the margin" amounted to four times the force of his Majesty's ships: and this was the whole account of the action. "Glory to God and the Empress, Ismail is ours!" is perhaps the shortest despatch on record: but Suwarrow never wrote much. The best answer to a desire to strike is that of Captain Jeremiah Coghlen, who was told to do so by a very superior force. "Strike!" said he, "that I will, and d—d hard too!" and so he did too, and took the vessel opposed to him. "Give me a certificate," said a French captain to Captain Coghlen, who had captured him without making the least resistance—indeed, he never fired a gun—"that I have acted *bravely*." "I can't exactly do that," replied the gallant Englishman; "but I'll give you a certificate that you have acted *prudently*."

The *Arethusa* had stood some distance from the land, and the second day after the action with the flotilla, the man at the mast-head reported a large ship; the signal midshipman reported her as a frigate, and Mr. Jones, who had perched himself on the top-gallant yard, reported her as a very suspicious sail. It was at daylight that she was first seen, the wind being north-east by east, the *Arethusa* standing on the starboard tack, the stranger bearing south-west. Captain Murray instantly bore up in chase.

As the weather was very hazy, some time elapsed before the stranger was properly made out. She was evidently a frigate on the larboard tack, with her royals set; but the difficulty of accurately discovering her course or her intentions arose from her having her mizentop-sail aback and her maintop-sail shivering. The rake of her masts was decisive of her nation: there was not the least doubt that she was a frigate from Toulon, which had crept along the coast, and was now apparently disposed to court an action.

Captain Murray was resolved not to disappoint her captain; and in his short energetic address to his men, he mentioned his regret at the loss he had experienced from the last action, and the absence of his men in the prize: "Not," said he, "that the victory is in the least degree doubtful from their absence, but that I regret such brave fellows should be excluded from sharing the honour with us. That, my lads," said he, as he stood on the carronade-slide, and pointed to the chase, "that is a French frigate: in three hours' time she shall be an English frigate! And now, my lads, we have no lee-shore to fear, and, thank God! no one to assist us. This will be a fine trial of strength, and our former *practice* will now become beneficial. I shall lay you close alongside; and I have confidence enough in the *Arethusa's* crew, although diminished in numbers, to expect the certain capture of that ship. We will keep our three cheers until we are near enough for the crew to hear them; and when the work is done, we will splice the main-brace."

Whilst this was occurring on board the *Arethusa*, the officers of the French frigate were passing their remarks and calculating their prize-money.

"She is nothing more than a corvette, and not a very large one either," said the French captain to his officers.

"She certainly does not look very large, although she is in the haze," replied the first lieutenant; "and there can be little doubt of the result."

"These English sailors," continued the first, "consider themselves invincible, and that no vessel has a right to sail the seas but their own: we must look large to her from our position, and with our royal yards aloft we must appear what we are. And yet the little vessel comes down as gallantly as if she were a three-decker. It is marvellous how some men walk to their certain destruction, and how coolly they tumble into a trap which with common prudence they might avoid!" He then addressed his men, who were at quarters, desiring them "to fire high, so as to hinder the escape of the rash captain who was coming down to sail with them into a French harbour."

It was eight A.M. The French frigate had remained on the larboard tack, waiting for the *Arethusa*, and keeping still under the same sail. She hoisted her colours, and fired a gun to windward. As this was considered a fair challenge—a kind of throwing down the glove, Captain Murray ordered the colours to be hoisted and a blank cartridge to be fired. "Mr. Stowage," he said, "after we have beaten that gentleman, he will try to escape; we will engage him to leeward to prevent it. We may have his smoke in the first instance, but we shall prevent any bearing up and making sail. Where is the gunner?"

"He is busy on the main-deck," replied Weazel, "priming the men, sir."

"What do you mean, Mr. Weazel?" said the first lieutenant.

"I heard him say that all hands were loaded with sin, and that he would prime them for heaven."

"This is no time for any nonsense, Mr. Weazel! Go down in the main-deck—ask him if everything is right in the magazine."

Mr. Weazel was down in a moment. "Gunner," said he, "the captain wants to know if your work is done in the magazine."

"No, my work is not done in the magazine, Mr. Weazel; but I have told the sinners of their state, and have given them some of the magazine to read, and I have not been sparing of the tracts: many of them who are here now will be there to-morrow," pointing to the sea,—"and to go with such a load of sin!"

"Holloa!" said Weazel, "has any one given you an acting commission of parson, and told you to preach? Why, if you talk that way, you will make half the men afraid of their lives! Hand here that rubbish!" said Weazel; and he began collecting the tracts, which the seamen had shoved into their waistbands, and said they would read when the business was over.

"Well, Mr. Weazel, what does the gunner say?"

"He says, sir, his work is not done; that all hands are fitted out for a hot cruise below; and that if we do not read these things,"—handing out the tracts,—"we shall go down stern foremost, and be stirred up with a long pole hereafter."

"Poor fellow!" said Jones, "he is half mad, but very sincere. You had better bundle that rubbish overboard.—But stop; even my curiosity gets the better of me now: let us see what they are. 'Wrappers of Wrath for the Cold in Christ'—'A Wet Blanket for the Burning Soul'—'A Comfortable Draught for the Thirsty Sinner'—'Crumbs of Comfort for the Craving Christian'—'New Steps for the Broken Ladder'—'A Tough Tow-rope for the Trusty Tar.'

Why, here is enough to make a mutiny on board of the Channel fleet! and some of his own trash amongst it. 'A Monkey's Tail to point the Gun of Salvation'—'A Blue Light for the Sinful Sailor'—'The real Rocket to lift the Righteous'—'A Spark to Fire the Devil's Magazine.' Bundle them overboard," said Jones: "a regular attempt at mutiny, and enough to damp the ardour of any man! That psalm-singing boy does as much mischief as his master!"

Whilst this was going on abaft the mizen-mast, the captain had visited every part of the ship: he was loudly cheered as he passed round the decks. He saw the signal-books collected, the weights put in the box, and having satisfied himself as to all arrangements both below and aloft, he came on deck just as the gunner's magazine, as Weazel called it, was drowned.

The French frigate, at a quarter to nine, opened her fire, directing all her guns aloft; then filled her main and mizen-top sails, gathered way, and wore, bringing a fresh broadside to bear upon the *Arethusa.* The wind being light, much time was required to near the Frenchman; and he, availing hiimself of his position, practised the above manœuvre three times, thus keeping almost his own distance; for when he got before the wind, he seemed much superior in sailing to the *Arethusa.* Murray's impatience soon became manifest; the shot of the Frenchman rattled amongst his rigging, and finding that many men must be sacrificed before he could pass to leeward of his wary antagonist, he altered his determination, and ran right at her to windward.

This gallant measure succeeded: by a quarter after nine both frigates being then on the larboard tack within pistol-shot, brought their broadsides mutually to bear, and an animated fire commenced. The *Arethusa*, being under all sail, with the exception of her studding-sails, shot ahead of the French frigate: the latter, immediately profiting by her opponent's damaged state of rigging and of her own position, bore up, and thus getting her guns to bear on the stern of the *Arethusa*, raked her. She then instantly luffed up and tried to bestow her starboard broadside in the same manner. This last intention was frustrated by Murray, who instantly ordered the sail-trimmers to the braces, threw the *Arethusa* right aback, brought the bow (or rather, stern) of the Frenchman against the starboard quarter of the *Arethusa*, and, foul of each other, they lay in a parallel direction.

"Boarders on the starboard quarter!" The word was repeated, and immediately the men, headed by their different officers, (the boarding-pikes and cutlasses gleaming in the sunshine,) rushed to the appointed place; whilst on board the Frenchman the cry was also to board, and her forecastle was crowded with a very superior force.

"Avaust boarding!" said Murray. "Mr. Weazel, jump down on the main-deck, and tell the officer of the after-quarters to get one of the guns through the cabin-windows. —Fire away, marines,—that's your sort; keep down all but the small-arm men!—Jones, jump below, and get that gun ready!"

The Frenchman, having tried three times to carry the *Arethusa* by boarding, and being beaten off each time, turned their attention to a long brass thirty-six pounder which was on their forecastle, and brought it to bear upon the English frigate: whilst the soldiers on board the French ship annoyed Jones and his party by keeping up a steady and well-directed fire upon the cabin-windows, killing and wounding vast numbers. Foremost amongst the most active was Weazel; he was now quite in his element—he cut his jokes as readily as if out of all danger: and the gunner, who was told of the position of the ships, finding the powder-boys did not come to replenish their boxes, was likewise conspicuous at the post of danger.

"Hand here the tackle, Pounce!" said Weazel: "there —bob your head like a mandarin in a tea-shop, or you'll go after your magazine with lead enough to sink a man of three times your specific *gravity*. That's your sort!" he continued, as the gunner worked in silence. "Now get a handspike—not that monkey's tail of yours, and handspike the gun round,—never mind the captain's lockers—down with the rudder-head—kick that rubbish overboard; hand here a cartridge—a rammer, you precious-looking cuckoo! I beg his pardon—he caught that shot right in his hand! Now, then, my lads! you are half of you indebted to the gunner for your wounds; for had he fitted a long tackle to the gun, instead of writing his 'Monkey's Tail,' we should have cleared away those precious Frenchmen half an hour ago: there they stand right along the larboard gangway, blazing away at us as if we were sparrows on a dung-heap!"

Murray, finding the whole fire of the French marines directed towards the cabin-windows, and hearing that the deck was literally strewed with the killed and wounded, went down himself, sent Mr. Jones on deck, and there saw Weazel foremost in all the danger, appearing to bear a charmed life.

"Well done, Weazel!" he exclaimed; "your promotion is sure."

"Thank you, sir," he replied; "the gunner thinks I shall never be exalted. Now, then, we are ready; hand here another canister, and just another bundle of grape: there's fruit enough for half Paris!"

The gunner, who had never said a word, but worked in the most exposed part, took as quiet aim as if he were practising at a cask, and fired right along the French frigate's deck. It stopped all the musketry—no less than twenty of the enemy were killed by the single discharge, and the ship appeared swept from stem to stern, since not a man was visible for a minute after that awful fire.

"There's D. D. for a lot of them," said Weazel. "Pounce, you have all this on your conscience; you have set those fellows dancing to a tune they don't like. Knock that powder-monkey's eye out! why don't you move?—hand here again." Again the gun was fired, sweeping fore and aft the Frenchman's deck, and creating a fear which even the gallant Frenchmen could not overcome.

In the mean time, the *Arethusa's* marines were not idle: their fire was so well directed that the French frigate was unable to use the forecastle gun, and both parties, from their vicinity to each other, were obliged to stoop under the bulwarks to load.

Half an hour had the two ships been in the position we have assigned them, when a light breeze caught the sails of the French frigate (her yards being braced up, whilst the *Arethusa's* were aback), and she forged a little ahead. As she advanced on the broadside of her antagonist, the jolly tars poured in the contents of the guns, cutting away the head-rails and gammoning, and seriously wounding the bowsprit. The Frenchmen were now all in their glory; again they gave a cheer as their frigate shot up upon the broadside of the *Arethusa*, and a most destructive action commenced, yard-arm to yard-arm,—the one party fully convinced of the superiority of men, the other firm in the belief that they could beat three French frigates.

Weazel was heard singing the song,

> "And when the foe shall meet our fire,
> Rather than strike, we'll all expire,
> On board of the *Arethusa*."

"Blaze away, my lads! never mind expending the powder; plenty more where that came from. If I can only catch hold of any mate of that ship, I'll see if his fingers will grow on my hand again!"

Murray's voice was likewise heard cheering his men, and the advantage of practical gunnery now came into play. Almost every evening the *Arethusa's* men had practised at their guns; and from being quite at home at their business, with the advantage of the real practice the two days before, they now fired nearly two shots to the French frigate's one. The battle soon exhibited sufficient proof of the good firing of the *Arethusa*, when, with her maintop-mast gone, her foremast tottering from its wounded state, the French frigate relinquished all hope of capturing her opponent, and passed ahead of the *Arethusa* and was soon out of gunshot.

On board the English frigate every brace and bowline had been shot away; her sails were cut to pieces, her main-royal mast, maintop-sail yard and gaff were in shatters; and although, comparatively speaking, uninjured in the hull, she lay on the waters perfectly unmanageable. The gaff had been shot away when the two ships first fell foul of each other, and the flag of the English ensign falling on the forecastle of the Frenchman, they instantly seized it, tore it from the gaff-end, and carried it aft as a trophy. Murray looked at Weazel, who directly got a boat's ensign, stuck on a boathook, and called out, "That's all the prize-money you'll make out of us to-day, my lads!"

"Now, then, Mr. Jones," said Murray, "turn the hands up, refit ship,—I have not half done with my friend yet, and he looks as much like a wounded bird as ourselves,—

let a party of men get a new set of sails up: hand up some coils of small rope—anything will do to reeve for the present: look sharp, my lads! Topmen aloft! unbend sails!—let the gunner look to the main rigging, and a small party of the marines go down below to remove any of the wounded men, and carry the dead forward out of sight—cover them over. See to this, sir," he said to the second lieutenant of marines. "Knot all you can aloft, Jones; reeve and cut the rest:—don't wait for orders aloft! —unbend as quick as possible! Well done in the foretop! —There, my lads, look ahead of you!—there's her foremast gone;—we'll have her before one o'clock.—Step out with the foretop-sail halyards. Well done, my lads,—trim sails! —Jones, here's a delightful breeze coming; the Frenchman's a perfect wreck, and long before they get clear of their foremast we shall be alongside.—That Weazel is a wonderful fellow, where is he?"

"He's down in the cockpit, sir," replied one of the youngsters, "very badly wounded."

"Go down and ask the surgeon about it, youngster. Weazel and the gunner," he continued to Jones, "although as opposed to each other as oil and water, are two of the finest fellows I ever saw."

"He is very badly wounded, indeed, sir," said the midshipman, coming on deck; "but he says he shall die contented if he only hears the cheers of the men when the French frigate strikes."

"He shall not be long in being so gratified," murmured Murray; "although if it is to be the last sound he hears, I declare I wish that ship to escape. To quarters again; we have her now, Jones!—Mr. Stowage, place us as close alongside of her as you can without getting foul of her. Stand by, my lads. Now, then, one and all, with a good will, give her three cheers!"

In an instant the lower rigging was crowded, and three such hearty cheers were given, that Weazel started from the chest on which he was laid in the steerage, joined in the cheer, and singing out,

> "Rather than strike, we'll all expire,
> On board of the *Arethusa*."

fell back and fainted.

The effect of these cheers upon the Frenchmen may be imagined: their ship, which they had fought and defended with determined bravery, lay a wreck upon the waters. The *Arethusa* was coming up on the starboard side, over which was the wreck of the foremast. The men, from the gallant manner she approached, became dispirited; and after a short council of war, in which it was resolved that all further opposition would be useless, the tricoloured flag of France was ordered to be struck; and at fifteen minutes after noon the *Arethusa's* men gave the cheer of victory; and poor Weazel, unable to speak from weakness, moved his fore-finger round his head, imitating the manner in which a sailor waves his hat when he cheers, and died.

The *Arethusa* ranged up alongside, hove-to, and received on board the brave Frenchman who had so gallantly defended and so excellently manœuvred his ship. As one brave man receives another less fortunate than himself, so did Captain Murray his former antagonist. He took the sword which was offered to him, and returned it with courtesy and elegance. "He," said Murray, "who has so gallantly wielded the weapon in his country's cause is the best man to retain it;" with this he offered it to his conquered foe, and taking him by the arm, led him to his cabin. The bulkheads had been run up the instant the French frigate struck, and the brave but unfortunate Frenchman found himself, by the generous foresight of Murray, effectually screened from the public view, which of all things is the most humiliating when a man is first led into captivity.*

Leaving the captain below, Murray was again at his post. He gave positive orders that the prisoners were to be treated with every respect, and their wounded with every care. He declared that any violation of his orders would be visited with a severity of punishment which should be long remembered:—no cruelties, no plunder; the enemy who has struck should be your friend, and he who has nobly defended his ship should never be insulted.

"Mr. Jones," said he, "change the prisoners, and let

* This action, which we have here given faithfully, is a just tribute to Captain, now Sir Thomas Baker, who, in the *Phœnix*, captured the *Didon*, in the manner thus described, and whose force was exactly that which is stated on the next page.

them be searched. We must be prudent; for owing to our loss and their superiority of numbers, it is not impossible that they will attempt to recapture the ship. But, by heavens! if they do, I will be just as severe for the breach of honour as I would against my own crew for a breach of trust!" Murray's face became pale as he repeated the last words; and with an impatient motion he thrust his hand into his bosom, as if feeling for some object, which, having found, his tranquil manner returned.

Mr. Jones was now actively employed: he was to take charge of the frigate, and he had to select his crew. It was impossible to work the prize with less than sixty men, and these were sent from the *Arethusa*; twenty prisoners were retained on board the *Didon*. This left the *Arethusa* thinly manned indeed, especially for the charge of the men she had now on board. The comparative force was as follows:—

		Arethusa.	Didon.
Broadside Guns,	No.	21	23
	lbs.	444	563
Crew	No.	245	450
Size	Tons	884	1091

The superiority was altogether in favour of the French. Her crew consisted of young, strong, active seamen, trained by as gallant an officer as ever walked the deck of the French navy. No man has since stood higher in public estimation than Captain Milius; and no man more richly deserved the praise which he has received.

By the affair with the flotilla, the *Arethusa* was twenty-eight men short of complement. She had now lost ten men killed and twenty-eight wounded, besides the sixty sent in the prize; she therefore had only on board, in an efficient state, one hundred and nineteen men to take charge of three hundred and fifty in sound health, besides forty-four who were wounded. Murray felt unusually anxious: in the first instance, he had to lend Jones a hand in refitting the prize; and he scarcely liked to confine his prisoners below, for that looked like cruelty.

Whilst pondering over his future conduct he received a message from the prize, saying that it was requisite to cut the mainmast away, as it was so badly wounded that it could not be secured. This settled his resolution: the prisoners were placed on each side in the cable-tiers; the carpenters nailed some rough wood from the orlop to the lower deck, which made the exit difficult; whilst some of the seamen lashed capstan-bars between the tiers and the after-hold. Sentries were placed at each part; and thus security being, as was imagined, effected, the mainmast of the *Didon* was cut away, jury-masts were rigged, and the *Arethusa*, with her prize in tow, made sail towards Malta.

There appeared a perfect resignation to their fate amongst the officers of the captured ship. They fenced in the gun-room, played piquet with their messmates, and, with all the liveliness characteristic of their nation, sought to amuse their less volatile companions. No thought of the future seemed to agitate them; every misfortune which might occur was put down to "fortune de guerre;" and, like good predestinarians, they seemed to take the rough and the smooth without care or regret.

Not exactly so the prisoners in the hold or tiers. They had no space to dance quadrilles—no light by which they could play cards; the only gleam of a candle which they could get was from the sentry's lantern, the man and the light being placed on the hatches of the hold, and separated from his charge by the cage-like prison alone which had been so hastily erected. A Jacob's ladder was fixed on the combing of the hatchway on the main-deck, and only twenty-five men were allowed on deck at a time.

At first some few sung songs, and appeared disposed to make the best of their condition. This soon gave way to low murmurs, then to hasty words; whilst the men began to congregate together, to whisper rapidly, and, by their uneasy conduct, to manifest a disposition to act on some concerted plan.

This was duly reported by the sentry; and the French pilot of the *Arethusa*, dressed as a marine, was sent down to relieve the guard. Believing him to be an Englishman, and unable to comprehend their language—for they first tried him—they continued hatching their mischief. He overheard their plot; which was, to rise, capture the *Arethusa*, and recapture the *Didon*. The whole affair was to take place on the first occasion of allowing twenty-five men to walk on deck to get a little air and exercise. The last man was to seize the sentry; a rush was to be made, and the barricade to be broken down. The twenty-five men were to make a stand, until others jumped up the ladders, and thus they hoped to gain possession of the quarter-deck, where there was a stand of cutlasses, and by cutting a few throats to effect their object.

The pilot was eager immediately to bellow out the intelligence, and nearly betrayed his apprehensions by his constantly looking up the hatchway. At last he was relieved, and rushed on the quarter-deck.

Murray heard his intelligence, and reported it to Captain Milius, who was disposed to recommend a little punishment at once. But Murray waited quietly; he placed the pilot on the main-deck, desiring him to seize the ringleader when he came up. This was done; and Captain Milius's coxswain was the man.

The French captain was sent for, and the culprit stood before him. "Have you any complaint to make of unkindness, of severity, or of want of food?" asked Milius.

"None," replied the man.

"I knew it," replied the former captain. "Had you cause of complaint, I would have joined your enterprize. As it is, you are a dishonourable scoundrel, and unworthy of the name of Frenchman!"

He was placed in irons, and in a few days the *Arethusa* entered Valetta harbour with her prize in tow, and was safely anchored.

CHAPTER XXX.

THE TRADER AND THE FRENCH PRIVATEER.

We leave the *Arethusa* at Malta to refit, and Murray to rejoice over the honour due to him, and the prize-money in perspective. Jones was made a commander, and some few promotions occurred.

We must now follow Corncob.

His voyage in the packet was prosperous, and in twelve days from the date of his sailing he found himself at Falmouth. There he found a vessel going round to Portsmouth: his money had run pretty short, and he found out that his liberality had left him with just sufficient to meet the demand of the skipper of a coaster, but not to satisfy the bookkeeper at the coach-office. He had no choice left, although having stepped on shore, he had vehemently sworn never to trust himself again on board of any vessel but the *Matchless*. He was soon, however, shipped on board the *Mary Henderson*; and the wind being fair, about four in the afternoon they weighed their anchors and put to sea.

The captain of the craft was a rough, hard-featured, short, stout sailor—all open and above-board; a man who never said a civil thing by accident, and never was known by any chance to coincide in opinion with those who exchanged a word with him. Corncob, who really loved his daughter with much affection, was now in exquisite spirits at the thought of again seeing her. The mate of the vessel had pronounced the wind as sure to last, and calculated that by sunset on the morrow the *Mary Henderson* would be safe enough at Portsmouth. The craft was under weigh, the sails set and trimmed, when Corncob, unable to restrain his feelings, said to the captain,—

"Well, I calculate now all my care's at an end, and to-morrow I shall see my daughter at Portsmouth."

"Then, old boy," said the captain, "you calculate wrong; you won't be at Portsmouth this week to come; and as for your cares, you'll have a cargo of them before you land."

"I expect, captain, "you're one of Job's comforters," replied the American. "Why, your mate there, who seems to know as much of the clouds as if he had made them, guesses this wind will last."

"I guess he's wrong now, for he never was right, and that we shall have the wind foul before long."

"Well," said the Yankee, "I expect one of these days I shall get to my journey's end."

"Just the contrary," said the captain; "for you'll never be there till you die: and then you have got a journey of eternity before you, so you'll never get to the end."

"Well, I expect you are a particular pleasant fellow," said Corncob, "and must know the gunner of the *Arethusa*."

"Wrong again—never heard of him."

"I think," said the mate, "we had better get a pull of the weather-braces, for the wind's coming further aft."

"Just the contrary," said the captain: "the wind's coming forward, and the yards are too fine."

"I calculate, mate," said Corncob, "that your captain there is like a Maryland pig—if you want him to go one way, you must pull him the other."

"He won't agree to that I'll be bound," replied the mate; "for ever since I've sailed with him he has never once agreed with me on any question. He fell overboard one day, and I got in the boat and picked him up; and when I thought I would say something to comfort him, by remarking that boats were blessed inventions, or else he must have been drowned, 'Just the contrary,' said he; 'for if it had not been for a boat I never should have been on board the craft, and therefore never could have tumbled overboard.'"

"Well, then," said Jonathan, "I know my man, and I expect I'll get him to agree with me."

"Not you," replied the mate. "I tell you, if you swore you saw a ghost as white as snow, he'd swear he saw it also, but that it was as black as the devil."

In the evening, the captain and Corncob were down in the cabin. The wary old American descanted upon the danger of smoking below: "Just the contrary," came out—and with it Jonathan's pipe. Rum was "tarnation rubbish;"—the captain had nothing else, swearing it was the best liquor of life; and Corncob, now finding himself quite at his ease, puffed away heartily and swallowed large potations, merely, as he said, to try and become a convert to the captain's opinion.

"There's a vessel standing after us, sir," said the mate; "she's right astern and under a crowd of sail: she looks very like a privateer."

"Privateer!" said the captain; "why, it's a light collier bound to the northward."

"I think," said the mate, "we had better edge towards the shore, sir, and clap on a little more sail."

"Just the contrary," said the captain; "I shall shorten sail and let him come up, and then we can keep company together."

"I guess you'll keep company with him longer than you like, captain," said Corncob,

"I calculate I shan't, Mr. Yankee," replied the bear; "for when I am tired of his company I shall leave him to himself."

It was a moonlight night, the weather beautifully fine,

and the four or five men who composed the crew of the *Mary Henderson* had not gone to bed. The mate asked them all their opinions, and every one seemed inclined to fear she might be a French privateer, which had stood across the Channel to pick up any vessel disposed to make a run of it, or which might have been separated from a homeward-bound convoy, and sneaked up along shore to avoid such intruders upon commerce as those vessels were known to be. She came up fast, and the mate was about to make some remark, when Jonathan took him aside and said, "Now, mate, you may be a very good sailor, and know a horse-marine from a stuffed alligator, but I guess you don't know how to manage that man; what do you want done?"

"Why, to edge in shore, to be sure, and see if that vessel is chasing us or not. If she is, she will alter her course after us; if not, why all the better—she will go her course, and we ours."

"I calculate," said Corncob to the captain, "that the vessel astern would just sail round your clumper, for she's got a lighter breeze, but she's coming up fast."

"Just the contrary," replied the captain, "for she's got a much stronger breeze, and does not gain an inch upon us."

"You'll get a stronger breeze if you stand further out to sea: the wind is always scant along-shore."

"Keep her three or four points *in*-shore," said the captain to the man at the helm; "it's blowing half a hurricane there, and we shall go along the quicker."

No sooner was this done than the vessel astern seemed to alter her appearance. She was a lugger, with her sails on each side, going before the wind, and, with the main-topsail set, seemed before a small sneaking brig. Now she altered her course, trimmed her sails on the larboard tack, and steered three points higher than the *Mary Henderson*, in order to cut her off.

"I think there's no doubt now what she is," said the mate. "If that's not a French privateer, and we are not prisoners before midnight, there's no canvas in a foretop-sail!"

"She is a Cawsand Bay fishing-boat," said the obstinate captain; "and before midnight we might have a dish of fish for supper."

"It will be a dish of French souls, then," said the mate.

"Mixed up, I calculate," said Corncob, "with some fish-sauce from Dieppe."

The skipper soon became a little anxious: his obstinacy, however, did not give way as the privateer came up. A shot whizzed over his head.

"We had better," said the mate, "heave-to at once: we can never escape, and we shall only get the men killed."

"Just the contrary," said the captain; "we will carry more sail, edge in-shore, and, if we can, run the craft high and dry. He won't like getting too close to Plymouth; for he might find a man-of-war outside of him to-morrow, and the more he fires the greater risk will he himself run."

"Then he'll run alongside of us and board us," said the mate.

"Just the contrary," answered the captain; "for he'll try and sink us."

"Well," said Corncob, giving a sigh, "settle it amongst yourselves: I guess he dare not touch a hair on my head, or he'll have Congress at him in a moment; he'll know me for an American."

"He'll know you for no such thing; and being an old man, he will make you sweep his decks until he gets into harbour; and then you will grin through the bars as well as the rest of us."

The old obstinate pig, as Corncob called the captain, was, with all his faults, a brave seaman. He saw the danger, and he made the best use of the *Mary Henderson's* sails to avoid a prison; he made a good calculation also as to the probable behaviour of the privateer; firing guns would only alarm the coast, and getting too close in-shore might get the vessel becalmed;—and although he contradicted everything which was said, he still did everything a seaman could do to save his vessel. He had neared the land considerably; indeed, so much so, that a long point was now seen on the starboard bow: the privateer was at least a mile and a half distant, and appeared a little baffled by the wind. The breeze had died away considerably with the *Mary Henderson:* but for some few minutes she seemed to hold her own.

Corncob, whose eyes had not deceived him during the chase in the Bay of Biscay, was the first who called out that the privateer was no longer coming up. He was met, of course, by a "'Just the contrary:' she's running up hand over fist, and will be alongside before any man has time to say his prayers. But I'll give him a run for it—and right on shore too; so, mate, get the boat clear for hoisting out; we might get a shot through the one astern."

Corncob now began to lose his usual good spirits, and complained most vehemently of all the tricks Fortune had played him. He recalled his former days, and then thought how happy he might have been if he had left the cargo of *notions* to be brought over by any other man but himself, and if he had kept his daughter at home to be married to an American instead of hunting up a lost midshipman. He was a little startled by the whiz of a shot, which came just clear of the taffrail, and went through the fore and main courses.

"That hit us," said the Yankee.

"Just the contrary," said the captain: "it went through the sails. He may fire as long as he likes; but he shall have some trouble to get the craft off the rocks."

A light now appeared, which soon grew into a large fire, blazing beautifully in the clear night. Another was seen in another direction. The privateer almost immediately bore round up, and stood out to sea; whilst the *Mary Henderson* hove-to close in-shore, against which the ripple of the water as it broke on the beach was plainly discernible. There she remained until the privateer was out of sight, when she again made sail, and taking a fresh fair breeze, anchored in safety at the Mother-bank.

Corncob was soon on shore. Having shaken hands with the captain, and in the fulness of his heart thanked him for his kindness, "Just the contrary," he heard as he stepped over the side: "you paid me—I fed you—no obligation—all's square fore and aft—good-bye."

To Jonathan's uncommon delight, he found that his *notions* had been well sold; that his daughter was snugly housed, his agent an honest man, and Sir Hector likely to have been as a father to his child. Having received some money, he immediately began to steer a course towards his daughter's abode, and, like a true philosopher, turned all his wanderings to a salutary effect! "It will teach me to be contented at home," said he to himself; "and I guess he's a considerable donkey who has got enough to be happy upon, to risk it in making more! If ever they catch me afloat again, except to go from James's River to Norfolk on market-days, may I be most particularly thrashed by my own niggers!"

At Sir Hector's house everything had gone on quietly and comfortably. Murray's letter had given new life and hope to Amelia: she would not consider her brother dead whilst a chance remained of his being alive,—neither would she despond. Maria Corncob still clung to her first love: in Hammerton she had fixed her hopes of happiness, and now that she had cemented a strong friendship with his sister, she felt very disinclined to think even of James's River. Home had no charms for her whilst Hammerton was away. For her father she felt no uneasiness: Walter's letter had pronounced him well, and on his way to England, and she confidently looked forward to his safe arrival. She regarded Sir Hector as her father; and Amelia as her sister, companion, and friend.

After dinner one evening, as Sir Hector and what might be termed his family were sitting in the drawing-room, a very unusual noise was heard outside: the whole household seemed resolved to resist the entrance of some determined man, who blustered and created no common disturbance. Sir Hector, old as he was, manifested a little activity, and believing his castle likely to be taken by storm, was in the first instance for sending the women to fortify their chambers, whilst he proceeded to head his servants. He opened the door, and the sound of her father's voice broke upon Maria's ear.

"I hope to be eternally eaten by cockroaches, if I don't mash your skulls as I would a cocoa-nut!" said Corncob; and suiting the action to the word, he dabbed his broad hand upon the cauliflower head of one of the footmen, dispersing a most ominous cloud of white dust, which the ingenuity of the then chancellor of the exchequer had taxed as hair-powder. "I calculate you're a precious set of powder-monkeys!" continued Jonathan.—"Whew! whew! —here's a precious fog come out of the lazy vermint's head! But now's my time: here's board him, I calculate, in the smoke." And in the manner he had seen negroes fight in America, making his own head a battering-ram, he ran right on, and capsized him clean over old Benjamin, who was coming to his rescue with the kitchen-poker, rather too hot to be handled; and jumping over his prostrate antagonist, stood in the hall, panting for breath.

The maids, ever ready to satisfy their curiosity, each ran to the spot, shrieked, and retreated; and whilst poor Jonathan stood flourishing his arms for another attack, John the footman had recovered his legs, and armed himself with the hot poker. At this instant Corncob found his neck encircled by the arms of his daughter, and, making a stern board, came in no very fashionable manner into the presence of Sir Hector.

The Yankee's wrath was disarmed in a moment. The kind baronet welcomed him as an old friend; his daughter nearly smothered him with kisses; and Amelia, who saw before her the generous man who had sheltered her brother in his distress, seized the unemployed hand and said, "At least, Mr. Corncob, you must yield to the ladies!"

The surprise of Jonathan made ample amends for the fear he had caused. In the whole of his life he had never stood in such a mansion; and when he saw his daughter's improved appearance, the elegance of her dress, and her altered manner, he gave vent to his feelings in his real vernacular, and exclaimed, "I guess I'm fixed clean slick in a conjuring-box!"

His daughter soon introduced him properly to the baronet; but before any interchange of civilities occurred, Corncob broke adrift by saying, "Avaust heaving, old gentleman, as they say on board the *Arethusa*—short accounts, long friends. I expect I owe you thirty pounds your son gave me instead of a flogging; and here it is, which at the rate of five per cent. for seventeen days will be one shilling and three farthings interest: and there it is, I calculate, principal, interest and all; and when you give me a receipt, then, you know, we start all fair, excepting that I guess you have me on the debtor side of your ledger on the score of gratitude. But, Corncob, why rot it! I need not make a boy of myself either; but a man may feel as a man, I calculate."

"Don't think of it, my dear sir," said Sir Hector; "your daughter has returned all obligations by giving us the pleasure of her company. We will not talk of such things; supper is ready, and you must give us an account of your adventures."

So passed the evening; Corncob convulsing Sir Hector with laughter as he told him his adventure as a captain of horse-marines, his impressment, and all the tricks of that devil Weazel, whom, nevertheless, he said he loved for his fun and his good humour. These anecdotes brought to mind all his mischief-making propensities after the wreck of the *Tribune*: and Sir Hector, taking a pocket-book from its usual place of abode, wrote down in it Weazel's name: at that time he little knew how useless were all endeavours to serve him!

"And now," said Corncob to his daughter, "you must be ready to start to-morrow and return to James's River. The *Matchless* will be all in trim order for sailing, and when I have cleared the account with the agent, away we go home; and I guess it will be many a year before I sail again on the salt seas, without I can walk along the sea-serpent, which reaches, I calculate, from Sandy Hook to the Bill of Portland."

Maria looked at Amelia: in that look she conveyed her wish to die in England, rather than relinquish the chance of seeing Hammerton again.

"You cannot go to-morrow," said Sir Hector; "I have something to say to you on that head; besides, the *Matchless* can get ready just as well without you as with you."

"I expect you're wrong there; I know something about a vessel now—a man-of-war 's the school for improvement."

"I know that," replied Sir Hector; "it is the best school to refrain the vicious, to instil honourable notions, to correct the covetous, in the whole world; and if I liked the profession before, I could almost use a woman's word, and say I love it now."

"Well, sir," said Corncob, "to-morrow we will talk over all that; but I calculate now I had better get back to Taunton, for I over-sailed my harbour before I made the land hereabouts."

"Taunton!" said his daughter.

"A fiddlestick's end!" said Sir Hector; "you are in a comfortable harbour here, and here you shall remain: you are under my command now, and you must follow the commodore.

Supper was brought in; and Corncob, willing to show his liberty and equality principles, and likewise that he possessed a forgiving heart, shook hands with the powder-monkey of a servant, and said, "I calculate your head will ache for a month; so, as peace is proclaimed, here's give your hand and welcome; and let's have a glass of wine on the signing of the treaty, as Washington used to say."

Corncob spent one evening of his life at least free from care. His cargo of *notions* with which his schooner had been laden was sold; every article of any value belonging to him had been preserved; and he found himself none the poorer, but much the wiser, for his first cruise in the *Arethusa*. He had learnt, though late in life, a valuable lesson: he was convinced that, in all places and under all circumstances, liberty and equality were not maintainable; and he had perceived that order and regularity were necessary to preserve discipline;—he was now aware that a captain must be an absolute monarch, and that anything in the smallest degree tending to weaken his power was certain to create distrust, disobedience, and neglect.

"I expect," said he to Sir Hector, "that your son will turn out a tarnation fine officer: he is none of your tippy-bobby, Jemmy Jessamy, pretty considerably d—me kind of cocked-hatted coxcombs; but he is a sailor, and I calculate a seaman; foremost in danger, and prudent enough to avoid it when the risk is more than the venture is worth."

He then described the gale in the Bay of Biscay. Sir Hector's eye glistened with delight at the recital; and Amelia could not withdraw her look from the speaker while thus lavish in praise of him whom she loved. However, she was not quite so well pleased when Corncob wound up his remarks by saying that he would have made an excellent merchant, for he took care to draw bills upon others while he kept his own money snug enough.

After two days Corncob, with his daughter, took leave of the hospitable old baronet and of his adopted daughter: the latter having promised Maria not to omit writing upon all opportunities. The parties separated, and Corncob and Maria arrived in safety in the Chesapeake.

CHAPTER XXXI.

MEETING OF THE TWO CAPTIVES.

In the mean time poor Hammerton had remained in captivity. His mind, naturally buoyant, never sank under his accumulation of grievances: the wholesome punishment inflicted on the obstinate mate was not lost upon him. He saw the necessity of exertion, and with a willingness and cheerfulness which pleased the old Turk who was placed over him, he toiled through the drudgery to which, as far as appeared, he was condemned until the day of his death.

Too active, however, to lose all hope, his mind dwelt on the future prospect of escape; with this view he turned his attention to learn the language of the people by whom he was held in captivity. Naturally quick, he caught their customs: and when dressed in a turban, and robed according to the costume of the natives, he might have been mistaken for a disciple of Mahomet. On religious points he had many arguments with his friend Mustapha: the latter imploring him to turn Turk, giving his description of the change as more the work of a minute without pain than as any operation of the mind. These persuasions, however, did not convince Hammerton, who preferred receiving the occasional buffets due to "a dog of a Christian," to forsaking his early faith. He smoked his pipe, allowed his beard and mustachios to grow, and by endeavouring to imitate the people by whom he was surrounded, he was soon convinced that if a chance occurred his escape was not wholly impossible.

Another strong inducement kept his curiosity alive. Mustapha had forbidden him ever to approach the western side of the house. The small windows overlooked a garden which was surrounded by a high wall; and although Hammerton had heard the shrill voices of females, yet he never had seen one. Sailors are always very curious, and the more danger there is in an enterprise, the more they admire it: Hammerton, having a full share of that commodity, resolved to avail himself of the first opportunity of doing what was so strictly forbidden.

Six months had passed, and the watchful eye was relaxed. Hammerton was declared the best of all Christian dogs, and bore kicks and cuffs, insults and buffets, with the most spaniel-like subserviency. He was now left more to himself.

Turks have holidays as well as Christians: further eastward, warlike amusements constitute their principal recreation,—further south, indolence and inactivity are termed amusements; in fact, perfect freedom from all thought, cessation from all labour, the liberty of sitting in the sun to smoke, to relate anecdotes which never occurred, and to tell lies on the most extensive scale, may be estimated as the chief amusements to which a lazy Turk can be invited. One of their religious festivals occasioned a holiday, and Hammerton was left at home to guard the outside part of the premises, which would have been as efficiently done by the score of dogs which growled and yelped whenever a stranger appeared.

"Faith," thought Hammerton to himself, "this chance is not to be thrown away! As to making my escape, that is out of the question; I am not quite Turk enough yet, and I should soon be detected in my garb, or my tongue would betray me: besides I have no idea except by the sun which way to steer towards the coast, where Christians resort: but I may as well take a peep at the forbidden fruit, which the old boy locks up in his garden and his harem."

Having carefully surveyed the premises, and finding the coast perfectly clear, he got a ladder, and placing it against the westernmost part of the wall, he cautiously ascended. When he reached the point where his next step would have raised his head above the wall, he took a good survey around him: no human being was in sight. Not far from him were some sheep quietly nibbling the short grass; and now and then the sharp bark of the dog disturbed the dead calm of the day. Hammerton listened and heard steps approaching inside the garden wall. His heart beat high: he knew the rash act he was about to commit, yet he could not withdraw; but he still kept concealed. Not many minutes elapsed before an air familiar to most English ears was hummed by a delicate voice; yet no words were uttered. No other person joined in the song, or sung in answer.

"Sure I remember that voice!" said Hammerton to himself; "it is that of the poor girl whose shriek I heard when I was placed in the dark cell. How shall I ensure her notice without betraying myself? I'll try, however."

He immediately turned his head away from the wall, so as not to appear too close, and whistled the air she had sung. Turks never whistle. Hammerton, when he had concluded the first part stopped and listened. His ear caught the word, "Hist—hist," whispered above the silence around. He answered it in English, by "Here—here;" when he heard the footfall rapidly retreating, and shortly afterwards another voice was heard.

"Too late, by all that is good," said Hammerton to himself; "but the day is young yet, and I can wait. I'll have a peep, however;" and with cautious prudence he raised his head to the level of the wall, and taking a rapid survey, saw two women walking towards the house. Having tried the first attempt without discovery, he became bolder. He now perceived one or two more lingering in the garden, and becoming sensible of his imprudence, he removed the ladder, walked back, and placed himself under the wall.

His ear was stretched for the slightest sound; for, in the calmness and silence of that sultry day, the very melody of the birds came in an enfeebled tone, as if worn out by the lassitude of the heart.

At last footsteps were heard, then voices—one, two, and three, and one which plainly bespoke authority was of deeper tone and more commanding than the rest. From the silence which ensued, it was evident that the party were either standing still or had seated themselves on the grass. Presently the twang of a guitar reached his ear, and after some time a young rich voice, clear as the thrush's note, broke forth in a song. It was in English, the pronunciation clear and distinct, and given out with a fulness of tone which might lead her companions to imagine it was a song of joy, except that the air was melancholy. It was intended to reach the ear of Hammerton, should he still be at hand.

Deeply did its words sink into the heart of Hammerton: all that was loyal, Christian-like, and brave, rose within him; he hardly noticed the words of one of the other captive girls, as she lazily remarked that the air was melancholy and the song unintelligible.

"All but the last verse," said another, "and then the Isauri heretic was animated: what was it all about?"

Hammerton resolved at all risks to let her know that her song was heard, and that her words fell not on inattentive ears; in fact, that he would aid her to escape if possible. Reflecting for a few moments how he could apprise her that a friend was at hand, he recollected that he still had about his person the envelope of a letter addressed to himself; wrapping this round a pebble, in order to give it the necessary weight, he threw it over the wall in the direction of the girls, and from the loud shriek which followed, it was evident it had been seen and taken as the signal for a general retreat.

It was now useless to peep into the garden: the old lady who commanded in that Ottoman paradise had taken the captives to their apartments, and no doubt a more rigorous surveillance would be practised. Hammerton, however, resolved to visit the ground whenever he could, trusting to the ingenuity of the girl to manage some mode of communication.

The Turkish festival was over—the rigid disciples of Mahomet had taken their last bath and performed their last ablutions—the sun had gone down, the evening prayer had been muttered, and all remained quiet. The old Turk had returned home; and as Hammerton was neither bastinadoed nor confined, he concluded his artifice had not produced any complaint. His mind naturally pondering on the occurrences of the day, he watched with painful anxiety until Mustapha and the rest of his half-confused companions should fall asleep, being resolved to visit the spot and make himself perfectly master of the ground. The opium which these fellows had smoked, a thousand times more efficacious than brandy, soon did its duty, or at least seemed to do; the snore of Mustapha was decisive as to the repose he enjoyed, and the rest of the slaves apparently followed his example.

When Hammerton had satisfied himself that all were fast asleep, he stole gently away, took the ladder, and placed it against the wall; he then carefully examined the ground, to see if any paper or Oriental signal had been deposited. None could he find; and therefore, with the elastic step of one resolved to face a danger, he surmounted the wall; then lifted the ladder, and lowering it into the forbidden garden, he cautiously descended and stood on the dangerous ground.

The moon shone clearly, and gave him sufficient light to see the garden. In the centre was a small fountain which bubbled into a marble basin: the continued stream, by the noise it made, was a kind of safeguard to Hammerton—his step could not be heard. There was a grass-plat near the basin; and here and there, small raised heaps of mould, which were used as seats. It was on one of these spots, no doubt, that the English captive had sung her song of woe: there seemed but few flowers, and these sprinkled about without much attention to art.

The back part of the house had two wings, which projected into the garden, and nearly reached the fountain: in one of these, no doubt, the girl for whom he was thus risking his life was quietly asleep. Wound up to a pitch of desperation, Hammerton, unarmed as he was, resolved upon making an attempt to gain an interview, or, if possible, to let the Christian girl know that her song had not been sung in vain. Slowly and cautiously he approached the building. There seemed no windows, but, instead, something like loop-holes; and the whole front, although it opened on a gallery, bore no signs of any egress excepting by the doors. To scale this would not have required any particular activity, but the folly of doing so was obvious.

He listened attentively; but not the slightest noise of any kind disturbed the night, except the fountain, which bubbled on in endless monotony. With the greatest caution, scarcely more audibly than the murmur of the fountain, he whistled. He then stood trembling at his own audacity: no fair hand unbolted the door to welcome his daring steps—no sweet voice whispered thanks for the attempt—no kind and counterfeited cough told him he was heard or understood; all save the eternal fountain was silent. Again he tried more loudly; and then instantly withdrew and concealed himself behind a small tree. It was useless to try again; she must have heard it, had she not slept, and slept soundly.

At length he emerged from his hiding-place, determined to retreat, when, at the glass-door which formed the entrance to the lower apartment, he perceived a female form: the cautious manner in which she placed her small naked foot upon the ground, the timid eagerness with which she looked around, and then at the galleries above, convinced Hammerton that this was the poor girl who had implored him to effect her escape. All was still—even Hammerton held his breath, and watched the approaching figure, who, holding a finger to her lips, had now gained the grass and flew towards him. Her scarcely covered limbs betrayed the beauty of her form.

Hammerton took her in his arms, and instantly led her to the ladder. Not till then had they spoken: they had known each other in the *Rover*, and now their common slavery and misery bound them closely together.

"Now, now!" said the impatient girl; "now for our escape!"

"Impossible!" said Hammerton, with eagerness: "let not precipitation ruin our plan. To take you away now is impossible: half the night is gone—we should be overtaken before noon; you have no change of dress to conceal your creed. Be advised; no opportunity shall be lost. I have examined the ground well. At the eastern angle of the wall there is a thick plantation: over that part I will throw a button when the day comes on the night of which we are to make the attempt. You must manage to make the Turk sleep soundly, and in his dress you must escape. We must wait our opportunity, for I am watched more closely than you appear to be. Do not waste your time; learn the language well, and strive to find out in what part of the land we are; when the nearest caravan passes; and glean from the old Turk, when opium makes him loquacious, before he sleeps, how far we are from Tunis, Tetuan, Algiers, Oran, or any port in the Mediterranean: lead him first of all to talk of the interior, of Fez, Morocco—any place or country, so that when we resolve to start, we may strike into the interior at first, rather than go to the coast, in which direction they will follow us. Return, return! Good night!"

"Return!" replied the girl; "to the man who bought me, to him who now slumbers overpowered by opium—to the creature whom I loathe—who uses me like a part of his household property, who threatens me with the whip! No! I will risk it now! I cannot—I will not return! If you are the same Hammerton who, like an English sailor, defended your ship to the last, you will not desert me, who now implore your assistance to save me from further misery and degradation!"

"You must return!" replied Hammerton. "Before another hour, the first gleam of daylight will be visible: you know at that time every slave is at work, and I should be missed; the ladder would betray us; and how, without horses, without knowledge of the country, could we escape! —it would end in your death and my future imprisonment. Be guided, then, by reason."

"Reason!" she replied; "can that guide me which I have lost! You are a coward, and afraid of a stick! You dare not do even what a woman dares! you cannot be the man who surmounted all the dangers of the boat, and who nobly rushed at the pirate as the only means of saving the ship!"

"You wrong me, indeed you do! Every chance is against us. Hark! a dog in the yard is baying the moon; it will awake the sleepy hounds, who would gladly gain a little coin from their master by exciting his suspicion of me. I am the same I ever was—I will sacrifice my life to save yours; but I will not allow a woman's precipitation to ruin my plan. Good night!"

Hammerton jumped upon the ladder and gained the wall: he turned to remove it, and found the girl endeavouring to follow him. Knowing that all would be lost if at such a time the escape was attempted, he shook her from the step, which she still grasped with all her force. In vain he endeavoured to raise the ladder: she implored him to rescue her, and falling on her knees, and lifting both her hands as if to heaven, said, "I will worship you, if you will but save me!"

At this moment Hammerton lifted the ladder clear of her

grasp, and removing it to the other side, said, "As I live, I will save you! Think not the worse of me, because I now leave you. Hark! that cursed dog again! his bark shall be the pretence of my being awake. Go! go!"

Hammerton replaced the ladder in safety, and creeping to the straw on which he slept, threw himself down and slept soundly. What happened to the girl was unknown to Hammerton; but from the cautious manner he was watched, and the extra blows and work he received, it was not improbable but that either the button had caused suspicion, or that the foolish girl, unable, after she had strung her nerves to the escape, to return to the bed she loathed, was discovered by some of those rivals so plentiful in a Turkish harem, who, by way of enhancing their own merits, make known the weakness of the Christian girl.

From this time no opportunity occurred of revisiting the garden: another sleeping-place was appointed for Hammerton, and he would have required the eyes and the agility of a cat to have crept from his straw unperceived. His cheerfulness, however, never deserted him. Aware that any precipitate measure would only rivet his chains for life, he never rashly attempted what he foresaw he could not accomplish; but he turned his attention and his talent to master the difficulties of the language, and when any stranger passed the house, he would enter into conversation with him, and from his remarks try to learn if he was suspected of being a foreigner, He was thus more than once enabled to accomplish his object, in discovering the place of his confinement: he found that he was much further in the interior than he believed, and that his master, although he occasionally visited Algiers, was a subject of the Emperor of Morocco; that the long tedious journey which Hammerton had been compelled to undertake with Mustapha had terminated near the town of El-Harib, which stands about two degrees and a half to the southward of Morocco.

These tidings, confirmed by many who passed the house on their way to El-Harib to join the caravan which every month journeyed to the southward, were by no means agreeable to Hammerton. He knew that to pass to the northward towards Fez, to reach Tangiers, was the most dangerous route; for Christian slaves brought from Algiers and Oran were common commodities, and if once detected, he was certain that even the little liberty he enjoyed would be still further curtailed, his life being spared solely upon the principle that no one (who is not mad) kills a horse because it has strayed.

In the mean time, days and weeks slowly passed away; the usual work of driving the camels or of attending the horses continued; working in the noonday sun in the fields, and constant labour from sunrise to sunset, went on unvaried; and before an opportunity occurred to escape, Hammerton had been a prisoner for upwards of five years. During this time, however, he had by his cheerfulness and apparent resignation won the entire confidence of Mustapha, and once or twice had succeeded in beholding from a distance the white handkerchief of the Englishwoman, and, unseen by others, had succeeded in answering the signal. He was now able to pass for a Moor or a true Turk—the language of both were even more familiar to him than the English; for, with the exception of humming the song of his fellow-captive, his own language had scarcely ever passed his lips since his captivity.

CHAPTER XXXII.

ESCAPE OF THE CAPTIVES ACROSS THE DESERT.

ADVERSITY is the school of wisdom. Taught by that rigid master, we all become either philosophers or stoics: we learn to submit to our fate, and be at least apparently contented with our lot. Hammerton had by his steady application to the duty imposed upon him by his master, and by a strict imitation of the customs of the people by whom he was surrounded, so deceived all, that not even Mustapha, who was generally suspicious, imagined he harboured the least idea of quitting the terrestrial paradise in which, by the blessings of Allah, he was allowed the enormous privilege of being a slave to a true believer.

Mustapha was a steady good Mahometan: he was as convinced of the holy embassy of his master the Prophet, as that the beard grew on his chin; he was very conversant with the Koran, and fervently believing that an angel, as mentioned in that work, was hereafter to weigh men and women in a balance, he resolved to weigh heavy himself, smoked his pipe without moving even a muscle, and grew fat as he grew more indolent. He had a wife—that is, one out of four—to whom he gave the preference; she was suspected, but Mustapha, like Mahomet, had a chapter from the Koran in regard to Ayesha which satisfied him of his wife's purity; but when, after six years' quiet residence in his master's house, he was desired to prepare for the long toilsome journey to Algiers, he lifted his hands and said, "Blessed be Allah, who transported his servant the Prophet from Mecca to Jerusalem in one night, and grant that he may do the same to Mustapha as far as Algiers!"

Previous, however, to his departure, for he was to accompany his master, he very strongly urged Hammerton to turn Turk; and Hammerton, quite conscious that no opportunity would offer like the present, appeared to acquiesce, which gave the greatest satisfaction to Mustapha.

"Why," said Mustapha, "will you remain a dog of a Christian, when you can have all the blessings of our religion? It is the ass which always eats briars, whilst the lamb is cropping the fresh grass."

"Because," said Hammerton, "I was born a Christian; and if you had been born in England, you would have been a Christian."

"Allah be praised!" replied Mustapha; "my head was not covered with the dust of such a misfortune."

"No," answered Hammerton, "and therefore you have shaved it and covered it with a turban. You may yet live to see the day when the Padishah will let his hair grow, and wear a hat."

"Holy Prophet! what blasphemy!" ejaculated Mustapha; "after your conversion, we would stone you to death for such words."

"—And make a martyr of me to the good cause. But come, Mustapha, before you go on that long, tiresome journey to Algiers, to buy more Christians,—and which journey, Allah be praised! I am not condemned to take,—tell me what I am to do to become a good Mussulman."

"I'll do that for you," replied Mustapha. "You must, besides the outward signs, bathe five times a day, pray at sunrise and sunset, learn the Koran by heart, never eat pork, believe in Mahomet, and have a few wives."

"It is a very pleasant belief," said Hammerton, "and whilst you are away I will study it. When do you go to Algiers?"

"In three days' time: we are to take with us, as far as the mountains, one or two of the slaves; the Moors have lately been plundering. Those dogs of the devil have no more respect for a true believer than that cur has for its grandfather: they would rob a Christian for the value of his unsanctified garb."

"That is bad," replied Hammerton, "and you ought to be well attended. How many of the camels will our master take?"

"Six," replied Mustapha.

"Is there anything," continued Hammerton, "I ought to give the camels before they go on this long journey?"

"No," answered the Turk; "if we were going south through the sands, it would be requisite to make them drink as much as possible before they started; but on our route there are good resting-places, and no want of water. No," he continued, as he smoked; "but you are a good lad to have thought of it. When we come back, I will bring you a wife; and as you intend to turn Mussulman, I will get you a copy of the Koran. And although I know that whatever is to be must be, yet I should like to borrow the wonderful camel Borac, just to carry me to Algiers in a day. You will learn all about that animal in the Koran."

"How is it," asked Hammerton, "that our master has never been to Fez since I have been here?"

"'Tis a vile road," replied Mustapha, "and nothing but tyranny and oppression along it: if soldiers were wanted, they would as soon take him as they would bastinado you. No, no, Allah be praised! our master is no fool; he spends his life as a great man ought to do who is preparing for heaven: he rises early, goes to the bath, smokes his pipe, reclines in the shade, has the terrestrial houris to sing to him, drinks sherbet, sips coffee, says his prayers, eats, drinks, has his choice of the beauties, goes to bed, and never condescends to think, or to do any work. Allah! Allah! what would I not give for one such day of real happiness, to lie by the side of the fountain and hear the birds sing."

"Yes," said Hammerton; "on those mossy banks to recline while the bubbling water lulled you to sleep!"

"What know you of this place?" said Mustapha, his mustachios standing out like a cat's whisker: "has the dog of a Christian dared to profane the retirement of the righteous?"

"Don't be angry, Mustapha: in my country we have books, which tell us that in almost all gardens belonging to the faithful there are fountains and mossy banks: and our master being a great lord, I thought he would have what all other great men have."

"Tis well, Christian," he said: "now go, and I'll make a Turk of you to-morrow."

Hammerton now saw that the time for action was arrived: he began cautiously to collect those things which would be of service, and resolved not to hazard a discovery by venturing to the wall until his master and Mustapha had started on their expedition. One thing alarmed him: it was the usual custom for men of his master's rank to travel with their women; the poor creatures were packed up in a coop like chickens going to market, cautiously excluded from the prying eyes of the curious;—he would therefore remain uncertain whether the English girl would be taken away or not. As inquiry would only provoke suspicion, like his Turkish master he left all things to fate, trusting that the girl by some female adroitness would contrive to avoid the journey."

The first gleam of the morning saw the master, Mustapha, four slaves all armed, with a hen-coop of women, ready to set forth on their journey to Algiers. Before they started, the master called Hammerton and addressed him: "Dog," said he, "Mustapha has told me that you have seen the error of your belief, and are willing to become a Mussulman: take this—it is the book of the Prophet; read it, for you can read, I am told. I leave you behind, for you are, Mustapha says, learned as a Hakem; if the women are sick cure them; if one dies," and here he made a sign with his hand that no one could misinterpret. "Abdallah, take charge of the house, and tremble!" With considerable elegance of manner he held forth his hand for his pipe, which his dirty-mouthed slave had puffed into a light; and giving his horse the rein, the clattering hoofs resounded along the enclosure, and in a few minutes he and his retinue were far away.

Now came the decisive time. Hammerton felt that quick pulsation of the heart which precedes all dangerous undertakings; he felt how absent he must appear in mind to all observers, and he endeavoured to blind the dishonest Abdallah, who, finding himself left behind as master, at once gave himself the airs of a great man (all emancipated slaves are tyrants), and threatened to bastinado Hammerton if his work was not better done. With increased alacrity Hammerton continued his labours; he offered his services to his imperious master, who, naturally indolent, now enjoyed the height of Turkish luxury.

In the evening, the camels that remained were brought within the enclosure, and, as usual, suffered to go loose on the ground; but the driver, having profited by Mustapha's advice, made them drink much. Often did Hammerton's looks wander towards the wall, and once he caught a hasty glance of the English girl whose life he was pledged to save.

Abdallah, finding himself free from all restraint, indulged in his love of smoking opium, and, like all those who carry that passion to excess, he became intoxicated even to madness: he rolled about unconscious of his actions, raved, stamped, and fell. The few remaining slaves, glad to get repose, and wearied from the heat of the day, and the oppressive labour they had undergone, crept to their sleeping-places; whilst Abdallah, having vented his impotent rage in endeavouring to kick Hammerton, sunk from the raving of a madman into the idiot's slumber. No time was now to be lost: Hammerton secured Abdallah's fire-arms and sabre, and with restless impatience watched the moon as it slowly declined towards the horizon.

All at length slept; not even the slightest noise was heard: the brightness of the night was partially obscured by some passing clouds. Hammerton now gently placed the arms in his belt, and having wound up his mind for any act of desperation, he offered up a hasty prayer, took the ladder, placed it against the wall, surmounted, and descended without fear into the garden—the earthly paradise which Mustapha had pictured as the retreat of Sloth fanned by Pleasure—and with the same signal as before gave notice of his approach. Again the English slave appeared: more anxious than before, she almost pushed her deliverer up the ladder; but again she found the calm reason of her rescuer at variance with her excited hurry.

"You cannot go in that dress," said Hammerton; "the very circumstance of a woman robed as you are, travelling without the usual preparations of camel skins for conveyance, would excite suspicion. Go dress yourself as a man; if you are disturbed, clap your hands. This night we must escape, or never. Be not over-scrupulous; take whatever money or jewels you can find. I have provided some food for ourselves and the camels,—I have made every preparation, and only wait now to hang the water-skins and place you on the camel's back. Do not trifle with time: I will not leave you, though all the old women of El-Harib come forth to claim you: armed as I am, I may perish, but I will not—cannot retract."

She immediately obeyed Hammerton, who spoke as one in authority, whose directions must be complied with. But little time elapsed before she again appeared, dressed as desired: she had, amongst other valuable articles, appropriated to herself a pair of pistols, with some cartridges, and although the dress fitted but badly, yet Hammerton made no objection, but, taking her hand, led her to the ladder. "You must mount first," said she, "or I doubt if I could ascend in safety: seeing you before me will make me brave any danger."

No seaman ever scudded aloft with more sprightliness than did Hammerton. When they had descended on the other side, the girl looked back: "I have," she said, "taken these pistols of the Turk with me, that in event of our being retaken, I may destroy myself with them, rather than again fall into that horrible captivity. Now quick, and let us away."

"Not quite so fast, young lady," said Hammerton: "before we go, I must borrow a spare turban and skull-cap from my new master Abdallah; his pipe and tobacco-pouch I must have also, and the spare travelling-tent and pole will not be useless lumber. We have a hard game to play, and we must be attentive to the customs which prevail in these parts: a man without a pipe would be like a Turk without a turban."

Hammerton soon reappeared: a camel was laden with the water-skins, tent, and a quantity of millet and barley-cakes: some dates and brans were also placed upon the animal; a pack-saddle, such as are used in that country, was covered with some linen, and the fair fugitive was placed on it. Hammerton warned her that the animal would, unlike a horse, rise with its hind-feet first. On the other camel he was soon astride, and both moved forward. When clear of the ground and on the road, Hammerton gave his companion this lesson of advice: "Never speak English if any one is near; keep this pipe in your mouth—never mind its not being lighted; and do not on any account complain of fatigue. Remember that the step of the camel is as light and as noiseless as a lady's footfall on the softest turf: keep a vigilant eye, therefore, behind you; for if I do not lead, the camels will not go more than three miles an hour. And now, fair lady, I must change your name for you,—for the future you must answer to Sidi Kalif: my own must undergo an alteration also, and you will remember me only as Abdallah Chebic. We have a desperate undertaking before us;—you must for a time unsex yourself, and be a man, or I fear you will sink under the severe privations we must suffer."

"Abdallah," replied his companion, "your orders shall be obeyed: I, who rebuked you with being a coward, will not sink under the imputation. Death is far preferable to the life I have led; and rather than again fall into the hands of that old Turk, I would encounter any peril or privation. This camel's motion," continued the fugitive, "is not unlike the disagreeable pitch of the *Rover*."

"The ship of the Desert," replied Hammerton, "although famed for the silence of its progress, does, as you say, pitch about like a jolly-boat in a head-sea. We shall get accustomed to it, however, before we arrive at our journey's end."

"And how distant may that spot be which we so anxiously seek, Abdallah?"

"That, fair Sidi, is as yet uncertain. I have resolved not to attempt to pass to the northward, because my namesake will mount the dromedary and scour the country in that direction; and those animals have gone more than one hundred miles in the day, whilst our dull sailing-ships hardly ever exceed thirty. I am now, if the stars do not deceive me, or my compass fail in its constancy, steering to the south; we shall leave El-Harib on the right, and by keeping the camels on their full pace, we shall overtake the caravan going to Timbuctoo. I propose to join it as merchants going to the Gold Coast. The rest we must leave to chance; we may be prisoners of the Moors before night, and then all our plans will be useless.—I must make these camels go quicker by singing to them; they require the voice to encourage them, and they know the song of their driver as well as I remember one sung by the fair sultana of a Turk when she rebuked me for not daring to save her."

"No more of that, Abdallah, I entreat you; if you knew what I have suffered, you would instantly forgive my hasty reproach: I feel now like the bird escaped from its cage, yet fearing that my wilder brethren may tear me to pieces. But why did you leave that dromedary for Abdallah to hunt us with?"

"For this reason: had I taken it, only one could have used it; it would have outstepped the camel, or it would have been fatigued by its one continued dull pace. I know Abdallah well: he will go the very route he ought not. Luckily we leave no trace behind us, or a Moor would follow our path as surely as the bloodhound does its prey. Try now to go to sleep; for we must continue our journey all this night and all the morrow without stopping."

"If I attempt to sleep I shall fall," replied Hammerton's companion; "for my whole strength is requisite to keep me in security."

"Custom, Sidi Kalif, is a great master: many an hour you will sleep on that faithful beast, if we do but escape to-morrow's danger."

Hammerton now commenced singing a Moorish song which he had learnt, at the sound of which the camels quickened their pace.

"It is hard," said Sidi, "to sing when life is at stake!"

"It is harder to be silent when hope inspires the song. On your left side you will find some dates; eat them sparingly, and take great care to watch the water-skins, that they do not leak: the long desert before us, if all be true, will try our courage and our patience."

"There are men behind us!" said Sidi.

"Keep cool," continued Hammerton: "it is God's mercy to us,—they are, like ourselves, going in search of the caravan, which left El-Harib yesterday."

Here Hammerton began another Moorish song, having enjoined silence upon his companion, and the camels again quickened their pace: their followers maintained their relative distance, without appearing to approach them.

In vain did Sidi endeavour to make her camel approach nearer to Hammerton's; the animal knew its station, and would not move one inch faster than its usual stride. Hammerton, watchful for her safety, told her not to jerk the rope, for the camel might lie down; and reassured her, by pointing out those behind, which followed one after the other like wild ducks in a flight.

It was now growing towards morning. The sudden gleams of light which lit up the eastern horizon ushered in the day, and already might a gray horse be seen a mile off (the Turkish way of estimating daylight), when Hammerton perceived his friends astern. Keeping more to the eastward, the country round about them was entirely open —there was no human habitation; the distant hills, with Mount Atlas overtopping all, were just visible behind them, whilst in front the prospect appeared like entering on eternity: there was no tree to guide them—all seemed one dreary plain; the grass, over which the camels had trodden during the night, from the time they had left the road to El-Harib, was now fast changing its verdure into sand: the strong refraction of light, as the sun shone, placing a shrub, as it were, high in the heavens, and enlarging it into a tall tree; whilst a camel in that direction, with a man on its back, appeared like a huge castle with an immense turret, convinced Hammerton that to the south-east all was sand. In front there seemed an interminable sea, behind them the mountains which greet the homeward-destined caravans after their tedious journey through the desert.

"There are but three men near us, Sidi: we will edge towards them; we must find out whether they suspect us. Keep you silent; from them I must glean their destination: we may find friends in them who may prove most useful. They will not be afraid of us; and the more we are, the less likely are the Moors to attack us."

With this determination, Hammerton altered his direction more to the eastward, the camel of Sidi following close in his wake. When within speaking distance, Hammerton gave the true "Salam Aleikoum," which was returned in the same manner, both parties rather distrusting their neighbours: indeed, the quick eye of Sidi saw the hands of the second and third men upon their pistols, and she nearly betrayed her sex and country by expressing her fears in English.

"We seek the caravan going to Timbuctoo," said Abdallah; "and, Allah be praised! we have encountered those of the true faith, who will not be misers of their intelligence."

The leading man of the strangers bowed gracefully after the Oriental manner, and replied, "We also seek the caravan; by night we ought to overtake it, for its first day's march is always slow, to allow those who have missed it through negligence to repair the error. In this case we cannot rebuke each other."

Here the old gentleman, whose face bespoke a careless disregard of danger and a glorious defiance of fatigue, took his pipe, and, after striking a light and placing it in the bowl, he drew in the smoke strongly, and then offered it to Hammerton. This calumet of peace and good will was eagerly received; the second man also proffered a pipe to Sidi. The incautious and yet watchful lady, not having practised this art, with eager breath drew in the smoke, and forthwith commenced a salute of coughs, which lasted some minutes.

"'Tis a bad omen," said the second man, rather displeased at this unfortunate cough, "to find the offering of friendship sicken in the mouth."

"He is young," replied Hammerton, "and my brother's sickness has been long. Our Hakem, who, by the blessing of Allah, is wiser than men in general, forbade him to smoke; his greediness to receive the proffered friendship, and the long restraint from it, occasioned the cough: may your hand honour the pipe of Abdallah Chebic!"

This set all smooth again, the Turk remarking that "the boy was indeed young and sickly to face so great a journey." Hammerton, although he saw that he could pass muster with either Moor or Turk, began to tremble for young Sidi: the great change from a harem to a desert, without preparation, without knowledge of the camel's stride, would soon fatigue her; and then what was to be done? To loiter behind the caravan would be to court destruction: pirates on shore hang upon the large fleet of inland ships as privateers do upon the ocean. Had the first day's march been trifling, and the fatigue increased by degrees, a child might be weaned from luxury to rough usage; but after the dull, unvarying monotony of a Turkish garden; to be placed upon a pack-saddle on a camel's back, and have to sit there from eleven at night until eight o'clock the next evening, with hardly one hour's intermission, would try the mettle of a huntsman. However, the excitement occasioned by the fear of being followed enabled her to bear up against the sensation of fatigue and desire of sleep.

"The boy," said the second man, "looks behind him at the mountains, as if he had left the black-eyed beauty to weep until his return; he sends a kiss on every breeze, and lifts his eyes to Allah, as if to pray for her he loves."

"'Tis nearly so," replied Hammerton: "beyond El-Harib dwells his favourite sister: our journey, if prosperous, will be the last we make; and the poor boy may well feel pain at leaving her he loves to face the dangers of the desert."

"Allah be merciful!" said the first man; "has the sickly boy been here before?"

"No," replied Hammerton, "nor myself either. Our trade was carried on at Algiers; but there no luck befel us. Almost ruined, we hardly even hoped for this opportunity to retrieve our fortunes: we must trust to destiny."

"The winter of sorrow," replied the leading man, "is succeeded by the reviving strength of spring, and the darkest night is followed by the brightest day: may your destiny be good!"

The two parties continued together, exchanging few

words. Whenever the camels grew short in their stride, the song soon cheered them onwards; and thus, until the heat of the sun became too oppressive to be borne, they journeyed forward. There yet remained some signs of vegetation, and here and there were still some small shrubs, and wells were not infrequent. On arriving at one of these the three men halted, dismounted, and, turning their camels adrift to feed, threw themselves down, and sought repose. Hammerton's camel instantly stopped, and it required some little persuasion to make it move on again.

"Whither go you?" asked the first speaker; "we are well provided, and in the name of the Prophet, who enjoins hospitality, the stranger is welcome."

"We thank you," replied Hammerton; "but the more we separate now, the more likely we are to gain our ends. If I see the caravan from yonder tree, I will wave my fold from its summit; and then we can repose together when the object is attained."

No sooner had they passed beyond the reach of voice, than Sidi said, in a weak, faltering tone, "We must stop, or I shall faint."

"Courage! now or never!" replied Hammerton; "gain but yonder tree, and underneath its shade you shall repose. To stop now, with the fiery sun upon us, would be fatal; your next ride shall be easier. See! see! it is near us; continue for half a mile, and then half your troubles will be over."

"Oh that I could die, and thus release you!" said the poor wearied girl. "I fear I shall now drag you to the earth in your generous efforts to save me: but I have the heart of a woman, and if I cling until my nails are torn from my fingers, I will endeavour to gain that tree. But pray urge the camels forward."

With a tremulous voice, for Hammerton was much fatigued, he sang the Moorish song; and the faithful creatures, apparently unwearied, soon gained the tree. He now dismounted, and making the other camel kneel down, took the fainting Sidi in his arms, and laid her in the shade. The skins of water were then taken off; and after bathing her temples, the poor creature awoke to experience all the miseries of life.

In the mean time, Hammerton, whose generous disposition prompted him to forget his own troubles in alleviating hers, got some dates and biscuits. With these and some water a spare repast was made. But Hammerton worked and ate at the same time. His prudent foresight had prompted him to take with him one of the skins used to carry women: this he arranged with sticks to act as stretchers, and with the rope he slung this uneasy bed on one side, and balanced it on the other with the water-skins. Having done this, he placed the saddle for a pillow, and covered it over with some of his friend Abdallah's garments. He then fell asleep himself; but even in that sleep he was sensible of all around him.

How long he slept he knew not; but he was awakened by a cry from Sidi for assistance. The drowsiness of over-fatigue almost overpowered him, when the sound of a pistol startled him into activity. Before him stood Abdallah, whose name he had usurped, and whose garments he had stolen. The ball aimed at him as he lay sleeping had missed him, and slightly wounded his companion. Before he could recover his surprise or find his fire-arms, his old associate had levelled a pistol at him, and but for the frenzied effort of the girl, he must have been killed. She had drawn a pistol, hardly knowing whether it wås loaded, and pulling the trigger, it went off. Abdallah fell, and Hammerton's defender fainted. The affrighted and wounded dromedary, which had been fired at and hit by Hammerton, turned short round, and with the corpse of him who rode it dangling by its side—for it was sustained by one leg being entangled in the trappings—it took its quick flight towards the mountains.

Having restored the warrior Sidi to herself, and with words which came from a feeling heart, expressed his gratitude, Hammerton bound up the wound which was on the left arm.

"We must be moving," said Hammerton; "our friends are already mounted, and I am anxious to keep before them; for they will be a rear-guard for us. I marked the course with my compass which we steered before. And now, fair lady, let me lift you into your bed; and trust to me to be vigilant in endeavouring to repay the life you have given me."

The slight pressure of Sidi's hand which held that of Hammerton was gently increased, as if she feared to make this first advance which gratitude to her deliverer prompted. He placed her gently in the skin, and, with apparently more solicitude for her comfort than when they first began their journey, said, "Sleep, sleep, pretty Sidi!" He gently placed his finger on her eyelids, and with a smile continued, "This will darken the day, which before was too bright for mortal sight." A blush came over the girl's cheeks, and a sigh escaped the ears of all but his for whom it was intended.

Hammerton, much relieved by his slight sleep, now mounted his camel, and directing it in a south-by-east direction, found he was going exactly to the same point as his friends behind him. The heat was oppressive, but every moment made it less so. The sun was fast sinking; still no sign of the caravan was visible; not a sound disturbed the profound stillness of the air; the camel's spongy feet trod silently on the sand. In vain, as the haze grew less, did Hammerton strain his eyes. Another hour and daylight would be passed: what then was to be done? "If we do not see the smoke by sunset," said he to his companion, "we must stop and keep close to our friends. By them we must be guided; and when night comes we must sleep near them. We will make the best use of this hour, and keep the beasts at their quickest pace. If we could but guide those near us to the caravan, it would be a service not easily forgotten."

"Hush!" she replied, as she raised herself up so as to look over the edge of the skin; "I hear the cry of an animal more on our right: listen! again I hear it distinctly."

"I cannot hear it," said Hammerton; "but no chance must be thrown away." He altered his course, as he jokingly said, "two points to starboard," and kept the head of the ship of the desert at south-by-west. Both now strained their ears, still no sound was conveyed to them: at length, charming sight! a column of smoke was observed to rise gradually in the air. Hammerton immediately waved a scarf affixed to his scimitar, and kept it in motion until his friends behind him had answered it, and altered their direction. The smoke was seen on the right hand, and shortly afterwards the camels lifted up their long noses, as if they had received intelligence through a different sense:—the caravan was before them, slowly wending on its way.

CHAPTER XXXIII.

ADVENTURES IN THE DESERT.

THE caravan had halted: and this was the last night of repose, as henceforth they were to travel by night and rest by day.

Hammerton had never seen a caravan before, and he became alarmed at the multitude with whom he was about to associate. Observing a vacant space between two loads of merchandise, he stopped his camel, erected his tent, and placed his wounded companion in safety. The strangers with whom they had conversed during the day pitched their tents near him, and came to make inquiries as to the cause which had occasioned the report of fire-arms. The story was related exactly as it happened, with only this addition—that the man was a predatory Moor, and in the act of getting off his dromedary when the sick brother awoke—that the Moor had fired at the one awake and wounded him—that Abdallah was in the act of defence when Sidi fired and shot him. The strangers were eloquent in praise of the sick boy, who lay quietly wrapped up in the corner of the tent, apparently seeking repose.

In all caravans, during the first day's march, there are camel-merchants and slaves; both the beasts and drivers being for sale, the price of each gradually increases as the caravans increase their distance. Being rid of the unwelcome presence of the strangers, the gold was produced which Sidi had purloined: there was ample for the purchase of a slave and a camel; and these two, themselves just released from slavery, were but too glad to buy a fellow-creature to assist them in their perilous undertaking. The lad whom they bought was a Moor, who was forthwith installed as camel-driver.

The water-skins were filled, and our two adventurers sat down to their first caravan supper. This repast, under the name of *Dokhnou*, which is the flour of the millet mixed with honey, was greedily devoured: to this was added a few kabobs, brought from one of the vendors of mutton-flesh in El-Harib. The Moor was lodged on the ground under heaven's canopy; whilst Sidi took possession of one side of the tent and Abdallah of the other. Hitherto all had gone on apparently well,—that they were under no fear of discovery was evident; and having associated themselves with their wandering brethren, although they looked forward still to many privations, their ultimate escape seemed now to be certain.

The caravan consisted of at least three hundred persons, and more than six hundred camels. The people composing it were a mixture of Moors and Arabs—merchants from Fez—traders from Tripoli, Tunis, and Algiers. All sorts of mongrel dialects might be heard; and on this night, as a kind of festivity before a general fast, the camp was in an uproar: rude music broke upon the ear: whilst vendors of flour, dates, beans, or millet, kept bawling aloud in pursuit of their occupation. Although considerably fatigued, the novelty of the situation and the excitement of their escape rendered our party indisposed to avail themselves of the hours so necessary to restore weary nature.

Hammerton had taken the precaution to fasten the entrance of their tent, and previously to the night's slumber proposed to dress the wound of his companion. There is nothing in an Englishman beholding the bare arm of a woman; but in climates where females are carefully excluded from sight,—where the face, excepting in slaves, is seldom seen,—the least exposure appears criminal. This was Sidi's first feeling; but familiarity soon wore off this restraint.

Hammerton forgot his usual caution, and spoke in English. It happened that when Abdallah pursued the fugitives, he came upon the three men who were reclining under the tree: one only was awake, and seeing the man approach, he walked towards his camels, in order to protect them. After the usual "Salam Aleikoum," Abdallah asked if two persons had been seen, one young and like a woman, the other with a cast of countenance resembling the infidels who sometimes frequented the coast. The stranger directed Abdallah to the tree. The curiosity of the wandering Arab was excited: and although he kept the secret from his companions, he resolved to ascertain if his conjecture were right, that the lad who was so cautiously desired by the learned Hakem to avoid tobacco was of the sex unaccustomed to pipes. Accordingly, whilst Hammerton was carefully dressing the wound of his companion, this man listened outside the tent; and not only did so, but, through a small hole not perceptible from the inside, was able to obtain a sight of the beauty of the Christian girl, as her white arm was displayed, and her countenance animated by gratitude. Satisfied that they were Christians, with the wily character of his countrymen he kept the secret to himself, and retired to his own tent, too fatally convinced of the secret.

At early dawn each party were busy preparing for the route. During this interval another consultation had been held, whether, having despatched their pursuer, it would not be better to shape a different course, and endeavour to gain some port of the Mediterranean; but fear that their escape had become generally known determined them at all risks to continue with the caravan to Timbuctoo, and then to endeavour, by joining another caravan, to reach the coast.

With this intention, they altered their garbs, so as to appear rather inferior merchants, which indeed their miserable retinue sufficiently attested. The Moorish boy, unused to the kindness he now experienced, already began to consider his slavery a blessing.

Their journey at first was over the hard soil covered with light sand and loose stones. The pathway made by frequent caravans had not been obliterated: except this slight trace of man, the whole scene was wildly desolate—not a shrub nor tree was to be seen—all around was bleak and barren. The desert was like the sea, occasionally showing small waves of sand, which, as the breeze increased, swept with frightful velocity over the surface of the earth: sometimes the sky was unclouded, and the rays of the sun became almost intolerable; the easterly wind caused the water to evaporate, and dry up the skins until the unmoistened bags cracked; sometimes, when the welcome spot where Providence had provided water was hailed with delight, upon being tasted it was found so salt as to be dangerous to drink.

Day after day was thus passed, and the companions ventured not to utter a word to any but their first friends and their slave, and night was the time when the cool air invited them to push forward. The different wells of Mayara, of Marabouty, of Ekseif, of Amoultaf, were passed, until they arrived at Telig, where the caravans occasionally met that came from Cape Blanc, near which the Great Desert of Sahara begins, and over a part of which the caravan had already journeyed. To accomplish the journey from Telig to Cape Blanc, it was necessary to go still further to the southward, to wells called Tichyt, and thence again in a west-north-west course to the sea : this information was gleaned from their Moorish slave, who, having made frequent journeys with the caravans, had passed over this track before.

The wells of Telig are situated in a valley formed by a long chain of granite mountains, sterile and bare, which extend from east to west: the soil immediately in the vicinity of the wells is of large yellow sand, having but little verdure. No sooner was the water scented by the camels than they broke away from all restraint and rushed to the spot. In vain did the drivers apply the rope's end—they would turn short round and rush to the place: the consequence was that the wells were soon nearly choked with sand, which the eager animals had trodden therein. It required much time before the Moors who accompanied the caravan could clear the pits of this incumbrance, and before the thirsty men could gratify the imperious wants of nature. In spite, however, of sand or human beings, the camels disputed the point of priority and gained the victory.

These wells are only four feet in depth; but they yield a plentiful supply of water. The taste is rather brackish; but this was not discovered for the first five hours. The sight was indeed curious. Hammerton forgot his charge; and Sidi, equally fearless of danger, rushed between the heads of the camels, and with outstretched arm filled the calabash. It was taken from her grasp, before her thirst was half satisfied, by the Moorish boy, who at this moment for the first time doubted her sex; there was a scuffle to retain the gourd, and the dress of Sidi being torn open in the affray, her bosom discovered her to be a woman. To remedy the disaster, she relinquished the calabash, which the Moorish boy returned to her after he had slaked his burning thirst, his eyes too plainly indicating the discovery he had made.

The mishap was communicated to Hammerton. To sell the Moor would not have made the business better; to make him a confidant would be to court treachery, for all of that nation are low, cunning, insincere, holding Christians in the lowest estimation, and ever ready to seize them and commit them to slavery. Could the Moor but believe Hammerton to be a Christian, he would have sold his master. It was resolved between them, therefore, to make no allusion to what had occurred, but to be more observant of the Mahometan hours of prayer; and from that moment Hammerton was never seen without his Koran. His memory being good, he soon learnt by heart many verses, with which he studiously embellished his remarks; and amongst the few who knew him, he was accounted a most rigid and exemplary Mussulman.

The caravan had now rested its usual time; the water-skins of the different merchants were filled, and the camels had recovered a little from the fatigue they had undergone. The near approach of the caravan from Timbuctoo now made it requisite to decide which route the travellers should take, and finally they resolved upon joining the caravan which was expected. In order to do this without suspicion, Sidi was announced as being very ill from his wound, which indeed had never properly healed.

The most constant visitor at their tent was the Arab who had directed Abdallah in his search: he watched them closely, and was often seen in conversation with the Moorish boy. The determination to wait was not conveyed to the slave; and when the usual announcement was made that the caravan would advance on its route when the sun went down, preparations were commenced by Hammerton as usual, and no doubt existed in the mind of the Moor but that the journey would be continued by them that night. During the bustle of removal, Hammerton continued to gain time by arranging the conveyance for his sick brother; and time crept away until they alone remained at the wells.

Far away along the inhospitable desert the track of the slow-wending caravan might be still traced in the sand, for no breeze arose to obliterate the steps of the travellers: still the ear could catch the distant voice of the drivers, as they cheered on their camels to increase their speed. Gradually these sounds grew fainter and more faint, until the dead silence of the spot made even the bold Hammerton tremble at the solitude he had courted. Left desolate in the midst of the great Sahara, their own voices sounded unusually loud, for the air was not disturbed even by a breeze; and Sidi sank into dejection, frightened at the plan adopted, and fearful of some unpleasant results. In the mean time, the last tinge of daylight had disappeared; the camels were picketed to the ground, or those sagacious animals would soon have followed their former associates; the Moor walked lonely and moodily round the solitary tent, and Hammerton betook himself to the hardest task in affliction—that of affording consolation when he needed it himself.

"It is a bold step we have taken," commenced Sidi; "we might be this night made slaves to the Moors, who not unfrequently hover about a caravan, and examine the place where it has rested."

"I do not fear that," replied Hammerton; "neither do I fear anything whilst Sidi is near me: her good fortune will keep us safe from danger."

"Good fortune!" replied the girl, with astonishment; "my life, like yours, has been one of suffering and misfortune."

"In this solitude," said Hammerton, "where the human voice is rarely heard, we must not be silent, or sleep may overtake us, and thus we may be surprised. To keep off the drowsy effects of weariness, we must continue to converse, and endeavour to find some theme whereon to engage our attention."

"Alas!" replied Sidi, "the sense of my misfortunes is ever present to my mind,—I can speak of nothing else."

"Confide then your sorrows to me," replied Hammerton: "in becoming acquainted with your grief, I may haply assuage it."

"Mine is a sad tale. I am the daughter of an officer in the navy. My father, after having distinguished himself in many actions, did not receive the proper meed of his exertions. I grew up under his eye, until, oh, fatal day! my affections became engaged to one who had no means of supporting me. My mother opposed the union. Opposition is fatal in love.

"I have no motive to conceal what followed: you have known me as the slave of a Turk, confined in his harem. In a word, then, my admirer having won my affections, basely deserted me and sailed for the West Indies, leaving me a prey to the deepest despondency. In vain I wrote, stating my despair: he had been removed to a floating sepulchre, the *Shark*, and having drunk as if courting oblivion, he died at the hospital, my own brother hearing from his dying lips his repentance.

"My brother's letters hardened my father's heart against me: I was driven from his house. With my own hands I was enabled to support myself. My mother endeavoured in vain to soften a father's anger: his honour had received a blow he could not survive, and he died.

"No sooner was he dead than I joined my only remaining parent. · Her brother held a situation at Malta, and being unmarried, was anxious for society. He wrote to us to leave a country in which poverty must be our lot, forwarding money to pay our passage. We embarked on board the packet:—I am here, and my mother a menial servant in Algiers.

"I feel relieved now that I have frankly told you all but my name—that is better concealed: for time may change our situations, and you might, perhaps, sail under my brother. His feelings should never be outraged by knowing the sad fate of his sister. But where is the Moor?"

Hammerton rose immediately. He had been so riveted by the simple relation of his companion's misfortunes, that, for a moment, he forgot his usual prudence. He called aloud for the slave, but he was unanswered: he rushed from the tent and found his worst fears realized—the Moor had gone, and taken with him one of the camels and the water-skins; the rest of the articles were safe, and were instantly removed into the tent. For the present the theft could not occasion much discomfort; it would be felt more as they advanced, when they would have no convenience for carrying the proper supply of water.

To follow the slave was useless: the night, though not dark, had already begun to show some disposition to be windy; the track in the desert would, no doubt, be lost; and in the event of not overtaking the Moor, or reaching the caravan, death from thirst must ensue. They had an ample supply of millet and of dates; with these they could hold out until assistance came—to move must be fatal.

Sidi's spirit rose with the necessity of the case: she now appeared more resolute than her companion.

"If we die," she said, "we only meet that inevitable fate which in a few years must be ours; but we will struggle to the last. Come, Hammerton," she continued, "you shall not despise me for my fears; by your side I am ready to live or die; and you will better support my resolution by showing me that hope has not forsaken you. Our case was much more desperate in the house of the Turk: six years did we seek for a propitious moment, and shall we droop now, when the caravan may be here to-morrow, and both of us reach England in three months?"

Hammerton looked at her with a steadiness of manner shown only in despair. "You shall not outdo me in words, although you are a woman: I will cling more closely to you now that our fate is inevitable; fear not that we shall fall into slavery without a struggle. I will not survive your fall.—But you only look, I fear, at the bright side: the Moor is leagued with the Arabs we first met; he knows we cannot move from the wells or we must die of thirst: he knows us for Christians, and he despises us doubly for having held him as a slave. Our fate is sealed! I cannot shut my eyes to what must follow. We cannot fly—we cannot escape: around us is the vast desert, a trackless sand, to guide us through which we require the experienced eye that recognizes every stone; the wind has blown the sand over the camel's tracks. It is useless to waste words. I almost fear to leave you whilst I take the camels to the wells: stir not from the tent, and I will soon return."

"No, Hammerton," replied the girl; "you have claimed me as a wife,—it is my duty to divide the toil with you. I must learn how to guide these unwieldy animals, for I would rather do anything than remain alone in this awful and mysterious silence; my voice seems to return to me, and there is a depression in our loneliness which nothing can cheer—not even those bright stars."

"They form the southern cross," replied Hammerton, "and are the only lamps which guide the caravan. Even now I almost feel inclined to try to escape, and trust to my memory of the position of the stars: but the water-skins are gone, and Death would ride behind us at sunrise."

The camels were taken to the wells, and drank freely. They were then allowed to browse about the side of the hill, and glean the scanty grass or herbs which still remained; while Hammerton, taking the hand of Sidi, led her to the tent, and after offering up his prayers, endeavoured to obtain some sleep.

CHAPTER XXXIV

A COMPANION IN THE DESERT.—THE SIMOOM.—DEATH IN THE SAHARA.

By daylight both were on the alert. The camels were ready, and seemed to welcome their masters. The wind had subsided, and Hammerton found, on examination of the track of the caravan, that not the slightest mark remained, and he and his companions were, like Adam and Eve, alone. Their conversation naturally turned to the expected arrival of the caravan from Timbuctoo.

"It ought to arrive by the day after to-morrow at the farthest," said Sidi; "and if gold does not fail, we will soon repair our error, and survive the difficulties by which we are surrounded. But I fear my strength is not equal to my resolution; I feel the approach of fever, and here in this dreadful solitude must I linger without the kind hand of affection which woman bestows upon woman in affliction. If I die, remember me as your companion in misfortune, and may heaven restore you to your country and friends!"

"Poor Sidi!" said Hammerton; "I have nothing to soothe your sorrows but words! You had better remain in the tent, and not expose yourself to the sun."

"How can I consent to lose sight of the only human being in this immense solitude!—the very camels seem aware of their dreary situation, and come near us, as if to borrow courage from companionship with their masters. I tremble when alone, and my mind sickening with my body, makes me fancy the deceptive water before us a sea rushing onward to swallow us up. Hammerton, do not leave me; I cannot bear to be alone: my fancy conjures up an approaching enemy on every side. See that large tower which appears rising from the lake!—Ah! as I live, it moves!"

Hammerton, who had supported Sidi in his arms, gazing with melancholy solicitude on her pale countenance, turned his eyes in the direction she indicated, and there beheld the large tower evidently moving in the refraction of the mirage.

The fear of an approaching enemy placed both upon their guard; they instantly drew nearer to their camels, and the sagacious animals, seemingly aware of the approach of one of their own kind, elongated their necks and screamed a welcome.

The stranger seemed unable to control his animal; it rushed to the well, and having slaked its thirst, rose suddenly and dismounted its rider. Hammerton instantly approached: the rider lay apparently dead; his eyes were sunken, his face thin, and, although life was not extinct, the pulse seemed to flutter in the last struggle before death. The stranger was removed to the tent, where the hand of Sidi chafed his burning forehead, whilst Hammerton bathed his heated face and moistened his parched lips. By degrees animation faintly returned; the stranger opened his eyes, but closed them almost instantly. Some millet soaked in water and sweetened with honey was placed in the stranger's mouth, and after a short time the action of swallowing was perceptible; but overcome by the unwonted exertion, he fell into a heavy slumber.

"Be careful," said Hammerton to Sidi, as he withdrew her from the tent, "not to betray either your sex, your country, or your religion. Every word spoken must be Moorish; our tale, that we are travellers from El-Harib, bound to Timbuctoo;—sickness had overtaken us, and we await the caravan going to Cape Blanco, in order to retrace our steps by that route, as no other to Timbuctoo will arrive for two months. This man must be an Arab: he will become our friend when once he has eaten salt with us. Remember, brother, you are sick."

"I need no friendly hint to make me feel that, Hammerton; although this incident has excited me much, and I feel better. We must ensure his protection by kindness."

"Most certainly: if we feared him, we could easily rid ourselves of our apprehensions; but I would rather live to fear him than reduce the living to our lonely selves. When he awakes, do you appear reading this Koran. He may extricate us from our miserable situation."

Hammerton searched the camel of the stranger. The water-skins were dry and hard,—they had not contained water apparently for some days; not a mouthful of food remained; the animal seemed almost starving. The saddle was removed and placed in the tent. Universal silence prevailed, and except the voice of Sidi, which occasionally broke into prayer from the Koran, all was a still, solemn solitude.

When the stranger awoke, he cast his eyes round the tent with some indication of fear: he arose, apparently in health, felt for his arms, remarked his saddle, and in a quick, hurried manner asked, "Where am I?"

"With friends," replied Hammerton, "who will relieve you: this pledge of friendship is offered."

The stranger took some salt and swallowed it: Hammerton and Sidi did the same.

"'Tis well," continued the stranger: "what brings you here?"

Hammerton related the truth.

"Natives of El-Harib?" said the stranger.

"No," replied Hammerton; "but natives of the sea-shore beyond."

Apparently satisfied, the stranger opened the tent, looked at the sun, cast his eyes towards the point from which he had come, and having for a moment watched his camel, took the water-skins, and walked to the wells.

Hammerton accompanied him, and asked him if it was his intention to stay with them, or if he could guide them to some better place.

"I came," replied the stranger, "for money, and nearly lost my life: you have restored the one, which shall be yielded up or I will have my due. I am one of the Trâkânt Moors: like the Arabs in their deserts, we are masters in that of Sahara; we exact tribute from all caravans passing through our sandy inheritance. I, with my men, was to have met the caravan going to Timbuctoo, here; but we were assailed by our own brethren who inhabit the desert farther eastward, who drove us from our encampment, routed and dispersed us. I fled, and arrived here.—Allah be praised! all is told. You have restored me; I will not leave the stranger to perish. In that caravan we have three of our men, dressed as merchants; they will exact the payment, and return with the caravan going to the coast, whither you seek to go. But we must away from this spot: our hostile brethren intend to attack the returning caravan, and are now within two days' march of us. The skins will be soaked by evening; prepare yours, and those of your sick brother: an hour before the sun goes down we must remove: for if our messenger has met with the returning caravan, it will turn to the westward, avoiding these wells, the best in the desert. Fear not for your guide; I know every one of the few shrubs which grow upon this moving face of nature. Load your camels: if the enemy come, you are slaves, and I a burthen to be easily disposed of."

Hammerton then related the flight of the Moorish servant, and the circumstance which had attended it.

"Fear not," continued the stranger; "from the description, those Arabs are our spies; none dare strike if Hossein holds up his hands. But I am no longer a chief; my skins must do for all; by to-morrow morning we will be better provided with food. Before sunset we move: go comfort your brother, — he shall be my son, and I will be his father. I was not quite so near death as you thought, and in my apparent slumbers I learnt that I was preserved, and felt the hand of friendship chafe the forehead of adversity. We have eaten salt; we must now shake off the black dust of misfortune, and cover our faces with whiteness;—I will lead you to the coast. Prepare some food, Abdallah: to-morrow we shall replenish from one of our secret stores.—Hark!" Hossein threw himself on the sand, and, keeping his ear close to the surface, listened without breathing. "The hunted lion fears the wind," he continued; "and hunted man the breath of human nature.—Go, get ready; I will prepare the camels for the journey."

In the evening they left the wells, and struck off to the north-west. There appeared no speck to guide them, and yet their route was in a straight direction. The camels stalked on quietly; not a word was uttered until nearly midnight, when Hossein abruptly remarked, "You are not natives of El-Harib, you say; neither are you from Algiers, Tripoli, nor Tetuan: your speech, though good, is not of the Trâkânt Moors, or of the people about Morocco; you have another language—what is it?"

"We have eaten salt together, Hossein," answered Hammerton,—"we are pledged to each other; why, therefore, this suspicion?"

"You doubt who I am," replied Hossein, "who thus leads you over the desert. I, seeing you have no merchandise, doubt your story; no man goes from El-Harib to Timbuctoo for the sake of the ride. I am your friend, your protector; without me you would starve—"

"And without us," interrupted Hammerton, "you would have—"

"—Died," continued Hossein, calmly. "It was not my destiny; Allah is merciful! When the day comes, I shall be ready. Whilst I live, I pray as I travel: and in robbing a caravan, Allah is never forgotten. What says the Koran, which you read? 'It shall be no crime in you if ye seek an increase from your Lord by trading during the pilgrimage.' Life is a pilgrimage; we trade with the strongest, and lighten the burden of the weakest. From this you know my life: be candid with me."

"I will," said Hammerton, "if by the sacred pledge, and by the Koran, you will swear not to leave us."

"I swear," said Hossein, "be ye infidel dog or true believer,—Moor, opposed to me by revenge,—slave, sold and escaped,—or leper-stricken Jew, never to leave nor harm you; but, as a man, a chief, and a Trâkânt, to do the rights of hospitality according to our creed. Speak!"

"We are Christian slaves, escaped from misery. We were taken in a ship, sold at Algiers, conveyed to El-Harib, or near it, and, after six or seven years' cruel bondage, have endeavoured to fly. Have you a father or a mother, a brother or a sister, whom you love? If so, would you not break from captivity to see them once more before you died? Would you, a man, a true believer in the Prophet, whose law you promise to fulfil, be a slave to a Christian, and not strive to shake off the shackle which bound you like a beast to its load? Speak, for you are a man—and a bold one too, or the eye of the hawk has been placed in the head of the dove; if *you* would so strive to be free, is it a sin in a Christian to have the feelings of a man?"

"Thou hast spoken well," replied the Moor: "what you have done, by Allah! was nobly done, and you have risked the long dreary march of the caravan to avoid the Moors of the north. You have acted wisely; but you are yet slaves."

Hammerton, whose ears had greedily caught every sound, at the mention of the word "slaves" felt for his pistol, and half drew it from his belt. The Moor saw the motion of his hand, and coolly said, "Abdallah, is your reason gone? If I die, who will guide you in this pathless sand? and would you spill the blood of the man with whom you have eaten salt? You, too, repeat the instructions of the Koran; but, being an infidel, you act like a perfidious Jew. I will guide you to the coast, I will show you the waters of the great lake; but as you have doubted my word, so also I doubt your friendship. To the coast I will see you in safety; then Allah protect you! for Hossein will leave you."

Hammerton had made up his mind not to be led back a slave without trying his skill with the pistols about him. He told Sidi, in English, that he doubted the fidelity of Hossein, and advised her to be on her guard: from that moment not a word was said. Hossein kept his eyes fixed upon a star; the hours of darkness passed, and the streaks of daylight appeared.

The sun had risen about an hour, when Hossein, looking carefully around him, said, "This way, Abdallah. See you yon shrub? fix the tent close to that: before you have done it, I will be with you."

"Stay, Hossein, stay!" cried Sidi: "you are a chief—you have sworn and repeated your friendship; will you leave a woman, a weak woman, to die in this horrible place?"

"A woman!" said the Moor, as he turned his camel towards her: "by Allah, it *is* a Frangi woman! Fright must have blinded me, or I could have told from your eyes that your heart belonged not to a man. Near this place we have provisions; I know where to find them; I will return with them shortly."

"You have with you the only drop of water," continued Sidi, as she stretched out her hands: "you will not leave us, Hossein! I implore you, I pray you, leave us not for a moment!"

"Holy Prophet!" said Hossein, with great coolness, "women are all alike,—Arab, Persian, Morocco, Frangi, or Negro; if once they get frightened, they would not believe even in a Turk. You rubbed my head and cooled my parched lips," he continued, as he addressed her; "I owe you the hospitality you have shown me: my word is pledged; before you are ready to eat in shelter from the sun, I will bring more food for you. Waste no more time in words: an Arab or a Trâkânt Moor never speaks falsely; for if I were inclined to deal treacherously, who could avert the blow?"

Hammerton made no remark, but guided his camel towards the bush. Near it was a small sprinkling of scanty grass, and the hungry animals scarcely allowed time for their masters to unlade them before they rushed to the green herbage and ate it. Sidi, fatigued, worn out, excited, was hardly able to stand. The tent was pitched, and both were soon under its shelter. Sidi, weakened by the fatigue, dispirited, wavering, uncertain, burst into tears, and Hammerton, who felt his tongue cleave to his clammy mouth, was conscious of his own indifference to life from the total want of power or inclination to afford the least consolation to his friend. Even hope scarcely inspired them, and they viewed each other with feelings of despair.

Some time had elapsed before Hossein returned. He brought with him a great increase of provisions, the water-skins had not leaked, and once more confidence was restored to the travellers. Hossein, by far the strongest of the party, acted more as a slave than a master, and by his kind manner restored the spirits of his companions.

"Allah is merciful!" he began: "our stores are not discovered; here is sufficient to carry us within two days of the great water,—there we have more in concealment. We have yet, however, the worst part of the journey to perform: for twenty-five long nights must we pursue our route; on the morning of the twenty-fifth, Inshallah! we shall rejoice—that is our hope. Tell me, Abdallah, what reward do you think is due to a man who preserves the life of another?"

"Whatever he can afford: all but to render him a slave is due to his preserver: his name should be cherished with gratitude until life be extinguished."

"'Tis well, Abdallah. What think you, Sidi, is the due of him who leaves his own tribe to guide two slaves through the desert and restore them to liberty?"

"All—all, everything," replied Sidi, "but life or slavery."

"Remember your words," continued the Moor: "now eat, and then take your rest."

With a liberal hand he gave each their allowance of water in a small calabash; and when the parched and cracked lips of the wanderers had been cooled, and they had drained the bowl of its last drop, they werc surprised to see the Moor wash out the calabash, and throw away a quantity which to them seemed inestimable. Hossein took less than the rest, and before drinking carefully turned the bowl so as not to allow his lips to touch the part which had been profaned by infidels. In silence he ate his food: and then, as if perfectly secure in the company of strangers, placed his head upon his saddle, and in two minutes was in a sound slumber.

The example was too good not to be imitated; and long and sound was the sleep of all three. Hossein awoke his companions, and, in a hurried manner, desired them to strike the tent directly and secure the camels. The order was promptly obeyed, although there appeared no reason why it should be given. It was about three hours after noon—the sun was on the decline,—not an object to cause alarm was visible,—indeed, they appeared alone in the centre of a far-spread lake; still Hossein became more eager as the preparations were nearer conclusion. "Drink," said he, as he offered the calabash; "this black misfortune I did not anticipate: drink largely, for it may be long before you are again so invited. Now cover each camel's nose and eyes, and keep close to the ground; do not attempt to stir, or you will perish. See there!" he said, pointing to a light streak of a yellowish colour which spread itself in the heavens from south-east to north-east, but which was so far from assuming a formidable appearance, that it looked more like the cheering rainbow.

Hossein kept his eyes fixed upon it, and Hammerton remarked that it looked less distinct than before. At this moment it was a dead calm: the hot breeze, which had blown with scarcely strength enough to move a grain of sand, had perfectly subsided, and the heat became intolerable. The camels turned towards the eastward, stretched out their long necks, and exhibited signs of impatience: they were made to lie down, their heads pointed to the westward. Hammerton, who was suspicious of every movement of the Moor, became alarmed at the fear which manifested itself in the countenance of their guide, and the remark he made concerning the streak becoming less distinct was answered thus:—

"It is the sand carried up in the clouds which darkens the view. Allah! Allah! but its force must be tremendous! When it comes, lie down close—close, and let its violence blow over you; keep your hand before your mouth and nostrils, and do not lift your heads until I call."

A low murmuring sound was heard approaching, and the wind was plainly audible above as it skimmed over them: a dark cloud appeared approaching like a pall to cover them. No retreat or flight could save them: to the north two or three pillars moving with great rapidity, and whirling round, were stalking along; whilst to the southward the whole desert appeared tossed into the air. The sand was borne aloft, and a current of wind carried it over the heads of the travellers: being there released from the viewless barrier of the wind, it fell like a slight shower of rain. Nearer and nearer the centre seemed to approach; the whirlwinds which occasioned the spiral columns of sand gradually became closer; when Sidi seized the hand of Hammerton, and throwing herself on her knees, offered a wild ejaculation to heaven, and sank upon the ground. Hammerton kept his eye upon the forthcoming danger; alarmed, but not daunted, he stood as if he could oppose himself to the fury of the elements and brave their force;—whilst the Moor, whose eager glance swept the horizon from north to south, had alarm and apprehension strongly depicted on his countenance.

"Down! down!" he cried; and scarcely had Hammerton

obeyed the injunction, when the sand was driven over him with fearful rapidity: that which supported him seemed sapped from beneath him. A difficulty of respiration succeeded, and, faint and weak, he kept his hand over his nostrils and mouth, gasping for breath, at each respiration feeling all the horrors of suffocation. The wind roared over the prostrate travellers, and the sand grated on the ear as it was propelled with fearful violence along. At last came one tremendous burst, and then all was calm again. The sand fell to the ground,—the air became clear; and at Hossein's call, Hammerton endeavoured to rise: he was so weakened, however, by overpowering lassitude, that he was scarcely able to stand; giddiness seized him, and he sank down again. In the mean time, the Moor released the camels, and took the coverings from their eyes: his prudent foresight had saved them; and the fabulous story of these sagacious animals burying their heads in the sand to avoid the storm was at once confuted by the knowledge of the fact, that they bury their noses to avoid the sand, which drives them to madness if propelled with force into their large nostrils and eyes.

"Awake! woman," said Hossein, as he advanced towards Sidi, and took her in his arms. As he lifted her, the head fell back, and the lifeless form of the unfortunate girl was supported by the Moor. She was dead!—not the slightest pulsation was evident to give the smallest hope; and with a kind of superstitious dread occasioned by touching a dead infidel, Hossein rather dropped than laid her on the ground.

The announcement of this calamity soon roused Hammerton into exertion: he flung himself over the dead body of his departed companion, rubbed her heart; but all was still—still as the desert around him! For some time he remained in perfect despair: the only human being to whom of late years he had been in the least attached, the object for which he had risked his life, was now a corpse by his side, and he a wanderer in the desert, with no companion but a Moor,—and a Moor of that tribe notorious for their perfidy. He sat by the dead in mute despair, unable to rouse into action that spirit which alone could extricate him from his perilous situation.

"Why weeps my son?" said Hossein, as he placed his hand upon Hammerton's shoulder. "Allah is great, and his will must be done: it was her destiny, and who could avert it? Why weeps my son?—when the treasure is gone, of what avail is counting the gold in imagination? This is no time for weakness or useless excitement: see how the hot wind which killed her has reduced us!—look! the water-skins are dried and cracked as if they had been placed in the oven; not a drop remains, and we have a long, long journey before we reach a well. I dare not return whence we came, for before this time the enemy is there. Arise, Abdallah! and bow to the fate you cannot avoid. If we are to succeed in our endeavours, our destiny will guide us; if not, Allah is merciful!—Arise, and let us bury the dead!"

Hammerton at length roused himself, and finding that it was useless to waste the precious moments which could not recall the dead to life, with his hands scratched a grave deep enough for the body: in this he was assisted by Hossein, who manifested some little religious awe as he flung the sand aside and worked in silence.

"Are there any beasts of prey to disturb my poor companion's body when we are gone?" asked Hammerton.

"They are too sagacious to come thus far: but I have known large birds of the desert soar over a spot far from vegetation. They follow caravans, and pounce upon the carrion when it falls,—but here she may lie in security."

They took the corpse and placed it in its narrow grave. But before it was hid for ever from view, Hammerton knelt down and prayed; even the Moor turned his face towards the temple, and kneeling down thrice, bowed his head to the ground: he then covered his face with his hands, muttered aloud some verses of the Koran, and remained in that position until Hammerton arose and threw the sand over his unfortunate companion.

"'Tis done," he said; "our last duties to humanity are performed. Death levels us all; the Padishah and the infidel must both cease to breathe; and you, Hossein, surely are not so warped by your faith as to deny that poor girl a place in heaven."

"Allah is great!" replied Hossein; "the thing is possible.—Now to the camels. We must go on by night and by day until we reach the well: there is not a drop of water left; and as neither could travel to the well without it, we must borrow a little from our neighbour here."

So saying, he took the camel which Sidi had ridden, and removing all the useful articles to his own beast, desired Hammerton to advance with the two animals whilst he killed the third and extracted the water. There was no alternative,—either the camel or themselves must have perished.

The Moors of the Desert are expert in the butcher's trade: the docile animal stretched his throat as directed, and was soon relieved from the toils of existence. Hossein knew the delicate anatomy well, and with surprising quickness extracted the stomach which contained the water. This he placed entire in the skins, and having reloaded his camel, and cut sufficient flesh for food from the one sacrificed, mounted his beast, and the lonely pair proceeded.

"I owe you much," said Hammerton, while they continued their journey; "and I swear by Allah and by my own God, that I will amply repay you; once return me to my country, and there I will be a more profitable slave to you than if sold into captivity here. I have gold—take it: I would rather be rid of the useless dross than weary my camel by its weight. Here are jewels—take them all. You are my only hope; and this is a trifle to the remuneration I will cause to be forwarded to you, if my father lives."

"You have done well, Abdallah!" replied Hossein: "here gold is an incumbrance, and to you at any rate it would be useless; the jewels are rare and valuable; you have sworn a good oath: hear me.—You have by this offer of gold eradicated the suspicions I entertained against you: once more you are my friend; I will be true to you, and trust you to remit me a ransom in the manner I shall hereafter relate: your life is safe now. I knew that you possessed this gold: we Moors have spies where few would suspect it. Had you continued with the caravan, you would have been robbed, and perhaps murdered. The Moorish servant, in his escape to warn his comrades of your unexpected delay at the wells, met me: it was fortunate, for I wanted a messenger. You, I knew, I could manage: I leave the rest of the caravan to them."

CHAPTER XXXV

ADVENTURES IN THE DESERT.

THE travellers proceeded on their exhausting journey; Hammerton revolving in his mind the adventures of the past, and his hopes for the future. Since the death of his late companion in slavery, all seemed to have changed: the journey, the horrible sameness of which was more painful almost than the fatigue, was performed without any particular misfortunes. As the travellers approached the sea, the appearance of the desert now began to alter,—the sand was found to be composed partly of sea-shells, bearing evidence that this great and gloomy desert had once been covered with water.

On remarking this change to his companion, Hossein replied: "We have a tradition amongst us, that, many moons past, the waters of the great lake, to which we cannot see a termination, once washed over this desert; but this was even before the blessed Prophet rode the miraculous camel. Amongst us who live here at war with the world these stories pass from father to son,—it was our only history, for when we go to the coast or towns for intelligence of caravans, we never learn to read those books which your countrymen the infidels send over to instruct us, as they say. We watch the starting of the caravan. to get one of our tribe a friend of the caravan bashi, and then we reap our harvest in the desert, where escape is impossible."

"But some caravans," remarked Hammerton, "arrive in safety to their place of destination."

"True," replied Hossein; "but they have paid handsomely for our protection: then we escort them, and our words once pledged for their security, we would die rather than rob them!"

"The caravan I came with," resumed Hammerton; "was that under your protection?"

"No," replied Hossein. "The ass of a bashi, who, under the advice of the devil, refused to give the trifle we required, has long since paid it eight times over, before he reached his journey's end: I warrant he and his cargo have changed hands. Those who refuse to give up their property are slain. We have with us men respectable from connection, who sell our plunder at Timbuctoo; and we therefore allow the poor devils, who, believe their property to be secure, all the trouble of the transport; but when they are nearly at their journey's end, we save them all further anxiety, and manage the rest ourselves."

"And then," interrupted Hammerton, "return home."

"We have no home but our tents. No: we share the plunder; go into some town, revel in the luxuries of life, until the means of satisfying our wishes are exhausted; then we mount our camels again, join our tribes, and soon replenish our stock. But, asses that we are; worse than the father of all fools are we! we now quarrel amongst ourselves. Some drunken owls stole some women from our neighbouring tribe, and blood once spilt is never dried up even by the desert. My scattered people," added he, "will meet me not far from our next resting-place. Fear not—my word is pledged; you shall be taken in safety to the great water."

The whole scenery now began to assume a different appearance. For twenty-five days had the travellers toiled over the sand, but now the sight was gladdened by occasional patches of verdure; the camels stepped out more cheerfully; birds were also seen whirling about aloft, and the travellers seemed, as it were, to be returning from the dead to the living. As they advanced further on, trees were seen in the distance; some hills reared their heads above the dismal plain; animated nature again assumed her dominion, and the scene appeared by contrast like a garden.

The spirits of Hammerton rose as he approached this termination of his journey; and those of Hossein in proportion seemed to droop. "You rejoice," said he, "at this change: my home is far behind me. It is true that I shall enjoy myself in the towns, for I shall return by Morocco to

El-Harib, thence again over the sands; but I shall have no companion. I have much to do to repair the evil which has come upon me; and yet, if man's heart is not like the stone dropped into the water, over which the endless sea runs its uninterrupted course, burying it for ever beneath its waves, you will occasionally think of her who lies now beneath the sand of our desert; and even when far away you will remember Hossein the Moor, who assisted at her burial. Ah! yonder is a man—one of my tribe most likely. Before we approach him let us listen. Our tribe will demand a heavy ransom for your life. I know you have given all you have. How will you silence these men, who consider infidels as marketable commodities, upon whom they put a price? What shall I say to quiet them?"

"I will pay any sum of money I can command," answered Hammerton, not very much pleased with the manner this unexpected communication was made, "into the hands of any agent you may appoint."

"'Tis well said, Abdallah; but when the bird has escaped from the fowler's snare, who shall insure its return?"

"You know well, Hossein, that I have no money. If you can believe in me, I will be as true to my word as an Arab. Of what use would my carcase be to you and yours? for if I am returned to slavery, I will destroy the hope of reward by terminating my own existence."

"Our dogs which bark, Abdallah, seldom bite," remarked Hossein; "it is the silent, surly cur who rushes undismayed upon danger. But my word is pledged: to you I trust to remit me three thousand dollars, to Israel Ben Achmet at Algiers. Say it is for Hossein, the Moor of El-Harib. Promise."

"I do."

"Swear by your Prophet."

"I swear."

"It is enough."

By this time the stranger had approached. It was as Hossein had conjectured, one of the expected tribe. He brought great intelligence of plundered caravans, of retreating enemies, and of prosperous events. "But," said he, "two prizes have escaped us. Berzroom has lost two slaves; one a woman of great beauty, the other a willing lad, who worked hard. Perhaps the old Turk might have borne the loss of both these without much repining had not his favourite slave Abdallah been killed,and a dromedary of great worth stolen. He has offered ten thousand dollars for both, or five thousand for either slave returned to him. All the malice of revenge—every cruelty that man has invented to torture his fellow-man, he vows shall be used, until the skin, wasting away by slow degrees, shall leave his victim a moving skeleton, to die of lingering starvation. They would be great prizes for us, Hossein, but they have eluded our vigilance."

"How long is it since these slaves escaped?" asked Hossein.

"It is now forty-two days. Our men have been active; and some report has reached us that they followed the caravan to Timbuctoo. If so, they may yet be ours; for minute descriptions have been given of them. The reward and known integrity of the old Turk have set us all on the alert. Such a prize would give us all the blessings of a repose in the towns."

Hossein seemed little to heed the garrulity of his comrade. He had one of the prizes in his power; and although his word was pledged, yet he was not quite so honourable in his heart as at once to forego the bait: the other was dead, still he could find the bones. He bent his head forward and seemed wrapt in thought; whilst Hammerton, who had paid the greatest attention to this unwelcome communication, was busy planning some mode of escape—even by a murder.

His pistols were still about him; the flints not likely to forego the spark—the powder dry. What was now to hinder his despatching both his friend Hossein and his avowed enemy? He was evidently not far from his journey's end: there was a freshness in the air unknown to the desert; and not far on their right some curling smoke rose, and on the left the trees seemed all to have an inclination one way.

This last circumstance was to Hammerton's mind decisive that the sea was not far distant. Yet to murder the man who had assisted to bury his companion—who had led him through a desert where no stranger could have extricated himself—who had provided him with provisions, slept under the same tent, drunk from the same bowl, and eaten of the same salt, was impossible! and Hammerton would sooner have died than have taken his companion's life:—to take the life of one who had been, moreover, his only companion in danger, who had sworn to release him, and who had appeared so open and so upright, was a thought not for an instant to be encouraged by such a man as Hammerton.

Very different were the workings of Hossein's mind. His life was a life of rapine and murder—he was an outlaw—a general vulture upon society—one who heeded not the screams or entreaties of the innocent. He was the privateer and the pirate of the desert: to him all were enemies who crossed his seas, and the camels (the ships of the deserts), their cargoes, and their crews, were all prizes. He reflected upon the uncertainty of the ransom on the one hand, the certainty on the other,—for he would have repaid himself had the Turk proved false to his word; the danger he ran with his own tribe; the ease by which this large sum of money would be made, and the folly of being bound by an oath when his hand had not scrupled at a murder; and yet Hossein had contracted a friendship for his companion, and such a friendship as adversity alone can create. Abdallah had reposed a trust in him; had given up, unsolicited, all his money; had fed with him, worked with him, and suffered with him: it was odd for a Moor, but a sensation of mercy passed over him.

Hossein, after having duly considered the matter, called the stranger, and kept up in a low voice an earnest conversation with him, during which Hammerton was occasionally watched by the new-comer. Whenever their eyes met, there was a kind of doubt upon the features of the Moor, and a careless disregard on the other. That he was condemned Hammerton had no doubt; and yet he was confident that had Hossein intended treachery, he would have shown his intention long since.

This consideration convinced him that the sacred pledge of the salt would not be violated; although he well knew that these pirates frequently shuffle out of an oath, and think the deceit laudable.

Hammerton had been the football of Fortune from the day he entered the navy to the present time, and had encountered little else but a succession of troubles and privations. Still he clung to life with all the ardour of a more fortunate man. He had now surmounted every peril by which he had been surrounded—had gained the coast, and was firmly resolved to leave his bones to whiten on the shore, or to try his old enemy, the sea, to restore him to his home.

It was now nearly noon: the heat was oppressive, and the wearied camels walked with difficulty. Hossein proposed a halt: the camels were as usual allowed to browse; the tent was fixed, and all seemed conducted with the usual confidence. The stranger ate from his own store; whilst Hossein and Abdallah shared the little which was left.

It was the customary habit immediately after the meal to retire to rest: but Hammerton was too much on his guard to do this. Hossein, as usual, threw himself down, and was soon asleep; but the stranger remained awake, and never took his eyes from Hammerton. He answered no questions, but in a surly, dogged manner examined his arms, then lighted his pipe, and smoked in silence. Hammerton thought the first example one very proper to be followed, and he likewise looked to his arms, which he found to be in good order. By way of keeping on the alert and awake, although fatigue nearly weighed his eyelids down, he rubbed his scimetar until the blade was as reflective as a looking-glass: at last he could no longer struggle against nature, and he fell into a profound slumber.

It was not till past noon that he awoke. The stranger was in the same position, smoking. Hossein still slumbered, and everything around him remained untouched. This disarmed Hammerton of any suspicions he might have entertained. The camels were now again prepared, and for the last time the party set forward. There came a freshness in the breeze as the sun went down; the night was cloudy, and occasionally squally; and Hammerton felt assured that this peculiar freshness of the air was caused by its having been blown over the ocean, and that on the morrow his eyes would be gladdened by the sight of the

Lake of Large Waters, under which denomination the Trâkânt Moors call the sea. There seemed no particular communication between the parties: Hossein went, as usual, first; Hammerton second, and the stranger third. Very few words were exchanged; but those few were highly gratifying to Hammerton.

"To-morrow, Abdallah," Hossein said, "you will see the large lake, and you will be freed from the necessity of using a tent by the day after. There is a small town not far from the cape, to which my friend will direct you. At dawn I shall leave you, after I have fulfilled my promise, and pointed out to you the waters. On your part, you will not forget your pledge. We may meet again, or destiny may separate us for ever. I shall not forget poor Sidi who lies under the sand; nor should you blot from memory the Moor who conducted you across the pathless desert. My people are not far, and I must join them. Have you anything to say, to offer, to give, or request before we part?"

"I have," replied Hammerton: "to repeat my gratitude; to offer you all that a poor wanderer can offer—my prayers for your safety. The tent which has shaded us is yours, my camel yours—everything I possess is yours. One favour only I would request:—if I reach this village which you say is so near, I must enter it a beggar; I have not one piece of money of the smallest value; should I go into the town a mendicant, I should be compelled from necessity to work, or become a slave. I ask just sufficient to keep me for three days; by that time my strength may be partially recruited, and I may be enabled to bear more fatigue."

"Here is money," replied Hossein; "you need not much:" and he gave back to Hammerton some coin with the air of a man who did not feel inclined to do a generous action.

At daylight Hammerton gave a shout of joy: before him lay the sea, and the dark clouds which settled on the horizon were to him perhaps the most glorious sight of his life. When he saw the curling waves foaming as they broke upon the shore, he tried to urge his camel to a quicker walk, that he might meet the breakers upon the beach, and feel it was no deception—no mirage of the desert—by plunging into it. Powerful indeed were the emotions this cheerful sight produced. All his past troubles and anxieties were forgotten: he looked no longer upon the perils he had encountered,—he looked forward only with hope.

"My task is done," said Hossein,—"my pledge is redeemed. There are the waters of the great lake: there," said he, pointing a little to the right, "is the village you seek. Farewell! I leave you this friend of mine as your companion: he will not desert you. Farewell!"

"Nay, stop," said Hammerton: "one word before we part. You will believe me sincere in my promises: inquire at Algiers within four months of this day. You will not deny me this favour: accept this ring—it belonged to Sidi. When we laid her in the grave, I took this from her finger and concealed it: it is all I have at this moment in the world; I ask you to take it as a pledge of friendship and of esteem."

Hossein took it without saying a word, and bowing with a graceful Oriental bend, he turned his camel to the north-eastward, and desiring Hammerton to follow his destiny, departed.

There was in Hossein's manner something which startled the suspicions of Hammerton:—there was a coolness and condescension, which ill accorded with their previous friendship. Neither did Hammerton much admire his guard and companion; he would rather have entered the town by himself, and he saw no necessity for burdening the stranger with his company. However, he concluded it would be as well to allow him to keep near him until Hossein was far removed; and with this intention he did not attempt to swerve from the course he was pursuing.

Well did Hammerton know the treachery of these people, notwithstanding their religious superstition in regard to the violation of any law of the Koran. He saw in Hossein's departure a subterfuge; he had conducted him to the spot, but he had left a man to watch him,—one who had eaten by himself, one who had proclaimed the bounty offered for his capture. Again an idea presented itself to Hammerton: the terms of the reward were for his capture alive, that lingering torture might glut the revenge of the old Turk;

for his carcase was not worth the powder requisite to kill it, and every farthing had been given to Hossein, with the exception of about two dollars which were returned to him. With this conviction, Hammerton's mind became more composed; he thought that, singly opposed to this man, he himself being armed, he would deserve to lose his life if he could not protect it. But it was evident Hossein had men within reach, and Hammerton felt he might be led back to El-Harib under the orders of Hossein, whilst the perfidious Moor would only appear when the reward was to be paid.

Whilst he was busied in turning over these thoughts in his mind, the day broke, and there at anchor off the town lay a large ship. Hammerton, although he had been so ong a stranger to his profession, knew her at the first glance to be too large for a merchant ship. The vessels employed in the slave-trade, and which are those which frequent the coast further to the southward, are generally low, sneaking vessels, built for fast sailing; this looked like a frigate: to whatever country she belonged, she was for him a sure refuge. The vessel was at anchor a little to the southward of the town, and in order to get down upon the beach so as to advance near to her, it became requisite to steer the ship of the desert more to the westward. Without consulting his companion, Hammerton altered the direction of his course. No sooner had he done so, than his careful friend reminded him that he was taking a circuitous route.

"I know it," said Hammerton. "I am going along the beach to the village."

"Pardon me," said the Moor, as he advanced; "I must see you in safety. This is the way I intend to go;" and suiting the action to the word, he caught hold of the rope which served as a bridle, and giving it a sudden jerk, made the camel resume its former course. Hammerton did not appear to heed this insult, but turned round to assure himself that Hossein was too far away to render any assistance. As he was still visible, he remarked to the Moor,

"Friend, you are too kind, and I fear I trouble you with my company."

"Not in the least," replied the surly dog; "I shall have

plenty of that before we part, so we may as well get used to it: make your beast walk faster."

Hammerton took no notice of this remark. His eyes were fixed upon the ship, the sides of which showed the ports of a frigate. He then carefully surveyed the coast. Along the shore, the high sea broke with furious impetuosity—wave after wave came surging and breaking; whilst the noise heard far off of the reflux of the sea convinced Hammerton that any escape from that part was impossible: his own element had tossed up an insuperable barrier against him. Continuing his search with a careful eye, he discovered, nearly in a line with the ship, a small part of the coast which seemed free from the breakers. Although nearly in a semicircle outside, there was a bar or sand-bank, over which the water foamed; the centre part was open, and afforded an inlet for boats. This, therefore, was the place which he was resolved to gain, and there by signs and signals to draw the attention of those on board the ship.

The clouds which had lowered over the horizon cleared away as the day advanced: a light breeze blew from the land, and the frigate was rigging with her head to the town. It was scarcely daylight,—at least, not broad day; the sun had not risen; and although Hossein was no longer visible, he might have been near enough to render assistance. Now came the trial—now came all arguments to Hammerton's mind in self-justification of the blow he seemed compelled to strike. It was for his liberty—his life; for without the one, the other was not worth retaining. Carefully he ran over the future prospects of the recaptured slave;—slow lingering torture, starvation, bastinado, the life of the brute with the thought of the human being; constant labour to increase the wealth of others, and no recompense for services; to live a slave—to die a dishonoured infidel, and his carcase to be given to the birds of prey, because no one could feel sufficient affection to scratch a grave. On the other hand was restoration to life by the renewal of all social ties;—again to see a cherished sister, to hear tidings of his earliest friends; to mark how Fortune, so adverse to him, had smiled upon others; to live with those he loved: but this great good was to be effected by a cool deliberate murder.

There was no doubt as to the intentions of the Moor; still Hammerton was desirous that the base conduct of the Moor should be made quite manifest before he proceeded to adopt this last cruel necessity. "Am I not free at this moment?" said he to himself; "and shall I at the beck or bidding of a Moor alter my determination? What right has this man over me? why am I subject to his restraint?"

The mind weakened by slavery and fearful as to escape, like the thief in the fable, trembles at every voice. "There is no time for delay," thought Hammerton; "I must now act." With this determination, he again directed his camel to the beach; at the same time, and with trembling hand, he drew a pistol from his belt, which he held ready for service.

"More to the right," said the Moor, as he perceived the alteration.

Hammerton took no notice.

"Dost hear me, Abdallah!—more to the right!"

Still Hammerton took no notice, but continued to sing the song of encouragement to his camel. The Moor now broke out into a furious strain, which convinced Hammerton that Hossein had not considered himself in honour bound to keep the secret.

"Dog of a defiled infidel!" said the Moor, as he advanced close up, "dost hear me? By Allah! if thou dost not turn that brute towards the town, I will lash thee on its back and scourge thee to make it walk the faster."

"Touch but that rope," said Hammerton, "and I will send you to your Prophet before you can loosen the lock of hair by which he is to take you to Paradise."

"By our holy Prophet!" ejaculated the Moor, "this would make a Persian laugh!—a slave—an infidel—a defiled dog, to draw a pistol against a Moor! Are you mad? or must I get my comrades here to hunt you to the town as they would a jackal? I tell you, more to the right, or I'll give a signal which will soon be answered."

"Raise but your hand, and you die. Walk on by my side, and you may live long to cut throats in the desert. Am I your slave, that you order me? I want you not more than as an escort. I see no danger to alarm me; and if you are left by Hossein to serve me, do as I bid you."

The fury of the Moor at the coolness of these remarks was uncontrollable: in a moment he applied a whistle to his mouth, and blew a loud, long, shrill note. The mischief was done, and there was no means of counteracting the effect; to have shot the Moor would not stop the signal too surely given. Both stopped on the instant. The Moor leant over on one side, as if to hear the answer; and Hammerton, tremblingly alive to his situation, heard distinctly the long shrill note which responded to the whistle of the Moor. He turned his eyes to the ship; there was his only hope of restoration swinging carelessly to the light flaws of wind which, in this country, are seldom steady before the regular breeze is established.

Almost without hope, Hammerton continued to gaze: at length he saw a boat push from the ship, and steer for the entrance above mentioned. "Is there not a chance of escape in that direction?" thought Hammerton, as he urged his camel forward: but the jaded animal, in spite of the goadings unmercifully bestowed upon him, refused to quicken its pace. The moment Hammerton's eyes were fixed in one direction, looking for the appearance of some expected enemy, the next he would turn again towards the boat; but the animal on which he rode still took its measured strides; nor could the goad of the sharp point of his scimetar, nor the hasty song (the best inducement), make the camel advance the quicker.

The boat was now fast nearing the shore; it was inside the reef, and in smooth water. The Moor, who perceived the object Hammerton had in view, again blew the shrill whistle, but in another note. It was answered nearer than the first. Hammerton turned his eye in the direction of the sound, and saw distinctly turning round a small hillock the forms of one or two men. He now stepped down from his camel and took to his heels, holding in each hand a pistol.

The man who runs for his life runs lustily: in spite of his cramped limbs, from the sitting posture he had so long endured, Hammerton soon passed the camel, and increased his distance from the Moor. The latter, seeing his prey escaping, drew a pistol and took a steady shot at the flying slave. The ball passed through the fleshy part of the leg. Hammerton felt that he was hit; but life was on the die—he heeded not the wound, but ran even faster than before.

The boat had by this time touched the shore; the seamen were employed in preparing the seine to catch some fish. Upon hearing the pistol-shot of the Moor, however, they immediately got ready their fire-arms: whilst, to be in greater security, they jumped into the boat, and kept her off on her oars.

In the mean time the fugitive saw in another direction a quick-footed dromedary advancing to cut off his retreat. It was evident from the long strides of the nimble animal, that he would arrive nearly at the same moment, if not before he could reach the boat. There was therefore but one resource left, and his resolution was instantly taken. As the Moor with his bared scimetar rode furiously at Hammerton, the latter, panting for breath, and nearly overcome with fatigue and pain from his wound, stopped short, took as quiet an aim as was possible to one so hotly pursued, and pulled the trigger. It missed fire! His hope was now reduced to one pistol; he took it in the right hand, and as his adversary continued to advance to within three yards, he fired and shot the dromedary. The animal fell with a heavy fall, and the Moor rolled off from her back.

The officer in the boat, who saw the affair, broke through the orders he had received, which were on no account to interfere with the natives, but on every occasion to endeavour to cultivate their friendship. "Give way, my lads," said he, "and save that poor devil!" The sailors, ever alive to do a generous action, bent their backs to their oars; the boat skimmed through the smooth water, touched the beach, and in a second was lightened of her crew.

Hammerton saw his countrymen advancing to his rescue: but although he felt the fainting weakness which the loss of blood occasioned, his heart still bore him up manfully. He was within a hundred yards of his friends; the Moors pursued him closely—he could almost hear them panting.

At this moment it occurred to him to try the pistol which had missed fire, and which he retained in his hand, although he had thrown away the other. The cartridges were in his belt: he succeeded in re-priming the pistol. He felt, however, he could not reach his friends before he should be overtaken. With the despair of the hunted stag, which stands at bay when the chase is done and the greedy fangs of the dogs are shining in its sight, Hammerton turned to meet his foes. Their numbers had now increased; there were seven or eight in sight, but only one near enough to interrupt him. This was the Moor who had accompanied him. With a glow of satisfaction on his countenance, as he saw the slave almost within his grasp and unable to move, the Moor sprang lightly forward to secure him. Hammerton now made a last effort—he levelled his pistol, and the pursuer fell to the ground a corpse, as Hammerton dropped down and almost fainted from fatigue and loss of blood.

It was now a race between the seamen and the Moors, each striving to arrive at the spot first; and greatly did Hammerton fear that he might not retain sufficient strength to tell them who he was. He heard the officer cheering his men: "Step out, my lads, one and all! There is some foul play here: get between the Moors and the fallen man before you stop."

The cry of the Moors, "Allah il Allah!" was heard from the other side; "the slave will meet his destiny—he is ours!"

At this moment the officer jumped across the fallen body of Hammerton, and heard distinctly the last words he uttered before he fainted, "Save me! save me! I am an Englishman."

There was now every prospect of a much better fight. The seamen, who heard their officer call out, "By heavens! he is an Englishman!" drew up in a line, brandishing their stretchers; whilst four marines, whom prudent foresight had placed in the boat, lest some surprise should take place, stood with their muskets ready and pointed. This checked the advance of the foremost Moors, who waited for a reinforcement. The time was not lost by the officer, who made three of his men take up the wounded man and convey him towards the boat, he himself, with the marines, retreating at the same time.

The signal-man, who had been desired to watch the boat from the frigate, had witnessed by means of his glass the whole affair; the officer of the watch had reported it to the captain; the boats were hoisted out, manned, and armed; and as the lieutenant who commanded on shore began to be apprehensive of the result—for the Moors like bees began to swarm, and to gain upon him so much that he was fearful of his own retreat—a long gun from the frigate was fired. The seamen, who turned to see the signal, which was the recall flag, saw also the coming assistance. The Moors pressed forward to regain their lost prize; the seamen cheerfully carried the body, which again manifested some signs of returning life; the marines retreated with their faces to the approaching swarm, and with steady determination seemed resolved to protect the wretched man they had contributed to rescue.

The increased numbers of the Moors had been seen from the ship. The boats neared the shore; and at the instant the parties reached the beach, and Hammerton was placed in the stern-sheets, the Moors prepared their long spears. The seamen and marines of the *Arethusa* now landed to assist their shipmates, and the steady fronts thus presented to them scared away the pirates of the desert, who, with a wild cry, tossed up their spears, and turned round, as the boats returned to their ship and placed Hammerton in security.

CHAPTER XXXVI.

A FUNERAL AND A WEDDING.

THE *Arethusa* entered Malta with her prize towing astern. At this time there were many English men-of-war in the harbour, and long and loud were the cheers which welcomed the victorious frigate to the anchorage. Over the tricoloured flag, which, previous to the action, waved in all its pride from the peak of the *Didon*, was hoisted the union-jack, which Weazel had stuck on a boat-hook; it was almost cut to pieces by musketry, whilst through the white part of the

French ensign two round-shot had passed. The welcome was returned by the crew of the *Arethusa*, as she passed slowly and silently between Valetta and Bonaparte's Bay; and a simultaneous cheer of all the shipping resounded along the harbour, as the anchors of both frigates were let go at the entrance of the Dockyard creek.

The boats of the Maltese, laden with oranges, figs, sausages, bread, garlic, melons, and other luxuries to sailors, crowded alongside, and excited the curiosity of the French officers, who, in defiance of all English naval discipline (but uninterrupted from their situation), peeped through the ports. The uniform was quickly recognized by those who had so long groaned under the yoke of France, and who had been compelled, in order to save their own lives, to sacrifice everything they possessed. The hatred—the inextinguishable hatred—of the Maltese broke out in their hissings and revilings: they called them by all those opprobrious epithets of which the mixed character of the Maltese language is capable; and all attempts on the part of Murray to drive away these screaming jackdaws, who, having found others to hunt the prey, were now ready to devour it, were unavailing.

There was an admiral in the harbour; and those alone can estimate the feelings of Murray who have experienced the gratification of reporting to their senior officer the result of a contest such as that already described. The interviews which successful enterprise entails upon the fortunate, and which are seldom inflicted upon the miserable, were soon over; and Murray, whose heart retained a strong affection for Weazel, resolved to bury him with even more honour than was due to his rank.

Of all the killed in that action, Weazel alone had been reserved for a burial on shore. The seamen, sewed up in hammocks, were consigned to the element on which they had so long served. Some, it is true, were thrown overboard during the action; but those who lingered until victory was proclaimed, were buried with all the impressive honours of the service. Murray, sensible that nothing touches the sailor more deeply than the respect paid to a departed messmate, took care on this occasion that no circumstance should be omitted which could add to the ceremony. The bodies of the seamen were carried round the quarter-deck and forecastle, preceded by the band playing the 104th Psalm, and followed by the marines with arms reversed, Captain Murray and his officers bringing up the rear. They were consigned to the deep four at a time, two placed upon one grating, and two upon another, the gratings being placed upon both gangways. Captain Murray read the service, and read it impressively: the messmates of the killed stood on each side of the gratings, their eyes resting upon the flag under which reposed for ever the bodies of their former friends and companions. When the words were read, "We therefore commit their bodies to the deep," the gratings were launched over the side, and the dead were consigned to their watery graves; the marines fired a volley, the gunner gave a long deep sigh, and uttered "Amen! amen!" and the water rolled over those who before were borne upon it, and who were the pride of the noble frigate which had now given them up.

"It's an awful thing to die!" said the gunner, as he put on his hat when the ceremony was over; "and it is no use expending powder over the body, as if they wished to salute a strange ship, fitted foreign. For my own part, I should rather like to go quietly, or be bundled overboard during the fight."

"Ay, ay!" said the boatswain; "I understand all about it. You think, if you can get launched overboard during the confusion, that you will get up to heaven before the devil knows you are dead."

"Shocking! shocking!" said the gunner, as he ran down to his cabin and shut his door.

On the day that Weazel was buried, almost every one in the ship requested they might go on shore and see the last of their favourite—the one who was always foremost in any amusement or in any danger—who was generous, liberal, and humane—who lived like a midshipman, and who died like a hero. To the request of the ship's company Captain Murray gave an answer in the affirmative; and the streets of Valetta never witnessed, as the procession went slowly along the Strada Reale to the Florian Gate, more propriety of conduct, more real regret, in a funeral parade, than in the downcast looks of the seamen, as they slowly followed their favourite to his last resting-place. They laid him near the entrance to the town, on a rising ground overlooking the quarantine harbour, then not used for that purpose, and little frequented by vessels; and when the marines had fired their three volleys, and the ceremony was over, many of the old weather-beaten tars took a handful of dirt and threw it into the grave, saying, "When the hands are turned up to muster aloft, poor fellow! you will answer your call like a seaman."

"He never did any harm to any one but himself," said the gunner: "he was very fond of the liquor-case, and I make no doubt——"

"That he will avoid bad spirits for the future," interrupted the boatswain. "Come along, Pounce, and let's drink him a safe voyage to the Great Harbour."

"Let us kneel down," replied the gunner, "and pray for him: let us sing a good psalm."

"No! no!" said the boatswain: "he never liked that music; but he was very fond of—

"'Here, a sheer hulk, lies poor Tom Bowling:'

and if you will just step into this rosolio shop, I'll give it you loud enough for Weazel to hear it."

"Come along on board to our duties," said the gunner. "We have done for him all we can do; he is gone, and now cannot repent. He was hurried from us, doing his duty to his country, but not to his——"

"Avaust heaving there, Pounce! He could not attend to his duty because he was wounded, or he was not the chap to lie down on a chest in the steerage when his shipmates were blazing away on deck. Don't you take the poor fellow's character away, Pounce; it's unchristian-like—very, Pounce,—that's what it is! I wonder that you, who are always turning up your eyes like a dying duck's in thunder, should say such a thing; but he can't hear it now, so you lose your labour."

The *Arethusa* required much repair after the injury she had sustained: she had many shot between wind and water, her lower masts were wounded, her sides riddled. There were no docks at Malta, nor could the dockyard supply lower masts; it was therefore decided that she should proceed to England. Accordingly, after a week's delay, she, with her prize in company, weighed her anchors and made sail. She shortly afterwards arrived safely in Portsmouth, entered the harbour, was dismantled, the crew hulked, and the ship taken into dock.

In those stirring times, the activity displayed in the dockyards was truly wonderful; nor were the seamen behind the shore-going labourers in diligence. The vessel without a mast might be seen launched afresh, as it were, at daylight in the morning; by sunset she might be seen in a forward state of equipment; and the following day, her top-gallant yards might be crossed, her guns and stores on board, and within a few hours of a proper efficiency to go to sea. No captain lingered in harbour; there was a stirring spirit in the navy of England, unknown to any other nation. The despatch with which vessels were docked and refitted was truly wonderful: nor was it at all an extraordinary event to see a frigate at anchor at Spithead on the Monday morning, docked, repaired, refitted, re-stored, and standing out of St. Helen's on the Saturday following, in a perfect state of efficiency.

On this occasion it must be confessed that Murray was not quite so eager to go to sea as he was on his first appointment, when he sailed away with old Jonathan Corncob. He applied for a week's leave, which was granted; but the Admiralty were very anxious to employ actively the young captain who had already given such an earnest of future greatness: the orders to the port-admiral were to hasten the refitting of the *Arethusa*, and Murray found that he was very likely to be married one day, and at sea the next.

He found his father in the full enjoyment of health: the adopted child was prepared to become his daughter-in-law—the correspondence between Murray and Amelia, which had been begun at Gibraltar, had ripened into a regular return of love-letters; and Murray, in the pride of the moment, when his greatest hope had been realized in the capture of the *Didon*, had offered his hand in the letter he had written detailing that event. On his arrival at Portsmouth this offer had been repeated. Amelia, although somewhat startled at the necessity for so sudden a celebration of the ceremony, frankly consented, without displaying any of those affected airs in which young ladies sometimes think it becoming on sueh oceasions to indulge.

We have known in the naval service a captain reeeive his sailing orders as he came out of the chureh; nay, before he had read his destination, whieh would sever him from her he had just married thousands of miles, his frigate was under weigh in obedience from the flag-ship, and the gallant eaptain had no time even to give his bride a parting kiss: she was earried to the hotel, and the bridegroom walked off to his boat—was on board his ship, and by sunset elear of St. Helen's, standing down Channel, to shape a eourse, when he had eleared it, which would forward the frigate to the Cape of Good Hope.

Walter was married, and thought he might answer with another when summoned to his ship, "that he was married, and eould not come." No one more strenuously opposed this than his wife.

"This is a hard trial, Amelia!" said Walter, as he impressed a lover's kiss on her drooping faee.

"I would not for the world mar your prospects in your profession," said the thoughtful girl, "and must not be selfish. No ehildish fears shall prompt me to detain you! If it must be so, go and realize the hopes of your country,—and the blessings of your wife go with you! Though far absent, my thoughts will be ever near you. Good-bye! You shall not see a tear start from my eyes: yet, God knows, I am very—very wretched!" Here nature, however, mastered her resolution, and, in spite of all her heroie determination, she could no longer eontrol her feelings, and burst into tears.

Not unmoved did Sir Hector witness this scene. "I will be a father to her, Walter," he began, his voice tremulous with emotion, "and will wateh over your treasure."

"Wherever you go," said Amelia, at length mastering the sudden outbreak of her feelings, "remember my brother! He may yet live. The uneertainty of his fate is almost worse than the aetual knowledge of his loss. Assure me that you will make every effort to learn the truth.—I shall count the hours while you are away," added she, playfully.

"You are my treasure, Amelia! you teach me my duty—the hard duty now—of submission to present circumstances. Cheer my father when I am away—you have ever done that as a friend which you now owe as a daughter. How long I shall be absent I cannot tell: perhaps I may be attached to the Channel Fleet, and then we can frequently meet at Plymouth; perhaps," he added, with a sigh, "I may be ordered to the East Indies, and then—but we will not anticipate evils. My time grows short, Amelia,—so short, indeed, that when I have left you I shall remember hundreds of things that I wished to say. Of your brother, however, be assured I will not spare any exertion to learn if he be alive. God bless you, dearest! Let me take you to my father, and beg of you not to witness my departure. Farewell! when next we meet, we must hope not to be so suddenly separated.

Walter took leave of his father; the old man, in a firm voice, bidding him to continue to do his duty as nobly as he had done. "We shall soon meet again, I trust. God bless you!"

The married life of Walter can scarcely be said to have commenced,—all was sunshine with him—the little bickerings and jealousies to which the most affectionate are sometimes subject had not reached him; the inflammation of the weekly bills, the torment of disobedient children, the eternal music of the nursery, the vexation of discontented servants, the prying curiosity of neighbours, the requisite attendance of the doctor,—these, and sundry other trifling annoyances of life, (for life would stagnate without annoyance,—we are told that spring would be but gloomy weather if we had nothing else but spring,) were yet in perspective; and as Walter returned to his ship, he had full time to consider how much one week had altered his situation. But that which gave him the most satisfaction was, that he was none the poorer by his marriage: his wife remained under the roof of his own father—all her personal expenses would come from that liberal hand; and Walter found he had now created a new idol, which he vowed within himself to worship with lover-like idolatry. In the mean time, the wheels rapidly performed their rotatory motion, and he soon found himself on board of the *Arethusa*.

CHAPTER XXXVII.

THE PIRATE.

THE *Arethusa* was soon ready for sea; and Walter, once separated from his young wife, felt more anxious than ever to be actively employed. His wish was soon gratified: ten days from the time the frigate had entered the harbour, she was standing off and on at Spithead, waiting for her captain. The maintop-sail was filled, the ship heeled over to the breeze, and his Majesty had another efficient frigate ready to meet an adversary. She was directed to join the Channel fleet; and in the latter part of 1807 she was one of the frigates employed in the blockade of the Rochefort squadron.

A new era was about to break upon the French Navy. Napoleon, notwithstanding the destruction of his fleet at Trafalgar, had, in the space of two years, increased his shattered navy to the number of eighty sail-of-the-line; twenty more sail-of-the-line were ordered to be built, some at Antwerp and Brest, and others at Toulon and L'Orient. And another Trafalgar might reasonably be expected, and the English Navy rejoiced at this growing fleet, which might again come in contact with the fleets of Great Britain, and offer the prospect of another victory to another Nelson.

Seven sail-of-the-line, under Sir Richard Strachan, formed the blockading squadron off Rochefort. To this squadron, as we have said, the *Arethusa* was attached, and was, owing to the necessity which obliged Sir Richard to put to sea, in order to meet the provision-ships, which had been ordered to rendezvous some ten or twelve leagues south-west of Roche Bonne, the only ship which witnessed the escape of Rear-Admiral Allemand from the roadstead of Isle d'Aix.

After apprising the English admiral of this event, the *Arethusa* was directed to cruise in the Bay of Biscay; but although Captain Murray was vigilant and active, yet no opportunity offered for any signal manifestation of daring, or gave an opening for any enterprise beyond the occasional capture of some merchant ships.

In 1809, the *Arethusa* formed one of the fleet destined for the expedition to the Scheldt; between which interval of time Captain Murray had not unfrequently put into Plymouth, and had been able occasionally to visit his wife and his father: and Sir Hector saw almost his last wish gratified, when a son was born, and the inheritance of the title insured.

After the affair in the Scheldt, Captain Murray was two years afterwards directed to accompany the outward-bound India fleet as far as Teneriffe. He was then to visit several parts of the coast of Africa, and to return to England at the expiration of six months.

He had parted company from his charge, and altered his course towards the Cape de Verd Islands, intending to touch at St. Jago, and had run some degrees to the southward, when a sail was reported a-head. She was felucca-rigged; and as this kind of vessel is generally found in the Mediterranean, some suspicion was excited—more especially as she altered her course directly she made out the frigate, and carried, considering the freshness of the breeze, a great quantity of canvas.

Captain Murray's orders were to search the sea between Teneriffe and the coast for a piratical vessel, the crew of which had committed unparalleled atrocities. The pirate had effected numerous hair-breadth escapes from the English cruisers, and had struck terror into the hearts of all the captains of merchantmen, whose memories were well stored with the cruelties committed by the low, black, sneaking craft, very properly named *Il Diavolo:* some called her by the Spanish name of *Diableto*, some christened her an English *Devil:* but no vessel sank from leaks or seas—no vessel was dismasted or disabled—no wreck floated, the crew of which had trusted to either rafts or boats, but the *Devil* had the honour of the deed. The snowball accumulates as it rolls, and deeds of cruelty are added by the timid and the easy of belief, to swell the catalogue of crime against the marauders of the seas. The felucca, however, manifested no wish to be overhauled, and kept under all the sail she could carry, nearly preserving her distance from the *Arethusa.*

About sunset the chase hauled up more to the eastward, standing towards the coast in the direction of Cape Blanco; and it was the opinion of some on board the frigate, that if she once gained the coast, her capture would be certain, for on that part to which she was steering there are no regular harbours: others, on the contrary, expressed their conviction that if she got into the baffling winds near the coast, she would be enabled to keep closer in-shore than the *Arethusa*, and thereby take those light gusts of wind which so frequently come after sunset, designated as the land-wind. As both vessels drew towards the land, the trade-wind evidently got lighter and more variable: the felucca was able therefore to creep away from the frigate.

For three days and nights the chase continued; and when the morning of the fourth day came, the low land of the coast to the northward of Cape Blanco was seen. The chase, far away north of her pursuer, had trimmed her sails to the light air from the eastward, and was hugging the coast, intending to creep back to Sallee, or gain perhaps an entrance into the Mediterranean. The *Arethusa* was becalmed, her head round the compass,—not the slightest air reached her to give her steerage-way. The boats were therefore hoisted out, manned and armed, and, under the orders of the first lieutenant, pursued the crafty *Devil*. The broiling sun of this climate soon rose to render the enterprise more desperate: whilst the cool of the morning remained, the men worked with a good will; but long before eight o'clock, when they had neared the felucca very considerably, and had left the *Arethusa* almost out of sight, the overpowering heat compelled the men to relax in their labours.

Resolved not to lose the chase, the boats were divided. One division kept languidly dabbling the oars in the water and still gaining on the chase, whilst the others refreshed themselves with some biscuit and grog; thus taking spell and spell about, and gradually drawing within gun-shot of the felucca. The *Arethusa* was by this time entirely out of sight. Captain Murray had directed his lieutenant, in the event of parting company, to run down under Cape Blanco, where he would find the frigate either in the offing or at anchor; but, at all events, not to give up the chase whilst a hope remained of her capture. The boats had each one week's provisions and water; and from the directions given to keep close alongshore, there was no fear of their being driven to sea should a tornado come on. With such orders, it was not very probable that the crews of the boats would return, without a breeze had sprung up and the felucca run them out of sight.

As the men were completely exhausted by the overpowering heat, and the felucca manifested a certain determination of resistance, by firing a round-shot over the boats, it was judged advisable to refresh them by a general rest for an hour. So weak, indeed, had they become from the long and hard pull, that one or two were scarcely able to lay in their oars. It was about two o'clock, P.M., the hottest part of the day, when the men, making the boats' sails into awnings, fell asleep,—the officers alone keeping awake. Never was more complete exhaustion manifested, and to run alongside of the felucca whilst the men were in such a condition would have been to insure certain destruction.

In the mean time, not the slightest air arose to counteract the burning heat: the boats and the chase both lay becalmed; but the latter availed herself of her sweeps, and began soon to creep away again. This rendered it necessary to have recourse to the oars; but to effect this, the language neither of hope nor contempt was of any avail: the men,—and those tried men too, who had faced so many dangers and difficulties—who had been in so many engagements, and who volunteered for this service,—were completely exhausted; they called for water, and declared themselves willing to die, but unable to work. One or two, more spirited than the rest, made a great effort to overcome their languor, but it failed: the heat had done more in eight hours than actual labour would have done in twenty-four.

It was with an aching heart that the gallant officer perceived the vessel slipping gradually from his grasp. The midshipmen in the other boats endeavoured to console him by the assurance, that even the men in the felucca, although under awnings, could not long continue the exertion; and that when the sun went down, the lost way would soon be made up, and the attack be conducted with more sure success in darkness. But the fear of the land-breeze springing up took away much of the balm such words offered. It was useless, however, to grow either morose or desponding; for such was the state of the men, that if the pirate had come alongside of them, it was doubtful if they could have made much resistance.

By five o'clock the intense heat had abated: the crews of the different boats, refreshed by their sleep and reinvigorated by some food, took to their oars, and with a cheer of contentment they set to work, declaring they could go on all night without complaint, but that to continue during the heat of the day had been impossible. By seven o'clock, the boats were again within gun-shot; but the felucca had prepared herself for a vigorous defence. Boarding-nettings were run up; she had lowered her long unwieldy yards, and had placed them fore and aft, leaving them sufficiently aloft for the crew to pass from side to side: she had substituted for these, square yards, evidently prepared for the purpose, and her bows were the only part not sufficiently protected: these were, however, so sharp and narrow, that there was less need of the netting in that part. On nearing her, the officers in the different boats beheld another mode of defence, which had at first escaped their notice: inside of the netting bristled a row of boarding-pikes from the hull of the felucca, whilst here and there a spar was run out so as to prevent the boats from coming alongside. She lay like a porcupine with its quills pointed, and offered herself boldly to any one who would have the courage to handle her.

Not a shot had yet been fired: the boats were within two hundred yards of the pirate, when it was judged necessary to alter the mode of attack, and for this reason it was delayed. To board her on the quarter appeared almost impossible: stout spars had been rigged out to boom off any invaders; the broadside looked impregnable: the bows alone appeared assailable, and to this point the lieutenant directed his attack

"We must board her on both bows," he exclaimed; "the first on board must make way for his followers. The two barges must take this position; the two cutters will keep one on each quarter, and endeavour to gain a footing on the quarter-deck. But, whatever you do, take care and be cautious: it will not do to rush alongside, and have the boarding-nets over us: and rely upon it, we shall not find the bows unprotected. Now then, my lads! three cheers, and a handful of dollars for the first on board."

The pirate appeared to consider herself perfectly secure against the attack: only one or two heads had peeped over the taffrail; but now, when the consultation was taking place in the boats, a loud voice was heard hailing the boats in English. It checked the cheer, and was thus followed: "Boats ahoy!" The lieutenant, standing up, answered, "Holloa!"

"The captain has desired me to tell you to keep off. He says he does not want your blood, and that you shan't have his felucca; and recommends you to follow his good advice, which is to turn tail and go back to your frigate. You will do so much better now, than when half of your men are killed, and the other half wounded; half your boats sunk, and the other half leaky. That's all; do as you like."

"What vessel is that?" said the lieutenant.

"The *Happy-go-Lucky*, or the *Devil's Playmate*," answered the first man.

"What is she?" demanded the lieutenant.

"A felucca," answered the pirate.

"Where are you from?" still continued the lieutenant, the boats gradually creeping up.

"From where you saw us," answered the man, "and I advise you to stay where you are, or you will repent it."

"Three cheers, my lads! and a yard-arm for that vagabond."

The cheers followed the words, and a peal of musketry, accompanied by the contents of two swivels placed on the taffrail, came whizzing into the boats. So well was the fire directed that the attacking force was considerably weakened; one or two oars slipped from the dying hands of those who endeavoured with their last breath to use them, and some confusion was evident from this unexpected and slaughtering salute.

"Give way, my lads!" said the lieutenant, "and board her before they load again."

The advice was good, and was not neglected; but another volley from a party of men on the broadside showed how well the men were trained who thus defended their lives. Undismayed by this second warning, however, the two barges pushed for the bows; whilst the cutter, in order to draw off the attention of the pirate, kept up a quick fire of musketry from the four marines in each boat, who, with the steadiness that ever distinguishes that noble corps, continued their fire, notwithstanding the shower of bullets to which they were exposed, and which must have been crammed by handfuls into the swivels. As the barges passed ahead of the felucca they faced about, and got stem on to the pirate. This was done to avoidtwo long stout spars, like sweeps, which rendered it impossible to get under the bows in any other way except by either backing the boat against the stem, or going stem on—the last was preferred. The boat which bore the lieutenant commenced the attack; and just as she was placed under the head, in order to be better protected, a huge stone, which had been swung close up under the bowsprit, was cut away; it fell in the centre of the boat, stove and immediately sunk her. In vain did some of the poor fellows endeavour to cling to the vessel; the bows had been covered with grease, and not a rope hung overboard. As they struggled to escape the death which appeared the nearest, they were savagely struck by boarding-pikes; the pirates shouting in exultation, and daring the other boat, which was endeavouring to rescue some of the swimmers, to continue the attack.

In the mean time, the shout of victory which the pirates gave enticed the men stationed on the quarters to forsake their posts: who, believing from the cautious manner with which both cutters acted, that they would not venture nearer the felucca, gratified their curiosity by going forward to observe the struggling seamen coldly butchered. The other barge, having rescued one or two of the men, now advanced in spite of the warm and steady opposition with which they were met. The cheering of the barge's crew was altogether too exhilarating for the crews in the cutters to remain inactive; they advanced boldly on the quarters, and cautiously avoiding the spars, which would otherwise have stove the boats, they succeeded; for they were but triflingly opposed in getting athwart the stern.

The few who had stood at their post now rushed forward and apprised the captain of the felucca of this unexpected success on the part of the assailants. With a coolness equal to his courage, he despatched twenty men to murder the boarders; who, in their turn, accustomed to surmount difficulties, and cheered on by those behind them, made good a landing over the taffrail. Not more than six got on board before the pirates rushed aft. The slaughtering struggle which ensued was not of long duration; overpowered by numbers of these desperate men, who knew that their own lives would be sacrificed if they surrendered, the *Arethusa's* men were beaten back—four were killed, and the others were glad enough to leap overboard.

Still they were undaunted; the animating cheers from the barge, as her gallant crew boldly endeavoured to board over the bows, were answered by the cutters' crews, who again and again came to the attack. The numbers of the assailants, however, gradually grew less at each repulse, the cheer became less and less powerful, whilst the hurrahs of the pirates increased in strength. The last great rush was, like the rest, unavailing; the barge backed clear of the vessel, the cutters extricated themselves from their insecure position, and the three boats, joining company about pistol-shot from the felucca, held a council of war. In the barge only six men remained unhurt; and of those in the cutters not more than ten could be called actually efficient; and although the crew were still eager to try once more, and the marines most cordially seconded the proposition, yet it was evident that the case was hopeless.

In the mean time, the same voice which had warned them not to attempt the attack, again offered its friendly advice. "Go back to your ship, silly fellows!" was heard. "I warned you not to play with desperate men. Do you think we are going to be towed alongside of the frigate, to be hung at the yard-arm? Go and tell your captain that the *Devil's* crew disdain to follow up a beaten enemy from whom no prize-money can be got; and you may thank your poverty (for your jackets are no use to us,) for your escape. Good night! Come, lads, give them three cheers!—Away with you!"

The blood of all the crew boiled at this insult—the men almost mutinied against their officers, who, seeing how idle it was to entertain any further hope of success, resolved not to risk a further loss; and with many murmurings, not loud but deep, the gallant fellows turned their boats' heads towards the appointed rendezvous, and slowly left the felucca to follow her piratical employment. No sooner was this perceived on board the vessel than the boarding-nettings were lowered, the square yards replaced by the long lateen sails, and *Il Diavolo*, catching a light breeze which sprang up from the eastward, stood alongshore to the northward.

The boats' crews gladly availed themselves of this light flaw of wind; they stepped their masts, and, placing their wounded messmates into the most comfortable situation, the weary and the wounded lay down to rest, as the boat, under the direction of the officer, slowly and silently slipped through the water, standing to the southward.

The *Arethusa*, when she parted company with her boats, stood in-shore towards Cape Blanco; and finding a bay, with good anchorage in seven fathoms water, Captain Murray resolved to await the return of his men, and, keeping his ship at some distance from the shore, he anchored the same evening. The next day was employed in examining the coast and sounding: the opening before mentioned having been observed, it was resolved on the following morning to send the jolly-boat with the seine, in order to catch some fish, and hence the fortunate meeting with Hammerton, already mentioned.

In the mean time some anxiety was manifested for the fate of the boats, since it not unfrequently happens, along the coast of Africa, that very heavy gales, which perhaps do not reach more than four or five miles in extent, come suddenly upon the traders, and blow them to sea. The gales rarely last more than eight hours, but during that time they might carry the boats far out, and render it very difficult to regain the land. The look-out man at the main-top-gallant mast-head was frequently hailed, and as frequently to the question, "Do you see the boats coming?" answered in the negative.

Captain Murray's attention was now divided between anxiety for his men and curiosity respecting the stranger. The long uncombed beard and grisly mustachios shaded half the face and features of the unfortunate Hammerton. He had fallen into an uneasy slumber: his limbs were constantly in motion, and to the inquisitive ear which was placed near his mouth, as his lips moved, he was distinctly heard to speak in English: it was a hurried expression of caution to a female. Then would follow words in another language, to which the listener was a stranger; but those in English were well pronounced, so as not to leave a doubt but that the unfortunate man was an Englishman. Every care and attention which hospitality or professional skill could contribute were lavished upon him, and the surgeon gave every hope that the poor fellow would recover, and that before another day had elapsed his history would be familiar to the seamen, who vied with each other in endeavouring to contribute to his comfort. Along the beach from which he had been rescued numbers of Moors were still occasionally seen; but from their cautious manner in secreting themselves behind some hillocks of sand, it was judged advisable not to venture on any intercourse with them, as the bright end of a long spear not unfrequently dazzled in the sun's rays.

Whilst anxiously watching the Moors, who now and then waved a rag from the end of their spears, as if courting an interview, the boats were reported from the mast-head. The glasses were soon in requisition—only three could be discerned, and those came slowly on—the sails flapped in the light air, and the languid pull of only two oars from each side, distinctly seen as the boats neared the frigate, caused the most painful emotions in Murray's breast. In a moment the truth flashed across his mind; he was not deceived.

CHAPTER XXXVIII.

THE PIRATE.

THIS was Murray's first reverse, and bitterly he felt it. He had lost one lieutenant, one midshipman, and six seamen killed; the wounded fortunately were not seriously hurt; but the vessel had escaped, and *Il Diavolo* was still the terror of the trade.

The *Arethusa*, immediately after the return of her boats, weighed and ran to the southward. To have pursued the felucca to the northward was useless, for Murray well knew that he stood a better chance of finding her anywhere else than in that direction, since no vessels, either homeward or outward bound, hug the coast between Cape Blanco and Sallee. If she had gone to the northward of the last-named port, the *Arethusa* would have been obliged to quit her station.

In order to act up to his orders, Captain Murray steered towards Gorec; and in the mean time Hammerton recovered. Great indeed was the poor fellow's gratitude for his escape. His first exclamation on recovery was, "Where am I?" The answer, "On board the *Arethusa*," caused a shriek of delight.

"The very ship my sister christened! Who commands her?"

"Walter Murray."

"If, sir," continued Hammerton, "your kindness is not exhausted, may I ask you to tell the captain the stranger wishes to see him?"

"I beg your pardon, sir," said the gunner, as the surgeon walked away to apprise the captain of this request, "but they tell me you speak English, and are a Turk. I have brought you a volume of the Truth, and a tract of my own. When you have read the one, and studied the other, you shall find yourself a happy man; and, by way of beginning, the ship's barber is come to take off your outlandish beard and mustachios." The gunner continued to pour out a stream of consolation to one whom he regarded as a benighted man, and gave vent to his honest feelings as he endeavoured to reclaim an infidel.

Hammerton's cot had been hung up under the half-deck in a screened berth, and Mr. Pounce's salutary lecture was cut short by the appearance of the captain, who attended this strange summons. Hammerton's eye brightened as he approached; but when he endeavoured to trace the features of the boy in the stronger outline of the man, he found them so different, that he fell back disappointed upon his pillow, closed his eyes, and said, "Alas! my fortune never could have been so great: it is not him."

With a kindness habitual to a gentleman, Murray addressed the thoughtful Hammerton. He mentioned his satisfaction at having been useful in saving him from the Moors; and after promising him every attention and kindness, he inquired his name.

"A name which in itself is misfortune! a name which I shall now reclaim, although changed for Abdallah—Frederick Hammerton."

"Hammerton!" exclaimed Murray: "by heavens! and so positively it is: I never dreamt that such good fortune awaited me! Now, indeed, will Amelia's happiness be complete.—Let this cot," he continued, "be removed instantly into my cabin." Then turning to the surgeon, he said, "I fear to tell him the truth, for he is yet half-wandering in his mind: he is my lost brother-in-law."

The surgeon began to think his captain himself a little deranged. The sick man was immediately removed; and the care and quiet of the *Arethusa* soon restored Hammerton to a convalescent health. His beard was mowed, his upper lip shorn, and when washed and habited like a Christian, the manners of the gentleman, in spite of the rough wear and tear of life, were soon visible:—so true it is, that early habits of propriety always remain deeply impressed, and that, however low may be our associates, yet the character once formed in youth is never entirely obliterated. Every moment now grew into an hour: Hammerton could not believe himself safe until he should shake hands with Sir Hector, and once more stand upon English ground.

During their frequent conversations, Walter confessed to Hammerton that he never had forgotten the blow inflicted upon him; he confessed to him that he had abstracted the fifty pounds intended for him; and he finished by thanking heaven that an opportunity now occurred of proving to his father that the last of his failings, which had clung to him from his earliest infancy, and which had prompted him to the disgraceful act he now endeavoured to atone for, was eradicated. "Your former life, Hammerton—your days of slavery and misfortune, are now passed. Do not despond because you are poor, and have not one cowrie in the world with which to buy your bread. I was the cause—the innocent cause, in the first instance—of all your misfortunes. It was to save my then worthless life that you risked your own; every calamity arose out of that: and yet," said he, "that very circumstance becomes your greatest good fortune. It places me in a situation which I shall be proud to hold and to acknowledge—that of returning the good by making you independent; and all the hard rubs that you have encountered, and the misery you have escaped, will scarcely be remembered, except to draw comparisons of the past with the affluence and security of the future. My purse, Hammerton, is yours; and time shall show how sincere I am in making the offer. In the mean time, write to your sister, as we may have an opportunity of sending it; but, thank heaven! our time is short on this coast, and we shall soon carry on for Old England." Having obeyed the directions in his sailing orders, and having accidentally touched on a rock off the Islands de Loss, the *Arethusa* stretched out to sea, in order to return to Portsmouth.

Not many days had elapsed before the same felucca was again discovered, and under circumstances not quite so favourable as before: she was dead to leeward of the frigate, and was discovered during a hard gale of wind. The frigate, however, instantly bore up, shook out a couple of reefs, and stood away in chase under all the sail she could carry. The pirate was not slow to follow the example; but the sea was high, and the unwieldy yards of that rig, intended only for smooth seas and fine weather, was much against an escape. She was obliged to keep the wind on the quarter; for had she kept right before it, the danger of jibbing the sails was evident. The little vessel seemed to fly before the breeze; whilst the *Arethusa* surged along, steadier and quicker than the chase. The felucca was nearly buried by the press of canvas she carried; whilst the frigate, avoiding that error of carrying too much sail, rattled merrily along at the rate of twelve knots an hour.

The capture was now a certainty. Murray's anxiety increased as he neared the chase: his object was to take her without a chance-shot killing one of her men. It was the wish nearest his heart to make those villains pay the forfeit of their crimes,—to see them dangling to gibbets, a terror to all such marauders, and a just retribution for their past conduct. "I have you now, my little *Devil!*" he said, as the frigate surged along between the seas; and as the coming wave lifted her up on its breaking head, it seemed to dash her headlong into the valley beneath.

The gale increased. Still the felucca stood on, until a shot from the frigate went far beyond her: then, indeed, escape appeared desperate. The long yards were lowered; Spanish colours shown; the felucca, watching her opportunity, rounded-to, and appeared resigned to her fate.

With the eagerness to grasp his prey which ever distinguished Murray, and in spite of the more prudent counsel of the wary old master, the *Arethusa* continued to run under the same sail she then carried, until, close alongside to windward of the felucca, she rounded-to. There were volunteers in plenty (some who had already been on board of her) to man the boats; but great caution was requisite, for the sea ran high.

Every sail now instantly was taken off the frigate, the men were sent aloft to reef topsails, as the boat, lowered with the crew and officer in her, were safely launched, and cleared the frigate's counter. The distance between the two vessels could not have been two hundred yards: she lay right on the broadside of the frigate, which, however, in rounding-to, forged ahead, and brought her on the larboard quarter.

No sooner had the boat cleared the frigate, than a man appeared on board the felucca with a rope's end, ready to assist the boat in coming alongside. As she passed under the stern, this was hove into the boat; instantly a small jib was set, the vessel paid off, and gathered way.

Imagining something was about to be done whieh would render the boarding more difficult, every exertion was used to get the boat alongside by the erew in her. Some were obliged to keep ready with the stretchers, in order to keep her off from the vessel as she rolled over to leeward; but every time the boat got up on the quarter near enough to attempt boarding, the rope was veered away. The felueea was now before the wind, and coming to the wind on the larboard taek; her elose-reefed sails from the storm-yards were now hoisted, the boat was cut adrift, and the pirate, whose situation before had been desperate, resolved to make another attempt to escape from the frigate.

The marines of the *Arethusa* opened a fire of small arms on the vessel; but shc was soon out of reaeh of shot. The men being on the yards reefing, it was dangerous to wear; and the boat being to leeward, and having to pull against a heavy sea, made but little progress. In the mean time, the *Diavolo* kept a point or two away, in order to inerease her distance; and before the *Arethusa's* topsails were elose-reefed, the boat hoisted up, and the frigate on the larboard tack, the little vessel whieh had attemptcd and sueeeeded in this desperatc manœuvre was out of gun-shot, and earrying sail in a manncr to eonvince every seaman how well she was caleulated for the serviee on which she was employed.

Captain Murray could not but admirc the seamanlikc manner in whieh he had been deceived: it was now evident that when the felucea saw she had no chance of escape before the wind, she lowered her yards, lashed them fore and aft the deek, bent her storm-sails to smaller yards, and was preparing for the manœuvre she so ably managed.

It now beeame a chase on the wind; and here again the frigate's superiority was soon evidcnt. The felucea appeared almost swamped from the watcr she shipped; whilst the frigate, although she bore her eanvas well, served out an allowanee of salt water to all on deck. Under her reefed eourses and elose-reefed topsails she gained upon the chase; every yard was well secured; and Murray, annoyed beyond measure at finding that night would come on before he eould be alongsidc of the ehase, was resolved to earry on in spite of squalls, however violent.

Before sunset the frigate was near enough to see into the felucca as she rose to the sea: there were only three men on deck,—two steering, and the other lying down. From the quantity of water she shipped, it appeared a choice of evils, either to be swamped or to be hanged: the pirates evidently preferred the former, and, in spite of a warning from the *Arethusa*, in the shape of an iron messenger, she still carried on.

"A chance-shot," said Hammerton, who was as much excited as any man on board, "may kill the devil. Let me fire the next gun." As it was evident that all shots with a ship pitching bows under must be chance-shots, Hammerton's whim was gratified. The pirate did not heed his warning any more than the rest; and when darkness came on, the *Diavolo* was about a mile ahead of the frigate, holding on most desperately, her lee-gunwale under water, with every sea breaking over her.

It now became rather a difficult task to keep sight of her: she was so low, that she disappeared every minute between the seas. The night-glass was of no use; and a looking-glass—one of the best modes of keeping sight of a vessel in the night-time—was soon so covered with the spray, that it was rendered unserviceable. Many eyes were still fixed in the direction of the chase: "There she is!—there she is again!" was heard every time she became visible, until at last those cheering words were no longer heard—not a soul could see her. "She must have capsized, sir," said one;—"She is gone to her namesake," said another;—"The Lord have mercy upon them all!" said the gunner.

"We had better shorten sail, sir," said the master; "the slower we go now the better. That vessel is not capsized; she is much too good a sea-boat for that: she is up to some other trick."

The courses were hauled up, and the *Arethusa*, released from her press of canvas, rolled easily over the sea. Men were placed to look out in every direction: a quarter of an hour elapsed, and still the felucca was undiscovered. At last a mizen-top man, placed on the lee quarter, called out that he thought he saw something black on the water; and the sharp eye of an eager midshipman instantly discovered the felucca, the captain of which vessel had tried another scheme to escape. He had lowered his sails, and trusted to his good fortune, which until now had never deserted him. The frigate had passed her without being aware of it, and every moment was contributing to his further security, when a towering sea lifted the little *Devil* on its head, which enabled the mizen-top man to discover her.

Directly the *Arethusa* began to wear, the felucca ran up some square sails, and once more tried to escape before the wind: she was now plainly visible, almost under the bows. The frigate was surging over the seas right in the wake of the chase; the marines were on the forecastle, and kept up a continued fire—successfully or not was doubtful. Occasionally the bow-gun was fired, charged with grape and canister; but still the little vessel continued her course. The fate of the chase was now reduced to a certainty; her good fortune was evidently on the wane; the frigate neared her—too fatally neared her. Another attempt was still made—to round suddenly to—again to try her speed on a wind. The frigate was so close, however, that before she could come to the wind she must shoot by her. The helm of the *Diavolo* immediately was put gently a starboard, and the little vessel flew round as her sails were lowered. The master, who was forward, saw the attempt, called out "Starboard a little," and that little was fatal:—the *Arethusa's* deviation from her former course was just sufficient to meet the felucca; a shock was felt on board the frigate, as if she touched the ground—the *Diavolo* was cut in half! and not one soul remained alive of that daring crew! the angry seas rolled over them; and in the moaning of the wind, as it blew through the rigging, something resembling a shriek was heard. Whether it was a shriek, the last effort of despair, which was heard, is uncertain; for there was an awful feeling throughout the crew of the *Arethusa*, akin to fear, at the moment the shock was felt, which would have rendered every ear deaf to the call of pity from the pirate.

In vain was every eye directed now around; there was not a vestige of the pirate left. The struggling crew were no doubt soon swallowed up in the rolling sea; nor could the last cry of despair be heard, for the wind blew loudly and heavily, and the water, as the frigate surged through it at the rate of thirteen knots, hissed and foamed so as almost to drown every other sound as it was dashed from her bows.

So perished the crew of that noted vessel. That the atrocities committed by her commander and crew were exaggerated there can be no doubt, but that the blood of many called loudly against them was true; and although, had she been captured, her crew would have met a more ignominious death, yet there was not a man on board of the *Arethusa* who did not shudder at the catastrophe they had witnessed. Had it been daylight, there was not one of the brave men of that frigate who would not have risked his own life to save those who had so gallantly defended their vessel from the boat attack, and who had shown in this last affair that courage which might have sprung, it is true, from despair, but which was manifested in the coolness and steadiness of the manœuvres.

The *Arethusa* now hove-to until the gale should subside; she then stretched over to the north-west, until out of the influence of the trade-wind. Two months from that date she made the lighthouse of Scilly, and entered the Channel with the intention of steering to Portsmouth, having never seen a stranger from the time of the destruction of the *Diavolo.*

CHAPTER XXXIX.

CONCLUSION.

THE arrival of the *Arethusa* off the coast of England was not destined to realize the anticipations of a happy meeting, indulged in both by Sir Hector and his son; for, alas! the health of the former was fast declining.

The break-up of old age is rapid—the additional furrows of time seem daily to become deeper. The visible alteration for the worse in Sir Hector's appearance produced much painful anxiety on the mind of Amelia: she feared that he might not survive until Walter could reach his paternal home. The medical attendant, an old and tried friend, recommended that Sir Hector should be removed to some place which might offer some more excitement than the dull retreat where he had so long lingered. After various suggestions and long consultations, it was decided that the old baronet should be removed to Torbay, there to remain two months; at the end of which time, if he held on his lingering existence, he was to return.

This was opposed with more spirit by Sir Hector than the medical man believed to exist in him. "He had," he said, "built his vault, and could look at it undismayed." As Nelson had his coffin made from the mainmast of one of his captures, and as he, before he left England to take command of the fleet so soon to be engaged at Trafalgar, called upon the undertaker and told him to keep the last tenement ready, for that he should soon want it; so, Sir Hector, having spent a youth of labour and an age of ease—having passed his life in doing good to those around him—calmly resigned himself to the will of Providence.

"Would that all had your feelings!" replied Amelia; "but in this world we must obey the doctor. To-morrow we go to Torbay. I shall write letters to Portsmouth and Plymouth, to be delivered on the arrival of the *Arethusa*, and Walter will thus learn, the minute he arrives, of our retreat."

"Mind, my girl," said the worthy old baronet, "that the poor are paid during our absence. There are some as old as myself who cannot walk to my door. I leave them pensioners upon your bounty."

Shortly after this the *Arethusa* entered the Channel. The report of land was re-echoed along the decks, and the very light air which scarcely set the royals asleep was coaxed to freshen by every man fore and aft, as he came on deck whistling to windward;—a sailor's mode of soliciting the clerk of the weather to be more generous of the breeze; but the light air grew less and less, until

"The idle sail hung useless from the yard."

As the sun went down and night advanced, the lights on the Lizard Point were seen; and when the watch had been called and mustered, there seemed an unusual silence on board the frigate. Hammerton had evinced much restless inquietude during the day, and now was leaning over the taffrail watching the lights, his thoughts fixed on all the happiness yet in store for him. Before him was his native land,—there the place from which he had so long been exiled,—there his sister, the only surviving member of his family; all were gone but her. His many days of misfortune seemed to have entailed upon him a certain continuation of ill-luck. From the day that he had placed his foot on board the frigate, the fortunes of Walter seemed to have changed: the ship had struck on a rock; the *Diavolo*, although destroyed, was not captured; not a vessel had been seen, although thousands of miles had been traversed; and even now, as he saw the Lizard lights, he could not persuade himself but that some unlucky catastrophe still awaited him. He looked over the taffrail and gazed upon the stars reflected in the large mirror beneath; although not destitute of hope, yet a fear—a melancholy fear—hung over him.

He was aroused from this reverie by the look-out on the starboard quarter, as the bell struck two, giving a warning to the man on the starboard gangway to keep a good look-out. These words were passed round to each man on the different stations, and were wound up by "Ay, ay!" from the man on the larboard quarter. A shout of laughter was then heard forward; and Hammerton, no longer inclined to fancy himself the boding raven, went on the forecastle, and listened to the yarns of the seamen as they sat between the guns, all lively and happy at their return from the coast of Africa, uninjured by that unhealthy climate. "They are not heaving round the capstan now at Portsmouth Point, at any rate," said one. "I suppose all the girls are gone to supper; but to-morrow, when the breeze comes, they'll tow us along merrily." "Give us a song, Tom: what ship from a foreign station ever made the land without the lads of the first watch having a glass of grog and chanting a stave?"

Murray was on deck, and heard the remark. Hammerton walked aft, and begged he might be allowed to give the jolly fellows a glass to drink his return, and to coäx them to sing a song or two, the last hc might ever hear from the lips of a sailor on his own element. The request was immediately granted, accompanicd by a warning in regard to prudence. Hammerton, with a bottle of rum in one hand and a jug of water in the other, was soon on the foreeastle.

"Now, my lads," said he, "here is the liquor of life: get a pannikin, and I'll bale it out to you. If it had not been for you I should now have been a slave, eondemned to lasting captivity; so herc's a drop to drink my safe landing, to wash the cobwebs out of your throats, and to clear your voices for a song."

"Now then, Tom, if you have not swallowed a topehain, tune up! That rum's good; but it's rather spoilt by the water. Begs your pardon, Mr. Hammerton, but I should be mighty obliged if you could give us a nip without the pump."

"No, no, my lads!" replied Hammerton; "half-and-half is strong enough to begin with. Let's have the song first, and we'll talk of the raw nip afterwards."

"Here goes!" said old Tom. "But my throat's precious dusty! I'm blessed if I don't think I've got some of the sand of Capc Blaneo sticking there yet, and I feel as if that black Moor on his long-legged, hump-baeked horse was shoving it down my throat with the butt-end of his spear. It was touch-and-go there, Mr. Hammerton. Do just try another toueh-and-go, to wash the sand down."

"There," said Hammerton, as he took the hint; "as you are to sing, you must have an extra allowanee."

"Then you'll have plenty of songs at that rate," said another. "But fire away, Tom!"

THE ARETHUSA.

"A sail in sight to leeward, boys, we saw at break of day;
We crowded all our canvas on, at once we bore away.
The stranger hove-to gallantly, which gave us great delight,
For she seemed to scorn to run away, and boldly stayed to fight.
To quarters, boys—to quarters,
The Frenchman thinks he's caught us;
But we 'll show them what we'll do,
With the brave and gallant crew,
On board of the *Arethusa*.

"Be steady now, my noble lads, don't throw away your fire,
But give three hearty British cheers, our courage to inspire.
And they shall hear the hearty cheers, for we 'll be close enough,
And make the Frenchman know my crew are made of proper stuff.
Now steady, boys, be steady;
Now ready, lads, be ready;
Now pour your broadside in,
And thus the fight begin,
On board of the *Arethusa*.

"We sarved them out in proper style—the grape-shot flew like hail;
When British hearts are firm and good, we know they never fail.
The colours soon came tumbling down, the frigate was our prize,—
An equal match in length and breadth, in crew, in guns, in size.
Now chorus, lads, the chorus;
How the women will adore us;
When they raise the welcome din,
As we tow the *Didon* in,
Astern of the *Arethusa!*"

"Chorus again!" said Hammerton, as he rubbed his hands with delight; "and hurrah! for the hope that we yet get a brush at a frigate, and tow in another prize to the anchorage at Spithead."

All hands joined in the coal-box, as the seamen invariably call the chorus: and the author of the song, who was the singer, had another glass of grog for his chant, and was perhaps better rewarded by Murray, who called out, "Well done—well done!" and as he came forward, he said, "I'm afraid latterly we have not given you much chance of another song; but before the war is over we may yet have another brush, and give another subject to make verses upon."

"To-morrow," said Murray, as he walked aft with Hammerton—"to-morrow may place you on English ground again: a calm is always half a fair wind, and I shall hug the shore and pop you into any fishing-boat which we may meet. However, to-night, if we get a breeze, we will stand over on the French coast: your ill-luck has not yet, I hope, overbalanced my good fortune."

"I am a regular Jonah, Murray: and I think, if you were to throw me overboard with a black cat in my pocket, I should whirl about like Macbeth's witches in the sieve, and be always in fear of drowning, without the luck of being so. But, good night, and good luck attend you!"

About eleven o'clock a moderate breeze sprung up from the N.W ; and Murray, according to his resolution, made a start over towards the enemy's coast. The night was fine and clear, and a very good look-out was kept. Daylight, however, came; and although a most anxious search was made by the midshipman of the watch, who from the foretop-sail yard swept the horizon with a glass, yet not a sail could be discerned. Hammerton was on deck early, and heard the report from the masthead with a heavy heart.

"I am," said he, "the most unlucky fellow that ever stepped. I would have given any sum I could have commanded to have apprised my sister of my restoration, in order better to prepare her for the meeting; but I shall herald myself, as I did to my poor father, and, I suppose, frighten her to death. But it is my destiny; and I still retain some part of the Turkish creed, which coincides so exactly with that of my poor father."

"I beg your pardon, sir," said Pounce, as he passed Hammerton; "but I should like to know if you have been converted, because I have some tracts very much at your service."

"Thank you," said Hammerton. "God knows, I would willingly thank the man who would convert me into a lucky fellow."

Noon came—the dinner was piped, grog served, mastheadmen relieved—nothing in sight. "Now," said Hammerton, "I'll go to the masthead, and there I'll stick until sunset, on the look-out for either land or a sail." The wind had been variable, but had now settled at S.W by S. with every appearance of that comfortable mist which generally is the forerunner of a S.W gale of wind in the English Channel in the month of February.

Hammerton went aloft, and sitting on the fore-topsail yard, the *Arethusa* being on the larboard tack, he began to run over his past life, and think of his chance for the future. He still liked the sea; but he was too old to re-enter it as a midshipman, and he was much too proud to be a pensioner upon Murray. They were, it is true, brothers-in-law; but brothers not unfrequently quarrel, and the word pauper is sometimes not inaudibly muttered.

Whilst thus carelessly musing over past scenes of his life, and humming the chorus of old Tom's song, which somehow came oddly enough upon his memory, he looked cautiously round, and was the first to descry a strange sail to leeward. He had taken a glass aloft with him, and steadying himself by a firm hold of the topsail-tie, he made her out to be a large ship, close-hauled on the starboard tack: Murray, who was an active man and a keen cruiser, at once decided upon overhauling her; and desiring the officcr of the watch to turn the hands up, make sail, indeed to set all the sail the frigate would carry, himself scudded aloft, and taking the glass from Hammerton, he remained steadily observing the stranger. At length he called out, "If that is not a French frigate, there are no snakes in Virginia, as you say, Hammerton." Again hc looked, was perfectly satisfied in his own mind, and giving Hammerton the glass, he added, "Luck's turned: you saw her first, and you shall have an opportunity of lending a hand at her capture."

Fore and aft the *Arethusa*, the word flew like wild-fire—"The captain says she is a French frigate. Hurrah! one and all, and let's work like Russians!" The noble frigate was now under all canvas; her well-disciplined crew obeyed the sound of the drum, as it beat to the well-known air which, in most ships in the British Navy, is playcd to summon all hands to quarters, of—

"Come cheer up, my lads, 'tis to glory we steer,
To add something new to this wonderful year:
'Tis to honour we call you, nor press you like slaves,
For who are so free as we sons of the waves?"

Then came a little noise in thc handing of shot, the placing of sponges and rammers, and in the preparation of all those articles used in naval combats.

It was two P.M. when the *Arethusa* first saw the chase and bore up. By half-past two there remained no doubt in the minds of any but that she was an enemy; for at this time the stranger, as if satisfied of the force and intention of her pursuer, bore up also, and made a great effort, by the crowd of sail she set, to effect an escape. This was decisive; any of his Britannic Majesty's ships would have been as eager to close the *Arethusa* and satisfy themselves of her nation as Murray was now anxious to ascertain more closely the force of his flying enemy. The excitement was intense: the seamen rubbed their hands as they caught a glimpse of the chase; and as they passed old Tom, they would give him a seaman's tap on the shoulder—a blow generally strong enough to fell an ox—and sing,

> "—— Now chorus, lads, chorus;
> How the women will adore us,
> When they raise the welcome din,
> As we tow the Frenchman in,
> Astern of the *Arethusa!*"

At four o'clock the wind veered to the N.W and fell considerably: the ship, to the eager minds of the seamen, scarcely moved; but yet it was evident to those who watched with coolness, that the *Arethusa* gained upon the chase, and that at this hour she was not more than four miles distant. But four miles, at four o'clock in February, in the Channel, is as bad as ten miles in August. The general fogs which pervade our unhappy climate are kinds of cloaks to conceal the fugitive, and many doubts began to be afloat as to the ultimate success of the chase. Indeed, there was a certainty that the action might be delayed until dark; when, to the gratification and surprise of all, the French frigate, then bearing E.N.E., suddenly shortened sail, and endeavoured to cross the hawse of the *Arethusa.*

The action was now certain: the manœuvre was welcomed by the crew of the English frigate by a loud shout of joy; that shout was given with louder tongue, when, at a quarter to five, the *Arethusa* fired a gun and hoisted her colours, and the stranger, as if far from wishing to conceal her nation, hoisted the large tri-coloured flag of France, and seemed not at all disposed to evade her antagonist.

There was a confidence in Murray's manner which was conspicuous to all: he spoke to his men, not under the slightest impression that he could be beaten; he called it a little amusement for his men before they went on shore at Portsmouth; he treated his adversary as already beaten;

but he was much too wise in reality to despise his foe. His men caught his words with avidity; they gave those cheers which English seamen always give before an action; and having the greatest confidence in their commander, they saw but a glorious issue to the approaching struggle, and stood at their quarters silently awaiting the order to fire. He wound up his speech in these few words:—"My lads, although we are as certain of that frigate as we are of going into Portsmouth, yet we must not let our confidence lead us to treat her with disrespect; we will hug her closely, and you will best show your coolness by the steady aim which you will take, and your caution not foolishly to waste powder and shot. Stand to your guns!"

At five o'clock, the *Arethusa*, having previously bore up, passed close under the stern of the French frigate, and having given her a cheer, poured in her starboard broadside, raking her fore and aft. She then luffed up close upon the quarter, and was welcomed by a very heavy, well-directed, destructive fire; and before she could reach the bow of the enemy, the *Arethusa* had lost her mizen-mast, which fell over the starboard quarter.

During the twenty minutes which elapsed from the first raking fire of the *Arethusa* to the moment her mizen-mast was shot away, the French frigate had been severely handled also. Her foretop-mast fell over the side, and she shot ahead, not at all dismayed from the fire of her adversary, but rather rejoicing that as yet she had not suffered so much as her opponent.

Frenchmen flushed with success are dangerous enemies: the national spirit rises with the apparent facility of conquest. Hence the rapid victories under Napoleon: they believed themselves invincible—and went into battle resolved upon conquest. The British Navy had the same feeling: they had scarcely ever met a reverse upon the open seas; one frigate opposed to another was considered a certain capture—the English went into action with a confidence amounting to temerity. The French met their enemies with a feeling of certain misfortune: throughout the whole war we have not one instance of a French frigate chasing an English frigate when the force was ascertained.

The very circumstance of being chased, and of endeavouring to avoid an action, was not likely to instil more courage into the flying ship's company, and they felt themselves obliged to fight when the superior sailing of the chasing ship had brought her nearly alongside; as a stag pursued, when fight is useless, turns and stands at bay, beaten before it is attacked.

The French frigate, finding herself in an advantageous position, and flushed with her first success in having shot away the mizen-mast of the *Arethusa*, endeavoured to recommence the action by crossing the bows of her adversary, and of returning the compliment of the raking broadside with which she herself had been saluted. To obviate this, which Murray instantly saw, the helm of the *Arethusa* was put hard a-port, and the ship luffed up, in order to run the French frigate on board, and at once to settle the conflict. In this, however, she did not succeed: the wreck of the mizen-mast prevented the ship from answering her helm sufficiently, and the *Arethusa*, as she passed close under the stern of her opponent, discharged her larboard broadside with good effect.

The two ships now fell broadside to broadside, and the action continued with increased fury. On board the French frigate all was animation—they stood to their guns manfully; whilst on board the *Arethusa* the seamen gave occasional cheers, and never doubted for a moment but that each gun would bring down the large tri-coloured flag which blew out from the French frigate's peak, and finish the action. The *Arethusa* lay close on the starboard beam of her opponent. Bravely, indeed, on both sides was the battle maintained, which at twenty minutes past six gave the French a hope of conquest, when they saw the mainmast of the *Arethusa* fall, which, fortunately for Murray and his brave crew, fell over the unengaged side.

The shout of the French crew was short, for their own mizen-mast soon fell; and this was welcomed by a deafening cheer from the English.

"Arrah," said an Irish seaman, bellowing through one of the ports, "don't make game of the stupid! you may be sthruck comical yourself. Blaze away, boys! what's the use of a mainmast when we don't want to move our position?"

Both ships' companies, if possible, increased their endeavours. The *Arethusa* had only her foremast standing, and there could be no doubt but that she was in one respect at the mercy of her adversary, for she had it in her power to shoot ahead and discontinue the action; but this the French captain felt no inclination to do. He saw before him great rewards from his liberal master, could he but tow the *Arethusa* into a French harbour. Napolcon would have advanced him to any honour; and had he at that moment used the caution of a good seaman, he would have shot ahead, and compelled thc *Arethusa* to put before the wind.

For ten minutes longer each ship remained in the same position, broadside to broadside; at the expiration of which time the foremast of the *Arethusa* fell, and the mainmast of her adversary went over the side. Now, had Captain Denis Lagardc, who commanded the *Clorinde*, for that was thc frigate's name, been but commonly prudent, there could bc no doubt how the action would have terminated. A dismasted ship is, of coursc, unmanageable: the *Arethusa* must have remained rolling in the sea, unable to alter her position. The foremast of the *Clorinde* was still standing; under the foresail and fore-stay sail the ship would be manageable to a certain extent. Hc might have placed himself in an advantageous position, and might have nearly insured his adversary's capture; but escape seemed more desirable than the chance of conquest. Bravely had he fought, gallantly had he maintained his advantage; and now, when the wings of the bird were broken, he was afraid to stop and pick it up. At ten minutes after seven the *Clorinde* set her foresail and fore-stay sail, and standing to the S. E. was soon out of gunshot.

There are some men to whom Fortune offers her gifts, and who are afraid to receivc them; there are others who refusc to float down the flood-tidc of success, but run upon the banks and are wrecked. Change the position of those ships: would the *Arethusa* have availed herself of her standing foremast to have escaped? Never: she would have made so certain of the conquest, that she would have hailed the *Clorinde* to strike, and to avoid a useless effusion of blood.

With a heavy heart Murray looked at his dismasted ship, his confused decks, his wounded shipmates; but his courage never sank. With a readiness to meet any difficulty, he addressed his men: he urged them to clear the wreck, and put the ship in that position which would enable him to pursue his enemy. The first lieutenant, an active, enterprising officer, repeated the orders: the boats' masts were stepped and the sails set. The heavy rolling of the ship, however, was a great impediment to their exertions; but the men placed at the different stations worked with willingness, and the wreck of the lower masts was cleared. There was no wish expressed by that gallant crew to sleep; they felt that accident alone had placed them in the untoward position they were then in: they knew it arose from no want of courage nor seamanship in their gallant captain; and with true English pluck they set about their work with all willingness, and by five o'clock in the following morning a spare maintop-mast had been rigged as a jury-mainmast. By a quarter after six a jury-foremast was standing, and a mizen-mast also.

Daylight dawned—and anxiously indeed was dawn welcomed. The *Clorinde* was seen about six miles distant, bearing S.E. She had evidently not profited by the advantage she had gained: the wreck of her main and mizen-mast were not quite cleared, and every moment gave the *Arethusa* a chance of resuming the action. By noon this gallant frigate was under jury-courses, and topsails, staysails, and spanker, going with a northerly wind six knots and a half; whilst her adversary, who had increased her distance to eight miles, had not up to this time cleared away entirely the wreck.

Captain Murray was not a man to forego any advantage: he had been wounded during the action, but his spirit was unconquerable. With every hope before him he received the cheers of his crew as he promised them shortly a renewal of the action. He was overhauling the *Clorinde* fast; his decks were as clear as the day previous to the action; and no words are sufficient praise for the unremitted exertions of his crew—the activity and seamanlike conduct of that ship's company.*

That Jonah, Hammerton, was on board!—the seamen, who have a superstitious horror of a parson, a black cat, or a regular Jonah, could hardly bear the sight of him. Every misfortune was attributed to him, whose ill-luck, they said, would founder a frigate. It was yet to be more strikingly evident. The *Arethusa*, under her jury-sails, was fast advancing to renew the action. The *Clorinde* lay almost a complete wreck—her chance was gone, and the only prayer on board the *Arethusa* was for a better breeze and no intruders. The first was heard, but the second was disregarded; for as the frigate increased her way through the water, with her men refreshed and eager for the contest, two English frigates were seen on the lee-bow. They arrived up with the *Clorinde* before the *Arethusa*, and the French frigate surrendered without further resistance. That she must have fallen a prize to the *Arethusa* no one can doubt—her flight was sufficient proof of her being conquered; but the disgrace of the capture was saved by the unfortunate arrival of the two strange frigates.

The *Arethusa* now took the French frigate in tow, and stood towards the English coast, with the intention of proceeding towards Portsmouth; having parted company with the two intruders, who had received some of the French prisoners in their ships.

In the evening the breeze freshened to a gale, and it was judged advisable, on account of the damage both ships had sustained, to run into Torbay, and anchor until more moderate weather should allow them to continue their course. It was midnight when they rounded the point and anchored in security; but before morning the wind had chopped round, and blew directly into the bay. Both anchors were let go, and, as it was impossible to get to sea, every precaution was taken to make the frigates ride out the gale.

Some fishing-boats belonging to the place, which were at

* The annals of the British navy cannot show more zeal, or greater promptitude, than was exhibited by Sir John Phillimore and the crew of the *Eurotas*, in the action with the *Clorinde*, which is here recorded under the name of Murray and the *Arethusa*.

sea the day before, came running in for safety; and Murray, most anxious to procure something fresh for the wounded, got a boat on board of one to purchase fish. When she returned, the midshipman who had been sent approached his captain and said, "The master of the boat, sir, says Sir Hector Murray and Mrs. Murray are living in that house," pointing, at the same time, to a large mansion over Fryingpan-row.

Hammerton heard it, and was almost frantic. He implored Murray to land, and the latter, believing that the gale would soon be over, and that, from the variable manner the wind had veered, its strength was at its summit, ordered the gig to be lowered and manned, and this was the only boat seaworthy.

In the mean time the fishermen had landed. The cry of "The *Arethusa!*—The *Arethusa!*" soon reached the house, and a handkerchief was seen waving from the window, at which stood an old man and a young woman.

Murray's willingness to gratify Hammerton's impatience made him forget his usual prudence: he stepped the mast, and carried the whole sail. The sea was at this time running high, and the boat, as she flew towards the shore, rolled heavily. Hammerton steered with a yoke, and Murray, who kept looking anxiously towards the shore, occasionally gave the man who held the sheet in his hand a glance, as much as to say, "Hold on." The sea rolled in heavily, and it required some—indeed the greatest—caution, to prevent the boat from being taken on the quarter and broached-to. To obviate this some strength was requisite with the yoke-lines; and it was whilst approaching rapidly the landing-place, and as the sea lifted the boat, that, as Hammerton endeavoured to counteract the effect of the wave, the yoke-line snapped, the boat broached-to, and was capsized.

The accident was seen from the shore. Amelia ran down to the beach half frantic, whilst Sir Hector used his utmost speed to overtake her. The boats from the landing-place were launched, hundreds who were making their remarks on the *Arethusa* and her prize rushed forward to assist, and all used their best exertions to rescue the seamen from the peril which surrounded them.

Murray and his crew now struck out for their lives. Some of them clung to the wreck of the boat, which floated bottom upwards; but Hammerton, who swam well, kept close to Murray, who, from his wound, was much weakened, and seemed fast giving up his first exertions. "I'll stay by you, Murray," he said: "fear nothing. Don't touch me; but let me get hold of that black ribbon round your neck. Strike out."

Murray gradually became more and more feeble, each sea washed over him, his struggles were nearly over, and yet he did his utmost. He could almost see his wife supported by others, his father tottering from fear; and as the last sea threw him on the beach, the ribbon snapped, and his mother's locket remained in Hammerton's hand. Hammerton instantly seized him by the collar, held him fast as the wave receded and nearly sucked him back into the greedy deep, and, before the following sea could secure him, he was safe on shore.

Amelia was the first to clasp him in her arms, and scarcely heeded the dark stranger who had rescued him. Murray was unable to speak, and as his wife thanked Hammerton for his kind assistance in carrying him to the house, Hammerton said, "I restore you a husband,—he restores you a brother?" The very words riveted her attention: she saw immediately through the darkness of his complexion the features of her long-lost brother Frederick! Seizing him by the hand, she fainted in his arms.

The recovery of Murray was followed by a restitution of the locket. Sir Hector, who was seated in an arm-chair, almost fatally overcome by the agitation, was gratified by the first words of his son. "Amelia, your brother has saved my life! Sir," he continued, as he looked at his father, "this locket has saved your son. Let me entreat you, whilst you have still life and strength, to secure an independence out of the property destined for me upon Frederick Hammerton."

"God bless you, boy!" said the old man: "that last request has cleared away for ever the only remaining blot on my son's character, and you have made me the happiest of fathers. You went from me a wayward child—you return to me an honourable and distinguished man: you were penurious—you are now liberal. You have caught the honourable feelings of all officers of the navy, and I may justly be proud of that shout which now welcomes you to me, and join in the cheer for 'The *Arethusa!* The *Arethusa!*'"

THE END.

J. Ogden and Co., Printers, 172, St. John Street, Clerkenwell, E.C.

Milton Keynes UK
Ingram Content Group UK Ltd.
UKHW041823141223
434388UK00003B/86

9 783752 534238